S0-ARM-876

EAST OF MANDALAY

A NOVEL BY

SUZANNE CLAUSER

Disc-Us
Books

East of Mandalay by Suzanne Clauser
Copyright©2000 Suzanne Clauser. All rights reserved.
ISBN 1-58444-117-8
Library of Congress Card Number: 00-102838

Published by Disc-Us Books, Inc. by arrangement with the
author and copyright protected under U.S copyright laws and
International treaties. Published in the USA.

Cover Photo Credit:
"Dramatic Mountains" provided by Peter Whittlesey.
For additional photos of Laos, visit his website at
http://whitney.bcoe.butte.k12.ca.us/poplar/Laos/default.htm

Cover Design by Carrie L. Starkey

PUBLISHER'S NOTE
This is a work of fiction. Names, characters, places, and
incidents either are the product of the author's imagination or
are used fictitiously, and any resemblance to actual persons,
living or dead, events, or locales is entirely coincidental.

Without limiting the rights under copyright reserved above, no
part of this publication may be reproduced, stored in or
introduced into a retrieval system, or transmitted, in any form,
or by any means (electronic, mechanical, photocopying,
recording, or otherwise), without the prior written permission
of the above publisher of this book.

For more information write:
    Disc-Us Books, Inc.
    Sarasota, FL 34233
    Email - books@disc-us.com
    www.disc-us.com

Grateful acknowledgement is made to the following for
permission to reprint excerpts from previously published song lyrics:

Excerpts from the song lyrics "I Get Around" written by Brian Wilson and Mike
Love. Copyright©1964(Renewed)Irving Music, Inc.(BMI) All rights reserved. Used
by permission WARNER BROS. PUBLICATIONS U.S., INC., Miami, FL 33014

Excerpts from the song lyrics "Help Me Rhonda" written by Brian Wilson and Mike
Love. Copyright©1965 (Renewed) Irving Music, Inc. (BMI) All rights reserved.
Used by permission WARNER BROS. PUBLICATIONS U.S. INC., Miami, FL 33014

Excerpts from the song lyrics "Snap Your Fingers" written by Grady Martin and
Alex Zanetis. Copyright©1969, Renewed 1998 by Acuff-Rose Music, Inc. All
rights reserved. Used by permission. International Rights Secured.

Throughout the novel, limited use is made of short
exerpts from song lyrics which is herewith gratefully acknowledged:

"Bridge Over Troubled Water" Paul Simon; Paul Simon Music (Publisher AC)

"Last Train To Clarksville" Tommy Boyce and Bobby Hart; Screen Gems - EMI
Music, Inc.

"Light My Fire" John Paul Densmore and Raymond D. Manzarek and Robert A.
Kreiger and Jim Morrison; The Doors Music Co.

"Monkees Theme" Tommy Boyce and Bobby Hart; Screen Gems - EMI Music, Inc.

"Person To Person" Charlie Singleton and Teddy McRae; Fort Knox Music, Inc.;
Jerry Lee Lewis Music; Trio Music Co., Inc.

"Sweet Hour of Prayer" William W. Walford 1842; Published by the Presbyterian
Church in the United States (1945)

"Words of Love" John E. A. Phillips; Universal MCA Music Publishing of
Universal Studios, Inc.

"Sweet Slumber" Lucky Millinder and A.I.J. Neiburg and Henri Woods; Fort Knox
Music, Inc.; Trio Music., Inc.

"When A Man Loves A Woman" Lewis Calvin Houston and Wright Andrew James
(U.S.); Pronto Music; Quincy Music Publishing Co.

ACKNOWLEDGEMENTS

Any errors in this novel are of course solely this author's. But there would have been far more of them without a lot of help.

First of all, to Liz Trupin-Pulli – good agent, good editor, good and open-minded publisher – my admiration, deep gratitude, and great personal affection.

Great thanks are due Mike Trajak and CW4 US Army (RET) Joe Licina. Mike first took me flying, letting me feel what it's like to fly a light helicopter, then read this manuscript and came back with lots of needed reminders. Joe provided the interior and in-flight specifics of the old LOH-6A, the Loach, and brought his own experiences as a Loach pilot in Vietnam to his careful vetting of the material on the Loach in combat, along with valuable insights into the structure and flavor of the U.S. Army in the Vietnam War.

In addition, many books, videos, and papers provided background. Among those covering the Vietnam War and particularly the helicopter war in the late 1960's were those books written by the brave and spirited young pilots who flew both the Loach scouts and the Hueys, especially Hugh L. Mills, Jr.'s *Low Level Hell,* Robert Mason's *Chickenhawk*, and W.T. Grant's *Wings of the Eagle.* Concerning the political and military involvement of the United States in Laos in 1970, the author is especially indebted to two books by Christopher Robbins: *The Ravens* and *Air America.* A number of ethnic studies, books and reports supplied the material on hill tribes of Southeast Asia.

The tragic story of Burma came out of several economic and historical studies, most notably Norma Bixler's *Burma, A Profile.* These were joined with my own personal experiences while living there and private talks and correspondence with American missionaries stationed there both before and after the military coup.

And, at last, I would like to thank publicly members both past and present of The Yellow Springs Writer's Group. Their constant interest, encouragement, stringent critiquing with editorial input, and not least the laughter running through the Group's meetings like a golden thread over the years have enabled me to maintain a long and rewarding writing career.

DEDICATION

Dedicated with gratitude and love to my neat husband
and best friend, Charlie, who was the first to see value
in this book, who has always been my best critic and
through thick and thin keeps his faith in me and what
I do, much to my constant amazement.

Through the jungle very softly flits a shadow
and a sigh –

He is Fear, O Little Hunter, he is Fear!

The Song of the Little Hunter

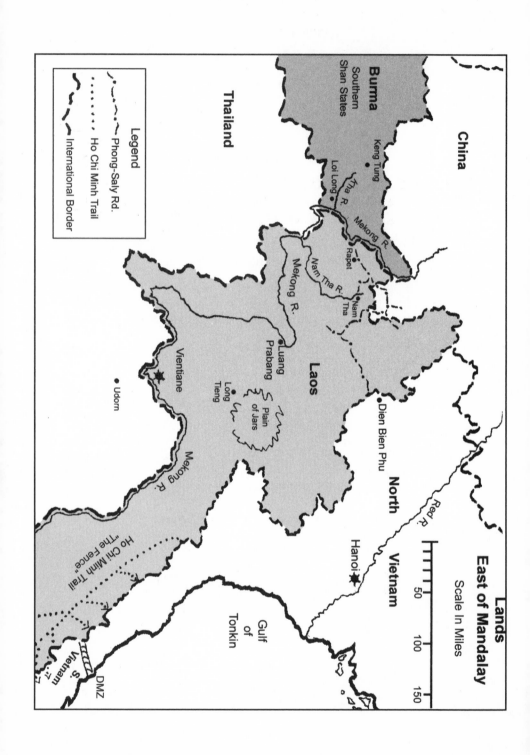

Lands
East of Mandalay
Scale In Miles

50   100   150

Legend

Phong-Saly Rd.

Ho Chi Minh Trail

International Border

China

Burma

Southern
Shan States

Thailand

Keng Tung

Loi Long

Tha R.

Mekong R.

Rapet

Nam Tha R.

Nam
Tha

Mekong R.

Luang
Prabang

Laos

Vientiane

Long
Tieng

Plain
of Jars

Dien Bien Phu

Udom

North
Vietnam

Mekong R.

Red R.

Hanoi

Ho Chi Minh Trail

"The Fence"

Gulf
of
Tonkin

S.
Vietnam

DMZ

PROLOGUE

They could see the monsoon haze hanging over Da Nang before they finished the turn around Marble Mountain. Not raining now, but off and on most of the day, the air fairly saturated with it by this time. A long day, as they'd all been for the past couple of months, nine, ten hours. Not enough scout pilots, only kids so new to helicopters and flying they weren't half safe, not in combat, anyway.

Settling easy to the pad, Michael shut down and took a minute to let the relief come. All day doing low and slow pop ups, drawing VC fire, Michael on the minigun, Hanny in the cabin working his M-60 until their Cobra gunship up above them could zero in and take Charlie out with rockets. Michael no longer was sure why he'd come to Nam, only knew that no way did it have anything to do with what he'd found here.

He sucked in a breath and swung out and down to the ground, giving his legs the chance to firm up, cramped from too long in the tiny Loach. They'd landed three times to refuel and reload ammo, but Michael had shut down only once, all those grunts out there waiting, looking to them for cover. And his mind each time seeking Kathleen. Was it possible he could see her again? Even see her soon?

Preceding Michael out, Hanny was already examining battle damage to his baby, talking to the ground crew, but his eyes caught Michael's and he sent him a wink, saying as he'd taken to doing lately, "Smooth sailing, Cam." No "sir" today. He'd started that business, insisted on it in front of others, the day they'd stood before the passing list of the phase exams at Fort Wolters, and Neal Hanrahan's name still wasn't on it after two efforts. He could fly but he couldn't handle the books. He sure as hell had learned how to take care of his helicopter.

Care of his pilot, too. And had, earlier just this day. Michael had said nothing about it – flying scared – but Hanny knew. Both of them on short time in their second tours, Michael scareder and scareder he'd make a mistake that would cost more than just himself, too many depending on him. Today it'd been close. Hanny'd had to key Michael on the intercom to nudge him, saying he was getting seasick back there in the cabin the way the boom was swinging back and forth. Yeah sure, Hanny goin' seasick. But until he spoke, Michael hadn't realized his foot was going heavy and uneven on the pedal, jinking the light observation helicopter too much like a sparrow between and over the trees.

Shortly after, Hanny'd started beating the rhythm on the bulkhead with his fingers, and had belted out, "Hey, Hey, We're the Monkees!", pulling Michael in. And then they'd vamped into "Little Deuce Coup", had let the Beach Boys carry them the rest of the day, Hanny on bass or falsetto in the bridges, Michael doing the melody. They always tried to keep it to the intercom and off the radio. Helped lighten the load, Hanny liked to say, but it tended to make the flyers up above nervous while below they were sneaking across the endless green in the quietest chopper alive, across the beautiful green where beautiful small people once ran in safety. A people so like those he'd learned to care about years ago. With Kathleen and Tom.

"Sir? Mr. Cameron?" Michael startled and pushed away from the side of the Loach, looking down at the young corporal. "The CO wants to see you, sir. Front and center, he said."

Shit. How had he managed to piss off the Major this time?

"Jeep's over here, sir."

Levering himself in, he heard Richard's letter crinkle in his pocket. No reason to read it again, he had every word memorized. The damned thing was only two sentences long, could've been a cable: Please get leave, go to Hong Kong and see Tom Howard soonest. Jesus.

Had to be about Kathleen. Only why couldn't Richard say so? Richard just being Richard, big brother throwing his seniority around.

While sitting on the ground off and on during the day, waiting for Hanny to fill up the tank, he'd tried and failed to raise a vision of her. Like one from the dead. Hell, he'd been avoiding it for four years. Now, for the first time he wondered if he might regret that.

The jeep stopped in front of the grey clapboard operations hooch, Major Niemeier gunning for him inside and Michael too tired to take shit about an overdue report or some fucking requisition filled out wrong.

But as he slid off the seat it came to him, suddenly and with surprise – today he'd eat anything that prick wanted to dish out. Otherwise no R & R, and he had to get to Hong Kong.

DAY ONE

1

The night air held a cold damp and gusted, the rains having settled heavily into these mountains for over two months, and at times the little lamp, nothing but a wick floating in a shallow dish of oil, flickered wildly. But she'd gotten the hang of it now, writing a meaningless journal in the poor light, not caring how literate, or even how readable it was. It was for Sawbwa Htin Aung's benefit, his only.

In four days he would be gone. Kathleen was counting them down. Her pencil jerked, and she had to take a breath, and the questions she'd thought silenced rose up and asked themselves again. Should she ask him? If she asked him, this one last time, wouldn't it alert him? He could lock her away. He could take the baby away. She already knew what his answer would be, didn't she?

Kathleen's head drooped under the weight of doubts, and her fear. She closed her eyes against the soft light, then turned them to see into the corner where U-pym lay on her mat with Cho resting on her breast. How she envied the woman. But at last Cho had gone quiet, seemed now to sleep, and she must not disturb him.

It was late. Midnight had chimed a while ago on the palace clocks, more than a dozen of them collected by the Sawbwa Gyi, the Great Prince, Htin Aung's father now dead. A man was paid a retainer just to keep them wound and all set to the same minute. Even so, the clamor was enough to drive all the ghosts out of Loi Long, or so the palace women joked. So why wasn't Htin Aung here? He kept close count on the days of the month. He knew, just as she did, that tonight was the best hope for what he wanted. She turned her back to U-pym, separated her knees and reached down inside her longyi and up into herself to make sure the little piece of oiled silk was spread and tucked properly. It had protected her before, except the one time that gave her Cho. She had to put her faith in it for this one last night.

Tomorrow, the buyers were to come, and there would be endless negotiating, some drink, much banqueting, and if she were lucky the Sawbwa wouldn't come to her again before he left with them. And on that day, that same day, the last opium train would leave for Laos. A day later, and she would follow behind it, the delay for safety's sake – there were always riders who returned to the town and others joining up belatedly – but the tracks of some fifty horses going before her would remain clear in the mud of the trail. More than a day or two of the monsoon rains and the tracks would be lost, at least in places, and so would she and Cho, the mountains and the jungle an indecipherable maze. In only ten days, the train's supplies running out and the refinery unable to feed them, all would be back, the town and palace crowded with celebrants. This would be her only chance. Cho's last chance.

Dear God. When she thought of it, that the Prince would be within easy reach of Bangkok and could so easily, oh, so excruciatingly easily take the baby with him – his son, *hers*, whom she loved beyond life, now held in the arms of another – when she thought of it, the great hospital that surely must be in Bangkok, and that he would not carry Cho to it, she wondered if she should just take a knife to Htin Aung. That had seemed her only choice until she had remembered the silly secret code she and Tom had created. So she had learned to embroider and had sent the homespun bag out with the Gurkha on the first opium train of the season. Cho was not so sick then. Then there had seemed to be time enough.

But no word had come back. Nothing. No news even of the Gurkha, who, for all she knew, had been discovered carrying her message and killed for it, or had just died in bad circumstance, the bag long since destroyed by fire or carried off down a river or buried in monsoon mud. Or it could be sitting on Tom's desk, its message unsuspected and unread.

Of course, even if she found the strength and the courage to wield a knife, she knew perfectly well that Htin Aung's death would serve nothing, certainly not Cho. Everyone in the palace – in all Loi Long – knew that the Prince's heir sickened more and more everyday. Cousins, nephews, Lord knew who else would gather round like cawing crows to claim the province, would finish off her baby boy in a trice if they thought it would further their ambitions. Kathleen, too.

4

Her writing hand went very still. He was coming, his bare feet a soft slap slap on the teak veranda floor. Quickly, she continued writing her nonsense in the journal for him to read when he stole it, as he always did. He'd read them all, beginning a few months after she had moved into the palace, taking them secretly like a thief, returning them secretly like a guilty child. He'd not bother with it tonight, nor did it matter. For what she was putting into it was that she'd ridden Maung Swe that morning. A freedom, the only freedom, he had granted her, and that always with a guard and a gun at her back.

She felt his presence the moment he entered the room, felt as much as heard him approach her, smelled the faint sweat of him, overlaid with turmeric and garlic and ngapi. He waited beside her, saying nothing. Slowly, knowing what she'd see, she turned her head towards him, towards the mound already swelling the folds of his longyi at the level of her eyes. As quietly as he, she stood up, not looking at his face, never at his face, he must never see her anger and her fear, and preceded him to the bed. He had been generous with that, a western bed for her.

She slid within the mosquito bar to stretch out on her back. He lifted the bar and sat beside her. Cho coughed, whimpered, coughed, and began to cry, then to scream. Oh, dear God. Of course, it infuriated the Sawbwa. He looked to the corner where U-pym and the baby lay. "Stop him, woman!" Though she had some English, thanks to Kathleen, he spoke in Shan. "It disgusts your prince. It sounds like a sick cat."

Even before he'd finished, U-pym was creeping from the room, the squalling baby cradled in her arms, Kathleen watching them go in the soft light, her hatred for him, her terror for Cho causing her to gasp as if being smothered, and she knew she'd been right not to plead again for Cho's life. As likely as not, his response might be to fling the baby against the wall. She'd watched him do that once to a cat.

He loosened her longyi and pulled it down with hard small gestures, down so that he could spread her legs. She no longer wore panties. They'd all worn out with no replacements, and anyway, she'd learned early they were of no use to her here, in this bed. His breath was hissing through his teeth, as always. And she could hear, as always, in a strange harmony with him, the light breathings and little whispers of the three gathering in the doorway. Witnesses. To provide him assistance if she should resist, as they had the first time. His three wives, and her only friends.

But she didn't resist. She must be clever. Michael had been the first to see that in her, and she'd had two years of perfecting the talent, of practicing how to feel nothing, and she no longer wondered anymore if she would ever feel anything of that deep bloom opening inside again. She knew she wouldn't.

Only once had it happened with Htin Aung. Only once had he wanted her to share the pleasure with him, had tried to arouse it in her. She had fought to quell it, but her body, too long without it and awakening to the memory of a more knowing touch, had betrayed her. Had misled her to lie to herself. And had nearly destroyed her, for on the explosion she had cried out Michael's name.

It had so diminished the prince he had pulled back and up from her, his eyes glittering in his lean brown face, and had carried the flat of his hands against her cheeks over and over again, each time with a grunt.

Since then, his readiness was all, hers nonexistent, so that he hurt her, even tore her sometimes. Her friends were gentle to her then, their soft hands ministering to her with fragrant salves.

She raised her knees as he preferred it before he told her to. Tonight, the only betrayal by her body was that her hands, unnoticed by him, balled into fists fierce and determined. Tonight, he must have no suspicions. She would see to it.

2

The jeep had come down the slope with a grinding whine as the driver used first gear to brake through the thick post-monsoon dust. But Michael hadn't seen it until it came around the dense clump of bamboo rising close to three stories high, and even then the light had haloed the driver so that he couldn't make out who it was. The jeep had stopped, the motor'd died, the driver got out, and Michael was on the brink of seeing her, finally seeing her, when he was jerked forward in the seat of his cab, which had stopped with a shrieking skid in the heavy Hong Kong monsoon rain.

The driver in the car beside them leaned out his window into the wet, screeching like the tires in high angry Chinese, giving Michael's cabby the finger. He, in turn, leaned across the front seat to screech back, and Michael figured one or the other'd be out of the car in three secs barrelling for a fight, so he smacked his hand down on the back of the front seat by his driver's ear, shot his arm forward to point through the windshield and in his best command voice said, "Go!" It worked, or maybe it was the fact that his passenger was twice his size, but the driver jerked the gear into first and they skidded off into traffic.

No dream. He'd been wide awake. Anyway, in Nam even the dream came seldom, the full memory never, but pretty obvious why the thought of it had come now, on his way to see Tom. Was she with him? Here, with him? He couldn't see her face, couldn't in the dream either. Always woke up too soon. Any old noise could do it – things seeming extraneous to him. But maybe just himself running away from the clarity. From memory.

Nothing really got forgotten, wasn't that what the experts said? And bits were restored to him. This about her eyes. That about her mouth. And her hair, oh, yes. A sudden smell, a little noise would do it, unwanted and without warning, like just now. Probably brought on by the snapping growl of a passing motorbike, seemed everybody in Asia rode one, never mind it didn't sound much like a jeep. Too long without trying to summon the whole. Even three years ago when packing away his stuff to store with Richard he hadn't fanned through the pictures from Burma, just tossed them into a box.

The cab was crossing Kowloon from Kai Tak Airport through the late rainy afternoon. The world's worst landing strip in bad weather. Michael stretched his neck against the unfamiliar collar and tie, his tightening throat. His foot locker had provided him with one polo shirt and a moldy pair of jeans. Enough to've gotten him to Hong Kong, but then while waiting for his connection in Saigon he'd found himself in the PX at Tan Son Nhut, ended up with a full uniform, including his ribbons. He was halfway to Hong Kong before he admitted the reason why: showing off. Especially to Kathleen, oh yeah. Walk the top of the fence, let her see how brave you are. Worse than a jerk. A total asshole. He almost took the ribbons off, but he didn't.

The wry thought occurred that if he'd really wanted to impress Kathleen he shouldn't have put Major Niemeier off two days ago. No dressing down but the offer of a Combat Direct Commission, a real jump for a Warrant Officer Two. He'd have to extend for a full third tour in Nam, but hell, he'd already been flirting with that, only down in the Delta winning hearts and minds with the new fast-growing rice. After the thing at Kent State three months ago, everybody knew nobody would be set free in the States looking like a hero, medals or not. The college degree that enabled the offer lay in third world agriculture, and working in the Delta might get him a start on some kind of future outside the U.S.

The Major knew about the degree, just not what field. With it and Michael's in-country record, he said he could almost guarantee Michael would take the promotion home, well on his way to an Army career. Almost guarantee. Hedging his bets, typical of Niemeier, as if it mattered. An Army career wasn't in Michael's plans – not that he had any.

He heaved a sigh, leaned his head against the cab's greasy leatherette seat-back and shut his eyes. Close to being a burnt out case was what he was. Which the Major suspected, but it hadn't stopped him any. So what if Michael put others in jeopardy? A field commission for one of his men would enhance his record, and Mr. Cameron was candidate of the moment.

"Not much combat, Mr. Cameron," said Niemeier. "Just a whole bunch of in-bounds coming in, and you'll be platoon leader."

His own platoon. In-flight instruction of the new guys. That wasn't combat? Half the kids already called Michael Pappy – you'd think he had thirty years on them when it was more like eight – because he was forever putting one or another in the peter seat to take him into shit heaven and get him up to snuff.

Pappy. And nobody worried that he might betray them. Too slow, maybe, or a hesitation that would spin the Loach down into the ground like a corkscrew.

How did the fucking Army ever give a guy like Niemeier a command in the first place? Talking about their shared "war weariness," when maybe once a month he'd take the controls and fly down to Saigon for a little overnight fun and games. Had to be exhausting.

The cab careened around a corner and Michael's eyes flew open as the gates of the All Asia Ecumenical College flew past on either side. Now on a single lane black-top campus road, Michael somehow spotted the drive and leaned forward to punch his insane cabby in the shoulder, shouting for him to slow down and turn. The Howards' house sat at the head of the drive – a Chinese house, low, closed in on itself, its roof tiled green with swallow-tail eaves, probably built around an interior courtyard.

Michael had called from Da Nang and reached Tom, just to say he was coming over. The line static was terrible, phone-time hard to come by, so he'd left the rest for later. Didn't even ask about Kathleen.

How changed would she be? Lord, right this minute he couldn't summon up anything. Not mouth, eyes. Not the way she sounded. Not the way she'd felt under his hands. Richard would have a lot to answer for when this turned out to be as awkward – hell, as absurd as burgeoning uneasiness informed Michael it was going to be.

The cab drew up before the house and Tom came out the door before Michael had finished paying off the driver. Looking around at him, in that flashing moment all Michael saw was Kathleen in Tom's face.

Anyone would have known them for brother and sister, yet so different. Same light hair, but hers catching red from sunlight and Tom's the color of dun-colored straw, no wave to it at all; the same tip-tilted noses, but Kathleen's finer, narrower; the same fair skin, Tom's more freckled, but raising the same fine down. The same cheekbones, hers slighter, and maybe higher, allowing Kathleen's smile to curl up the sides of her mouth and slant her eyes. That's where the difference between them really lay. The eyes. Tom's a washed-out blue. Hers a true green, deepening or brightening with her moods. No matter. Looking at Tom now, Michael saw her. Just like that, the whole of her face. As if she'd been in his head all along. Coming around the bamboo clump towards him, the hill village at his back, her hand reaching out, and her hair glowing around her face.

The recognition of it shook Michael so that he could hardly respond with any sense to Tom's reaching hand, his thanks to Michael for coming, calling him "Mick." Immediately, Michael was looking beyond him, but no one else came out the door.

Tom led him in to a hallway, and Michael had it together enough to take in the parlor beyond an arch, eyes searching. And his hand went loose on his duffle so it landed on flagstones with a small plop. The room was empty and so close to ugly, so sparely furnished with what had to be hand-me-down mission furniture – scarred-up teak-wood, seats and arms both, not a pillow to soften any of it – that he knew.

"She's not here." He said it aloud, not meaning to, half-whispering.

But it brought Tom, who'd been heading along the hall, around in a spin to stare at Michael. "Is that what you thought? That she's here? No. No."

Michael looked at him, saw more than regret, saw pain in Tom's eyes. "Leave your kit for later," Tom said, nodding to the duffle, "come back to my study. There's a lot – a great deal – " A shake of his head and he turned once again to lead away.

There was something not just wrong. It was something bad. Dread, a new familiar in Nam, now filled him here. Four years he'd managed to thrust her away, but she'd always been alive somewhere, that was a thing he'd always known.

Slowly, he followed Tom down the hall to the room at the end where Tom entered and held the door for him. Inside, Michael stopped, turned to face Tom with it almost asked, when Tom said, "Kathleen remains in Burma, Mick. At Loi Long."

Michael damned near sagged with relief, then disappointment swept it aside. He firmed up against it, to hide it. Tom was watching him again. Michael had determined on the plane that no way were the Howards going to suspect what they'd put him through four years ago. He may not have succeeded, for Tom looked away, out of kindness perhaps. But he also looked oddly thoughtful, as if surprised. He stepped past Michael to cross the room.

Mick. A long time since anyone had called him that. The name he'd always insisted on as a boy. Had he been that young when in Burma with the Howards? Now it jangled. Kathleen had called him Michael from the first.

Still in Loi Long. All this time? How was it possible? Hadn't that crazy dictator closed Burma to the whole world?

Tom had gone to a small cabinet under a window. He pulled out a bottle of liquor and two glasses. "Scotch all right?" he asked, casting a glance Michael's way.

Michael managed a short nod. There had never been drink available at the farm in Keng Tung Province. Tom wouldn't have wasted truck space on transporting it up country from Rangoon, not to mention the cost of whiskey in Burma.

While Tom poured, Michael at last summoned the interest to look around. No more elegant than the parlor, this room at least welcomed with comfort. Cushioned wicker chairs and couch – stuff from the farm? But no, these cushions were bright. Fresher, too, Michael would bet. Still, once you'd got used to the lumps, the faint mustiness, that old fraying reed furniture back in Keng Tung was cozy enough. You could read a book clear through by the gasoline light, or sit talking into the night, making plans, your arm around Kathleen . . . Books had been stuffed into two or three rickety bookcases or piled in corners on the floor. The bamboo basha walls couldn't support the weight of hanging shelves. Somehow Tom could always find what he wanted when he wanted it. Michael never had figured out his system. Here, the walls were lined with crowded bookshelves broken by one space where hung a panel of old Shan silk, its reds, purples, rich blues woven through with gold thread.

Turning from the little bar, Tom caught Michael's bemusement at the glasses of Scotch in his hands, and he nodded as if Michael had wondered aloud. "Oh, yes," he said, "lots of differences. Everything . . . me." Michael could see some of them. Tom's body softening a little, hair going gray. At only thirty-four? And when they'd shaken hands outside, his were no longer that of a farmer. "Your expectations of me had best change, too." Tom sounded dogged.

That was too much. "What expectations? I haven't had any expectations of you in years, Tom." Tom's eyes widened, startled. How come? More than anyone else, Tom had to understand the edge in Michael's voice.

Tom handed him his drink. "There's ice if you prefer," he said. Michael shook his head. Tom raised his own glass in a little toast. "Michael," he said. Well. Michael, now. Tom sipped, and glanced around the room. "An improvement over the parlor, isn't it? A friend helped me with it. She very much would like to meet you."

She? Michael wondered.

"Though I shouldn't complain. Everybody at the college pitched in with furniture. The house is set aside for the chair of economics. Come on, sit down," he finished, taking a seat himself.

Struggling for patience, Michael sat opposite him. "Economics," Michael said, to keep the chit chat going, though only God knew why. And then he remembered. Sure. That's how Tom and Richard had met as undergraduates at Cornell. Both econ majors. But Tom the chair of a college department? He was a farmer. Used to be. And a pastor.

"Yeah," Tom was saying. "No reason for you to know, of course. I got a double doctorate. Divinity and economics. Odd combination, I guess, but the two schools went along, cross-over credits, whatever. Your brother was in law school, then. We were already out of close touch."

Even so, Michael thought. But all Richard had told him was there was this missionary guy out in Burma, a friend of his, running a demonstration farm and he needed some pure-bred stock. This was after he'd hauled Michael out of the Haight and had waited with him in a suite at the Mark Hopkins 'til Michael came down off the maryjanes and hash. "You always said you wanted to be a farmer," he'd said. "It'll be the saving of you." For awhile, Michael had thought it was.

"You're thinner than I remember," Tom said, eyes again too sharp on Michael. He smiled a little. "You look taller."

Hardly, Michael thought. He'd already been going on twenty-two, back then. "Army rations," he said, trying for lightness, wondering when the hell they'd get to whatever it was had brought him here.

"Exhaustion, too, maybe?"

Well, he had that right. Michael swallowed some Scotch. A blend, not the best but not the worst, either. As uncomfortable as he thought he'd ever been, he sent his own eyes roving the room again, spotted some pieces of Burmese lacquer. So few when there had been so many. He remembered these. The layered tiffin carrier and a tray and a little covered box, maybe fifty, sixty years old, Tom had told him once, their rusty-reds and greens and black still glowing. There was a pile of books in a corner behind a table holding a sloppy bunch of magazines. Not everything had changed. And then he saw it. Sitting on the battered old desk – obviously another hand-me-down – the framed photo of Kathleen.

He was on his feet, crossing to it without thought, helpless, drawn as if by a rope.

Tom said, "I like that picture. I don't have that many of her – it was

12

too difficult to get them developed, remember?"

Michael managed barely to nod.

"Aren't you going to inquire after her, Michael?" There was a hardness to Tom's voice, and Michael let the old anger show, swinging around and the hell with it. "How come she's still in Burma and you're here? It's a lousy place for a girl alone!"

Something flashed in Tom's eyes Michael had thought never to see – a deep anger of his own. "Your concern's a trifle late, don't you think?"

Michael stood dumbfounded, flooding with a resentment that he was damned if he'd admit, even to himself, was part guilt. About what, for Christ's sake? He didn't deserve it.

Tom looked as if he'd like to bite his own tongue. A moment, a long draw at his Scotch and, "How much do you know about Burma these days, Michael?"

"Not all that much, I guess," Michael answered, simmering. "We don't see many newspapers in Nam." He tried to calm down a little, get rid of the sarcasm. "The last I heard, the military dictator had kicked all Americans out. I mean, I knew from your Christmas card to Richard from here three years back, in what, '67? . . . " Shit, he really hadn't forgotten any of it. " . . . that Kathleen had stayed in the Shan States. But surely by now . . . I just assumed – "

Tom held up his hand in a plea for patience. "In '67, General Nei Win was already ripping off the country . . ." – his voice was going ragged with a bitter humor – "calling it the Burmese way to socialism. And then, on the pretext of unification, he moved against the hill tribes. My Kaws, the Pa-o, even the Wahs. He used artillery for the love of God against those poor reformed headhunters." He finished off his drink before he continued. "But not the royal Shans. The Sawbwas were still dickering with him, so he left them alone for awhile."

Michael set his Scotch aside, determined to cut through all this, but Tom didn't give him the moment. "I managed to hold on longer than most Americans. Partly the livestock you brought in. It made the Rangoon militarists think I might have some value to Burma." He gave a little half snort, stood up to go after another drink. "But finally they accused me of fomenting rebellion, so I had to get out."

"And Kathleen stayed," Michael said. "I get it, but – "

Facing Michael, Tom nodded. "A man came to see me two and a half weeks ago, Michael – from Loi Long. Not a Burmese Shan. I work with

13

them, the ones that make it here, so that's how this man knew to find me. A Gurkha." He hesitated, maddeningly.

Michael had had enough. "What is all this, Tom? Time to get to it, about Kathleen." His voice sounded as raw as it felt.

Tom set his own drink down and went to collect a shoulder bag lying on a table. He held it out to Michael. "Take a look."

It looked like any Shan bag to Michael. He'd brought several of them back from Burma – even one for Charlotte, Richard's wife, though of course he'd never caught sight of it after he gave it to her – not Charlotte. Didn't match her kid pumps. But he'd used one himself as a carryall back in school. Long gone, now. This one in his hands was the traditional red – did all Asians love red? – with jagged multi-colored interweavings – and, now he peered closer, some figures were running along the bottom, not woven, embroidered. They looked like Burmese script.

"Nonsense squiggles, mostly – except for these." Tom drew his finger along the edge of the bag, pointing out the five in a row he meant. "These are Burmese numbers. Remember them?" But Michael didn't. He'd learned them while there – for street signs and whatever, prices of things. Forgotten, now.

"The Gurkha who brought it said it was given him by Kathleen. Shan weavers don't usually embroider their bags. I wasted more than a day before I figured it out. Those numbers." Tom pointed as he went on. "This figure, and this and this and this, they are real, not just – doodles. This is eight. This five. Twelve. And sixteen."

Michael had to wait for him to continue. Tom's voice was low. "I suppose she was hoping that if the bag took somebody's notice on its way to me, the numbers would seem like astrological signs."

"And they aren't."

Tom shook his head. "No. When Kathleen was very little, I'd come back from the States for school breaks and I'd try to teach her the alphabet and her numbers. I did it by telling her we had a code nobody could decipher except us. She was so . . . she had such a crush on her older brother, sharing secrets was – . " He swallowed. "It's simple enough, of course. A, B, C, D, one, two, three, four." He pointed at the Burmese numbers on the Shan bag again. "Eight – H. Five – E. Twelve – "

Michael had counted on his fingers. "L," he said.

"Sixteen," Tom continued, but Michael cut him off. "Help." Jesus. What the hell was this?

"Kathleen embroidered them." Tom sounded as sure as if he were proclaiming the presence of God.

Michael was spinning. It was – crazy. Wild. "She hated sewing," he said, as if that offered some kind of reality. But it was true enough. She'd complained, only half kidding, the whole time she'd sewn up his longyi for him.

"It's probably a thing she's learned to do lately, embroidery – out of God knows what, boredom maybe." Tom caught Michael's eyes with his own, holding them steady, firm. And again, that odd accusation. "Prisoners do get bored, don't they, Michael."

Stunned silent, Michael pulled his eyes away, drew the bag away from under Tom's hand. He ran his fingers across those Burmese numbers, then crumpled the rough homespun cloth in his fist as if to catch the warmth of its maker. But there was no warmth. Only the memory of Kathleen – homespun and clever Kathleen.

Eyes lifting sharp like flint against Tom, Michael ground it out: "How could you not send word!" If Tom was trying to speak, Michael was blind to it. "You had to know I was frantic. I wrote her constantly for months through you, and no answer, she just quit writing me, she – . In prison?"

Now Michael saw, Tom's eyes gone horrified. "She didn't quit writing," he stumbled it out. "You did."

Feeling a tremble in his hands, Michael struggled to get hold of himself. Finally he said, "Never." He got to his drink, picked it up, couldn't stomach it, banged it down again only to have the Scotch slop over. He fished out a handkerchief to mop at it. "Michael," Tom had started, but Michael managed to level his voice and swept over him. "Never, God damn it, not for eight months hearing nothing, and always writing every other day . . . " One shake of his head and he continued, "I tried to go back, Tom. I wrote you. I had Richard pull strings. Rangoon wasn't letting anybody in. The Ecumenical Mission's head office said your station letters hadn't stopped and they would know if anything was wrong." His voice was gravelling now, anger in full spate. "So, shit. I plowed on through ag school to my BS, trash in the mouth, and figured the hell with it."

And her, he didn't say. Increasingly sure she'd come to doubt her own feelings, to doubt his, but how could she just dump what they'd wanted so furiously to do together, without a word? It had fed their own fire, so Michael had thought, and thinking so, he'd had to conclude that none of it had been real.

"And all the time she was – God in heaven, down in Rangoon Prison? Still?"

"Michael, if you'd be quiet a second. You haven't understood. Your letters just stopped. She wrote for months with nothing back. I know. Every week I went out to Loi Long, saw her, and mailed her letters to you from back in Keng Tung so they'd go out quicker."

The two stared at each other. But it was surely Michael who felt the cruel twist of it the more. Four years lost. Four fucking years. He licked at his dry lips. "The government? Why should they care about two kids writing love letters . . . "

"Right. Not the government. It would've been the Sawbwa."

"Sawbwa – " Michael started, then lost it.

"Sao Htin Aung," Tom filled in. "He was still negotiating with Nei Win then, trying to outwit him." He studied over it a moment, then, "Intercepting Loi Long mail in the Keng Tung post office would have been simple wisdom for him. He probably figured it belonged to him anyway. He had droit de seigneur for everything in his province."

Hell. Oh, hell, thought Michael.

Tom had suddenly stopped, no doubt hearing his own words and the significance of them. But he picked up in a moment, struggling a little. "Even stuff between you and me – must've, because I did write you. I felt like an interfering old goat, but Kathleen's misery was so profound . . . And after I left – well, there never had been regular mail in or out of Loi Long, and with the political situation . . . People do come out, bringing reports, sometimes of Kathleen. That she was still teaching. Once, that she had become a member of the Sawbwa's household, I thought for safety's sake."

Both were held silent, appalled at the waste. Tom continued at last. "No bars to her prison, but I think – from the bag – a prison nonetheless."

Michael had started down his own track. "He didn't just happen to steal our mail," he said softly. "And damn it, I knew, Tom. Not about Kathleen or the letters. About him. First time I saw him, when Kath took me up to his palace. Standing there on the veranda at the top of those wide wooden steps, all in his Shan robes looking like – some potentate out of *The King and I*! And hungry for her. I saw it in him." The fucker stopped my life dead, Michael thought. Just coolly shredded both our lives.

"I didn't see it, God help us all," Tom said. "And he is a potentate, Michael. All the Shan princes are – were. The rest are either dead or languishing in that horror of Rangoon Prison, their states absorbed by Nei Win into Burma. But not Sao Htin Aung. He's holed up in the mountains of Loi Long."

"With Kathleen," Michael said.

Tom took a deep breath. Was there worse to come? "He's one of three drug lords that are known in the west, the one Burmese Shan," Tom was saying. "The others are Thai and Laotian, though *he's* said to be an American. They all bank huge profits in Switzerland from opium sales in the Golden Triangle."

"And you just left her there," Michael said. So did I, the thought followed immediately, even as Michael heard the terrible condemnation in his voice continue. "With him. Knowing all that."

The tendons in Tom's neck strained. He'd gone white, looked sick. And then, the clock that Michael had recognized from the farm, now standing in the hall here, chimed its Westminster quarter hour. It had rung twice maybe already, but neither of them had paid it attention, 'til now. Tom looked at his watch. "Almost time for the ferry," he said. "I go up to Macao several evenings a week, to seek out displaced Shans and hill people, Burmans, too. We keep a clinic and some cheap apartments there we've turned into dormitories, even a means of livelihood for some. But they have to be pulled off the streets first, most of 'em on opium. Tonight's one of my nights."

Michael was outraged. To be left like this, and nothing clear?

Tom saw, spoke quietly. "It's what I do, Michael. Of course, you must come." He turned and headed for the door.

Michael watched him go. Then grabbing up the Shan bag, he followed.

3

Not much was said most of the drive to the terminal. The rain had stopped, people moving again on the streets, but Michael saw none of it. Burgeoning up in his mind and having to be smacked down again and again were the insistant questions of what could he do about Kathleen, and what did Tom want him to do about Kathleen, and worst of all, was she all right? Except for the last, he had a pretty damned good idea what the answers were. Plus which, coloring those questions red was the shit fact that except for that Shan bastard, he wouldn't be killing people in Vietnam, and Kathleen wouldn't be – doing what? He kept having to swallow against whatever it was he'd eaten hours ago.

"A lot of villages in eastern Upper Burma took a cash crop from a tiny opium field, back then," Tom said suddenly. As if there'd been no interruption. "But anything like the size of what Htin Aung must have them harvesting nowadays . . . if that was going on, I didn't know it. The poppy fields would had to have been far away from the main tracks, the ones I travelled certainly. Kathleen didn't know, either, though she must, now."

All right, Michael begrudged him, he hadn't known. But how could a man – Tom, of all men – just ditch his little sister? Again the thought came, I did, too. And with it, this time, the sound of Kathleen's weeping, smothered, so nobody would hear her from the small bore latrine toilet attached to the back of the farmhouse, the only place she could find some assurance of privacy. He'd thought he was doing the right thing. Had been sure of it, it never occurring to him that he might be wrong, or mistaken, or . . . Talk about changes, mistakes're what he thought about all the time now, flying scared he'd make one, the fear beating all around him on the wings of the adrenaline.

But with Kathleen. . . so full of his own certainty back then, so damned eager to go on his own self-determined course, he'd betrayed her. Hadn't even known it, in all these years. But maybe not all that different, then and now. A mistake in Nam, and people counting on him would be betrayed, too. Only, in Nam they might not come back. And Kathleen either.

Tom braked and turned into the car park, again startling Michael into the present. They found a slot and entered the terminal, Michael with the bag bunched in his pocket. They couldn't talk there, it was too crowded, and that served Michael fine. He couldn't put it together right: here and there, now and five years ago with Kathleen, the wonder of that and his uncertain foot on the pedal day before yesterday.

But it wasn't a long wait until they were admitted to the ferry, maybe not long enough. Tom led the way to a sheltered spot by the railing behind the wheel house. The engine noise would smother their words, he said.

The ferry got underway quickly. It had turned into one of those recurring monsoon evenings when later in the day the rains drift off and the sunset is a glory: deep ochers, magentas, and at the end, blood red. The harbors and island reaches from Hong Kong on up were busy with cargo ships and boats. Painted junks sailing, bobbing; anchored private yachts and garishly lighted restaurant barges; the big island crowded at the shoreline and running part way up to the peak with tall white buildings showing rosy gold in the sunset. And everywhere the sampans slid across the reflecting oily water, propelled by boatmen weaving their long stern oars back and forth, back and forth, so languid it was close to lascivious.

Tom had pulled out a handkerchief to wipe the railing dry of the leftover rain drops and lean on it, to pick up with what he'd started to say in the car. Only this time, as he spoke Michael's name to get Michael to look at him, his eyes were pleading. "I was trying to save thirty-seven hill-tribe villages from the Army of Burma, and my own farm. And she was fifty-odd kilometers away, refusing to leave Loi Long, telling me how she'd found a life for herself trying to bring those remote valley Shans into the twentieth century, teaching them English and history and – it was like a calling, after our parents." His voice was rough. "Or her big brother. She believed it was her part to see to her Shans. To make things better for them."

He cleared his throat. Had to, probably. "All this she said to me the last weekend she came home. I was after her to leave right away, right then. I may have missed some things, but I knew it was going to get bad. I'm sorry, Michael, but – she said she didn't want to go live in some city somewhere or go back to the States. 'I'd go live anywhere with Michael,' she said, 'but without him . . . this is where I must be.'

"She trusted Sao Htin Aung as she would an uncle – or older brother." He swallowed as if he, too, felt some rising nausea. "And so did I trust him, to protect her. Not long after, two and a half weeks I think, I had to leave. In such a hurry, I couldn't get back out to Loi Long. Oh, damn it, she'd turned twenty, and she was changed!"

Michael looked out across the moving water. Because of me, he thought.

Tom finished in a kind of sad disbelief. "Was there ever more of an innocent than she was then? Maybe than all of us were."

After all our loving, Michael thought, the way she was with me was not innocent. Nor was I. What did I do to you, Kathleen? Make you think because you were wise with me, you were wise in all things, could be safe in all things? Something else I should've known.

Michael pulled out the bag and smoothed it across the top of the railing. "Tell me about the Gurkha."

"One of Htin Aung's mercenaries. He rode guard – " But the ferry was slowing down, out in the middle of the bays, finally stopping dead while the deck hands used a boat hook and hauled a man out of the water.

He was lacking a shirt, his pants loose, his body stringy. Swimming for freedom? Or a suicide off the ferry? The hands tipped over a barrel, chocked it and draped him across it belly down, head dangling, and left him, water leaking from his mouth.

As the ferry got underway again, Tom and Michael passed a glance at each other. Tom was the first to move, going to the drowned man to squat beside him, the man's face turned towards him, and he took hold of his wrist.

Michael came to the other side of the barrel. "Pulse?"

Tom looked across the barrel at him. "A flicker," he said.

Michael said, "Come around to this side, Tom." Tom looked a trifle startled, perhaps at the command in Michael's voice, and obeyed. Michael placed his hand spread wide across the drowned man's back, above where the diaphragm would be, and shoved down hard, twice. A moment, the man coughed, and suddenly in a whoosh, the vomit spurted out of his mouth. Tom's pants and shoes would have received the lot. He smiled at Michael, and the two hefted the man up by his arm-pits, supporting him to make sure he could stand. But he shook free, ducked his head and darted away. Michael and Tom exchanged shrugs and returned to the railing.

Tom might be somewhat soft in the middle, but his legs must still be in shape for that easy squat. Silly, but it cheered Michael. At least some of the remembered past had come with him into the present. Tom had had a farmer's body, muscles that could do most anything – jump, lift, run from an enraged water buffalo if need be, or scythe a high-hills wheatfield, or balance astride two bamboo beams high in a field with a winnowing basket to let the wind blow the chaff from the rice. Michael had watched him, knowing he had to do that. He fell five times, while the bare-chested village farmers squatted around their fire, noisily sipping salted green tea, and laughed at untranslatable jokes. But he did it, and one of the farmers rolled him a cheroot and made him smoke it, and they all laughed some more when he inhaled and coughed his lights out.

"Okay, the Gurkha," Michael said. He took out cigarettes, and automatically offered Tom the pack, belatedly surprised when Tom accepted one. He knew Tom didn't smoke – or hadn't used to. After a couple of pulls, Tom tossed it away with a grimace. "Never did like 'em," he said. And then, "He guarded the opium shipments into Laos. Kathleen apparently got the bag to him on his last turn-around trip. Smart girl. He wouldn't harbor the loyalty a Shan would for his Sawbwa, so she took less of a chance in trusting him. But how she knew a Gurkha soldier had plans to skip out and come here . . . " Tom shrugged. "Maybe she'll tell us when we see her." He caught himself short on that one. His eyes flew to Michael's, then away.

Tom was hatching a real pipe dream for himself. And for Michael. No doubt most certainly for Michael.

Michael snapped his cigarette out over the railing. What kind of desperation dictated sending a message in a code learned in childhood? Pictures of Kathleen kept rising up, after so long of not being able to raise pictures of her at all – crouched in some corner of that wooden palace in the deepest night, her hair catching copper in the light from an oil lamp, stitching, stitching, her breaths coming in little scared puffs, so afraid . . .

Not her breaths but the soft humid air of the bays and harbors brushed against his face. Salt air, warm. It felt good. And sometimes moving on it from the shore came the thick smell of Asia: charcoal cookfires, rotting fish, wilting pagoda flowers and incense, spit and urine and garlic and sweat, open sewers. The smell had struck him like a blow when the old freighter carrying him and the hogs and the chickens had chugged up the Rangoon River to dock opposite Strand Road. Like other first loves, he thought, it seems the memory of it is never lost after all. It had welcomed him again a year and a half ago when he'd first landed in Saigon.

The silence grew heavy. Michael drew breath to confront it all head on, when Tom sighed and said, "So. How is it, Michael?" He gave a short chuckle. "I'm not even sure what your rank is."

Michael turned his head from the view to look at Tom, face ruddy in the sunset, his gaze on the ribbons.

"And I certainly don't know what all those colors signify," Tom went on. "But the V's dangling from them mean medals won in combat, that I do know. And the purple bars mean wounds."

Trying to avoid all this stuff, Michael answered truly about the other, eyes fixed on nothing. "How is it? Fun, to begin with. You won't like hearing that. But it's come to be . . . mostly ugly. Every day a death of something." He stopped there, but Tom was waiting, so . . . "I'm a chief warrant officer two, Tom. Fourth is tops. It's an appointed rank the Army's using to fast track the training of helicopter pilots. Commissions require more education. So it hangs in a kind of Army limbo, between non-coms and commissioned officers." He tried a rueful smile. "But it gets me into the officers club, along with some command responsibility. About the best rank going."

Staving off talk about decorations which most in Nam figured to be a crock anyway, Michael asked, "Were you, Tom? Fomenting rebellion?"

Tom's eyes slid away as if ashamed. He took his time answering, and then was oblique. "If it weren't for my busted eardrum, I'd've been drafted. I always knew if that happened, I'd declare a conscientious objection. And it would've been the truth. But now, I couldn't do that anymore, Michael."

Michael couldn't help it, he started a grin. Well, well. Tom had fought for his people.

Tom's smile was less triumphant. "I couldn't let it – just happen. That S.O.B. Nei Win had beaten our lovely little Eden down into a lost world filled with nightmares. God damn him. Burma was once the rice basket of South East Asia. A main rice exporter. And now the people starve. And then to turn his filthy troops against the tribes . . . My Kaws wanted to fight, came to me to show 'em how." His smile now was bitter. "The soldiers were killing their chickens, their hogs, started burning the stored rice from last year's harvest. What were they to eat all winter? So I joined them. I had the vehicles. They got hold of some Kuomintang guns. But what did I know about how to fight a war? It was a farce." He shook his head, mouth tight. "The Burmese started shanghaiing the young men. Using them as human shields to fight the other tribes. My presence was only making things worse."

Both men avoided each other's eyes, Michael without any words at all, but wondering if Kathleen had known about what her brother was doing, and how she had felt.

Then Tom resumed. "Made me question everything, of course. Questions without answers." He surprised Michael with something close to a grin, if wry. "And I haven't figured out yet what I'm supposed to do about it."

They let it rest. "They do Sally, too?" Odd that he really wanted to know, hadn't thought about Fat Sal in a very long time. He'd been remarkably fond of her.

"Sally?" Then Tom remembered. "Sally. Yes, afraid so. But she'd had some five or six litters by that time. Her blood line's in every pig-pen in Keng Tung Province, probably – if considerably diluted. Due to you, Michael, both the pigs and the pens. And to me. I take pride in it."

That moment they shared, and again fell quiet. Both of them too overloaded all at once, probably. God knew Michael was. But now and then he glanced at Tom, looking so troubled. Shit, how not? He was full of troubles, wasn't he? And now and then, his glance got caught in Tom's, almost as if Tom were watching him, speculating. Was there something more? Something else?

Just what he wanted from him, that's all, Michael thought. But if Tom didn't want to push for it, why should Michael make him? It could have no good ending, anyway.

Tom spoke only once for the remainder of the ferry ride, to point out a Taoist pagoda sitting on a hill, its red roof tiles shining. "Full of idols," he said, "and people – women mostly – clapping pieces of wood together, flinging them to the ground, looking for the right answers. Better at it than I am, let's hope."

It was still light though close on seven when they landed. With the empty Shan bag dangling from his shoulder, Tom led the way from the ferry terminal up into Macao. They turned and walked along a main shopping street with elegant little shops, banks, even a casino or two with burly doormen barring entry. Tom's pace was picking up, he seemed energized, eager. They turned off the street running parallel to the harbor into the winding back alleys of what now became a purely Chinese city.

Saying they'd eat dinner later, Tom bought them spicy tidbits off cooking braziers on the street, the crispy heat burning their fingers and

24

tongues, while radios wailed with the shrill violin-like stringed instruments and wrong-scaled xylophones of Chinese music. Cobblestones were slimy underfoot with old rain and God knew what else. Men squatted in doorways clattering mahjongg tiles and toddlers squatted across curbs to relieve themselves. Sounds and sights Michael knew from Chinatown in Da Nang, the smells of frying fat and poor drains filling the nostrils and clinging to the hair.

Walking more slowly now, Tom's eyes roving, seeking the smaller, darker people, his people, among the lighter skinned Chinese, Tom started in.

"Why did you enlist, Michael? Richard wrote you were in medical school, wouldn't't've been drafted, so why?"

"Habit of mine, dropping out. Didn't Richard happen to mention it?" Tom glanced at him quickly, smiled a little, eyes continuing to scour the narrow street. "Before I came to you in Burma, I'd dropped out of pre-law. Surely you knew that. My father's idea to join the old family firm. But I know you do know, I wanted to be a farmer. So, naturally, I dropped into a commune out west. I told Kathleen all this. We opened up to each other, Kath and I."

No reaction from Tom because he seized Michael's arm, turned him into an alley, and Michael saw ahead a small figure in black homespun trousers. Still wearing his hill clothes even here, but maybe they were all he had. Tom hurried to him, began speaking softly, urgently in a language unintelligible to Michael. The man's eyes were glued to Tom's face as if heaven were opening up hope to him. But then they flickered beyond Tom to Michael, and he turned and ran away on down the alley. Tom made no effort to go after him. He returned to Michael, not cast down. "I'll find him again. It's all right."

So they returned to the street, walked on. "A commune, huh?" Tom pursued him, eyes roving again.

"Rainbow Farm," Michael said, and had to chuckle. Right name, all right. Rainbow. "Dropped some acid there. But even in the midst of a good trip I still could smell the stink of diapers – among other things. Nobody bothered to weed much, so the vegetables went all to hell. I got tired of the squabbling – man, you wouldn't believe how those flower-power peaceniks squabble!"

"Wait here," Tom interrupted, moving quickly forward to encounter a Burman wearing a longyi, the sarong both men and women wore in Burma fixed at the waist. So Michael stepped out of the hustling throngs and

25

waited against a wall, watching.

But the memories marched on. That last day at Rainbow, when he'd glanced into the small tarnished hash of a mirror tacked to the window frame to see himself. A thatch of a beard and long curls frizzed out like a clown wig. His grandmother's voice saying, "Goodness, dear, you look a fright!" Right then he'd cut the lot to go cropped and beardless ever since, and he'd shoved off and gone to the Haight.

"Let's go." Tom back, already turning to walk some more, the Burman gone.

"Maybe he got a glimpse of me," Michael said.

"Maybe. Americans are still loved in Burma. But you are very much the soldier, Michael, and a big one."

"Look, Tom. I'm bushed anyway, so – "

"I'd like you to see the clinic, so let's head that way, see what happens." He turned around a corner, Michael dogging his heels. "Richard did say he'd found you in San Francisco, so obviously you left the commune."

"You ever hear of the Haight, Tom?"

"Oh, sure," he said, and cast a smile at Michael. "A street like this – for dopeheads."

Michael let the laugh rise and Tom joined him. Best moment yet of this whole crazy deal. "I crashed in a pad with five other guys and whatever girls – nevermind. I quit the acid. Got hooked on pot. It made everything happy, so why not?"

"You still using, Michael?" Tom stopped and faced Michael.

Michael hesitated, knowing the truth would just buy more trouble, turn him even more into fine dependable Michael. But when he answered it was honest. "No. These days I leave pot to the kids. We've got so many of 'em in Nam. They're the ones with a need for it."

With a nod, Tom started on.

"Never did know how Richard found me. He swore I'd sent him a postcard of the Palace of the Arts with my address on the back." Michael shook his head, a short shake. "No way would I do that. Anyway, he got me clean and hustled me onto a slow boat to you. Even had my passport ready. Stupid me, goin' on board that boat all I could think of was how was I going to pack along some grass – maybe I could tuck it into the chicken feed, or – " He gave a little laugh. "I gotta tell you, Tom, that had to be the longest trip I ever hope to take, because I never did figure out where to stash the grass. I just kept telling myself nevermind, pal, you're going to where they grow the stuff. There I was, on my way to opium heaven, and I'm worried about a little grass!"

"So why did you drop out of med school?"

Had to know it all, didn't he. Fed up with the questions, Michael answered full out. "Hell, I never in my whole life wanted to be a doctor. I wanted to be like you."

He was never sure whether Tom heard that, because his eyes were fixed on another hill man, this one dressed in ragged shorts, and Tom was already striding towards him. Tom took the man by the arm and led him into an alley. But as the man turned he spotted Michael watching, and he jerked free and went. This time when Tom returned to Michael, he admitted it. "Not going to work, I'm afraid."

"Just point me towards the ferry, I'll get a cab at the other end, and if there's a key somewhere – "

"Forget that," Tom said. He reached into a pocket, pulled out a key-ring. "You pick up the car. Go out Queen's Way to Margreave, turn right and you'll find the college. But for heaven's sake, remember to drive on the left. The house key's on the ring, too."

So together they walked out of the Chinese quarter and back to the street heading to the terminal. Michael started down it, but on Tom's call he turned around.

"What are those ribbons for, anyway?"

"Campaigns, mostly." Tom just looked at him. "I fly scout, Tom," sounding patient. "We're always short of pilots, have to work double time, and the Army thinks to keep us happy with citations." But Tom wasn't going with that, so in irritation, Michael finally reported them out. "Two purple hearts. A silver star, two bronze stars and three DFC's. See you back at the house." And he went on his way knowing he'd just handed Tom the expectation of a miracle to add to the pipe dream.

The roof of the ferry terminal was in sight below when it occurred to him that he couldn't remember the color of the car. White? Beige? Or, Christ, maybe it was light blue. Nor did he have any fucking idea where it was parked, he'd been so distracted. He swung around. Tom was gone from the corner, but he'd said he was going to cross the main street and head up harbor. Hadn't he said that? Michael started back up the hill.

4

Michael reached the corner at the top of the hill and looked along the street to see nothing but pleasure-seeking Chinese. Crowded, but Tom was tall enough to be spotted above the Asians. Michael moved quickly in what he thought was the right direction, peering into each narrow cross street, finally turning down one to start combing. On a pass down his third alley, halfway along it he heard scuffling, thuds, grunts, coming from behind a wall where a door stood open and yellow lantern-light fell out onto the cobbles.

Not your business, pal. But he slid along the wall to look round the door – two guys mugging Tom. Shit. Michael barged on in. Tom was bent forward, trying to protect his belly and his head. One of the muggers danced in front of him with a knife that gleamed enough to show what it was, the attacker about to arc it up into Tom's gut while his partner bludgeoned Tom's head from behind. And Tom was going down.

Michael leaped, grabbed the wrist of the hand already thrusting upwards, got it and twisted the arm to the mugger's back, hearing something pop. Not sure if it was a dislocation or a broken bone, Michael heard the little creep cry out. For he was little, and Asian, both assailants were. The one beating on Tom quit, backing away, even as the one Michael held hissed something. But his pal suddenly spun around and disappeared through the wall, his running steps echoing down the alley.

Tom had straightened by now, was leaning back against the wall struggling for air. Michael wrapped his left arm, still holding the knife, across the thug's chest to press him close and under control. He smelled the dank oil in the man's hair, his breath fetid with garlic and bad gums.

"Where're the police!" Michael rapped out.

"Where'd you come from?" Tom managed.

"Tom, for God's sake!" It was the first time Michael had disarmed somebody since basic, but that could've been yesterday it was so easy, even to figuring the assailant was too short compared to him so that if he kicked back and up, his heel wouldn't reach Michael's balls. Still, he didn't want to hold him here forever.

"No police," Tom said, panting less now. He was rubbing at the back of his neck, his shoulder, which must've taken most of the blows. Until he'd bent over, he was probably too tall for the sapper to do more than stun him a little. "They weren't robbers. They were speaking Shan. Here to kill me."

"Why!" But Michael suspected he knew. "Ask him, damn it!"

But now Tom was just looking at the little man, devastated, bewildered somehow. "Tom!" Michael was sharp. They didn't need Tom going into shock. Dazed, Tom just went on as if without Michael's interruption. "They must have followed us from the house and – and waited for you to leave and – mugging's common in Macao, but not on campus, so – "

"Ask him, Tom," Michael said, his voice as even as he could make it.

And at last, Tom spoke in some Asian tongue or other. The creep said nothing. Michael twisted his arm higher up his back, and the guy's head went back with a groan. Startled, Tom's eyes lifted to Michael's face.

"Tell him he doesn't talk to you I'll break another bone," Michael said, and watched what had to be horror rise in Tom. What did he think, for God's sake? Flying choppers in Nam, if a little dangerous, was a white collar job? There was the old man they'd interrogated in that VC temporary camp, only three jerry-built hooches. Interrogated him hard. They'd taken out the four charlies running away before they'd landed, and he was all that was left. Finally, with a shaking, bloody finger the old man had pointed to one of the hooches, and hidden there in the dirt floor they found a trapdoor, and beneath it a hole and the two American airmen from the downed Cobra. They had been interrogated hard, too, tied up, gagged, left struggling to breathe and to rot to death by the VC. It had haunted Michael's dreams for a while. Not what they'd done to the old man, but that stinking hole in the ground and the little horrors it surely had harbored.

"Do it," Michael said. "It could happen again, whatever we do with this guy. You need to know."

Tom talked fast, now, in a sharp questioning mode, as Michael kept twisting and inching that arm up and up, until finally the Asian burst out a long speech. Tom translated with him. "He's from west of Chieng Mai. Thailand, up by the Golden Triangle. The man he works for – his 'lord' – he keeps talking about 'allegiance' – he says his lord owes a cousin, another Shan prince, a debt, and killing me was repayment. Let him go, Michael. His life is ruined in any case, because you stopped him. He and the other one will be running forever."

Tom's eyes were kind of dead, else it was still horror, Michael wasn't sure. But it angered him. He shoved the little Asian forward and planted his foot on the small flat butt to send him flying. The man stayed upright, twisted around and kept going through the open gate. Only afterwards did Michael think they should have asked about Kathleen. Except the guy wasn't from Burma, what could he know?

"You're not the same after all, are you," Tom said.

Michael's eyes had been on the knife in his hand – its point a stiletto and curving upwards from the blade. A real gutting tool. Now he looked up at Tom. Just looked at him. The same? Of course not. At least now Tom wouldn't think him all that great a white knight.

"If Htin Aung wants you killed," Michael said, "he's afraid of you. Afraid of losing her to you, one way or another. If she matters that much, he won't do her harm." That last, pure bullshit, and what he didn't say was that the Sawbwa must know Kathleen had tried to contact Tom. No telling what that S.O.B. Fu Manchu could be doing to her, but if it comforted Tom . . .

The house behind them remained silent. Hear no evil, see no evil. He picked up the Shan bag lying in the mud, slipped the steel gutter into it. "Let's get to the clinic, have 'em look at you." But Tom wouldn't have that either. "It'd scare Ma Hla Swe to death," he said. Whoever she was, Michael thought. But instead of arguing with him, he took Tom's arm beneath the elbow in support and they headed for the ferry. In silence.

The boat was at the dock, only a short wait before it left. Rain had come again, so they sat on one of the high-backed wooden benches in the cabin. Under the flat white light, Tom looked drawn. Awful. Michael wished he'd stretch out, there was room, but Tom only laid his head back, closed his eyes, and now Michael worried whether he should keep him awake in case of concussion.

"What is it you think I can do for you, Tom?"

Tom opened his eyes, turned his head toward Michael. The question hung there, loud like thunder, unable to be retracted.

"Kathleen," Tom corrected softly. "For Kathleen."

Michael looked away, trying to bank his impatience at the lack of realism here. But Tom was continuing. "There's no way to get her out overland. The Burmese army's conducting forays and major battles through-out those mountains. Not to mention Htin Aung's forces guarding Loi

Long Province and the capital."

Armed patrols on the rivers, trigger-happy locals everywhere, and betrayal on all sides, Michael thought. Forget moving through that shit-house of a jungle.

And then Tom finally got to it. "Helicopters can get in through those mountains. And don't need an air strip. I'm told they fly into the palace from Chieng Mai to buy opium."

He'd known it was coming, what else could Tom want from him. But the bald statement of it still took him short. Tom went on hastily, "I've learned some things, haven't wasted much time since I understood Kathleen's – message."

Her cry for help, was what he wanted to say, Michael knew. But he's trying to be – undramatic, maybe – so I'll consider it seriously.

"I have maps," Tom was saying, "made by people who know the mountains and the rivers, travelling them most of their lives, and – "

"Stop." Michael sucked in air. "You don't understand. No heli-copter has the range for the distance, South Vietnam to eastern Burma. My Loach scout is the smallest chopper made, you can be damned sure it doesn't have the range. Plus which, it would mean overflying Laos. Setting aside that I'd be AWOL and flying an airship short of fuel, Laos is a no-fly zone." He shut up. He was saying too much, as if asking to be reasoned with. And he was right.

"No, no, Michael, can't be. Air America's there."

"Right," Michael said, wanting this over. "It's C.I.A. owned and operated, Tom. The scuttlebutt is, everything Nixon is saying about Laos is phony. Sure as hell there's a war going on, and AA's running it – or the C.I.A. is. Without flight orders I'd be shot down by an AA plane not ten minutes across the fence."

Tom was looking at him with sick eyes, maybe with pain and head-ache, maybe just emotionally drained. But spinning this out was no good either. "I'm going home, Tom. Probably within the next three weeks." Tom drew breath audibly, and Michael could have gasped himself. Was he lying? Or was it decided? He ground it out with finality. "I'm sick to death of it, flying around, trying to find people so they can die. That's what I do for the Army, Tom." The small brown men you taught me to respect in Burma, Michael didn't say. The thought ran on, a surprised recognition: I thought to help them fight their war, that's why I came. Shit.

But Tom was offering a little smile, for God's sake. "And you make it safer for the grunts. I know what you do, Michael."

"Sure." He was angry again. "Scout it out, show yourself so the VC gives fire, the Cobra does its job, and down the grunts drop into the landing zone you've cleared for 'em. A month later, the dinks're back, same LZ, same job, different grunts but same body count. About the third time you're sent to clear the same LZ, you know it's no fuckin' way to win a war."

Tom had straightened on the bench. Maybe the bitterness in Michael had restored the pastor in him. His voice was gentle. "What will they have you doing in the States?"

Michael studied him. Tom just looked back at him. This man had to know all there was to know about steadiness.

"Train cadets," Michael answered, "until they rotate me back to Nam. And they will. Maybe in six months. But I'll've been free of it for awhile." And then they might let him do green rice. But he didn't say that. Saddened, he remembered he hadn't told Major Niemeier about it. Niemeier would've blown all to pieces, his habit when something threatened his own agenda. But Tom – Tom mustn't know any caring was left in Michael. Tom's hope had to die.

The trip going up to Macao had seemed quick. This seemed long. Michael found himself wanting to ask Tom what he would do now about Kathleen. Stupid and cruel. For God's sake, he'd just rubbed Tom's nose in his own terrible certainty that nothing could be done. Nor could it have been easy for Tom not to pursue it, but he didn't. Whatever was changed in Tom, he still put Michael in awe.

Then Tom asked, "Do you still love her?"

What did he want to think, that Michael had joined the Army to be closer to Burma? Eyes meeting eyes, Michael wondered if Tom'd see his were as blank as he felt, like a child's slate the years had wiped clean and ready but with nothing to write on it. What kind of question was that for him to ask, anyway? As he had for a fleeting moment on the ferry going up to Macao, Michael wondered if there was something else Tom had to tell.

"Is Kathleen sick?" he asked, his own sharpness startling him. God, so damned many fevers, malaria, dengue – but Tom just shook his head.

* * *

When they reached the house, Tom showed him his room, pointed to the bathroom, took the Shan bag from him, said a brief goodnight and left him until 7 AM breakfast.

Michael couldn't get to sleep, drifting in and out of a doze, voices and visions making him turn and turn again. His room, like Tom's, was on the second story of the back wing. The house was built four-square, the front and two sides having only one floor, around the courtyard. Even in the dim light thrown by lanterns hanging in the inner corners, the yard looked unkempt – mostly bougainvillea grown a little wild and a couple of small shade trees, with a dry fountain in the center going black with mold. Tom said he was dependent on the college gardeners and that they came only a few times a month. They always fixed the fountain, he said, but inevitably in a day or two it quit working again. The Burma Tom would have transformed this place.

The night was warm, and the sheet had gotten so tangled Michael had finally thrown it to the floor. He lay sprawled in and out of sleep.

"Oh, baby," she murmured, "these dark curls of yours. They spring into my hands. They feel so good, baby. You feel so good, all brown and earthy and warm like your hair." He was inside her, moving. "Kath," he groaned. To smack with shock and pull off her – and damned near off this narrow bed in Tom's house as he came awake.

He was damp with sweat, panting. Kathleen had never called him baby. Diane had. Poor Diane, no fair. That was the night he'd known he had to get out. She'd never said a word about it, not then, not the next day either. Maybe it had never happened before. He didn't think it had. But he had been devastated that Kathleen was still there, her name still there, in him.

Maybe Diane already knew it was winding down, even wanted it to. She did her part to keep the sex good, nice lady, he had to give her that. But he was beginning to know she resented him – school had always been a sail-through for him, and they made med school twice as hard for females anyway. Plus which, her dreams of a partnered big city practice, rich and fashionable, a dream she'd talked him into on beery nights that last summer of his ag degree, indifferent as he'd become about most things by that time, had begun to jade on him soon after they'd moved in together. And in short order, so had med school. It had seemed to Michael, as he'd lain awake that night with Diane by his side, that he was forever letting other people plan his life, until the only way he could get out of it was to run.

He withdrew from Case the next day, packed up his stuff in the apartment he shared with Diane, all except for the med books. She could use them. And drove the boxes to Richard's for storage. Charlotte was at the club, according to the maid, Richard was at the office, and he managed to dump the lot, scribble a note to Richard and get away before anybody could ask questions. Then he had to go back to the apartment and wait for Diane to come home. After which, he'd gone into town to the Army recruitment center and enlisted for Vietnam.

He curled up on his side around the pillow. "It's your eyes, you know," she'd said, quite solemnly. She was sitting astride him, a little oil lamp casting a wavering golden light. They were in some sawbwa's guest house built on piles over the water in the center of Inle Lake, the mountains all around. Tom had gone to Lashio for three days. "They're like pools, deep, and the light comes up from the blue depths as if through shivering water. That's why I can't look away from you. How could anyone? But it's not just that. It's your brain." He'd started to laugh. She slapped him on the chest, trying not to laugh with him. "Damn it!" It always surprised him when she swore. "It glitters, Michael. It's hard. It cuts like diamonds to the heart of things. It –" and he'd rolled her over and shut her up. Kath. Oh, Jesus. He turned to his other side, the pillow too hot.

It'll never work, he thought. He couldn't get assigned a Huey, not on his detail. And while a Loach would bear his weight and Kathleen's and a crew chief's, if Hanny could be talked into it, and God knew they'd need him on gun, that left not a hell of a lot of kilos free for extra fuel – fuel enough. No matter how fast and loose he got with phonying up orders, once in, how would they get back? Shit, he'd just finished convincing Tom it couldn't be done, so why go over it and over it . . .

The realization that *he* didn't want to be convinced brought him upright in the bed. It was just the puzzle of it, that's all. Everyone had always said of him growing up, "Michael responds well to challenge." Damn it, he didn't need this. Sure as hell, he didn't need Kathleen sneaking in on him at every whip stitch. He got up, rummaged and pulled on his pajama pants, found his cigarettes, and went down to the courtyard.

5

Light was coming from Tom's study window, partly closed for fear of rain, which once again had quit. He walked to it to see Tom inside, holding the Shan bag. Michael turned away and stumbled over a stone bench darkened by moss, sat down and lit a cigarette, took some deep drags.

How much disillusionment did you have when the letters stopped, Kath, knowing about the times before when I'd walked away? And you so young. I was the one who should have realized and kept the faith. I should somehow have gone after you. God damn it, God damn it, I never should have left you there.

There among the poinsettia and huge leaved teaks and the bamboo. She had come around the towering clump of it, that very first time, and he hadn't been able to see her face. The light was wrong, but he'd known it was a girl from the way she ran, hitching up her longyi to lope down the hill towards him. Tom's sister, had to be. What other female would be driving a jeep around the eastern Shan States, back of beyond. As she closed with him, she let go the longyi and reached out her hand. Now there was enough light behind her that her hair glowed. Soft as a baby's, he would discover, wisps of it loosening from the pony tail, sun-caught like copper. His hands rose to meet hers – and immediately she was looking down at them. "Oh! Your poor hands! Doesn't Tom give you gloves?" She was on the brink of a storm. On his behalf.

Michael was enchanted, and he stuttered somehow that he'd forgotten them this morning, that it wasn't Tom's fault.

But she was galvanized, tucking the longyi under her fanny and against the backs of her thighs to squat, reaching into her Shan bag to pull out a folded white handkerchief, not ironed but clean. Shans, Burmans, the hill people, everybody in Burma squatted like this, feet flat, back straight, knees up and sometimes out a little. Kathleen's long legs made her knees almost obscure her face, but somehow she looked comfortable as Michael never managed to be. He'd been trying all the week since he'd arrived to squat, and within a couple of minutes had to rise up on his toes or lift his ass or both, leaning forward to crouch instead. Tom had laughed, seeing him at it.

"You have to be born to it," he said, "and your legs are too long." But Kathleen's were, too, and she was as Anglo as he was.

"Don't you know you must never work split bamboo without protection? You'll slice all your skin away!"

She had torn the edge of the hanky with her teeth and ripped it in half, and was now tearing off narrower strips. All quicker than he could have thought it through, much less accomplished it. It seemed to him she hadn't even looked at him, only at his hands, but now she did, squinting against the light, a little frown between her green eyes, and she delivered that smile, and Michael had laughed with something rising inside him that only later he knew to be wonder.

"Well," he'd said, "Sally over there's tired of being tied up so I figured I'd best get her into a pen and nobody here to make it but me. The men're all off harvesting the wheat." Her eyes seemed caught looking into his.

"Yes," she said, as if dazed, "I know." She gulped. "It would help, don't you think, if you'd come down here?" So he crouched before her and she started laying out the white strips on his thighs.

She was facing down hill. Maybe that was how she did it. A couple of times he'd been on a hill with his feet slanting down and the squat had come a little easier. He looked to see if hers were on a slant, and discovered she was wearing boots, the laces running up under the hem of her longyi – walkers, practically clones to his own. The combination bemused him, boots and a longyi. From the moment he'd stepped ashore in Rangoon and seen women wearing the long, flowered, wrapped skirts he'd known they had to be the most graceful and feminine clothing in the world. Of course, Burmese men wore them, too, but they tied them differently and the checkered patterns were different, and anyway . . .

She had taken his right hand to wind the white strips around each of his frayed fingers. "The trick to twisting bamboo splints," she said, "is never to grasp them along the edges where they've been cut. Always hold them on the flat. It'll become second nature after awhile." Again she looked up at his face, cocking her head to one side. God, those eyes, tilted like a cat's. "You don't look at all like somebody named Mick," she said. "Micks are Irish. And brawlers, aren't they? Besides, Cameron's surely a Scottish clan."

It was as if his mind were stalled, and he hadn't even started to reply when she went on, "Are you a brawler, Michael?" And she smiled, her teeth milky white, only the incisors slightly uneven, and the corners of her mouth ran straight up her cheeks with that smile. It was her nose that saved her from classic beauty. It pleased Michael very much, that nose. He always avoided looking at the reflection of his own, considering it to be a ski-nose and unaware that it leant grace to the planing cheekbones, the straight brows, the deep set eyes, the hard line of his jaw.

"No," he said, finally. "I'd rather just – beat it on out of there, I guess." Their eyes held, something serious now between them.

Shouldn't've said that, he thought. But she might as well know up front how he could be, sliding out to leave things incomplete.

She only turned her attention to his left hand. "We'll put something on the worst of the cuts when we get home."

"You've ruined your handkerchief."

"Tom's really. I get them from Row and Company down in Rangoon. Load Tom up with them at Christmas," she gave a little laugh, "and then steal them back one by one all the rest of the year. They come in handy for all kinds of things. There." And tying a last knot, she dismissed him as patient. "All done." She rocked forward and stood up as did Michael. Tall as she was for a girl, even standing up the rise from him, he was taller.

She looked over the pig-pen. "You finished it in just one day? I ran into Tom, did I say that? Out on the road. He was on his way in to pick you up, but since I've dismissed school for the weekend and he wanted to drive on out to Long Gyi village – "

"It's not," Michael broke in. "Finished. There's still Sally's nursing crib to build. She had her litter aboard ship, and the babies are still small enough to be crushed if she rolls on 'em, which she will do – she's a lazy one. They're over there in a crate under the monkey-tree."

"Well then," she said, looking over the pile of bamboo poles, all thicknesses, and the sheaves of bamboo splints, long and thin and so flexible they curved across the ground like wires, "where do you want it to go, and what's it to look like?"

This time, he was quick. "Oh, no," he said, and he grabbed her hand, turning it palm up as she had done with his. "No way am I going to let you – " But then he saw. A palm smooth, yes, but hard, and callouses on every segment of every finger.

"It'll only take half as long," she said.

A moment, he sighed and stepped through the little gate he'd made into the pen. He pointed across to where the dirt lay in shade from a young bamboo clump he'd left standing just outside the fence. "There," he said. He looked back at her, shook his head, laughed. "Who'd've ever thought Mick Cameron could fall for a missionary girl." The words echoed through his head. And he knew he'd spoken out loud. "Michael," he amended hastily, as she frowned a little, head cocking again – habitual clues, he was beginning to have no doubt, that she was turning solemn. What would she say back? That's the dumbest thing any boy ever said to me? Or, what's wrong with being a missionary girl? Or even an anguished adolescent, I am *not* a missionary girl! She was, after all, barely going on eighteen.

But no. What she said was, "Not all missionary girls can build a house of bamboo, or a school." She walked over to the pile of bamboo poles. "Or a pig's nursing crib." She nudged the pile with her boot so that the poles loosened, and some slid apart. "What size do we want, Michael?"

"Michael?" Michael jerked his head up to see Tom, standing there in the courtyard.

"Sorry," Michael said, "the smell of my cigarette disturb you?"

"No, just told me you were here." He sat down on the bench next to Michael. Michael dropped his cigarette to the ground and saw there were three other butts around his feet. "There's something else, Michael."

He knew it, had known on the ferry.

"There's a child," Tom said.

Bewildered only a moment, Michael was shaken by a disgust rising in him like bile, pushing him to his feet. "Good God, man, you've been out of there for close to three years." His voice was so constricted he was nearly hissing over the growl. "Forget you thought I hadn't written – "

"Michael . . ." Tom stood up, too, as Michael swept on. "How could you think I didn't have the right to know?" He shoved Tom in the shoulder, rocking him, his earlier beating forgotten. "The fuckin' right?!" His fists clenched, close to decking Tom.

Tom stepped back, nothing done to stop Michael except to speak his name again, rapping it out. "Michael!"

Michael's head felt like it might explode, but he managed to shut up.

"He is perhaps four months old by now."

He couldn't swallow it. Wouldn't. Here he'd been trying to figure out a way . . . and she'd been out there doin' it . . . He turned his back on Tom. So where do you get off, Michael? Shit. Diane could've got knocked up, too, only she was in America, not Burma, and had the pill.

Tom went on, speaking softly, perhaps to give Michael time. "So.

Now I know. I wondered if you had – if you and Kathleen were –. She wouldn't tell me, of course, not her big brother. Nor could I ask. That was when I was sorriest, I think, that our parents had died. Kathleen, so young, needing a mother then more than ever in her life. No way to prevent you, of course, and I trusted you wouldn't hurt her, not deliberately. And I know you didn't. Only when the letters stopped."

Michael took a long breath, and his voice came hard. "He. Htin Aung's son, I suppose. Or – " He shrugged.

"Stop it," Tom said. "According to what's come through over the past half-year or so, there was much rejoicing in Keng Tung Province. The Sawbwa's only child."

No point in carrying on with this. Michael turned back to face Tom. "You've misunderstood her, Tom. She'll never come out."

"She's asking for help."

"Not and leave a baby."

Tom just looked at him.

"Ah. So. Of course. I rescue the damned kid, too." Michael said wearily.

"It's impossible, you said so."

The two just looked at each other, then Michael started back to bed.

"He's sick," Tom said after him. "According to the Gurkha."

At the bottom of the steps leading up to the gallery, Michael looked back at Tom still standing there, still looking at him. And went on up the stairs.

* * *

Sleep didn't come any easier than before. He skittered his mind around, trying to get off the treadmill. He thought of that sweet belly swollen, the pain that must've come because of it, and knew all that would've been good and wondrous if it had been his kid inside her.

Hell, he wouldn't even be here, with all of this sitting on his shoulder, if he'd had any of the sense Richard had found so lacking in him. He and Richard hadn't spoken since Michael's last leave before coming to Nam. They'd talked – or tried. Richard hadn't gotten it, the precipitous enlistment after still another drop out. He could hardly be blamed for that, since Michael didn't altogether get it, either. Richard had just shaken his head at him in bewilderment. "Jesus, Michael, Vietnam?! Next time you feel you have to do something like this, don't jump all the way to the bottom of the well, okay? Do us all a favor and try a lateral shunt instead."

At one point – how many hours into the night? – Michael found himself sitting up in bed, running his fingers through his wet hair, knowing Richard was right again. Nothing and nobody would be served, not Kathleen, not himself, nobody, by jumping down the deep well. What he had to figure out was a damned lateral shunt. But all he came up with was a vague possibility based on wild rumors that he wasn't even sure he wanted to try.

He looked at his watch, saw it was still not yet midnight, just felt like hours later. Noon in D.C. If he hadn't gone to lunch, Richard would be in his office. Not that Michael had the number, but maybe Tom did.

Lanterns still burned in the courtyard, out of consideration for a guest. Michael found his way into Tom's study. The phone stood on the desk as he remembered, next to a tabbed address book. Two numbers in it for Richard in Washington, one an office with an extension, the other probably his flat. Weekends, he commuted back to Cleveland.

After college ROTC, Richard had been a weekend warrior for years. Then suddenly, several months after Michael's enlistment, he'd turned up a light colonel with an office in the capital doing God knew what. Probably something aristocratic like intelligence. Michael never considered he himself might have been the kicker for Richard's "going off to war". Had to've been Charlotte. Who wouldn't want to get away from her? Talk about lateral shunts.

It took awhile to get through to him, lots of sentries at the gate. Michael stood waiting, eyes glued to Kathleen's picture until finally put through.

"Richard?"

There was a little silence. "Michael. Where are you?"

"In Hong Kong, with Tom."

"It's the middle of the night over there. Isn't it? What's the trouble?"

A moment, and Michael asked, "How are you, Richard?"

"Michael – " Irritated. Then, "I'm fine. How're you?"

"Okay. I'm okay. Richard . . ." Michael had to catch in his breath. "It's complicated. Tom's received a message from Kathleen. His sister."

"I know who Kathleen is, Michael. He wrote she's still in Upper Burma, so – the message came from there?"

"Yes. She wants to come out. We believe it's urgent."

"Michael . . . it's not your problem."

"Well, yeah, Richard, I'm afraid it is."

"I thought you had rid yourself of her."

"I didn't know you knew I was trying. But in the last twenty-four or so, I've found out I haven't. All that aside, I'm hoping you'll wangle me a transfer to Laos."

Michael could almost hear Richard roll his eyes. He wondered if his brother could hear his heart pound.

"We aren't fighting a war in Laos, Michael – not that anyone'll talk about."

"Air America's there, Richard."

"The military stopped approving transfers into AA some time ago."

Shit. But Richard would know, all right. Next option. "Well if things are goin' on in Laos, whatever they're sayin', the Army has to be around someplace. Right?"

"Whatever, it mightn't be flight duty."

Michael kept quiet.

"Michael, you steal a chopper, go AWOL, cross the Burmese border illegally and get caught, you'll be in prison for years." And articulating it very carefully, "Years, Michael."

"I won't get caught. Thing is, it's got to be ASAP. The Army wants me for another tour, with a commission – it's either that or go home. I've got to tell them when I get back."

"I see. I take it you've acquitted yourself well. It'll help. You're sure you want this, Michael?"

"Yes."

"Then give me your stats. I could get them through records, but it'll be quicker."

So Michael dictated his rank and serial number, Hunter Killer platoon C Troop, and Richard picked it up with a murmured, "The Sixteenth CAV, 92nd Division Air Assault out of Da Nang."

"Sixteenth squadron," Michael added. But he wasn't able yet to accept the relief. "Richard, um – another thing."

"Your servant, little brother."

"Yeah. See if you can find a slot so I can take my Crew Chief with me. He doesn't exactly know anything about this yet, but I'm pretty sure he'll go. Hell, he can work the motor pool if he has to."

Richard groaned.

"I can't do it alone, Richard. And there won't be time for me to make new connections, find somebody to trust. I know I can trust Hanny – I do it with my life everyday. That's Spec 5 Neal Hanrahan, same platoon, but I don't have his number."

Dead quiet, then, "Anything else?"

This didn't come easily. "Well, since you say it'll help . . . you might point out to whomever that I've won some commendations."

"Why am I not surprised? But you might write sometime. Of course they'll help. Even the Army likes to reward its deserving. I'll start greasing skids before end of work today. But I'm not God, Michael."

"You can do it, Richard, I know you can." Lord, he sounded like he was up in the air talking to a new guy in the peter seat.

Richard gave a grunt. "I want a promise from you. When – *if* you get to Laos, I want you to sit down and think very carefully before you do anything."

Easy. "I promise."

"How long are you in Hong Kong?"

"It's a three day leave, but – I'm sorry, sooner is better. Tom and I think things are bad for Kathleen."

There was a long silence, then Michael heard Richard sigh. "At least you're not diving off the deep end, as usual."

"Just what you advised, last time we talked. And Richard? Thanks. You always come through."

"You're the one who does that, Michael." He hung up, even as Michael just stood there, disbelief crowded out by old visions. High school wrestling regionals, he was on the team, and it was the final match. He and his opponent had each taken a fall. The boy was not as tall as Michael, but was dense, thicker muscled, carrying as much more weight as their class allowed, and Michael was spent, or thought he was. And he heard Richard, calling from down by the bench. First time anybody'd been there cheering for Michael, just Michael, since their parents had been killed the year before flying down to Florida in a friend's Cessna. But here Richard was. God, what a charge. Suddenly the other boy went down and Michael was holding him tight to the mat. And then Richard was hugging him stinking with sweat. "You came through, Mickey! You always do!" Had that life ever really happened?

Michael hung up the dead phone, still smelling his own sweat. If nothing else, he could get Tom a space air-conditioner for this room, anyway. He headed for a shower hoping to pick up some shuteye afterwards and wanting to yelp like a cowboy with triumph. No matter how he'd managed to sound on the phone, Richard always made him feel sixteen. The age he'd been, matter of fact, at that once in a lifetime wrestling match. It hadn't changed a thing between them. One drop does not an ocean make, and while placing the call to Washington, he'd been more than half convinced that his brother would laugh him off the line or read him a lecture and flatly refuse his request. Air-conditioning would've helped.

DAY TWO

6

Early morning, the sun already streaking across the mountains from Laos, carrying a Cho who was full of U-pym's milk and cleaned up by herself, Kathleen went beyond the palace grounds up to the natural shelf she had found long ago almost atop the big rock. There she sat cross-legged in the lotus position, the baby in her lap, the stallion Maung Swe cropping grass just below her in his pasture. This was her place except during the height of the monsoon, her place to quiet herself and find the silence.

It had been her savior for years, even back when she was still a school-girl. She'd been taught it when only thirteen, home with Tom for the summer, in a tit for tat with the Shan boy. A rare thing for any boy to do, especially when just out of the pongyi chaung and his own retreat, but he had ambition and a quick mind. When she had proposed the trade, it took him a week of shyness to get over the shock and then he had agreed. He'd teach her to meditate, she'd teach him English.

She had been practicing it ever since, had even tried to teach it to Michael, though half the time they were reduced to giggles because more than half the time the lessons came after making love and they weren't even dressed.

Michael. That was why she needed the quiet this morning. Michael. And U-pym. The wet nurse had come upon her when she'd returned to the room after morning tea. Found her kneeling on the floor by the trunk, separating out things to take. Her passport, long out of date but proof of U.S. birth. A couple of longyis for her and of course cloths for Cho.

She'd already slipped those few secret journals from their hiding place, journals not meant for Htin Aung's eyes ever and seeming a measure of her years here. Of herself, perhaps? Mottled black and white school spirals, now tucked into a Shan bag. She couldn't leave them.

U-pym had walked in and seen the lot. The passort lying on top of the pile of cloths couldn't be missed. The two of them had looked at each other a long, long moment, both of them knowing.

"Please," Kathleen had said, softly, clasping her hands in front of her.

"You cannot go!" U-pym had said, panic in her voice. "You must not, Lady!"

The baby, lying close by in a soft blanket nest, began to cough. "There, you see?" Kathleen said. "Yes, I must!" Quickly, she had scooped up the baby to pat him, quieting him. "Not for four days yet," she went on, rushing it, so frightened all could be lost here, "and but three until the Prince leaves."

U-pym had reached her hand to pat Kathleen's, looking very sad, not wanting to give up Cho, the child raised at her own breast, her own babe dead at birth.

"You need only tell them I am sick," Kathleen had said. "Say the baby cries less because he is better, and throw out the food they bring. I must save him, U-pym!"

U-pym had nodded, but Kathleen realized she might be stretching U-pym's loyalties too thin. She wasn't really a friend, not like the three wives. The Sawbwa had brought her in from a village, paid her husband and family. She'd have to be convinced that Kathleen's brother would restore Cho to health. That's what she'd say next, Kathleen thought, later today, tomorrow. Over the years, Tom's name had taken on the quality of legend in the Southern Shan States, so . . . So had Htin Aung's, and like all in the palace, all in Loi Long, U-pym lived in awe and fear of him. But maybe she'd hold out long enough to let the Sawbwa leave, let Kathleen get away.

Oh, damn her own impatience. She had been going to wait to pack, but she knew they'd have to leave quickly, silently, so she'd started, thinking she might change her mind about taking this or taking that . . .

This, after Michael had come to her memory during the night as he had not for a very long time. She had mulled that over, his coming to her that way, as the night had lingered on, Cho now beside her, no fear of the Prince coming again. He was done with her until his return to Loi Long in a month, so sure she'd be there.

Had Michael been waiting to rise from the deep ever since she'd sent the message to Tom? A hope secret from herself that it would be Michael who would come to get her? Could she truly still be so foolish? Michael was long since married, with a family of his own, in some poor land working with the people there. Surely it was only because she was going back to his world. He'd doubtless be coming into her thoughts a lot, during the next few weeks. No matter.

Since losing him, over the last four years the meditations had rescued her from that grief, had trained her how to engender a calm centering, the light of her awareness turned inward when the Prince came to her bed. And until the baby, any stirrings evoked by memories of Michael had come to be only the thoughts themselves, not the pain, nor any of the rest.

Cho's birth had begun to unravel that cocoon. She should have realized the first moment she'd heard his cry and held him on her breast, filled up with joy, that once you open the door again, anything can enter. So the battle had had to be fought all over again, just once in a while a lapse, when this son of the wrong man would startle her, frighten her with little knives. The brightness blazing at her from his green eyes even as his tiny body dwindled away with her helpless to stop it. His fingers reaching to her lower lip, to grasp and hold onto it, how that twisted inside her, bringing to life in that one familiar touch what she had quelled with such struggle.

But recently, the exercise had given her something else: the clarity to embrace her desperation and discover the solutions hidden in her mind. Like jewels waiting for the light. It had come like that, the reminder that it wasn't karma or fate that had kept her in Loi Long in spite of Tom's pleas to go with him, but her own self-determination. That this had been inspired by Michael. And became the source of her courage to find a way out.

Kathleen took in a deep breath, releasing it slowly, fully, releasing herself. She looked across the valley where the morning sun was now burning away the mist. Everyone shouted praises when the rains finally came. And felt a lifting of spirit when they ended. Missionaries sometimes likened the season of the rains to a long Christian lent, the light festival in October to an Easter rejoicing.

Maung Swe whickered. He was eager for the run. "Soon," she said to him. "We'll go for a ride soon." Her guard Lim Pong, a Shan now that the Gurkha was gone, squinted up at her from his squat, his cheroot coiling smoke. He was next to the rock and outside the fence like her, his pony on a tether, his rifle over his shoulder. He wasn't used yet to her speaking English to the horse.

Kathleen had named Maung Swe that, Mr. Gold, because of the color of his mane against his mottled chestnut coat. Htin Aung had given the stallion to her when she still lived outside the palace walls in the little house he'd had built for her of basha, like the houses of those she was teaching, attached to the school by a walkway covered against rain. So kind, he'd been then. And the glorious horse had made so many things possible for her, or that's how it had seemed. Did now again.

The stallion was descended from an Arabian Htin Aung's grandfather had bought from a British district magistrate before the turn of the century. Htin Aung rode his brother, by this time the two brothers not pure bloods, but better for the Shan hills, part mountain pony, sure-footed and rough-coated. Wonderfully intelligent, Maung Swe would come to her morning call from clear across the pasture. And his back was broad enough for her to feel safe astride it with the baby in her arms. Which was the first and last concern.

The casting about for escapes had started when Cho was going on a month old and not prospering. No earlier. If things changed in Burma, and they could, overnight, Cho's future would be rich and *he* could create changes. Besides, what was there for Kathleen to escape to?

The first schemes were silly day dreams concocted each time Htin Aung left Loi Long for somewhere. How she would put the baby in a sling and ride Maung Swe like the wind for . . . where? She knew better. How would she lose her guard? And even if she did, she'd only lose herself on the mountain trails which never went due east or due south but every which way. And what would she do if U-pym didn't go with her? How could Cho live without U-pym's milk? And how would Maung Swe, strong as he was, ever manage to swim the Mekong? Always she would bog down in fears and questions, and she never tried. But now, for a short time, a very short time, perhaps, Cho might manage on her own limited milk supplemented with her own chewed rice, and she could leave U-Pym behind. Women fed infants that way in the villages, a poor diet, children died of it if it was all they had. But if it got them free . . .

Six weeks ago, she remembered to the day, Cho had started a cold, and still the coughing never let up. It had caused her to send the message. Stupid. What had she thought, in some craziness she still didn't understand in herself, that Tom could do, even if the Gurkha had reached him? And then two weeks ago, days after the Gurkha had already left, the green diarrhea had begun. More than three months old, and hardly heavier in her arms than when he was born.

All children in these mountains got bronchitis by the end of the rains. Then they had a month, two, to get over it before winter set in. Either they did or were dead before a year old.

Htin Aung knew it better than she. He said that the first year was a test. If the child lived, he would have a naming day and be a fine prince. If not, it was his karma. The baby name hadn't fooled the bad spirits and interfering would doom him to live a weakling, and a dishonor to the house. In a terrible way, he was right. A child who survived beyond his first year here had a good chance at another thirty. Until killed by a fever, intestinal parasites or government bullets.

Pleading to take Cho to Bangkok or even to Hong Kong seemed only to intensify Htin Aung's distaste for his son. He said that soothsayers had predicted his first born would die. At the birth, he had propitiated all the nats, both evil and good, with a great festival and much gold leaf for the pagoda, hoping her western blood in the child would bewilder them. But he'd come to fear that those things had foolishly kept the baby alive, was coming to regret it. Perhaps it would be better for it to fulfill its karma, "it" being his own child, "it" being a betrayal of his own blood, and so he denied "it" western medical care. If "it" didn't survive, his shame would stop. If "it" did survive, "it" would be the stronger for that.

She was the only woman who'd ever given him an heir. And that was the only reason he kept her. The only reason he timed so carefully his once-a-month night visits. She was sure of all these things, though of course they didn't speak of any of them. More than a year had passed from the first time he'd taken her until she got pregnant. So long ago he'd had some feelings for her, at least a need to believe she had feelings for him, a need to be of importance to her. But she had never been able to pretend to feelings for him, and another thing she was sure of was that finally accepting that, along with what he'd read in her journals, had caused him to despise her. And still he wanted to father another son in her, and so she believed he had come to despise himself, blaming her for it. Thank God for the silk pessary one of Dr. Seagraves' nurses had explained to her. Though she would forever be grateful for its one-time failure. Grateful for Cho.

Kathleen came down off the rock. No less uncertain about U-pym, there was a calmness now, and she was more certain in herself. She would make it work. She would.

She went to the gate in the fence and through it, called to Maung Swe who came, and together, Kathleen still with Cho in her arms, they walked to the shed where his blanket saddle was kept. Four days, and the opium train would lead her east. She had the rubies. Some sapphires, too. She would follow until the great river and not worry whether Maung Swe could cross it. She would set him free to find his way back to Loi Long, and the stones would pay some boatman to take her down the Mekong. Buy the boat, if needed.

Riding up the ridge on beyond the orchard, Lim Pong's pony, like Maung Swe, was kicking stones down the scree, the Shan trailing her always at a steady distance. This opium shipment was the end of the final harvest of gum and the smallest in years because of Burmese depredations. Htin Aung had been storing it up the mountain behind the palace in the caves, pushing up the price by withholding it, to trade it out of season at the end of the monsoon when the demand would be high, the price higher yet. It was the reason the buyers were coming, from Thailand yes, but Chinese even so. The load was headed for the refinery that fed China, and he needed to bargain for the Laotians. He enjoyed it, he always claimed, and the Laotians were like children, bored too quickly to get the best deal.

The number of pack animals plus the goodly number of armed guards meant that Lim Pong's pony and Maung Swe would be the only dependable mounts remaining behind, once the train departed. All the rest were either too old or gone lame.

Lim Pong, always dogging her heels, surely would accept a ruby, some sapphires, not to betray her. There was a transmitting radio here in the palace. How could she trust him and be sure?

There were Htin Aung's pistols, kept in a display case. Could she do it, shoot a man? If he were hurting Cho, to save his life, oh, yes. Or her own. But to prevent that, when she wasn't even sure?

She looked back at the Shan guard, small, very brown, black homespun wrapped in a turban hiding his black hair, his eyes impassive looking back at her. Small, perhaps, but with the strength of three of her should he have time to move against her.

Her mouth rushed with saliva. She had yet to eat this morning, but something wanted to come up. She tightened a hand on the reins, clasping the baby more tightly, and kicked Maung Swe into a canter. Lim Pong

behind her did the same. Dogging her heels, all right. Wiping out a little of the certainty of only a few moments ago.

A step at a time, must take it a step at a time. But oh, God, what was it best to do about the Shan?

7

Tom was already gone in the morning when Michael made it down to breakfast. Which worked. He didn't want to tell Tom about the call to Richard, not until it paid off. The young woman who was the cook's wife and spoke limited English said "Missa Howard go school-side, leave keys to car, say go see Hong Kong. We fix Hunan for you tonight." And she beamed. He took a second cup of coffee, left her to the cleaning-up, and drifted into Tom's study. He figured it'd be death-defying to sit for more than ten seconds in that front parlor, and it was still too early to go out, even sightseeing. Besides, he had other plans.

He needed addresses and went looking for the phonebook, hopefully in English, under tables, on top of shelves, and at the last was pulling out Tom's desk drawer when, for the first time, he noticed on the corner opposite to where Kathleen's picture stood another photo, this of a Burmese woman. Had to be Burmese, her long highlighted black hair coiled to the top of her head where was tucked a frangipani blossom. The color film had managed to catch the Burmese quality of her skin, dusky, with that warm hint of rose just beneath the surface, too light to be hill-tribe, her face too long to be Shan. Her smile was warm, too, brown almond eyes direct. Burmese women often seemed to be shy but rarely were. Nor was this one.

No phonebook in the drawer, but a light sheaf of hand-drawn maps, those Tom had mentioned. Michael glanced at one or two. Better than he'd expected, sweetly made really, and no doubt excellent for a jungle trek. But not for flying. They reinforced what he'd decided to do this morning. He put them back in the drawer.

Phonebook, phonebook. Glanced around, saw the table piled with magazines, maybe it had got mixed up . . .

He started dealing through them, when Tom's name caught his eye. On the cover of FOREIGN AFFAIRS. "The Common Market and the World Balance of Trade" by Thomas Howard, Ph.D. He went back to look more closely at the covers of journals he held already shuffled into his left hand, and there, table of contents on the cover of THE INTERNATIONAL REVIEW OF ECONOMICS, Tom listed as Editor in Chief. No wonder they'd given him the chair here in economics. What in hell had Tom ever been doing in Burma running a demonstration farm?

He bent over to straighten up the pile, swivelled and saw the phonebook on the floor under the desk. English, too. He zipped through the yellow pages, got some addresses, tore out a map of Hong Kong. The clock chimed nine, and he left – telling himself, drive on the left, drive on the left.

It was steaming outside, no AC in the car, the roundabouts were terrifying, so Michael's jeans and polo were close to drenched by the time he reached the Star Ferry over to Hong Kong. Even with all that, he hadn't stopped marvelling at Tom.

In Michael's few weeks at the farm they'd talked about it again and again, and Michael had thought he'd come to understand Tom and the missionary spirit. There had been no hint of someone hidden, stifled. None. Evenings without electricity, the white light of the gasoline lamp catching in the weave of the basha flats, shadowing the bamboo beams against the whitewashed ceiling – and those damned black long-legged spiders skiing down the woven walls, Michael hated spiders – he and Tom, and Kathleen on weekends, would sit and talk and talk. And while Tom never preached, never even lectured, Michael knew he was privileged to see first hand how strength of purpose could fire a man.

But he hadn't suspected the depth of devotion. A double degree? So Tom could get ordained, just as his father expected of him. Had gone back to Burma where he'd been born, to missionize the hill people. As his father'd expected. Tom being Tom, not Michael, he hadn't dropped out of semi-nary. Or walked out on his father. He'd stuck it out. But Tom, unlike his proselytizing father, saw everything in terms of economics – why wouldn't he, for the Lord's sake, editing an international journal – saw the poor lives of the Pa-o and the Kaws, and decided to make a difference his way: show not tell.

Obviously, his involvement in insurgency in Burma had saddened him. Because he believed it to have been wrong, or because he'd failed? A little bit of both, maybe. Most certainly, it had freed him up from a life that may never have been his choice.

And how Michael had envied him. Begun by envying him, anyway, and ended determined to follow in his footsteps. Not the God trip. Michael had some time ago put religion, if not God, away. But a demonstration farm, an experimental farm, in the third world somewhere.

The ferry opened up, he drove on board, and since it was now pouring, he remained in the car for the short ride.

He'd shared it all with Tom in that basha farmhouse and out in the villages and jeeping it through the mountains, as he'd never shared with his brother back in Shaker Heights or, God knew, with his father. It had seemed to him that he'd found in Burma the way to merge childhood dreams with his almost unrecognized and certainly unexplored need to do something right. That's how they'd left it. He'd gone back to school, studied agronomy, until along with losing the girl he'd lost the fire in his gut. Maybe Tom had, too.

* * *

After putting into the British Colonial Office where they provided some topos of eastern Burma and the Southern Shan States from World War II and the construction of the Burma Road, he found the shops he wanted in spite of the phonebook street map which really wasn't good enough – maybe no maps were for Hong Kong, especially down along the wharfs. The shop interiors were dusty and confusing but he kept looking and uncovered what he knew were probably the best he was going to get, old French Indochina maps that included Laos.

Barely noon, and the car was like an oven, so he slid in and left the door ajar, opening one of the maps across the steering wheel. He peered for a date. 1953. Seventeen years old, for God's sake. The topographic lines and the elevation meters became rarer and rarer north towards the Chinese border. And west, too. He let the map roll itself up, and laid his head back. He was too tired, too tired, and didn't know if it was because of the two years he'd spent flying in the stupidest war in the world, or because of the nearly five years he'd been without her, four believing her lost to him. He'd have to find more current maps, better ones, when he got to Laos. If.

He jerked his head, afraid he'd go to sleep right there in the car. Sight-seeing, Tom had suggested. God. Michael decided to go to the beach.

He cruised and found the right store, bought a towel and swim trunks, and headed out along the coast road. Not looking for a Vung Tao, no comparable beach in the world anyway, so any old beach would do. And that's what he finally discovered, way, way out from town – a little old beach, not a big strand, and not many people, either. He parked so he could change behind the car, walked down towards the water on sand still damp from night rains, spread the towel out, bunched the sand up at one end for a pillow, and stretched out on his back to soak up the sun before a swim.

As they'd done on the blanket Kathleen had spread on the bank by the creek. "Do you know how to dance?" she asked.

"Sure."

"Teach me?"

"Oh, well, I don't know about that. Anyhow, Kath, you know you know how to dance."

So she'd told him about the dancing classes at her boarding school with some boys from across town, when she was taller than anybody else, and nobody ever asked her. "Except Jimmy Glover. He never failed to turn up for the lucky number dance. I guess it made us both feel better. He was short, and danced worse than I did."

Michael said it was the saddest story he'd ever heard, jumped up, pulled her up after him. He put his hand at her back, took her right hand, and started humming Percy Sledge. But it was a silly way to dance altogether, he thought, and he put both hands on her hips and began to shift his in time to the music, pressing hers to do the same, and before long she was shifting and dipping sideways, bending her knees, as if she'd never done anything else. She was the one who broke into the lyrics, almost in a whisper, "when a ma-an loves a wo-man . . .", and he swung her out, swung her back, their eyes locked together.

Remembering it now, Michael was astonished he'd ever been surprised at her immediate abandon and ultimate grace in loving, she had danced that day and afterwards at the farm listening to the BBC World Service on Tom's short-wave Phillips with such unselfconscious sensuality. Not so astonished perhaps, he suddenly discovered his tongue was running slowly back and forth under the edge of his upper teeth, his upper lip. He wanted the clean taste of her, every part of her, and he had tasted it all, as she had tasted of him. Places neither had known existed in themselves until awakened by the other, the mix of salt and sweet making of him a starving man at a feast.

At the beach in Hong Kong, on a belated thought Michael looked down on himself and hastily rolled over, hoping the cold hard sand would discipline the lump growing under his trunks.

He waited a few minutes, managed to get into Hong Kong Bay for a swim, and afterwards got the maps from the car, spread them out on the towel with rocks at the corners, and did some homework.

It was late in the afternoon before he returned to Kowloon, and picked up an air-conditioner. Turned out, installing it in the study window was the real trip. The cook's English, like Michael's Chinese, was non-existent. So it took the cook's wife to help. She kept getting the giggles, but they managed, and while the room got more pleasant, Michael pulled out Tom's small Shan maps and started trying to key them to the larger maps he'd gotten across the Bay. Impossible without Tom to translate names of mountains, rivers, landmarks. Anyway, he would need some that were visible from the air, not just this big boulder or that old jungle-covered stupa. A pagoda or two would work. But what it meant was, he'd have to change his mind and tell Tom about the call to Richard.

* * *

"Well," Tom said, a smile widening on his face. "Some difference!" He was barely into the study when he'd stopped, not noticing the maps spread across his desk, enjoying the de-humidified air. He nodded to Michael. "Kind of you. Very."

He crossed over to the little bar. "Looks like you found the Shan maps." So he had noticed. He poured himself a drink, turned, glass in hand and gestured, "Help yourself, won't you? Whenever. How was your day?" But his eyes kept seeking the desk. Was he aware of the big maps lying beneath the small ones?

Tom looked ten years older than he had last night. Before Michael had come. Before Michael had ended the hope. Michael wanted to see that face lift. And they really couldn't waste the time waiting for Richard's call-back. "I talked with Richard this morning."

Tom's hand froze his glass to his mouth. He lowered it slowly, carefully. "Oh? How is he?"

"He's, um, working on getting me transferred to Laos."

The face didn't lift. It damned near crumpled, and Tom had to close his eyes. When he opened them, they were wet but not flowing. He'd controlled it. "When did you think of that?" he asked, and had to clear his throat. Not, when had he changed his mind. Good thing. Because Michael wasn't sure when or if he had, only that he was taking whatever steps possible to be on the ready.

"Richard may not be able to pull it off, Tom. Plus which, my commanding officer will want to block it." That's if he doesn't go stark bonkers first.

Tom nodded, set his drink aside and blew his nose.

"Just so you know," Michael said. He sighed. "So. We better get to work. Because if it happens I won't be able to get back here."

Michael would have moved for the desk, but Tom stood blankly, until he looked at Michael.

"Don't," Michael said quickly. "It's a horrendous long shot, Tom – all of it, from now 'til – " 'Til it's over, Michael didn't say, couldn't finish it, scared to put into words this crazy thing they thought they could do. That he could do.

It had pulled Tom back to the moment, so Michael eased up a little, poured himself a Scotch. "I got some old topographics today, and what you need to do is help me key the hand-drawn ones to pertinent areas in the biggies, especially confluences of the small rivers with the Mekong. The topos're ancient, but no better to be had, I'm afraid."

Energized at last, Tom moved to the desk, pulled out a pad. "I can draw you a floor plan of the palace," he said. "And I can spot Kathleen's room on it for you."

"What *was* her room when you were last there," Michael reminded softly. "Can you be sure, now?"

Tom looked at him steadily. "Lots of long shots, Michael. I know." He smiled. "But I somehow trusted that you weren't going to be one of them. And I was right."

Michael was already searching through the Shan maps, slipped a couple out from the rest. "These are great in any case." They showed the palace, the walled portions of the compound which backed into a mountain of its own, and the mule tracks leading out of it. "But none of them tell me the kind of canopies there are for me to put down in, the heights of trees . . . Could we get hold of any of the guys who made these maps? Especially that Gurkha. He'd know more recent stuff."

The cook came in to call them to dinner. Tom led the way out, for the first time in obvious avoidance.

"Hey," Michael said, halting him.

"There's a problem," Tom said finally. So what else is new, Michael thought. Tom went on, as they entered the dining room. "If emigrés coming out of Burma can't hook up with family members already arrived or can't get a work permit in short order, they grab any chance to slip into the huge maw that's Hong Kong, and that description fits almost all of them. We've got the maps, but their makers're gone. The Gurkha, too."

Dinner was piping hot, pepper hot, and the best Chinese food Michael had ever tasted. The beef was more tender than the mushrooms cooked with it, the whole baked sea bass fell away from the bones, and the Chinese broccoli was crisp and redolent of garlic, ginger, and tart lemon grass. They washed it all down with pitchers of Tsingtao beer from the mainland.

Tom waited until the platters were all on the table, started spooning up the food. "He was terrified, stood outside the door the whole time we talked, a bloody rabbit caught in headlights."

"Afraid of you?"

"Unh, unh. Htin Aung. Or short of that, his connections with the Chinese triads." And Tom busied himself with the food.

Sweet Jesus. *Triads*? What was he buying into, not just flying in and flying out, but – once there, damn it. Michael looked down, away from Tom's eyes, not saying it because Tom knew it well enough. If anything went wrong, if he made any mistakes, it could be Kathleen who paid the price.

He jabbed at a slice of mushroom with his chopsticks. It slid away, and slid away. It had been too long since Michael had tried to eat a full meal with them. "Would you like a fork?" Tom asked. Michael shot him a look, to find too much innocence in that face. And suddenly, it seemed okay. Which for sure was crazy, too. But right now, this minute, he knew they'd all be okay.

He grinned. "I'm damned if I'll eat Chinese with a fork," he said.

Tom broke out a grin of his own. "Welcome back into my life, Michael."

"Same to you," Michael said. He made another attempt, and this time got himself a piece of mushroom, if small. "So," he said, chewing it down, "tell me about – what's her name? Something Swe – the lady in the photo on your desk. She's lovely." And he watched, charmed as Tom smiled sheepishly.

"Well," Tom said, "she's a nurse. Schooled by the bunch Seagraves trained – remember hearing about him?" Michael nodded. The American missionary doctor in Burma before WWII, who found and taught the only western trained nurses Burma had for years. "She runs our clinic." He smiled softly again. "She's the friend who made me comfortable in my own house." He drank some beer. Looked up at Michael. "Michael? I knew when I saw her . . . can you believe that?"

Could he? Oh, yes.

"Just the sight of her gave me . . . joy, I guess." Tom chuckled. "I didn't even know what it was I was feeling. When I did, I came back home that night and read the Songs of Solomon. I hadn't looked at them since seminary." He met Michael's eyes, his own gone shy. "And she continues to give me joy, never ending. Stupid man, I didn't know loving could be what she makes it, just thought it was . . . holy, I guess."

Michael had to look away. He knew.

Tom pushed away his plate. They hadn't begun to finish all the food. He refilled his glass from the pitcher, offered it to Michael, who refilled his.

"The Burmese people, all the tribes, they have to be among the earthiest in the world. You remember pwes?" *Pwes.* A word Michael had forgotten, bawdy open-air shows lasting all night long that went on in villages all over Burma during the dry season. Their dramas and dance stories were low-down humor, and so was the laughter they evoked. "My father used to be in despair over it," Tom went on wryly, "and the questions he'd get during Bible lessons." He shook his head. "I am quite sure my father never guessed – he would've been totally unable to guess what it is, *how* it is to love a Burmese woman. All the way around, Michael . . . every which way, I've been happier the past year or so than ever in my life. Until, uh – all this about Kathleen." He sighed, spoke ruefully. "Self-pity isn't becoming, is it? My father would say, we must bear what God sends us. Like Job, my father would say."

"That's trash," Michael said without thinking. Then, hastily, "All due respect to your father, but Tom, damn it, we make the choices, whoever sends 'em. Even Job must've had one or two." Michael had to grin again. "Course I can't say I've ever really read that story clear through."

"That's still there, isn't it, Michael, inside you. And unchanged. Can't stand the chaff. Do you remember how we talked?"

"Yeah. But unfortunately, you never converted me."

"My father would've. I never was as good at it as he was. Never will be." After a moment, he added, "Still preach, though. Have to. Those of us who're ordained rotate Sundays."

They were silent, and then Tom picked up again. "Anyway, nothing to do with this thing about Kathleen, Hla Swe and I don't talk about a future. She believes it's her calling to stay in Macao for the refugees."

Michael wondered if Tom were aware how like Kathleen his lady was sounding, more with every word. "And she's convinced me I have to stay here and earn the money to pay for it all. Medicines, food, housing. Part of her name, Swe, means gold. And she is. Purest gold." He chuckled again. "In case you're wondering, I'm not sure either what she sees in a body going soft and half the time sunburnt like a lobster."

"Not so soft," Michael said, thinking of the ferry.

"She once told me she loved me for my mind." Tom blushed.

Michael burst into a laugh. "Your sister once told me that, too. A very seductive thing to say to a man."

A moment, Tom cocked his head, frowning a little. Michael had forgotten that was another way they were alike, Tom and Kathleen. "You telling me my little sister seduced you?"

Was he teasing? Michael thought he'd better have a care. This wasn't some locker-room jock talk, after all. He managed a chuckle. "No, no." But she sure did put me in the way of it, he thought dryly, thought better of saying it. Tom waited. Michael sensed he could chance a little more, maybe. "You remember that time, I don't know, four weeks or so after I got to Burma, you went up to Lashio? I was at Long Gyi village building 'em a hen house, when Kathleen turned up in the truck. She'd dismissed school for the day – three days, she said. She'd filled a picnic basket with gobs of western food – potato salad, chicken salad – she knew I wouldn't want to live on curry for two solid days – that's what she'd planned, two days. She'd managed to get hold of the Younshwe Sawbwa to use his guest house, she made my excuses to the chicken farmers with great ceremony, and off we went. She had sleeping bags in the back and I don't know what all."

He sat there a moment, lost in the memory of that long, long ride, with him knowing full well what was ahead, had to be, and going a little nuts with it. She was the most determined female his short experience with females had ever provided him. He'd managed to control things the last time, managed to turn it off when she was so damned eager. But here she was, calm and easy, full of tales from her week at school, laughing the laugh that always caught at him – two notes up and a little hoot, before she broke into an over-flowing low laughter that was contagious. And he knew that unless he jumped out and ran like the wind, this time he'd be lost.

The cook's wife had brought in tea. Tom poured and shoved the cup across to Michael along with salt – green Shan tea, which Michael had come to like a lot five years ago.

"And?" Tom asked.

"Um," Michael stalled. "There was an outboard motor dugout waiting for us, and we crossed through the floating gardens. The day was gorgeous, mountains clear, men fishing with those huge triangular nets . . . shoot, you know better than I do about Inle Lake. Anyhow, the Sawbwa had opened up the house. Some house, huh? Up on stilts, blue water underneath and all around. There was a cook, and a by-God punkah boy – 'dyou ever have that, Tom? – pulling on a rope to wave the basha mat back and forth over our heads against the flies." Michael shook his head in the remembered wonder of it. Those tiny birds on toast roasted whole, including the beaks. Fish out of the lake . . .

Mosquito bars over the single-sized beds. The first thing Kathleen had done was to push the beds together under one net, and spread the sleeping bags – three of them – across the crack still dividing them. She'd planned everything very, very well, damn her hide.

He'd watched her without a word, knowing his conscience was doomed, only hoping some control would remain to him. And then she'd pulled out the longyi she'd sewn up for him, maroon cloth lightning-struck with silver. And they spent some time while she taught him how to tie it, giggling and telling him she knew it was a waste of time, he wouldn't be wearing it all that long. He kept trying to stay her hands, because they were being very casual down there below his waist.

"You remember that Mandalay longyi she bought me at the Keng Tung five-day bazaar?" he asked Tom. Stitched it up herself, which she never did let me forget. "She showed me how to tie it, that day." Evening. Night. "After we ate, the sun went down, the cook and the boy left, the moon came up and – " He looked at Tom. "One of those incredible experiences, you know?" And then, Michael blushed. "I don't mean –. What I meant was, all the Intha silk and bag weavers, the silversmiths with their worked belts and bowls and – they all arrived in their dugouts, brought by leg-rowers, and gathered at the front deck and lined up on either side of the path made by the moon on the water, knowing the beauty they were creating, each boat lit with little oil lamps, the light catching in the hammered silver. Their voices were so soft, just little murmurs, like music . . ."

"I know," said Tom.

They both looked away. It was too close to too much, and that ended dinner.

8

Tired as they both were, Michael close to true exhaustion, neither wanted to leave the phone in case Richard called. So Tom had coffee brought to the study, now very comfortable with the AC, and while he translated map-names, Michael desultorily leafed through one of his journals, finally started to read an article by him: *British Banks and the Future of Hong Kong*. The house was quiet, and they could hear the clock tick, hear it chime off the quarter hours. The third try at page two, neither page understandable, and Michael tossed it aside, belatedly laying it more neatly on the table.

What would she say when she saw him? "What are you doing here, Michael?! I never wanted to see you again!" Christ, why hadn't he let her come back to the States with him? No answer, just a round of good reasons. Just the mistake of a lifetime.

"Tom?" Tom looked up, waited. Michael got up, started pacing. Tom set his pencil down, leaned back in his chair, watching now, and wary. "See, she'd been so unhappy in school back in the States. Did you know that? She felt like an alien. And all those little vacations when everybody left but her. We both got through high school on the fast track, did you know that, too? We both graduated a year ahead of ourselves. Academically, it was a breeze for me, even if I was a disaster every other way. But Kathleen thought it was the best thing that had ever happened to her, to get out of there a year early. She was still so young. All I could think of was how isolated she'd be in married student housing at OSU, babies everywhere, everybody older and – I don't know, full of themselves, the way American students are. Or even worse, some apartment off campus and me gone all day long."

"She could have gone to school, too," Tom said. Finally said something, slapping it at Michael though perhaps not meaning to.

He'd known that, of course. "Yeah, well, sure, except – it was only going to be a year and a half or so, I'd come back. We'd get married – you'd perform the ceremony, I had it all worked out. We'd know where we were going, and . . . I thought, in the meantime, her life would be better with you, doing what she had a gift for. Did you ever watch her teach?"

"Yes, of course I did, Michael." He sighed.

"She never listened to me about it, about not coming with me," Michael said. "She wouldn't. She just cried. Or threw things. Or stomped off."

He picked up his cup of coffee, half empty and cold, oil showing on the top. He set it down again.

"I don't know whether you did the right thing," Tom was saying, "but if you hadn't, I would've forbidden it. Of course, come her eighteenth birthday she'd have gone after you like a shot, so you saved me from being the villain. Because I'd have forbidden it more for your sake than hers."

Michael stared at him, totally confused.

"You were older than Kathleen, but you were still very young, yourself. You needed time to surface from all that exotic romanticism you'd been immersed in."

It floored Michael. Of all the fucking things to lay on him on this second night in Hong Kong and decisions made. It hadn't been like that. He hadn't lost himself in Burma. He'd found himself. The memories awakening in him here, reawakening him after so long, had recalled him to what had been. The truth of it. All the feelings of it. He hadn't just fallen like a callow boy for Kathleen. He had admired her, had laughed with her and had had fun with her, he had adored her body and treasured her spirit and he'd determined to spend the rest of his life with her even if it was on some desert island at the back of beyond.

"So that's what you thought," he said, voice so raw he had to clear it, "when my letters stopped. That it had all been some adolescent fantasy, and I'd outgrown it. Just what you'd expected, right?" Now, he was afraid to look at Tom for the sadness rising in him. "Oh, I'll bet you were a great comfort to Kathleen."

Tom got up and crossed to the coffee pot, his cup in hand. But it rattled on its saucer, and he only set it down. "Nothing would have comforted her," he said.

Michael had to see him, moved to stand right in front of him, to see a sadness in Tom's eyes that mirrored his own. "Believing that of me," Michael said, his voice the kind of low hoarseness of calm, of hard-won self-control his crew heard from him flying in Nam, "you took some gamble, sending for me now."

What Tom said now was without apology. "There was no one else."

Michael slumped with it, the thing he'd known of course since almost the beginning of the few hours here. Why had he begun to hope otherwise, that somehow he was special here, that he and Kathleen would still be special to each other?

Rain had started again and slapped at the windows. Lord, Lord, he thought, what kind of chance can we possibly have if I do get her out?

The phone rang. Tom answered. It was Richard's secretary. Tom handed the phone to Michael. The secretary said she'd put the Colonel through and Richard came on.

"Your orders are cut and on the way to Da Nang," Richard told him. "You're posted to the embassy in Vientianne."

"The embassy?" Michael drew in a deep breath, looked straight at Tom. "Thank you, Richard." He watched Tom's face flood with relief. "What about Han – "

Richard was overriding. "Your Crew Chief, too. Promoted to Staff Sargeant with flight pay." Now Michael felt the relief. And glad for Hanny – might even soften his resistance, if there were any.

Richard was going on. "You should know, Michael, there's a new attaché." Well, they could both learn on the job, no problem there. But Richard went on, sounding a warning. "A light Colonel name of Wisby. You got the job because of him, I think. He's an Army pro, starting with Korea, is transferring like you from Nam, very hands on. He wants to have someone at his beck and call to fly him around, see what's what. You will go from Vietnam through Bangkok up to Udorn – you know it?"

"U. S. Air Force Base in Thailand."

"Yup. There'll be a light observation helicopter waiting for you there."

My God, Michael thought. A Loach. We can play pop up. Get down through the green, softly, softly. And maybe nobody in Burma'll see or hear.

"You're to fly it up to Vientianne," Richard continued. "And forgive me if you don't want the advice, but I've been looking into this guy Wisby. Be very careful how you diddle him, he's tough and no pushover."

"Warning appreciated," Michael answered.

"Good, 'cause I've got another one." Michael ducked his head a little. Just because he'd asked for Richard's help didn't mean –. "Your commendations are just plain scary. Foolhardy's the better word. From now on, have a care for yourself, Second Lieutenant. And write, will you?"

Michael softened inside a little. "Okay, Richard, yeah. I will.

Lieutenant, huh? Some clout you've got."

"Well, one of us does," Richard said. Tom was holding out his hand for the phone and Michael gave it to him, turning away for the door.

"Hello, Richard," Tom said, "I gather you brought it off." He listened, then sent a glance at Michael. "Tired, I think. I couldn't say what else." *He* sounded tired. Sad. "Oh, yes, Richard. He is. More remarkable than perhaps you can know." And Michael's sadness transformed. He was plain angry. He started out of the room. Tom ended the conversation hastily with, "Right, certainly I will. And thank you, old friend." He hung up before Michael was gone, so Michael looked back.

"I'll go out to the airport early in the morning," he said, "hang around, see what kind of service I can get to Saigon." He moved again into the doorway.

"You're angry," Tom said, "I know. Yes, I misjudged things back in Burma. I apologize for it, but you *were* young, Michael, and you were only a few weeks with us – what else was I to think?"

Michael almost choked on it, finally spit it out. "Damn you, how can you not understand?" Tom held silent. Good thing. Michael grabbed a swallow, and now his voice was trembling. "I believed . . . dear sweet heaven, I believed I could *do* it – all of it – because of your belief – yours and Kathleen's, that I could. Because of your faith in me." He pushed out a little breath. "Or the faith I thought you had in me. *It* changed me, oh, yes. Not the fucking war. Even after I lost Kathleen, I finished ag school because I thought that's what *you'd* expect. I knew I couldn't make it on a third world farm without her, no way, but I figured there'd be a use for agronomy somewhere. So I didn't run out. For once, God damn it, I didn't. Took a little detour afterwards, med school for five weeks, but that's all it was." Now the breath left him in a hard chuckle. No longer angry. Bitter. Tom was looking sick. "And you know what? When I enlisted, some- where inside me I thought you'd think it was right to go fight for Vietnam."

But he wasn't done with it yet, or with Tom. "See, with you and Kathleen – Burma – I thought I'd found some people who . . . my *own* people, that's what I thought. Yeah. You know, folks of my own I'd been waiting my whole life for." He went silent a moment, and his next sound was pure disgust, maybe as much with the wetness he felt on his cheeks as with the man listening to him across the room. "What did you tell her, Tom, when she was grieving for me?"

"I told her . . ." Tom took a breath, no tears in his eyes, just immense sorrow. "I told her what turns out to have been close to the truth. Something had gone wrong, had changed – obviously – but you were both very young and she mustn't blame you for it."

Michael could only stare at him, his eyes quite clear now. Finally, he managed to get it out. "Mustn't blame me?" A long silence, feeling very quiet inside. "Who then? Herself? Tom. She'd know you wouldn't mean that. She told me once she always knew what you were thinking. 'Poor Tom can't hide anything, not from me,' and proud of it. She'd have known full well what you meant. Oh, it's not the boy's fault. He just got carried away here in Shangri La and was too young to know his own mind."

"Michael." Tom's face held an agony of pleading.

But Michael let the silence run, heavy with the bitterness. This time, it tightened all the tendons he had in his neck to swallow so that he could finish it. "Don't worry, Tom. Come hell, high water, or the whole fuckin' Burmese Army, I'll get to Kathleen. She has to know. God damn it, she does."

This time, he made it out the door.

* * *

He expected to sleep the night through when he went to bed, what else was there to think about. But he didn't, waking at two-thirty out of a dream that he was certain was of Inle Lake but in a light that was blinding white instead of the wavering muted glow of the oil lamps they'd left out on the deck to draw the mosquitos out from the house. Odd.

And he had an erection. That wasn't. I knew it, he thought, the minute I let her back in, I knew . . . damned body acting like a pubescent teenager's. And then he decided the hell with it, shoved his clasped hands between his legs and let the memories run.

"I thought they'd never leave us alone," she said, "and you kept asking to see more things, you idiot!" He took her hand and drew her inside off the deck, and across to the bedroom. No lamps in here, but the window shutters were raised and the mosquito bar was white in the moonlight. This time, when she untied his longyi he let her, then stood there in his BVDs, stirring inside them, feeling silly. She reached, whether to slide her hand through the slit in the briefs or to slide the briefs down he didn't know, but he took her hand and stopped her. "No," he said. She stared at him. "Me first," he said.

So she stood quietly while he unbuttoned her eingyi, sliding the almost transparent cotton off her shoulders, pulling it off her arms. She had a camisole on underneath. He'd get to that.

He slid his hands along her waist and pulled her longyi free so that it fell in folds to her ankles. Now she looked as she had that day, that first day between them, at the creek after the dancing lesson, dressed in her underwear. But not quite. When he looked back up at her face, he saw her eyes were gone half-closed, her lips apart, and in the muted light her skin was ivory, the hair silver on her arms. He leaned and kissed her, not touching her otherwise, sliding his tongue in between her lips, her teeth, to find her fresh and clean inside. She always was, sweet as rain he'd discovered not all that long ago to tell the truth, so that he wanted to drink from her. Until her tongue curled round his and her mouth grew hot.

He leaned back slightly, their eyes caught and holding as he pulled the camisole over her head, then bent to pull down her panties to the floor. Her breath was coming in shallow pants, now, and she placed her hands on his shoulders. "Michael, please." But he only took one of her hands and led her to the bed, lifting the netting for her to slip under it, where she waited for him – to be shocked when he turned away.

He'd forgotten where he'd dropped his damned jeans, but he found them, dug into a pocket for his wallet and pulled out the one condom he had there. He'd only brought one pack from the States, and now didn't know what he'd do when they were used up.

"What're you doing?" she asked, still shocked. He showed her the little disk, wondering if he'd have to explain or – God, his cock was getting huge, felt like it anyway, he didn't look.

"Don't you dare put that on," she said. So, no explanations needed. "I've taken care of it, it's the right time of the month."

"Kathleen – what are you, some kind of secret mackerel snapper?"

"Don't talk like that, and in any case, you don't have to be Catholic to know about the rhythm system."

Jesus, he was likely to fade away if they kept this up.

"Michael," she said, soft now. "I don't want anything between us when you're inside me."

In the bed at Tom's, Michael began handling himself, something he hadn't done in a long time, his hand playing as if detached.

She was sitting like a Burmese woman on a pagoda platform, knees bent, legs to one side, and back as straight as an arrow. Now she lifted her hands to her hair, her lifting arms lifting her breasts as she loosened the twist she'd worn this day almost on the crown of her head. It fell heavily, coiling over one shoulder.

My God, he thought, do all women know this by instinct, or has she been reading beyond her years? Suddenly he heard the lapping of the water below, like the ticking of a clock, and he knew that before the night was out he would regret every minute he had spent without her, outside the net.

He dropped the condom, pulled off his briefs, and her eyes fell to his groin, but this time without the amazement he'd seen in them that day by the creek. He got under the net, and sat beside her as she was sitting, turned so that his erection lay across his upper thigh. She reached for him, and again he stopped her. He was going to make damned sure this was right for her, and he knew that once she touched him he'd be on short time.

"Just let me look at you," he said, so softly, and his eyes moved down that slender body, tinted gold in the light, the small breasts with the dark nipples seated above the curve, the belly rounding below the hollow of her navel. And now his hand followed his gaze, trailing around her throat, drifting his palm over the firm nipples, and moving down and into the triangle of curls. Her hands, planted flat on the bed on either side of her hips to do as he'd asked and not touch him were clenching now, and when he slid his lips down to her breast, took her nipple into his mouth, her sigh became a whimper.

He found her wet. She moaned and grasped that hand to press it against her, pushing her pelvis to it. Begging, now, leaning back on one hand, her head tipped back, eyes closed, mouth loose, legs loose, "Please, please, please, Michael, please . . ." She didn't know what she was pleading for, he knew that. She was so small he was going to hurt her, he knew that, too.

He laid her back, and this time she had her way. She took his penis into her hand, God, how did she know to keep her touch so light. She opened her eyes, looking at him. "Michael . . ." And even as she was spreading her legs, he was parting them to kneel between them. He looked at her dusky soft folds and up that open body waiting for him and groaned.

"I love you, Kath," he said.

He saw her eyes clear as she recovered herself. She reached for his face, running her finger along his lips. "You must know, Michael . . . you do know . . . you make my life real."

He felt flooded with the recognition of the fragile thing they were beginning and, leaning forward above her, too full to wait any longer, he pushed into her slowly, with her eyes wide open on his face and the pressure on him almost overwhelming. He turned his head to kiss her, her tiny breaths filling his own throat. And then, he was stopped.

He rocked against the barrier, gently, gently. Jesus. Her first time and his first virgin. Was this why they called it banging? Is that what he should do, just blast on into her? But she took it away from him, driving herself onto him with a small cry to press against him, grinding, legs clasped around his hips. Then, easily, his body insisted on a rhythm. But once again, her frenzy ran away. Her cries fast growing, she rose, finally arched and went over the top in spasm after spasm. In the seconds before he followed her, Michael had an experience unknown to him before, that stopped his breath and almost his heart. Deep inside her, the muscles moved and grabbed against him, all around him, all the length of him. When he exploded, it was close to agony.

In Kowloon, Michael had come in his hand. He lay sprawled on his back, wringing wet, recapturing his air. The release was enormous. He hadn't known he'd been in such need. And knew he would now be in unforgettable need of her. Better watch out, Cameron, it'll grow hair. Shit.

His last thought before falling off to sleep was to wonder if he'd moaned at the climax here, the way the kids did sometimes late into the night back at the hooch. And he wondered, too, without caring very much, whether Tom had heard him.

DAY THREE

9

Tom insisted on driving him to the airport, but it was in almost complete silence.

They found a flight out leaving soon, and Tom stayed to see him off, still little or nothing said between them. At the gate, with a hand on Michael's arm, Tom stopped him, his other hand outstretched to him. "God speed," he said.

Michael hesitated a moment too long, then grasped Tom's hand briefly. "I'll be in touch," he said, and headed towards the plane.

But then he knew he couldn't leave it like that. He turned around, blocking the way of the passengers behind him, managing to find Tom's eyes, and mouthed, "Watch your back."

Tom was unsure, but only a moment, then nodded and started to call something. But Michael turned, kept on walking, and didn't hear Tom's answer.

What he had to do now was figure out how to convince Hanny.

* * *

It was mid-afternoon before Michael reached Marble Mountain. He knew he should probably break the news to the Major before he heard it through channels, but his leave wasn't over until tomorrow morning. Even Niemeier wouldn't expect his decision on the other thing until then, and channels were always slow. Anyway, he had to talk to Hanny, first.

He got lucky three times, hitching a ride to the hooch to change into fatigues, on to sergeants' country to learn that Hanny was still flying, on to OPs to find out when he'd be coming home. Then the luck left. Yeah,

Hanny was down, and in trouble.

The OPs room was almost empty as Michael walked over to the board. Through the open door he could see the Major talking on the phone, his back turned. Michael read the reports chalked up, and he must have made some kind of sound. The Second Lieutenant who'd pulled Officer of the Day duty looked up to see him and said, "Sorry, Cam. About an hour ago."

Impatience running away with him, Michael said, "And nobody's gone out?"

"A couple of slicks making a drop over towards Ha Tan are gonna see what's what on their way back. But the Loach took hits over deep canopy, so . . ."

"What you got on the pad?

A voice behind Michael spoke up. "Me." Michael turned. Sergeant Wilbert, a Loach Chief. "Been sittin' around here all day waitin' for a pilot. Where you been?"

"Let's go," Michael said. The two of them grabbed their flack vests and helmet bags and were almost out the door when Michael heard Neimeier shouting "Cameron!"

No way was that prick going to stop him from going after Hanny. Michael was already swinging into one of the stand-by jeeps, Wilbert with him, when Bobby Zinc, a Cobra pilot, came pelting out of the building, followed by his co-pilot. They jumped in the jeep, Zinc saying "Want company?" And the four headed for the flight line.

* * *

Pre-flight done in record time, Sergeant Wilbert out on the pad with the fire extinguisher waiting for Michael to crank, after which, the Chief clambered into the back and Michael keyed Zinc in the Cobra gun-ship. He was ready. Flying the scout made Michael the Mission Commander. On his "Go!" the Cobra was out of the revetment, over the perimeter fence and up, Michael hard on its boom almost close enough to lose way in the downwash. Then both choppers went high and blistering, Zinc having to hold back to let the Light OH-6A keep up.

They flew past Marble Mountain and turned west and south, leaving Da Nang and the sea coast behind. The radio began to talk. Hanny's Loach, piloted by Lieutenant Farber was in triple canopy. No way could a Huey get to it, not according to their gun, Warrant Officer One Shelby, who was doing a three-sixty overhead in his Cobra. Shelby had yet to complete one month in-country.

Michael informed him that Rook 5 and King 4 were on their way.

"That you, Pappy?"

"Yup," Michael answered. "What y'got here, Tim?" steadying his own voice, deepening it for sureness, wishing he felt it.

"Crew Chief reports Lieutenant Farber caught it, Sir. Neck broke." So they were in contact with the ground and Hanny. Thank God. Shelby's voice spilled out of him, tone rising. "They took some .50 cal, .37mms, a few rockets, went down through the canopy and no sign left. I hit the fuckin' rocket launchers too late! Damn it – "

"Okay, now, Tim," Michael cut in, smooth and easy. "Keep altitude, cruise around, we'll be along. You might tell Rook 5 Alpha that, too."

"Well, uh, I've used up my ammo, Sir, and I'm just about shit creek on fuel. Don't know how long I can hang out here." Maybe not, but he sounded calmer. Until he overrode himself, "I see you!"

Michael switched to FM. "Rook 5 Alpha? Alpha, y'hear me?"

A moment, and then Hanny came on, whispering. "Yeah, Sir, and welcome. How was Hong Kong?"

"Have I got a story for you, pal." Michael switched back to UHF. "Fly home safe and sound, Mr. Shelby. Good work." Then back to Hanny with, "What shape're you in?"

"Bad ankle. Cut some and sprained." Still whispering. "I'm not goin' far with it. Not that it matters. No clearing in sight, and no way can you get down here."

Michael ignored the warning. He'd have to get down, period. "You got any smoke?"

"Yeah. The bird hung up in branches, but I angled out the door and brought some flares with me. 'Course the smoke'll spot you to the Charlies."

Again, Michael ignored the warning. "Your gun lost track of you. You've got to mark where you are for us. King 4's's up here, too."

No more hesitation. "Right," said Hanny, "smoke comin' up." And there the purple cloud rose, almost immediately drifting sideways across the canopy.

"Confirm Goofy Grape," Michael said. "See it, King 4?" and got two hisses back from Bobby Zinc as he keyed his mike twice for a yes. "Okay," Michael said, "we're doin' it."

He keyed Wilbert on the intercom, warned him to hold on, and put the bird close to a ninety-degree bank to the right, circling. "Bridge Over Troubled Water," – leftover from the jukebox last week at Li Li's – S and G singing sweet through his head. "I will lay me down. . ." If Hanny were aboard they'd be duetting it.

Again, Michael keyed Wilbert. "See any openings, Chief?" He'd be focussing his eyes down below the treetops to somewhere unseen in hopes of spotting an open space, Michael knew, while Michael kept his eyes on where the smoke had first appeared.

"No, Sir."

Back at what he hoped was that spot, Michael shoved on the cyclic, pitching the Loach forward, and shot down to within a few feet of the canopy. The grape had drifted far off to the right by now. He keyed FM and Hanny. "Rook 5 Alpha, I'm on the canopy. Can you still hear me?"

"Not well. Damned trees. Poppin' smoke."

And there, almost right under Michael, came the yellow. Michael immediately went up a little and spiralled down, looking for dirt down there. The Cobra jumped in with, "Tracers, Rook 5. I'm going after the source, but you might try a little zig-zag." Michael already was. The tracers went past big as baseballs. It complicated things. And then he spotted it – a slit in the high canopy beneath him. He keyed in Wilbert. "Chief, another fast drop, keep your eyes on the tail, we'll be choppin' wood, it's gonna be tight."

He pushed on the cyclic, the little bird leveled, he lowered the collective and the Loach fell like a stone, bits and pieces of branches swirling around it, Michael hoping to God the blades would hold up. One two-inch limb and they were dead. They held, and he brought the Loach under control, settling onto the small clearing he'd spotted as brown ground from above the canopy. And Hanny came on air.

"Christ, li'l sweetheart, how you gonna get out?"

"You saw us?"

"Heard you. So did the bad guys."

Michael opened up the intercom so Wilbert could hear Hanny, too. "Can you get to us, Hanny?"

"Not soon enough, Sir. This damned leg's draggin'."

"Where are you?"

"'Bout one hundred yards northeast of you – I think."

Michael felt slow, too. So damned slow. What was the matter with him? Before he could issue the order, Wilbert came on air. "I'm after him,

Sir. Just please do stick around, okay?" And the Loach rocked as Wilbert leaped out to the ground.

"Rock 5? Rock 5? Where are you, damn it?" It was Zinc.

"AOK, King 4," Michael answered. "My Crew Chief's out gathering up our package."

Something exploded off to the east. Michael saw it, felt the blast through the open side of the Loach. "Cam? Cam?"

"I know, Bobby, I know. Mortars. Puckered my ass, don't they always." He sounded weary. Watch it. Nobody needed that. "Signing off."

Almost immediately, he could hear Bobby starting to work his own rockets and minigun, bless him. There was another explosion from the dinks, closer. They were beginning to get range.

The weight of the Loach's minigun plus three men dictated a running take-off to get up. He scanned the forest, for bad guys, yeah, but if he could find an opening between the trees wide enough, he could hover over and head back here to the path they'd just cut down through the canopy. Then maybe he could grab clean air – enough to lift up and up, enough to break free. The little bird lurched to the right and settled deeper into the ground.

Wilbert came on. "Go, Sir, go. We're on – and he's bleedin' some."

The Loach strained, finally raised enough to hover through some trees, away from the closer and closer incoming VC mortars. He'd have to head straight back into them, no help for it. He turned the Loach, beeped a little more power, started back. Approaching the cut, now, turbine beginning to cry, the rotor RPM threatening to decay, and he waited and he waited. Shit, was it going to burn out? Was his fucking hand frozen?

At last he deliberately pulled up on the collective, got all there was, the N2 over-torqued by seven pounds but she held, and up they went, chopping a wider column this time. The poor little bird shuddered, but Michael was committed, so was the Loach, no turning back. And here came the light.

* * *

He slouched on the inevitable lime green bench by the nurses' station, waiting for the report, but he wasn't really worried. Hanny'd walked into the med unit okay, with only an arm around Michael's shoulder for support, both men of a size.

Had he waited too long? Had he sent the tachometer into the red for too long? Shit. No. No. He'd done it right, damn it. No mistake this time. At least there mightn't be combat in Laos. Not so much, anyway. Maybe. And not so fuckin' many people looking to him for wisdom and righteousness.

"Any news?" Bobby Zinc, come to inquire. Michael shook his head, told him not to worry. Bobby stood over him a moment. "I'm putting you in for a commendation," he said.

Startled, Michael gathered himself to stand and smiled wryly. "Thanks, Bobby, but it's a waste of time." At Bobby's raised eyebrow, Michael explained, "Niemeier's about to have my head. You'd best try to keep yours."

"The man's a no-brain," Bobby said. "You were a fuckin' classic out there."

"Tell you what," Michael said, "recommend Wilber. He's the one deserves it."

"Yeah, well . . ." Bobby again, shaking his head, turning for the door. "Tell Hanrahan I inquired." And he left.

Michael drifted after him to the door, looked out onto the late day. It had showered earlier, and the tarmac was lifting mist. How in hell had Niemeier gotten the news so fast? He obviously had, from the fury in his voice earlier. Via Alexander Graham Bell, you asshole. Probably on the phone that minute with the Head of Division down in Saigon, getting reamed for wasting the Brigadier's time on useless paperwork, not to mention having been brown nosed on behalf of an ungrateful chopper pilot.

"Got three stitches and three days grounded." Hanny talking at his back. Michael turned, Hanny started a grin.

"Yeah?" Michael said, grinning back. "Don't count on it. You up for Li Li's?"

* * *

They'd wrapped Hanny's ankle and he favored it but only a little. They got a ride over to the motor pool, scrounged a deuce-and-a-half with a sick transmission, and headed towards Da Nang.

Set about a hundred feet off the road, Li Li's offered beer, something approaching red eye, girls, and a Wurlitzer. There were a few customers Li

Li would let go straight through and out back to what she called her Florida lanai. She hadn't the best idea of what a lanai was, much less one in Florida – hers had an earthen floor and a slanting plastic roof which kept the rain off but let in some light, as did the canvas walls, raised or lowered to accomodate the monsoon – but she saw to it the girls didn't bother you if you didn't want them, and would keep you in Glenlivet if you knew to ask, along with fresh dim sum from a Chinese noodle shop on down the road.

Michael and Hanny didn't need to ask. After two tours, Li Li already knew. Hanny hadn't access to the "O" Club, and Michael was inappropriate at the NCO Club. Matter of fact, as a Warrant Officer, he felt out of place at either club.

The Wurlitzer had been their contribution to good times and a sense of home. They'd found it one weekend down in Saigon and bought it from the hotel bar on Tu Do street for three cases of frozen steaks out of the back of the Tan Son Nhut commissary. Every trip since they contributed new records. Never enough to replace all the oldies, because Michael spent time here alone and used them to think against, sitting at the small rusty round table in the corner where he and Hanny were now, the single malt set aside while he made two beers last through the evening, listening to Redding or Sledge or Rawls and figuring out how to nurse the FNG kid who'd blown it that morning into doing what Michael was pretty sure he had it in him to do. A lot of time spent doing that.

Sometimes, one of Li Li's tiny girls would come out onto the lanai and perch on his knee, turning one of his ears into a toy, and rarely, he'd dance. He missed dancing. But though they moved well enough, these girls were so small he kept wanting to set them atop his feet like a child.

This evening, Li Li brought out the forever open bottle of Glenlivet and two smeary glasses right away, leaving the bottle. They'd keep their own tab and pay her, but it was her way of saying they were special and could have it for free. Not meaning it, of course. She looked about fifty, was probably forty, her hard road to success tracing her face, her hair showing grey, her hips and buttocks pressing against her ao dai. Hanny pulled her down for a big kiss on her cheek as usual, saying, "You boku diep," his accent horrific as usual,making her laugh and act shy, and when she waddled away, she carried with her the smack of his hand on her behind. "Dim sum soon," she said.

"So. How about Hong Kong?" Hanny asked. The Temptations were doing "My Girl". Easy to talk over.

"Yeah well," Michael started, "um . . ." He got busy pouring Scotch. He lifted his to Hanny, popped it down, poured himself another.

Hanny watched him. "Your friends okay?"

Finally meeting his eyes, Michael decided to just out with it. "I'm transferring to Laos, Neal. A commission, with the military attaché at the embassy in Vientiane."

Hanny took a breath, ducked his head. He lifted his glass, set it down again. Unlike most Irish, he didn't flush when angered. Instead, his skin went white, deepening the freckles imprinted across his twice-broken nose and making the black hair hanging straight on his forehead catch light like coal.

"Hanny," Michael started, but Hanny overrode, his voice even – Hanny was good at that. "I figured – damn it, Cam, here I've been waiting around, putting it off with all kinds of excuses, waiting to know if you were gonna stay in-country or go home, what the hell – "

"There's a slot for you. A staff sargeant's stripes, flight pay and your own Loach." Jaw half-dropped, Hanny's eyes flew up to meet Michael's. Michael had convinced himself on the return trip that Hanny'd for sure kick back his chair in exasperation before the story was half told, to head inside and find himself a girl. Not for a lay. Oh, a couple of times, soon after they got to Nam, they'd gone into Da Nang looking for it, but on his last leave home Hanny had met the right woman, he'd said, who'd make a good mother for his little boy, so he'd up and married her before returning to Nam, and he stayed faithful. All he wanted nowadays, he said, was to put his arm around some little dink-ess and nuzzle. According to Hanny, get past the fish sauce and they kind of smelled sweet. The only times Michael came close to agreeing with him was when he'd had a couple of six packs and all he could smell was the beer.

But exasperation would have been far easier to deal with than what Michael saw building behind those black eyes. The wrong-side-of-town hang-up that hardly ever surfaced anymore. Michael always wanted to say, "Come on, Hanny, come on, get over it, it's a waste of time." But he never said anything to the point, just waited for it to pass. Because it wasn't a waste of Hanny's time. It mattered. And it always did pass. Only Michael had the feeling that if Hanny got up and walked away from this here and now, it wouldn't, and something unmendable would be torn. So he planted his feet squarely under the table and tightened his thighs, prepared to leap, wrestle Hanny and pin him down to hear it out.

Not that it would be a walk. Hanny had boxed all through high school. That's how they'd met. Sort of. Addresses had been posted at Fort Wolters, and they were both listed from around Cleveland. Hanny grew up in the east city, close to the flats, and blue collar. The only way Michael, rich boy from Shaker Heights, knew anything about the flats was from intramural sports – Polack hunks, little Eyeties who played dirty, and hot-tempered Micks. Or so he'd joked Hanny. "You got that last one right, anyway," Hanny'd retorted.

The minute they'd seen each other at Wolters, they'd agreed it was not for the first time. But they couldn't zero in on it, except it had to be some high school athletic meet. Two years older and shorter by only an inch, Hanny had some fifteen pounds on Michael, and when they entered a bar together, other men were likely to hold aside until one or the other of them cracked a smile. They used to call it the cowboy trick, but had some time ago outgrown it, to their occasional regret.

Michael had fought him once. He didn't want to connect with those fists again. So he plunged in, hoping to cut it. "There was a girl. I mean, there *is* a girl."

"Uh, huh. In Laos."

"Burma."

"Uh, huh."

Michael's breath was shallow. He sucked one in, and then the kid brought their dim sum, and Michael had to dig out a couple of bucks for him. He always took the first batch. Not that it lit up the kid's face. It was what he expected from these two. Even before the kid was gone, Hanny started, his voice soft.

"Let me understand this, Michael," he said. He never called him Michael. "You got the hots for some bird and for that you think you can make my decisions without talkin' to me first, shit, run my whole fuckin' life practically, and toss me some stinkin' promotion to shut me up?"

He was waiting for an answer. He didn't want it torn, either.

"There wasn't time," Michael said. "Not to get back here, sound you out about it, and then try to call my brother in DC. Hell, it's struggle enough to get through to Saigon from here." Hanny was still listening. "I thought . . . nevermind what I thought. No way am I running your life. Refuse the transfer. Tell 'em the truth, it wasn't at your request."

Hanny's upper lip was beaded. He didn't look away from Michael, just wiped it dry with the back of his hand.

"But I gotta tell you, Neal," Michael finished, "it won't work unless you're with me." Suddenly, he was flushing with anger of his own. "And she's not a God damned bird." Jesus, cool it, you jerk.

A long, long moment, one Michael would remember for a long, long time, and Hanny gave a short nod. It's a step, Michael thought.

Hanny lifted the lid off the steam basket and speared a dumpling with a chopstick. That's what he did with dim sum – jab in the yellowing plastic stick and hope the dumpling didn't slide off before he got his teeth around it. He claimed he didn't like Chinese food, except for dim sum, and wouldn't even try to use two chopsticks.

He made it this time and while he chewed and blew because it was too hot, Michael carried on. "That time I was in Burma? In '65? The farm belonged to this girl and her brother. He's the one I went to see in Hong Kong. He left Burma three years ago. Truth is, the government kicked him out – kicked everybody out. Except – Kathleen managed to stay, that's her name, only now she wants to come out, but . . ." This was sounding crazier than Michael had even thought. He sighed. "We think she's being held against her will."

Hanny's eyes were gone flat now, looking at him, and Michael couldn't tell what was alive behind them. What he said was, "Uh, huh," and he swallowed the dumpling. "So you're gonna go get her."

"Yeah."

"How?"

"Well," Michael said, "there is the Loach."

"Oh, right, God's little chariot," Hanny said, "and here with all this stuttering around, and you being you, I was figuring you to raise an army and invade the fuckin' country."

Well, he'd chilled out enough for sarcasm, anyway. An improvement. Time to drop the bomb, Michael thought. "Can't do that," he said, "the baby might get hurt."

Hanny's eyes stayed flat. "Any other little bits you'd like to share?" he said.

"I've got maps," Michael said.

"Well, there's a mercy," Hanny said.

Watching him, Michael saw his eyes begin to crinkle, a grin start, and suddenly the two of them were laughing, gasping, until the tears ran. It quieted, gusted out again, quieted.

"Shit," Hanny said.

Michael wiped his hand down his damp face, not too sure the tears were all from laughter. He picked up some chopsticks to get himself a dumpling. His hand shook and he couldn't manage it. He looked up to see Hanny noticing.

"I guess you'd better tell me about Kathleen," Hanny said. "For instance, where she is in Burma exactly."

That was easy. "Eastern. Shan Hills. She's um . . . at present, she's – " Not so easy. " – living in the palace of a Shan prince. They call him a sawbwa. He's a drug lord, actually." Talk about shit.

But Hanny again surprised him. No laughter this time, no resentment, either. He just studied Michael, until Michael could have killed him he wanted to look away so much.

Suddenly, Hanny speared up another dim sum and stuffed it in his mouth, pouring himself more Glenlivet. He leaned back, aimed his voice towards the inside and hollered through his mouthful, "For the love of Mary, put on some Dylan!" And muttered, "A man can't hear himself think."

In a flattering shortness of moment, The Doors went dead and "Blowing in the Wind" came up.

"She must be some lady," he said. And then, "Baby and all, huh?"

"Yeah," said Michael. "We've been out of touch for more than four years. I have to bring her out."

"Well I gotta say, what with one thing and another, you've made that pretty clear," said Hanny. "So. No more debate. Only question is how soon."

10

They stayed late at Li Li's talking strategy. But lacking the maps which Michael had left back at the hooch, everything was speculative, and they went round and round on time and distance and fuel supplies and whether the best shot would be night or day. Neither was anything but hazardous, with mountain locations and altitudes iffy and searchlights a giveaway.

On their way out, they tallied up their tabs at the bar and had almost reached the door when Michael turned Hanny to a stop. "How much y'got?" Michael asked. "I have about three hundred left from Hong Kong."

"Eighty or so," Hanny said.

Both turned back and joined Li Li at the bar, one on either side of her.

"Hey, darlin'," Hanny said, "we won't be back."

And he tucked his roll down into the left side of her cleavage. She looked at him, bad news taking her slowly. Michael tucked his larger roll into the right side.

She looked at Michael. She looked at Hanny. She looked down at the bar. "You good boys," she said. "Numbah one boys." She started a grin. "Save much Glenlivet without you boys." But suddenly, she started a wail. Her head tipped back, eyes closed, she covered her face and it went on and on. Hanny and Michael looked at each other, bewildered but also a little sad. Michael shrugged. They headed back towards the door. Just reaching there, they heard her hoarse but clear voice: "Is bad here. Maybe worse where you go United State?" They turned around. "You good boys make it bad here, maybe make it bad there, too? How we know such thing is true, or not true, in far away place? We say, go home American, we want you go home. But Li Li love American boys. Li Li very mixed up. She say, you good boys. You come back, is okay." She was looking after them, her eyes hot, but no telling whether with hatred or sorrow, pleading or just anger. So they left.

* * *

Hanny drove back. They could feel the concussions of incoming rockets on the far edge of the base. The rain had stopped, and the explosions brightened the horizon like northern lights. They were quiet, smoking. The road glistened, not just with old rain water but with tiny migrating frogs. Hundreds, maybe thousands, going across. It was usually in August they did it up here near Da Nang, but late for some reason this year. The truck tires went splat splat as they drove over them. "Poor little buggers," said Hanny, "I hate killin' 'em." Suddenly he swerved the truck, but there was a thump under the left front fender anyway. "Damn," Hanny said. "Humongous bastard."

"You tried," Michael said. He slid down in the seat, managing his legs, to lay his head back and close his eyes.

"What'll we be doing in Laos?" Hanny asked now for the first time. "Aside from this main deal of yours, I mean. I thought they were using one or two-seater fixed-wing STOLs for reconnaisance there. Engineering scuttlebutt is they got short take-off and landing dirt strips all over the place. What do they need us for?"

"All I know, the new attaché – a Lieutenant Colonel Wisby, ever hear of him?" Michael cracked an eye to see Hanny shake his head. "He wants to go see the country low and slow."

"Uh huh. We turn up at the right time, he wants a tour guide, so whammo, we get orders in under two days. Convenient all around. Just what the Army tries really hard to do, be convenient for folks. You suppose they already had the Loach or are they gettin' one in especially for us?"

Michael opened his eyes and sat up. Would he ever feel anything but tired? It should've struck him the minute he heard from Richard, would've except for being so blown away by all the rest. And he should've known, too, how Hanny would feel. Should have known. He'd better get his head together or the whole lot would go down. What he said was, "You're right. My brother has pull, sure, but they have to be the shortest orders ever cut. For the quietest machine in the air. Nothing better for secret little trips, and don't we know that. You don't suppose the Colonel – what, the Golden Triangle? Drugs, for God's sake?"

"Unh unh," said Hanny. "Not a colonel, heaven forbid. More like China. What do they call 'em – black operations?"

And here he'd figured all the clandestined shit belonged to AA. It could be he'd landed them in an ocean of it.

They were waved through the gate. Hanny knew everybody. They left the truck at the motor pool, with a note from Hanny under the wiper saying the transmission was at death's door, and hiked across the flight line to the hooches, Hanny showing more of a limp now.

"When do you see the Major?" he asked.

"Tomorrow, first thing, God help. He already knows, I think."

"Want company?"

Michael shook his head. "Stay clean of it, Neal. It's not your doing."

They reached Michael's digs first. The two looked at each other a moment, but there wasn't a hell of a lot else to say. Michael went into the hooch, found his cot and crashed.

*　*　*

Michael got to OPs at eight the next morning, to find Hanny seated in a jeep at one side of the building. He didn't even seem to know Michael had arrived, just sitting there, smoking, bad foot up on the seat.

OPs had been alive for a couple of hours. As he walked across to the Major's office, he was aware that men's eyes kept sliding to follow him. Great. They knew something was up and exactly who was to blame. The door was open. Michael tapped on it, and when the Major looked up, he stepped into it. "I, um – I need to talk to you, Sir."

The Major used a silence, then said, "You may want to close the door, Mr. Cameron."

Michael closed it, returned to attention.

The Major picked up a stapled thin sheaf of paper, and slapped it hard down on his desk. "What is this, Mr. Cameron?" His voice was low. Not for long as he answered his question, his voice going higher and higher. "Orders that came with Classified Distribution from Saigon this morning. For you. For *you*? What the fuck is this!"

Michael hesitated, not knowing how to answer him. The Major leaned across his desk toward Michael, suddenly whispering – probably thought it was more menacing. It kind of was, especially the words he whispered. "You snake. I've spent the night coming up with names to call you. First the call from the Brigadier and then I come in here this morning and find this – *this* sitting on my desk! I offered you the best deal in the Army, God damn it. I went on record for you and massaged every REMF in Saigon for you!"

Oh, boy, thought Michael. Not only that, he'd come to attention hastily and any moment he was going to have to shift balance. The Major would love that. He dug his heels into the floor.

"That's what Hong Kong was about, was it? Pull strings, go over my head? And for what?!" Again he let his voice rise. Purposefully, Michael was well aware. This man never did anything by happenstance or without forethought. "So you can go be a rear echelon mother fucker . . ." and now he was booming it out, "pushing papers in some backwater embassy with a commission and combat pay?"

Everybody in the OPs room had to have heard that, Michael knew. As well as what was coming next, because the Major was standing now, shorter than Michael, needing to look up at him across the desk, a good way to pitch his voice over Michael's shoulder at the door. "You disappoint me. You disappoint the squadron. You disappoint the Army, Mister."

Michael managed to keep his eyes fixed on the Major's, whose voice now lowered again. "I told you minimal combat. I promised that to you *and* the commission, and you fucked me. Your name ever crosses my desk again, your record will not be well served." He let loose again. "Men will die here because of you, *Lieutenant*. I want you and your toady the hell off this base by tonight."

"Yes, Sir," Michael managed, and he was in the midst of his salute when the Major slung the orders at him. They fell to the floor. In a tone of utter disgust, almost whispering again, the Major said, "Pick 'em up, you fucker, and get out."

Michael drew the office door closed very quietly behind him. Everyone, in one direction or another, was turned away from him. His first steps across the floor were the hardest he'd ever taken. And then the sound started, soft, low, like a grumbling. "Good luck, Cam." "Good for you, Pappy!" "Luck, Sir." "Good luck." "If it's what you want, AOK!" Michael's eyes flickered from one side to the other. The men still were not looking at him, faces lowered, voices pitched into their chests.

Not quite sure how, he finally reached the outside, and was held by a shaft of sunlight new in the air, almost blinded by it. He didn't hear the steps coming out after him. "Cam?" Startled, he looked to find Ed Miller beside him, his hand held out for a shake. He was a Wobbly 1, the newest FNG, most of the time either too eager or scared to death. "You remember that day? When I froze up – absolutely. Lookin' for my first long range patrol? You found 'em – saved them and me, too. And then didn't report it." His hand was firm out there, and waiting. Michael took it, and the kid grabbed on as if it were a lifeline.

"Hey," Michael said, having some difficulty. "That was a long time ago, couple of weeks, right? You're doin' fine, Ed."

"Yeah. And I won't forget it."

"Get in, Sir." Hanny had pulled the jeep up in front of them, thank God. Michael got in, slamming down into the seat, sending a half salute back to Ed as Hanny started driving.

They were quiet. Then Michael waggled the orders a little. "Got 'em," he said.

"That's good," said Hanny, driving. "The extra money's gonna come in useful. Did I tell you? Barb's pregnant."

It swept Michael away. "Aw, shit," he said, "stop the jeep, Hanny." Hanny kept driving. "Stop the damned jeep, Sergeant!"

Hanny pulled the jeep over, halted it, but kept the motor running. "You gotta go home, you know you do," said Michael. "So turn around, and I'll go back and get you out of it."

They sat there, Hanny not budging. "And why the hell, I might ask, didn't you tell me before? God damn it, *turn around!*"

Hanny swivelled in the seat to face Michael. "Now you listen to me, Michael. I thought about it during the night, sure I did. If I finish out my enlistment back in the States, it'll be down in Texas, where else? And Barb living in tiny non-com quarters on the base, ballooning out in all that heat. And my boy back in Cleveland, by himself with my folks the way it was before I met Barb. It was hard on my folks, and Eric hated it. So they're both with them now, it's a big house and that's where they belong. And when she's due I'll get compassionate leave and go be with her. And the money is good, no two ways about it, okay? Over, done, *finito.*"

Michael held in indecision long enough that Hanny got the jeep moving again, straight ahead. Hanny chuckled suddenly: "Holy Mother, there was hardly time between the ceremony and the end of my leave to jump in and out of the covers even once. How the hell d'you suppose it happened?"

"Oh, well," said Michael, rising to it, "see, it's like this. First you – "

"Shut up," said Hanny. Just like that, it was raining, sun gone, and coming down like a waterfall. "I'll drop you off to pack, come back for you. We better step on it, find ourselves a flight out, or the bastard'll have us in the brig."

Michael tightened. "You heard?"

"He had the shutters up. I always have wondered what it's like to be a toady."

Right then Michael didn't have a laugh in him. He'd guess Hanny hadn't heard it all. Michael doubted he'd ever tell him or anyone about that walk across OPs, but it was a thing he knew he'd never forget. Especially since that son of a bitch had been right. Ed had just driven it home. Men would die for lack of him.

"Y'know what?" He almost had to shout for Hanny to hear through the noise of the jeep and the rain on the roof.

"What!" Hanny shouted back.

"Kathleen better be by God glad to see us."

Hanny shot a glance at him. Michael just stared at the rain.

DAY FOUR

11

Kathleen stood just inside the reception hall, looking out across the roofed veranda to the courtyard, watching the last of the ponies go out through the gate, Cho suckling contentedly. Htin Aung would be leaving shortly for Ban Houei Say and the Golden Triangle. The helicopter waited in the plaza, the pilot, the three dealers already aboard.

This afternoon, she would try to get through the palace gate and go down to the town, to the bazaar, sell a sapphire and buy things she would need. She had thought to send U-pym, but not now. She was still unsure of her – asking too much, perhaps. Kathleen hadn't been off the grounds in many months. He would no longer permit it, not since the pregnancy and baby. He read her too well. But with him gone, she would take the chance.

Cho let her left nipple slip from his mouth and his cry mewled up. He'd earlier drained her right breast. There never had been enough for him, and less and less now. She jiggled him, tiny face screwed up in hunger, as she turned for the corridor, and headed to her room at the back west wing to find U-pym.

Cho was coughing, wracking coughs, and she laid him up against her shoulder as she walked, patting him to release the congestion, the rattle in his chest under her hand rattling her heart. "Tomorrow, little love, tomorrow," she whispered.

U-pym was there, always there in Kathleen's room so the two of them could share comforting the baby during the night and U-pym could feed him. As Kathleen handed Cho to her, U-pym turned her eyes away in avoidance.

Should she speak to her? Plead again? Even if U-pym let the Prince go, it would take only a word to the Shan guard tonight, and it all would be lost. But how could she keep her prisoner in the room all those hours? The women wandered in and out at will, full of giggles and tales and little bets for gambling down in the town. She decided to say nothing more, but took U-pym's hand, clasped it in show of good trust. The woman lifted her eyes to Kathleen's for a moment, then she freed her hand and reached for the baby.

Not wanting to watch Cho touch another's breast with his fingers, take another's nipple into his mouth, knowing she herself, his mother, was the fault for his hunger, Kathleen did as she always did unless it was pouring – she pulled on her old jeans, some spots so threadbare she'd patched and repatched them, and her old boots which she kept oiled and now tied with rawhide, and went up to the pasture. She saw Maung Swe clear on the other side. No heavy rains today, the sun seeping through the clouds, thin and cool. Auspicious for the pack train, everyone said. And for her and the baby.

She would ride the ridge a ways. Lim Pong, her Shan guard, leading his pony as usual, had followed her up the hill, his automatic rifle over his shoulder. With the late start this morning she hadn't meditated and she wouldn't now.

When Htin Aung was in residence, she walked up the mountain always wondering if it would be her last ride. He could take that away, too. As he had the school, and her own house, and as he'd tried to stop the teaching that had made her life . . . a life. He didn't know it, but when he was gone or distracted by things like the Burma war or the opium feud with Chan Shee-fu, she held secret classes for the women of the palace, even his three wives – ABC's, one-two-three's, and the history of Asia, which Tom had made sure she'd grasped by the time she was twelve. She would miss that, and they would miss her. But maybe they'd learned enough to keep their minds alive at least a little.

Walking along the fence to the shed, she called to the stallion. His head jerked around in her direction, so quickly. She watched him start to walk towards her as she called again. Now his pace sped up and he broke into an eager canter and a shot fired, echoed. He took two more strides, his head went up in a scream that came from hell. His left leg buckled and a black-red rose spread across that muscled chest and he went down. He had almost reached her, and the ground shook with the crash of him.

She was over the fence and running towards him. His head reached up towards her, then fell. She landed hard by him on her knees, crying out his name over and over. Then, to understand she looked up and back at the Shan. Had he fired? But his rifle was still over his shoulder. She looked around the edges of the pasture – and there came the Sabwa astride his own blooded stallion from behind the tall poinsettia tree, not in flower now, maybe twenty feet high. He walked his horse steadily to her, looked down on her.

"How could you!?" It was a cry in a voice she'd never heard before in herself. "He was your own breed!"

"Let the child go, Miss Howard," he said, quietly, so gently, in his perfect Cambridge English, and thrust his rifle into its sling below his saddle.

A growl rose up from deep in her chest, bringing her to her feet and across the few steps to him, grabbing for him, wanting to fell him off his mount to the ground. She didn't hear the pounding of hooves, only knew Lim Pong was there when she was spun away by the shoulder, and he was off his horse and hitting her across the face, tumbling her to sprawl backwards in the grass, the breath knocked out of her.

The Shan bent, reached to raise her up, hand still lifted to strike again. "Enough," came the calm voice of his Sawbwa. And then as she watched with dawning horror, he whipped the belt from around his jodhpurs and tossed it to Lim Pong. "Don't use the buckle," he said in the man's own language, "and stop at first blood."

Lim Pong ran the belt through a hand and coiled it in the other. Kathleen was scrambling on hands and knees to stand up, to run, but the Sawbwa spurred his horse to block her way.

"You will accept, Miss Howard, or I will ride you down."

She stared up at him, high above her like the god so many believed him to be, this man with a cruelty she had seen only once or twice, and then more against others, and felt shame for him, and for the Shan, and for herself, God help her. She would not run from him. And abruptly she found herself sprawled across dead Maung Swe, tripped and shoved there face down by the Shan. He tore her eingyi away.

She heard the blows, swishing and cracking, more than felt them, at first, and then heard her own gasps, her own grunts, digging her fingers into the great flank and russet coat beneath her. Uh! Uh! Gasping with them, together now. Huh . . . huh . . . huh! The pain had started and it burned, oh God, and the voice in her could no longer stay silent, and was pushing up a scream come next hit or next, and she raged against that as much as against the belt and Lim Pong and *him*.

It stopped.

"Look at me," Htin Aung said. Slowly, she turned her head towards him, not caring any more what her eyes revealed. "The wives must see to the cut, or it will infect," he said. "And they can ease the stripes." He smiled a little. "How long I wonder before you screamed, Kathleen? I would not have waited for the cut to end it, if you had screamed. Always you are too strong for yourself." He reached out and retrieved the belt from the Shan, turning his horse, only to stop again. "Give the child up, and get me another." He kicked up his horse and cantered away across the field from where he'd come.

She didn't know how long she must have lain there, trying to take comfort from her dead Maung Swe. Her back was on fire. It was only the sound of the helicopter taking off, the fear that it might fly over the paddock, that brought her to her feet. She would not, *would not* have him see her like that, still down, still helpless.

She bent to collect the remnants of her eingyi to cover herself, and found her every motion hurt not only her back but so much of the rest of her body that every muscle in it must have strained and grabbed while it was happening.

Lim Pong was gone. No need to guard her any more.

She started forward, her legs weak and trembling, stumbled over a tussock, righted herself, heading down to the palace to submit herself to the ministrations of the women and make plans. Now, she not only wanted Htin Aung's pistol, she needed the Shan's horse. And a way to steal it without getting caught.

12

There she was, a little OH-6A. She'd been cargoed in to Udorn from Okinawa yesterday. Her Army brown skin gleamed with fresh paint, but that was all. No serial number on her doghouse, no bright yellow star and "ARMY" on her side. And she had her doors on. He hadn't thought about it, but of course they had to be transported with the aircraft. Sitting out there in the sun, it'd be hot enough to fry inside. He guessed he wouldn't fuss about their weight for the short trip they had ahead of them to Vientiane.

"Well," said Hanny, "one thing's answered, anyway. They brought her in special for us."

"Without insignia," Michael murmured, "so God knows what else she's special for." Looking at her – and that's all he could do at this point thanks to the hard-assed Air Force, which wouldn't even permit them out on the ramp until they'd been logged in – he wondered how the cockpit was equipped.

"Things're pretty loose where you're going," the Staff Sergeant had said, "but at Udorn Air Force Base we're on security alert at all times." Typical bullshit. Particularly when it came to Army pilots, who they were convinced had no business flying, and especially not helicopters which weren't real airplanes anyway.

Michael had managed to maintain his patience through the long night and through the day at Tan Son Nhut and in Bangkok. But the adrenaline had started working when they'd boarded the passenger plane bringing them up here, the rush he hadn't experienced in a long time, not since his first months in Nam. It was the feeling of being on the edge and knowing he was good for it. It came with its own tension, its own sweet life, and it put the war, that war, anyway, and what he could or couldn't do in it, behind him.

Hanny never had a problem with it, impatience, but now finally in northern Thailand, so close, Michael was fast over-loading the driving need to get on with it, his gut at full churn. "I'll be around," he said to Hanny, and drifted away.

He and Hanny had spent the long airport waits studying the maps, their inadequacy socked home for Michael by seeing them through Hanny's eyes. But they plowed ahead anyway, using the crude scales the maps provided.

The old royal capital of Luang Prabang was a hundred miles closer to eastern Burma than was Vientiane. If at all possible, they should leave from there. Explaining away what might be a good many hours' delayed return from a purportedly standard mission would be easy – a mechanical failure, their radio out, Hanny able to repair the one but not the other. If for some reason they had to admit straying from their flight plan, blame it on the monsoon. Assuming, of course, that they had managed to leave the attaché behind in the first place.

The maps, if they could be trusted, indicated that only a couple or three mountains along their path would be higher than 8,000 feet. They decided to go in during late daytime so they could see what the hell they were doing whether flying low or high. Unseen and unheard 'til the last minute if at all, they hoped to track the best way into and out of the palace – assuming they could find Loi Long, that is. Nothing but assumptions here. Anyway, they'd put down and wait until nightfall, do the job on the ground, go high and blister for Laos in the dark. One good thing seemed sure, according to Tom: Htin Aung had no anti-aircraft ordnance. And figuring out what to do once inside the palace was a problem belonging solely to Michael.

So. Approximately a three-hundred-mile round trip, 2.8 hours at least, and dreading their ten-minute warning. No question, they needed to find themselves a STOL strip in western Laos that stocked fuel, or they could be suckin' air at the end. It would be nice to gear it to the moon, but the rains made moonlight unpredictable, maybe non-existent, so they decided not to take it into account.

A thing they hadn't dealt with yet. Once back in Luang Prabang or wherever, how to explain Kathleen. Or the Eurasian kid.

A half-empty Dr. Pepper in his hand, Otis Redding wailing around in his head about wastin' time in Georgia, Michael fetched up at the doors where he and Hanny had entered the Quonset hut and dumped their stuff. Michael would've gone on outside just to keep moving, restlessness riding him, but the sun's heat halted him like a wall. He wondered if it ever got as hot in Georgia as it was here right now. He lit a cigarette, drank his Dr. Pepper, and watched the dirt road shimmer. They'd been grateful at first it wasn't raining, but this heat had worked up a real sweat.

He turned, found a trash barrel for his empty bottle, and saw a girl squatting outside against the wall. She wore her sarong wrapped to the left like a longyi, tucked up under her in her squat the way Kathleen always had, but her flat, round, child-like face proclaimed her a Thai. Probably some kind of cleaning maid, day's work done and waiting for a ride off base, it was about that time. She was braiding her hair. Though deft, her small brown fingers were nowhere like Kathleen's.

Still, his eyes clung to them, working, busy. Watching Kathleen eat rice in the villages, her long fingers quick and delicate like birds, he'd envy how her small ball of rice would cling together with never a leaking grain. His always dribbled, both rice and curry. She'd pop hers into her mouth, and hands and chin and lips would be spotless.

Something else flashed through his mind and was gone. The Thai girl had nearly finished braiding her hair, smooth and black. But he'd never watched Kathleen do that, so . . . what was it?

This girl looked up with a smile that inquired if she could be of help. As if she'd asked the question aloud, he shook his head apologetically, hoisted the big duffles onto his shoulders, grasped his small one and his helmet in one hand, Hanny's helmet in the other, and started back to where the Loach was.

The Duty Sergeant was there now with Hanny. They saw Michael coming, came to relieve him of the duffles. "I was just telling Sergeant Hanrahan that you're cleared, Lieutenant – "

"And I was on my way out to look her over," Hanny was saying, and the Duty Sergeant overrode, "and I've called the base at Tak Le to send over your escort."

Half gone, Hanny stopped, looked back. "Escort?" Michael said. Now what the hell.

"Yeah, a couple of Hueys. Kind of lead you in to Vientiane."

"That's very kind of the Air Force," Michael managed, "but I'm sure if ground control can supply me with course and coordinates – "

"Not us," the Duty Sergeant said. "The Hueys are under contract to the Government of Laos . . ." and at last, the Air Force in him eased a little. "AKA," he said with a grin, "the American Embassy. AA flies 'em."

One glance at Michael's face, and Hanny had hit the ramp for the Loach, dragging the duffles behind him. Michael and the Duty Sergeant looked at each other. Still grinning, the Duty Sergeant added, "Sorry, Lieutenant. I'm sure you're capable of flying the forty-six miles to Vientiane on your own. If you'll follow me, Sir, some fire power's been requisitioned for you." Well at least he wouldn't have to argue with the Air Force over that.

A low cement building, bunker was more like it, housed the armory. The Master Sergeant brought forth the personal weapons set aside for them. The .38 revolver was standard for Michael. And the M-16 was fine for Hanny. But Michael exchanged a second M-16 for the Carbine-15 he could more easily stash in the cockpit. And he insisted on a .45 for Hanny, who liked the reminder the weight of it gave against his hip. The only problem that arose was when the Master Sergeant denied him the M-60 that all crew chief gunners used aboard ship and a 7.62 minigun kit for Hanny to install under the Loach.

"Not available," he said. "We fly clean going up into Laos, self-defense only."

Sure, Michael thought, picturing the fighter-bomber Phantom jets they'd seen out the window of their plane at the end of the runway. Not supposed to be engaged at all, this side of the fence. And closer in, they'd seen some Cessna O-1 spotters. Used as FACs, they'd figured. God, Michael thought now, were those little props forced to fly with nothing but assault rifles?

The two Air Force sergeants were exchanging a look. The Duty Sergeant said softly, bitterly, "And our hospital here at Udorn is full of Forward Air Controllers to show for it." Well that answered that, didn't it. Same shit here as there.

Michael strapped on his .38, said his thanks, shouldered both rifles, picked up Hanny's .45 and the survival kits, saw the Duty Sergeant had already collected the belts and boxes of ammo, was turning with him for the door, when the Master Sergeant reached to some shelves behind him, started laying grenades on the counter. "There's some smoke for you," he said, looking at Michael evenly. When Michael looked down at the eggs, he saw that at least half of them were either explosive grenades or frags. He smiled his thanks, the Master Sergeant found a box for them, even added some stringing wire, they packed it all up, and Michael and the Duty Sergeant trudged back to the Quonset hut and the Loach.

Finding the Air Force a deal more human than he'd thought, Michael decided it wouldn't hurt to try. "I suppose you guys have a pretty good idea what it's all about," he said. "Us, the light helicopter, the whole bit. We sure don't."

The Duty Sergeant got caught in his surprise. But a moment later, he shook his head. "Sorry, Sir."

Hanny was on his back under the belly of the Loach, pulling on the struts to the skids, testing strengths among other things. He'd slid the doors open, locked them back. At least they wouldn't burn their asses off. "How is she?" Michael asked.

"So far so good, Sir," Hanny answered.

Michael laid Hanny's weapons in the aft cabin, tucked his Car-15 away in the cockpit. "Got you some toys," he said.

Hanny slid out from under, looked in the cabin. "Where's my M-60? Sir."

"No luck, Sergeant," Michael answered. "We got us some eggs, though." The Duty Sergeant set the box and the ammo down next to the weapons and Hanny jumped in and started stowing it all. Michael went around the Loach, started unscrewing the cap to check the fuel.

"I checked it, Sir," Hanny said.

"Too bad about that senator a week or so ago, wasn't it, Sir." Screwing the cap back on tight, Michael looked around at the Duty Sergeant, utterly blank. "You know," the Sergeant continued, "went down over Nam and they still haven't found the aircraft."

Oh, yeah. Armed Forces Radio carried on about it for a couple of days. "Senator Beaumont, on one of those fact-finding junkets, right?" Michael said. Then he prompted the silent Duty Sergeant. "Crashed somewhere in the Delta." Hanny had gone quiet.

The Sergeant was looking at Michael steadily, gave a nod. "They came through here on their way," he said. "The whole shit pot from Washington."

Through Udorn to get to Vietnam? Come on.

The Duty Sergeant looked skywards. "Your guide-dogs have arrived, Sir."

Michael looked and saw the two Hueys coming in and down. He'd heard them and paid no attention, used to the wop-wop-wop of the big blades. He looked back at the Duty Sergeant, who was already turning away for the Quonset hut. "I'm grateful, Sergeant," he said. "It helps to have a purpose in life."

The Duty Sergeant sent him a grin. "You ever get back down here, Lieutenant, look me up. Always interested in a little gossip." He flipped his hand, and disappeared inside.

Hanny was leaning out the cabin doorway, and he and Michael looked at each other. "So there it is," Michael said. "Secret mission to Laos." Theirs and ours, he thought.

"Inconvenient how planes can get lost anywhere, even China," said Hanny.

Michael wished he'd get off the China bit.

The radio was making noises. The Hueys were hovering out about a hundred yards and up about fifty. "We ready to crank?" Michael asked.

"Yup." Hanny put on his helmet and hauled out the fire-extinguisher.

Michael levered himself up into the right seat, found his helmet on the left seat where Hanny had set it, put it on, and plugged in the mike and the headset. Before he switched on the radio, he called out to Hanny, "You're in the Peter seat today, Sergeant."

"Yes, Sir," came back to him. He keyed on VHF to send, UHF to receive, the intercom while he was at it, and spoke into his mike. "Hello, up there. This is the Light OH-6A sitting at your feet."

"Hello, hello!" a pleasant English-accented tenor said. "Good to hear from you."

"Same here," said Michael. "We'll be along pretty quick, but I'd like a couple minutes to see how my new baby drives. All right with you?"

He got a double signal back in an affirmative. He belted up, ran his pre-flights, and cranked. The igniters clicked, the turbine whined, and they were ready. Hanny stored the extinguisher and clambered into the left seat of the cockpit, belted up, plugged in his helmet, keyed on the frequencies. And like any good co-pilot, he rested hands lightly on the controls, feet lightly on the pedals, and waited. Michael knew he had to suspect what the hell he was doing up here, and undoubtedly didn't like it.

Michael lifted to a hover about four feet off the ground, taxied and did his little dance, looking for tail rotor authority. The left pedal gave him plenty. The Loach slewed a little. Damned foot too heavy again? But no. Shit, four days out of the cockpit and the feel of it blunted already. The main – the only problem with pilots going on R & R. The feel went so fast.

He halted the Loach, keyed the radio. "All right, Gentlemen. The command is yours."

"Thank you very much," said the English tenor briskly.

"But first," said an American baritone, "how about introducing ourselves?"

"I'm Sherman Darnell," the Brit cut in, "Sherm for short. And my friend over there is Jedediah Zimmerman, nothing for short. And you'd be Lieutenant Cameron, am I right?"

"Michael Cameron. Cam'll do fine. And my First Sergeant Crew Chief is Neal Hanrahan."

"Well, then," it was Jedediah, "what we're going to do, Cam, is fly a reverse delta. We'll point the way and keep an eye out for the bad guys. You fall in behind us as close as is comfortable for you."

"Not that there will be any," the Brit added hastily. "Don't want to frighten the gent to death, Jedediah, just in from the States."

Michael's eyes slid and met Hanny's. "Most thoughtful," Michael said. "Here we come," already lifting up, banking around. The Hueys were a tad slow kicking out of hover, probably because he'd caught them by surprise, but then they moved on ahead, taking formation. Michael picked them up, neither too close in nor below them enough to feel their double downwash. Those two together could tumble the little Loach straight into the ground.

Nevertheless, closer to the Hueys now, he could see that *they* sure weren't weapons-clean. A gunner sat in the open door of each, an M-60 slung in front of him, the barrel steadied against a leg draped out the door and already pointing down in search of those non-existent bad guys. The gunners were Asian.

Things were stable in a couple of minutes, the edge coming back. Michael knew Hanny had to be getting jumpy, thinking through what to do when the order came. And what not to do. He'd probably have Michael's head for it once on the ground, especially with two, as he would put it, fuckin' mercenaries to see the damage. But no way was Michael going into that palace without being damned sure Hanny could get himself out of Burma if Michael didn't come back, and Hanny hadn't flown for too long, longer than four days, for sure. Not since Michael had taken a bullet in his left leg and bled all over the damned cockpit, and Hanny had hauled himself forward from the cabin along the outside of the aircraft, not exactly the safest maneuver, had made it to the left seat and flown them home. The thing was, this looked to be an easy trip, few distractions, and Michael wanted to know sooner, not later, about Hanny. So, he'd give him a little warning, and then hit him with it.

He keyed off the VHF to the Hueys for privacy, and used the intercom, "Heads up, Sergeant."

Hanny's head jerked a little. "Bastard," Michael heard him mutter over the intercom. But Michael was watching Hanny's hands, still light. He went light on his own controls and said, "You got it."

Hanny clutched and the Loach dipped a little, swung a little, but then held steady and nice. Michael still periodically glanced at Hanny's hands, but didn't worry. Over the radio came the polite inquiry, "Everything all right back there?"

"Just testing out a few things," Michael replied happily. "And everything's dandy."

"Bastard!" Hanny said, a little louder this time.

"Well," said Jedediah's voice, "now that we're comfy cozy, we thought you boys might like to know something about our colleagues who went down on the Volpar. What to look for, maybe."

"Where to look's more like it," said Sherm.

It was like coming in on the end of the wrong conversation. And Michael had the feeling it was going to stay that way, full of undefined ambiguities unless he jumped in.

"Um, guys? Sorry to interrupt, but I think you ought to know you're talking to an air load of pure ignorance back here." There was silence. Michael went on, just so they'd know they weren't spitting totally into the wind, "See, we haven't received our local duty orders yet. No kind of mission statement at all."

"Shit," said Sherm. Hanny said into the intercom, "Didn't think an English gent would know that word."

"That being the case," said Jedediah, "you're going to have to stay ignorant 'til we're on the ground. Specifics are out, over the airwaves."

"We can still be of help to you, though," said Sherm. "More than anybody at the fucking embassy will be." Hanny turned his head this time to cast a look at Michael. The Englishman was shocking him altogether. "After you settle in tonight, you chaps up for a little pernod?"

Jedediah was chuckling. "We're staying over, and a place called Mam'selle Josie's is great for carrying on a conversation. Best Pernod and best blow jobs in Vientiane." He pronounced it more like Viangchan. This time, Hanny kept his reaction to himself. Michael wasn't sure the AA pilots weren't just putting them on, fucking new guys that he and Hanny were. But he said, "Mam'selle Josie's, huh? We'll be there if we can find it."

"Any cab driver in town," Jedediah said. "Oh, and by the way, if you can avoid it, don't get billeted out at K.M. 6 – the embassy's residence heaven. Unless, of course, you like musical beds, ladies' choice, always hazardous to an officer's health. Get them to put you up at the Phou Bia Club in town."

"Thanks," Michael said. Phou . . . what Club? Maybe Hanny'd remember. His mind was spinning at this point.

"Since we have a little way to go, why don't Jedediah and I give you a guided tour," Sherm offered. They were now flying over jungled hills close to the size of low mountains. Didn't look all that different from Nam.

"See up to the northeast?" Sherm asked. The mountains looked higher there. "That's where the Meo and General Vang Pao hold out. Hard for us to believe, but you probably haven't even heard of him back in the States."

Michael kept it light, enjoying it. He said, "'Fraid I wouldn't know about back in the States, Sherm. But we sure have heard about him in Vietnam."

"Oops," said Jedediah.

And, in a moment, "Oops again, I'm afraid," Sherm said. "We're lying down on the job. Gentlemen from Vietnam, you have just crossed the border into Laos. Welcome to wonderland!"

Michael felt the charge rise clear from his boots, like a shout right through him: "We're here! And comin' to get ya, Kathleen!"

This time when he looked at Hanny, Hanny was grinning at him and gave him a thumbs-up. Michael returned it. Blessed Hanny.

13

He saw them, clear as day, Kathleen and himself lying naked and spent on her unrolled mat. They were in a basha hut where the village petered out. Michael was building a hen house there for Tom's Rhode Island Reds. The people whose hut it was had left to build another better one, and no one had taken possession except, for this afternoon, Michael and Kathleen. It was so rickety it squeaked with their rhythm, and the palm fronds on the roof undoubtedly shook and quivered even as they did. But nobody cared, not even enough to gossip about it to Tom. Young people made love. Marriages were arranged, usually for the same couple who were already coupling, because the young as well as the elders knew the familial and clan taboos and abided by them. And if pregnancy followed, they got married sooner.

Kathleen had driven over from Loi Long, bringing lunch in a tiffin carrier – lacquer bowls full of food set one on top of the other in locked layers. Not curry that time, thank goodness, but kausswe. Michael didn't like much Burmese food, or Shan either, but these noodles swimming in a mild coconut milk sauce he was crazy about. Plus which, he could eat them with a spoon. He and Kathleen would sit looking out on a mountain or down to a creek and slurp them in like Chinese eating rice.

They called it their discipline. To eat before loving. Before touching even. Kathleen said they had to have some or the memory of it would someday eat away at them like sin. Which was nonsense, of course, but there were some things Kathleen wouldn't hear. The fact was, putting it off, controlling it, made it better. They played with discipline a lot, teasing each other, testing each other. Most of the time it drove them crazy, so that the game was forgotten in the rush to climax. Or it broke them up. Think we can do it? he'd say. Well I can, she'd say, can you? Sometimes it was lying face to face, with him erect inside her, and they would see how long it would be before her muscles would have to grab around him or he would have to pull back and slide in again. Sometimes, they managed to hold it for quite awhile, playing tongues against each other to tease. Sometimes, she would suddenly start giggling while he struggled not to, wondering if this was part of the challenge, but not really, because he knew what dissolved her. The odd ways their bodies were made to fit so perfectly together, and the peculiar things their bodies wanted to do which gave such miraculous ways of feeling – God had to have had a sense of humor, she said. Both knew that if they both laughed he'd lose it and they'd have to start all over again. Which wouldn't be all that bad, naturally.

So many nights he had lain awake and alone in his bed at the farm – of course alone, this was Tom's house and without exchanging a word about it he and Kathleen had never betrayed that – considering her, how she was, what she was. As he was doing now, lying alone in this new bed in Vientiane, remembering it. She had effectively destroyed every given he had ever believed about girls. Women. Girls were innocent, after all, and he had taken that from her forever. Anyway. Anglo-Saxon girls were cold, apt to be frigid, weren't they? But if ever there was an Anglo-Saxon it was Kathleen Howard, even to her name. Innocent girls were fearful and shy. Kathleen never had been, not with him, only eager, curious, her self-awareness never self-absorbed. You had to be serious when making love or girls wouldn't think you respected them. It was one more revelation that Kathleen had lit up for him how funny sex could be.

Michael got out of bed and found his way through the dark across the strange room in this whatchamacallit club to the bathroom and a cold shower. Not because he had turned once again into a wet-dreaming boy but because of tears oiling his face, like an old man sad for things he knew couldn't be recovered. Maybe something else would come, if he could get her out, but what had been for them in that short young time was gone.

It was only when the needles of spray hit his chest, his rear, not cold but warm, probably from coming through a gravity line from a water tank on the roof that got hot during the day, only then did he feel the anger seated at the bottom of his mind telling him that what was gone hadn't just slipped away with the years. It had been killed by Sao Htin Aung.

He couldn't find the towel in the dark, so he switched on the light – a real incandescent light – and saw two cockroaches scurrying away. On the way back to bed, he checked the kitchen sink and found only one there. Small, too. In the hooch, they were so big you couldn't tell what was rattling up and down the walls at night, the roaches or rats.

There were real screens. On an impulse, he turned off the window air conditioner, turned on the ceiling fan and opened the French doors, like those at Major Novack's house where that party'd been held earlier, his presence mandatory when hardly off the Loach with time to change. He stepped out onto the tiny balcony. Lights reflecting off the Mekong shimmered through the drizzle. It smelled acrid, fresh.

Standing there, he started again, working it over and over. If he wasn't escaping back into their time together, it was all he could seem to do – try to figure out a way. And after tonight, it looked to be as much of a pipe dream as when Tom had first proposed it. Just how was he going to break that news to Tom? Tom had never really said it, but he had to be terrified for that little nephew he might never get to see. He should call him soon, at least to tell him they were here. That's if he could find a phone with some privacy.

Walking back from Mam'selle Josie's, which turned out to be closer to the Club than he and Hanny had known when they'd cabbed it to the place, Michael had reported on the party, all the stuff he'd finally found out even before their meeting with Sherm and Jedediah. Hearing it, Hanny had come through, as always. "We could go tonight," he'd said. "We've got the AA maps, now."

Riding in the staff car back from the party, Michael had already considered going into Burma this night. But he'd decided against it. And Hanny knew as well as Michael it would be self-destructive for them both, not to mention hopeless. A night flight over strange country, no first-hand knowledge of fuel dumps, a trip twice as long as out of Luang Prabang, and the Army due to pick them up here before dawn. AWOL with a dishonor-able discharge inevitable. He might've chanced it somehow by himself if he thought he could do the impossible and bring Kathleen and the baby out under those circumstances. Thing was, he didn't. And no way would he chance it for Hanny.

How long was it going to stymie him, Michael wondered, getting damp out on the balcony. Flight duty day after day after day, looking for a plane lost in the mountains, the jungles, forget the guerrilla war. Only one thing in the entire evening had offered any hope and that was what the AA pilots believed, and the maps they'd handed over.

Putting his mind elsewhere – anything to put his mind elsewhere – he thought of those Meo they'd passed coming in from the airport. Talk about being stymied, heaven help them. He hadn't spent time wondering about refugees in Nam. Not much time, anyway. But these people . . . crouched in their huts – hardly that, bare shelters – trying to find a way to keep their children dry in the relentless monsoon . . . It was pouring again, a wind coming up and slapping the rain at him. He could go inside, and did. They couldn't. He stretched out on the bed, fixed his mind on them, locking out the rest. Maybe, somehow, this way, he'd get to sleep.

The road in from Wattay Airport had taken them right through their squatters' city. It had the shacks and huts and lean-tos of cardboard and palm leaves, grass rushes and scraps of tin, the stench that Michael had grown used to running from Marble Mountain on into Da Nang. But there was a difference here, like that between movie film and a set of still photographs. The Vietnamese, even in terrible straits, were striving for life, bargaining heatedly over the small piles of wizened chicken gizzards or half-spoiled vegetables spread out on little pieces of cloth as if they were precious jewels, women animated in gossip, their children kicking a wicker ball or riding bikes with metal rims for wheels.

But the people outside of Vientiane, tiny dark men in tied calf-length black trousers and women in black skirts and leggings, squatted or sat with their knees drawn up to their chins in silence. Even the children were quiet. Hanny had his handkerchief to his nose. He swore he had a better sense of smell than anybody else. Michael had given up trying to convince him that a broken nose would preclude that. Hanny tried never to listen when he'd rather not know something. Like Kathleen. On the other hand, Michael had to admit that Hanny could smell out Charlies through the canopy quicker than he could.

Michael would like to have known who these people were, but the Sergeant who was driving them in from the airport had been talking non-stop since he'd driven across the tarmac to meet the Loach, periodically reminding them to call him Willy. Right now he was informing them that there was only one traffic light in Vientiane – he, too, called it Viangchan. "They keep saying they're gonna put in a second one, but it still hasn't happened, so you gotta lay on the horn." Which he had done constantly since leaving the Loach, shouting above it, as he was now, to be heard. His hair showed gray and he had a paunch. Late thirties, and a Master Sergeant. A pretty senior NCO to be sent to fetch a lowly 2nd Lieutenant. Odd. Unless the embassy wanted some relief from his run-on mouth.

Michael decided enough was enough. He leaned forward from the back seat of the jeep where the Sergeant had put him and Hanny and cut into the word-stream with, "Who are they – these people here?"

Didn't phase the Sergeant, or stop him either. "Refugees, Sir. Meo tribesmen from the Plain of Jars and mountains farther east towards

Vietnam. They keep losing battles against the North Vietnamese and the Pathet Lao – the local commies – so we evacuate 'em, and then when the enemy retreats a little, we carry 'em back to plant their rice, and then when they're overrun again and lose their crops, we bring 'em out again. These people here have probably been moved on and off their fields four, five, six times, even."

One of the women squatted to urinate. Nobody else watched. Michael and Hanny looked away to preserve her privacy, and Hanny lowered his handkerchief. Michael knew why. Bad smell or no, Hanny wouldn't want to insult a people so trampled by bad breaks. Easy, once you knew, to identify their silence, their lethargy. Rock bottom despair.

"Who's we," Michael asked, "the Army?"

"No, Sir," the Sergeant replied. "AA choppers, mostly. Forever having to make food drops out there. Hard rice drops, too. For all the good it does, might as well be sand."

Hard rice? Ammo. We feed it to 'em, thought Michael, they use it, somebody shoots back, and they die instead of us. They need more than hard rice, they need well-fed soldiers and fast growing green rice so they can triple-crop with protection and half a chance at a harvest.

Hanny cleared his throat, and Willy for once was quiet. "Wouldn't you think," Hanny said reasonably, "that we'd learn how not to get into these messes or at least how to win the war and get outa Dodge?"

The refugee settlement was dwindling, and they entered the outskirts of the town. Flowering shrubs mixed their fragrances with an occasional whiff of a broken sewer. Big lawned compounds surrounded pleasant houses. Lazy traffic meandered around pot-holes, a few old Citroens and Chryslers but mostly tuk tuks and tri-shaws, donkey-carts and now and then an ox pulling a wagon or a brightly painted laboring bus with passengers hanging out the windows or clinging to the roof and horn blaring. The roadbed was badly pitted, maybe from use, maybe from war damage, most probably both, and occasionally there was rubble spilling into the way from tumbled down shop buildings or more impressive what-looked-to-be government buildings, so undoubtedly it was all war damage.

There was a feeling about it, like a shift in time for Michael, reminding him of Rangoon five years ago – a kind of shabby Victorian elegance amidst a war-torn infrastructure that might never be adequately repaired. In Rangoon, it had been old British colonial buildings, graceful in spite of the whitewashed stucco being cracked and battle-scarred and draped with mold.

The same colonial grace was here, undoubtedly French – the stucco was yellow, and equally moldy and cracked, but fronted by iron balconies streaking rust. Laotian music rang out over loudspeakers from time to time. Music with a Southeast Asian sound, a Burmese sound, as Michael remembered it, quite different from that in Nam. And interspersed with it, this late in the day, gongs were struck by monks begging for their evening rice. Bonzes, the Sergeant called them. Different pronunciation of the same word, it suddenly occurred to Michael. The Burmese word for Buddhist monks was pongyis.

Michael could feel Hanny relaxing. No matter what your purpose in being here, he thought, this world works a magic. And then Hanny said it. "Kind of nice. This could be all right, y'know it?" Talk about a mercy, as Hanny would put it. Michael was becoming more and more convinced that he'd brought Hanny into something that could go bad. If he liked the place, it would help.

The Sergeant by now had moved on to billets. "We're putting you up at the Phou Bia Club, gentlemen." That's a mercy, too, Michael thought. At least he didn't have to remember the damned name, or request it, either. "Of course, if you'd like to move out to K.M. 6 – that's the American residency compound six kilometers out of town – and there are some singles' apartments, just not available at the moment – you can put your names on the list." The place the AA warned them off.

"What I thought," the Sergeant – Willy – galloped on, "I'll drop you there, go on to the embassy, it's not far, leave off your weapons, and log you in, then come back for you, Sir." Michael was a little slow on the uptake, staring forward at a concrete monstrosity spanning the road ahead. But that was all right, Willy was already explaining. "Major Novack is expecting you. The Air Attaché? He's giving the party tonight."

The party? Jesus, Michael thought, exchanging a quick look with Hanny. Once a week? Every night? He jumped in. "Well, uh, Willy, um – I think for this evening anyway I'll beg off, if you could make my regrets to the Major."

Willy looked at him over his shoulder, making Hanny point out with the patience of a saint, "Bus is coming."

Willy snapped around forward, twisted the jeep out of the way. "Permission to speak, Sir?" Which almost ended it for Hanny.

"Sure," Michael said.

"You're expected, Sir."

110

And Willy'd been sent to make certain Michael went. Odder and odder.

The Sergeant wasn't interested in a discussion, if Michael had had it in mind. "By the way," he said, moving right along, "the arch we're going under is the Vertical Runway. U.S. A.I.D. gave the government too many tons of cement for the airport runways, so the Laotians decided to build an arch of triumph for the army to march through when they win the war. Sad. Except for when you get drunk enough to try to run up it, which some pilots do regularly. Not Army pilots, Sir," he added hastily. "You're the only flying military formally stationed in Laos."

Great, thought Michael, the need to be inconspicuous flushed down the toilet.

"You're on the ground floor, Sarge, and officer's country along with GS 7's and up is on the first floor, Sir. At the Club." Honest to God, the man never stopped. "I've got the keys right here. They're labelled like that, the floors I mean, because of the Frogs."

In mind of the other night in Da Nang, Michael and Hanny both looked out and down to the ground and then realized, glanced at each other and away as quickly as they could to avoid losing it completely as Willy continued, "The French influence here is extreme." He was still on a roll. "Apartments are all pretty much the same, living room, bedroom, kitchen and bath. You get a balcony, Sir, with a river view, and you get bars on the windows, Sarge, though it's kind of silly since crime isn't much of a problem in Laos. And just so you'll know, opium is legal and so are the girls. After I drop you at the party, Sir, I'll come back for you, Sarge, and we'll take in the best steak this side of Honolulu." At this point, Hanny slid down onto his spine and closed his eyes. Michael covered his mouth with his hand, coughed, and realized he'd have to shave. Shit.

* * *

Not taking the time to really look the place over, Michael had hauled civvies, uniforms, every damned thing he had out of his duffle, and none of it was wearable. Wrinkled and smelling of mildew. An iron would take care of both if he could find one. He'd located the ironing board when there was a knock at the door. Lord, he thought, Willy already. But it was Hanny, who came in and did look around.

"You okay with downstairs?" Michael asked.

"Damned near identical," Hanny said. He turned into the kitchen. "Where's your iron?"

"I don't know, I was just looking for it."

"Hell of an improvement over a hooch and five other horny guys," Hanny was saying. He found the iron, plugged it in, and flared out the ironing board to stand. "Bring that summer undress over here."

"What're you doing, Hanny?" Michael asked, getting irritated.

"If you're in uniform and all the rest're in civvies, it's good," said Hanny. "The other way around, not so good."

Michael started into the little kitchen. "Damn it, Neal, now – you're not doin' my God damned ironing!"

Hanny faced him and put his hands on his hips. Nobody could look bigger than Hanny doing that. "You don't get it, Cam. This is a tiny posting. These people here don't have regular parties just so they can play together. Hell, they see each other at the office every day all week long. I'm tellin' you, parties here have to be for business. Alcohol eases the way so they hear things, they say things, they get things done that don't get done at work. You're wanted for some reason and you better be up for it. Now bring your stuff here."

"You don't know all that, Hanny," Michael now annoyed as hell. "I don't, so how come you think you do!?" He was feeling wary enough about this damned party.

"I go to the movies a lot," Hanny said. Michael rolled his eyes in exasperation, but Hanny just glared until finally Michael got the trousers and shirt, went back to the kitchen and slammed them into Hanny's gut. Suddenly, Hanny was jabbing his finger into Michael's chest, sounding as if he'd been interrupted right in the middle of it. "And don't you ever pull shit like that on me again! I need flyin' review, we find the time and do it private!" He quit jabbing, but his chin was still out there. "What the hell did you think you were doin', God damn it!?"

Michael grabbed a couple of deep breaths and answered quietly enough, "I wanted to know, and sooner was better. So, I know. No review needed." He smiled a little. "And you set her down soft as a butterfly."

A last glower and Hanny turned for the ironing board. "Hit the shower," he said, shaking out the short-sleeved shirt, "you stink."

Michael gave it up and he headed for the bathroom. Hanny hollered after him, "And shave!"

14

A Laotian servant in white jacket had opened the door for him into Major Novack's house, beamed and gestured him in. Michael glanced back to see Willy give a loose salute and turn the car down the long driveway to the gates and the street. Some layout. Willy had said it once had been a royal residence. "'Course," he'd added, "royalty are as plentiful as ants in Laos."

The servant took his hat, and gesturing again, this time like a teacher pushing a child out onto a stage, he urged Michael forward into an archway through which came a lot of party noise. He hesitated there. Shouldn't have, because the noise dropped, people turned to look. Hated it, he really did, and if it lasted much longer he'd bug out and the hell with the command appearance. He flickered his gaze around as if looking for someone.

From its size, the room had to have been a receiving room once, the opposite wall nothing but French doors out to a garden, wet now. Comfortably overstuffed striped silk and teakwood furniture everywhere, and one wall at the end sported a white tableclothed bar. Not a uniform in the place, except his own.

People started talking again as a woman came towards him. Hips swaying, blonde hair swinging across bare shoulders, a sundress made of a blue and silver weave that had to be local, and legs to stop the heart in high-heeled silver sandals. What had those AA guys said? Musical beds?

"Lieutenant Cameron!" she exclaimed. "I'm Sandy Novack. Welcome! We're so glad you arrived in time to come." She grasped his hand in both of hers, holding it a moment too long, or so Michael thought. "Now you'll have a chance to meet everyone. We're all just family, you know." She suddenly dimpled. "Have to be, don't we. Nobody here but us chickens!" And she leaned towards him to loosen the tie Hanny had just pressed. "No need to stand on ceremony," she said. He could smell gin, but she seemed sober enough, if a little full blown. Close now, he could see she'd laid on the pancake. Probably older than she wanted to be.

Quickly, he took over the tie business, and she signalled the servant to come get it, which he did. Michael had twice murmured a "Thank you,

Mrs. Novack, Ma'am," and now she got around to that. "You call me Sandy," she declared, "and you'd be what? Mike?"

"Michael," he said.

She pulled his arm through hers so that he had to move off the shallow step into the room. Did she mean to do it or was it by accident that his arm was pressed against the swell of a breast? Immediately, three other females clustered. "Meet Michael," Mrs. Novack – Sandy – said, and went on with, "This is Ruth Ann, Marielle, and Drew." He really ought to get some lessons in remembering names. "Now, girls, give the boy some air, while we go get him a little drinkie!" And she steered him towards the bar.

A long night ahead. He insisted on a long Scotch with soda. Sandy made a little turned down mouth that labelled him a poor sport, but he got what he'd asked for, was turning with it when a light-haired fortyish man with a mustache came up, hand outstretched. "Lieutenant, I'm Wilson Novack, glad you got here." Michael shook his hand, called him Major, of course, and, of course, got told not to.

Hanny would no doubt have said it was all very predictable at parties like this – since he'd been to so God damned many movies. To its detriment, it reminded Michael of Shaker Heights and what he had shunned since old enough to know anything at all. And like Shaker Heights, if these people had any kids, they'd been banished.

Anyway, Wilson moved his wife away. Needed in the kitchen, he said. Was it his custom to cool things off that way, cool her off? Find something wrong in the kitchen? Poor bastard.

Looking after them, Michael suddenly caught sight of the back of a gleaming head, hair clubbed to the nape of the neck by a barrett, and as the girl was swivelling around towards him, a glimpse in silhouette of a tip-tilted nose. His breath stopped until he saw the blue, blue eyes in a pretty face, the hair not firey but honey-colored, and he could breathe again. But now the girl was walking towards him, smiling, her hand outstretched. He kept his breath, but it hurt to take her hand and find the difference. Not only was Kathleen invading his mind and body at night, he was beginning to see her at every turn.

"Hi, Lieutenant," she said, "I'm Joanie Osborne."

Letting go her hand, he managed a smile and nod. Perky little frosh was what she was.

"I just got in last weekend," she was saying, "so you and I're the newest guys in town. How about exploring the place together?"

"Oh, well," he started, and as he went on he saw the perkiness die a little. "Um, I'm not even sure what my duties are going to be, yet, so . . ." He hated this, too. "Give me a week or two to get my feet, Joanie, then maybe . . ."

She was studying him now. "Taken, aren't you?"

Lord, how do women, even babies like this, get so wise, he wondered. She went on. "We could still be friends, couldn't we?"

He had at least ten years on her, and she was primed to get a crush. Not knowing what to do about it, he hesitated too long and she got tired of waiting for an answer. Insulted maybe, or maybe just impatient, she gave a little shrug, turned to walk away, but then she looked back with a grin. "Your loss, y'know."   Yeah, he thought, y'got that right.

She met up with a girlfriend and started to giggle. Good. No putting her down for long.

He noticed a small wiry man, very weathered, his brown hair matching his skin, leaning against the wall in the corner, a drink of neat whiskey in his hand, watching him. Great. Probably her father. But now Novack returned, sans Sandy – still in the kitchen? – and took Michael in tow, started introducing him around.

They might all be in civvies and one big family, but not an introduction missed a title. It was "Head of A.I.D." or "C.I.A. Station Chief" or "keeps the consular wing going." That last was Jim Osborne, with his daughter's blonde hair. And not one lieutenant. With or without uniforms, Michael obviously was the lowest rank here.

They finally approached an older man, grey hair, looked like a mix of academics and tough know-how, which he was. Presenting Michael, Wilson said, "Ambassador Godley. A trouble shooter from way back, including Patrice Lamumba."

The Ambassador gave Michael's hand a firm cool shake, his eyes quick and appraising. "See you at the team meeting in the morning," he said. "Lots to learn in Laos." He smiled a little, bowed his head a little, and moved on. A smoothie, and plain all-around scary.

After exchanging some chitchat with an Air Force captain Wilson dumped him on, Michael managed to ease himself over to one side. Damn, he'd about finished his drink – soda or not, it was still a full jigger of alcohol, and he needed all his wits. He turned to set it aside, and saw again, still in the same corner, that guy watching him. This time, Michael tried a smile, a nod, got a minimal acknowledgement and gave it up, letting his eyes drift. Shouldn't've. They connected with – who? Ruth Ann and Marylou? Marielle? Or what was that odd – oh, yeah, Drew. They'd started his way. And there was a touch on his arm.

Thinking it yet another female, he looked to one side and down to find it was the small man from the corner. Usually Michael disliked towering over other men, but oddly, though considerably shorter, Michael would have bet a million this man felt in no way diminished.

"Lewis Wisby," said the man, his voice deep, belying his size, "Lieutenant Colonel, U.S. Infantry." Michael stiffened, came damned close to a salute and just managed to avoid it. "Been looking forward to your arrival, Lieutenant – in Laos, and to this party, too."

"Michael'll do, Sir, if that suits you."

"Suits me fine. Willy did a good job. I'm sure you'd have as soon begged off. I'm barely over culture shock myself – " his eyes scanning the room – "and not just from the Laotian culture. Willy's my main man. Like you, Michael, we're just in from Nam, only ten days ago."

Michael blinked a little. "Willy, too?" he asked. "I, uh – well I got the impression he's been in Laos forever. He seems to know just about everything."

The Colonel sipped his whiskey, hiding amusement with it Michael was sure. "He does his homework," he said. "Listens well, when he wants to."

"Yes, Sir," Michael said. Beware with Willy tonight, Hanny, he thought, sending a message. Things are not all they seem, here. But Hanny'd had that figured out first shot back in Da Nang.

And this guy. How many tours had he delivered in Nam? They came off him like the smell of lightning. Richard had warned not to try to diddle him, it might not work, but even if it did, Michael didn't want to. Damn it.

"Lieutenant?" and voice softening, "Michael?" It was the Colonel.

"Yes, Sir!"

"You and I are going to skip the country team meeting in the morning, so – "

"Um, Sir? Ambassador Godley just said – "

"I know what the Ambassador probably just said." His dark quiet voice in the midst of the brittle laughter and chat surrounding them kept his words a secret to all but the two of them. "Fact is, we're gonna go flying instead. Which leaves a lot you don't know but need to."

"Yes, Sir." Every step of the way, it got more complicated.

The Colonel looked out through the French doors. "The rain's stopped, for the moment anyway. None of these sweet petunias would dare leave the air-conditioning for fear of melting. We'll have privacy. Give me a couple, four minutes, and then follow me out." And before Michael could answer, the Colonel had turned and slipped unobtrusively out a corner glass door into the garden.

Marielle and Company, having started Michael's way, had hung back while he talked with the Colonel. Hanny was right again. The party was for business, and the women knew it. Now, before they could reach him, pretending not to notice, Michael moved for the bar and ordered a soda and ice. A waiter offered him a tray full of paté canapes. Without thinking, he picked one up, then looked at it, set it down. He'd found drop zones for troops to get shot up in while people like these played like this in Saigon. And here, in this sweet little city, hill people squatted on no future at all, unable even to get away from their own stink, while only six kilometers away, these people ate imported pate and drank imported whiskey and, if AA was right, hopped beds. Michael started for the garden. Sandy caught him. Finally back from the kitchen.

"All alone, Michael? We can't have that!"

"Just um – heading out for a breath of fresh air. I'm feeling a little queasy," he said, telling the God's truth.

"Oh," she said, grasping his arm, her sympathy raging like her hormones. "You come right upstairs with me, and we'll find you a bed and you can – "

But Michael disengaged himself, thanked her, said the fresh air would work just fine, and in a tone close to command, he finished with, "Excuse me, please," and he walked out one of the French doors, no doubt leaving her in minor shock.

He stood on the terrace above its two wide steps letting down to the garden, unable to see the Colonel. Then he noticed the hibiscus and bougainvillea bushes jutting out before the back of the garden was reached, and he knew the Colonel would be behind them.

He was, just lighting a cigar. He offered Michael one. Michael showed his pack of cigarettes, got permission to light up. And the Colonel didn't wait to lay it all straight out.

"We're here, Michael," he said, "to screw the C.I.A., the State Department, and every damned politician in Washington before they can finish screwing us. The Army doesn't deserve the blame, and you and I are here to find the truth and prove it. But we've got to be quick about it, and quiet, or they'll stop us dead. So, we talk now and get to it, first light tomorrow." He drew on his cigar, blew out smoke, and grinned. "Got your attention, did I?"

"Yes, Sir," said Michael, smiling back. "But, um, Sir?" Michael wasn't thrilled to have to say this. "I think I may already know something about it. About Senator Beaumont?"

"Oh, shit," said the Colonel. "Fucking leaks. Watch how they blame us for them, too. If the press gets hold of the truth, it's to the Army's advantage after all."

He looked around. Michael had already noticed the small stone bench close by, probably some kind of lover's nook here, and had been wondering how he could maneuver them onto it. Never look down on your commanding officer any longer than you can help.

The bench was wet. The Colonel pulled out his handkerchief, Michael jumped with his own, they wiped it off and sat down.

"Okay," said the Colonel. "What do you know and how did you hear it?"

Until just now, when the Colonel had said that bit about the Army being blameless, Michael had forgotten that the news reports had identified the downed aircraft, purportedly in the Vietnamese Delta, as an Army transport helicopter. So it seemed the whole story was a fabrication. Except that the mission had been lost. He told the Colonel the little he'd gathered from the Air Force and AA personnel. That they knew Beaumont had gone down in Laos, not Vietnam. And AA, at least, had identified the plane as a Volpar, not an Army aircraft.

The Colonel listened, thought, and made a decision. "There wasn't time to get a thorough security clearance for you, Michael, though Lord knows your brother has enough clearance for three. And your combat record, your years in the Army . . . all spotless. So. I'm only going to ask you one question. Just because it is a very neat coincidence, isn't it."

Here we go, thought Michael.

"Why are you here?" asked Colonel Wisby.

Not to show even a second's hesitation, Michael started his answer before thinking. "About five years ago, Sir, I spent some time in Upper Burma and fell in love. With the people." He started again. "I stayed on a demonstration farm, Sir. It kind of changed my life. I went back to the

States, got a degree in agronomy. And then, because of – you'd have to call it a failed relationship, I guess, I enlisted. By the end of my second tour I was thinking about doing the hearts and minds thing with green rice down in the Delta. But they're plains people. And I'd really like to get back to the hill people, Sir. It's a different bunch of tribes here in Laos, but they're basically similar in one regard. They're anachronisms. Doomed unless they adjust to this century somehow. Anyway, Sir, that's why Laos. Tell the truth, I've been hoping that as this tour goes on, I'll be able to get out to the villages. A lot." Wonderful how telling nothing but the truth could obscure it.

One more moment of appraisal, and the Colonel began. "Beaumont's a dove," he said. "Was. The only one with any seniority on the Senate Armed Services Committee. He'd been receiving intelligence from people sharing his sympathies about the war here. The war everybody denies, from the White House down through the State Department to the C.I.A., and include A.I.D. They didn't want him or his fact-finding mission anywhere near Laos, and as I understand it from my intelligence – I don't have much, but some – they stalled him for several days here in Vientiane, pleading monsoon rains and fog and God knows what else. He knew enough, apparently, to want to see the Plain of Jars, to want to visit the hidden city in the mountains."

"City, Sir?" Michael cut in. Hidden? It was beginning to sound like H. Rider Haggard's lost Solomon's mines. What had AA Sherm called Laos – wonderland?

"More like a fortress," the Colonel said. "General Vang Pao's, but with several thousand people. We'll probably get there, Michael. You'll find a good number of American advisors. So called. C.I.A., of course. Some A.I.D. And Army Special Forces. They're training the Meo, and with the help of Air Force FACs, they call in strikes. This is a very full-fledged war, Lieutenant. Which probably our country would forgive, if they knew about it – helping some poor hill tribes fight the North Vietnamese and Chinese-armed communists. But of course they don't know about it at home, though many suspect. But what nobody's going to admit publicly is the secret that's got the administration so scared – the heavy bombing, growing heavier every month. Not to mention that we're shoring up a very corrupt Laotian government.

"I managed to requisition a flight for myself three days ago. Out to the Plain of Jars. You can see it from the plane window. The craters, the brown devastation. Anyway, the country team, as they call themselves, couldn't stall Beaumont forever. They had to let him fly. And he never came back."

Michael didn't have to ask, the Colonel saw his reaction. "No, I don't think so," he said. "Not sabotage. Not a U.S. Senator. Not even the C.I.A. – though embassy talk is admitting that all would be easier if the entire mission were permanently lost. The Delta in Vietnam was wishful thinking at its best. Because one thing is very clear here. The Company is scared. So is State. If Beaumont should have survived a crash, he could be imprisoned. And if he should be taken to Hanoi, be made to talk, made to lie publicly, hell, even tell the truth publicly about what he saw before the crash, the shit will hit the White House fan. And it won't do the country any good either, coming out like that. Certainly the Army would prefer he tell it like it is in Senate committee."

The Colonel's cigar had gone out. He relit it before continuing, then said, "Whatever the Laos team wants us to do or not to do to cover up their mess, we're gonna find that fuckin' plane, Lieutenant. It was a Volpar, yes. The AA have been searching. But their little reconnaisance propellor jobs can't compete for low and slow with your helicopter, or immediate landing capability. And if it turns out that anybody from the plane is still alive, you and I are gonna have to do something about it. That's why we're both here. The boss's head's on the block."

The boss? Who – oh, shit, Army Chief of Staff. Michael sat silent, half stunned and totally appalled, while the Colonel allowed him the time to assimilate it. Finally, Michael said, "Well, Sir." He cleared his throat, gone thick. "The first thing we need, Sir, is the Volpar's flight plan. Will you be able to get it before tomorrow morning?"

"They didn't file one."

Michael just looked at him. Then he said, "Sir, if I may?" The Colonel just waited. "There's no pilot in the world, flying in a war zone like this, who doesn't file a flight plan. For rescue, you see, Sir. And believe me, the pilot flying that particular mission would – "

"It doesn't exist, Michael. Not now, if it ever did. Or so I'm told."

"Have you talked with the airport traffic controller that day?"

"He was Laotian Royal Army, hasn't worked since, and hasn't been located."

"Well, but – excuse me, Sir, but – Jesus Christ all over."

"Yes indeedy, Lieutenant." They sat there looking at each other, letting the silence run, until the Colonel said that they had to get back to the party. They set a time for Willy to drive them all out to the airport, and the Colonel sent Michael inside first.

He got through a soupy plate of curry on his lap without spilling it, assiduously avoided the Colonel, and when everybody was gathering to the bar again, this time for the largest display of liquers Michael had ever seen, he managed to reach the foyer, had gotten his tie and hat from the servant who then went out to round up a staff car for him – but too late. Sandy came down the stairs on the arm of some guy or other, both of them looking every bit as caught out as Michael was sure he did, only they looked proud of it.

The servant came back inside to get him, Sandy smiled and said, "'Til next time, Michael," and Michael finally escaped.

Halfway down the drive, he remembered he hadn't told the Colonel about the meeting ahead with the AA pilots. He thought about going back in to the Novacks' and finding the Colonel, but he couldn't face it. Plenty of time in the morning to tell him whatever came of it.

Hanny opened the door at once when Michael knocked. One look and he said, "Back from the wars, from the look of you."

"More like the zoo," Michael said. "You ready for a blow job? The staff car's waiting."

"Get rid of him," Hanny said. "I got a cab out back, and no need for the embassy to know how we spend our time. Especially where we're goin'."

Michael shrugged, headed back down the hall to do the bidding, then looked back at Hanny. "I'm beginning to think you were born to this shit."

"Yeah." Hanny grinned. "Me, too."

DAY FIVE

15

Michael looked at his watch. Close to four. He swung his feet to the floor, sat up. He didn't know how much he'd slept. They said people always slept more than they thought they had. But it sure hadn't felt like a whole lot to him. And Willy and the Colonel'd be here in little more than an hour. Might as well call it a night and get something done.

He went into the little sitting room, pawed through the junk he'd dumped on the floor when he was unpacking earlier, and found the remnants of the plastic sheeting he'd bought at Tan Son Nhut and that he and Hanny had taped front and back to the maps they'd brought with them. Dug through the small duffle, got out his knife and his duct tape, cleared off the coffee table, unrolled and anchored with ashtrays the maps the AA pilots had given them, and then thought of scissors for the plastic. The knife didn't work all that well. He rummaged around and found some in a kitchen drawer. Whoever equipped this club did a decent enough job. Only problem was everything was beige – wood, uphostery, blankets, bedspread, everything. Hanny's apartment, too. Must've got a cut rate. Of course, there were a couple of orange prints on the walls, for which he guessed he was supposed to be grateful.

He cut and taped, and as he did he studied the maps. They gave him the very stuff he'd looked for and didn't find in Hong Kong – the locations of the Lima sites, those short take off and landing strips called STOLs, as well as whatever fuel dumps anybody knew about. Both the Limas and the dumps were rarer to the west and northwest towards China than in the Plain of Jars or the mountains towards Vietnam. But there were a couple of strips rumored to have fuel supplies not far off the path to Burma. If they ever were lucky enough to get up to Luang Prabang to start that journey.

123

Everything was getting weirder and wilder. In Hong Kong, he'd started out convinced Tom was crazy. That didn't hold a candle to tonight. Yet somehow, in an odd reversal, it gave the scheme to reach Kathleen a validity it had lacked before. First that incestuous party. Then the Colonel's tale out of a spy novel. And then, sweet Jesus, Mam'selle Josie's. Michael had to chuckle. Hanny'd had his share of shocks tonight, too.

They'd had to halt inside the door to accustom their eyes to the dim light. Nobody'd noticed them, which was a change. Softly, but nevertheless vibrating the floor, came a rhythmic beat, and against it, down and dirty, groaned a saxaphone. First they saw figures weaving, gyrating gently on top of the bar, silhouetted against the wall in back. Then, that wall became a reflecting mirror. And then they saw that the girls were both topless and bottomless, powdered white, even their shaven crotches. All they wore were high heels. There were five of them, and at any one time three of them were going into a spread-legged squat, thrusting pelvises forward in display to the men sitting at the bar less than two feet from the view they were paying to see. Asians and westerners alike, they waggled bills at the girls, pleading for closer, baby, closer. Nothing new to Michael – North Beach wasn't all that far from the Haight.

Still just inside the door, other groans came to Michael and Hanny. And their eyes now afforded them a view – dark booths along the walls where men sat, heads back and rolling, eyes closed, smiling some of them, and black heads, hair short and permed curly, bobbed and wove, rose and fell and rocked face down in their laps. Like black furry spiders in the throes of death, thought Michael. Damned spiders.

Hanny had gone taut, ready to pull out. Michael could feel it. Hanny never went to church, but he'd been born and bred a Catholic, and his gorge must be rising full. Michael grabbed his arm. He couldn't lose him from this meeting. Moving forward together, more or less, Michael still with a grasp on Hanny, they started looking for the AA pilots. And the smell hit them, the place stinking of it. Sin, thought Michael. Not just sex, but by God sin. Even more than the opium den he'd once gone to in Da Nang. Of course, there, everybody'd been asleep. They sure as hell weren't sleeping here. Though as a matter of fact, this air was smokey and did hint of something more than pot.

At the far end of this – what? bar? sex parlor? – hung a curtain of wooden beads, which suddenly split apart and revealed Sherm sticking his bald head through. He saw them, waved them to come on back. As they did, Hanny damned near stumbled over his own feet, his eyes roving back over his shoulder at those writhing girls on the bar, Hanny probably figuring that what they were doing was a lot more wholesome than what was going on elsewhere around here.

Michael let go of Hanny's arm when they stepped through the second bead curtain, having walked through a short coridor. There was more light here, western men mostly, seated at tables, some of them Indian wrestling or throwing poker dice, some just talking, telling jokes, and in a corner, a bunch were playing pick-up-sticks. Michael wondered about the stakes. Lots of cigarette smoke. A few maryjanes here and there. And a few local dollies floating around lending their light Asian laughter to the sense of a private club. A far cry from the room out front. He'd've bet that most of the guys were airmen of one kind or another. American airmen. It just felt like it.

Jedediah was standing up at a table against the wall, and both he and Sherm held out their hands for a shake. Hanny and Michael introduced themselves. They hadn't met at the airport after landing that afternoon, just waved across the tarmac as the two Huey pilots headed for the AA shack, and Willy stood by, waiting for them. Sherm was short, stocky, going on for fifty, and utterly hairless, including a lack of eyebrows. Jedediah had enough facial hair for both of them and was a good twenty years younger. A bear of a man.

Everybody sat down, and a girl came over, standing closest to Michael. At once, she looked down at Michael's and Hanny's groins, and started a big smile. "You want blow job?" she asked. "I give best blow job at Mam'selle Josie's. Special for big boys."

Hanny leaned forward over the table. She, meanwhile, had laid her hand on Michael's thigh, was sliding up it. He grabbed the fragile wrist before she connected. "No, thank you," he said, politely.

"You sure?" she asked in surprise. "I got good tongue, good throat, we go upstairs, very nice."

Jedediah interrupted, sounding a bit weary. "Dam Dzi, bring 'em a drink, okay? What do you fellas want?"

"How's the Scotch?" Michael said.

"I wouldn't," Sherm said. "Try the Pernod."

"Beer," Hanny said.

"Two," said Michael. "In the bottle, with the cap on."

"And bring a church key," Hanny said.

Dam Dzi looked confused. "You can't expect the girl to know that," Sherm said, and he pantomimed it to her, saying, "bottle opener." She beamed and left. Hanny was looking at Sherm. A lot of condescension there, coming out of Sherm. Michael hoped he wouldn't keep it up. Sherm'd be sorry, but so would he and Hanny. These guys might really come through with some help. But Hanny was just studying him, maybe trying to decide whether – or how much – to take offense.

"So," Jedediah said, looking at Michael, "you got briefed?"

Michael looked him back, not happy about this either. The Colonel hadn't cautioned him about discretion, but then the Colonel hadn't known they had a late date.

"You said, flying up, that you could tell us where to look for the Volpar," Michael said, temporizing.

"Yes, we did," said Sherm. "But we could save a lot of time if you would deign to tell us what you've learned."

Deign? Hanny shifted in his seat. Thing was, even Hanny didn't know what Michael had learned. The cab ride was too short. So the hell with it. Either they fished or cut bait. "The flight plan's missing," Michael said.

"Yeah," said Jedediah, "but it was phony anyhow, so what's the difference?" Hanny looked as incredulous as Michael had been feeling most of the night. "See," Jedediah was going on, "they were supposed to be flying out onto the Plain of Jars and on into Long Tieng, at least the Senator thought they were. I mean, that's where the secret war's being fought, right? And since it was cloudy, half raining, no sun, well – wherever they headed, nobody on the plane'd know the difference. And that suited the company fine. First a fly-over of the old royal city – you know, Luang Prabang – to entertain the Senator, and then they flew north and west and got in trouble."

"And how do we know all this," Sherm picked up smoothly, "you most assuredly must be wondering? We all had drinks together the night before. Right here. The Volpar's pilot Curtis Semler, his co-pilot Johnny Dorn, the crew chief Rene de Vere, and the two AA attendants on hand to keep the drinks and cheezos moving for the Senator and his mission. Unimportant as those two young men were, they had to be in on it in case they happened to look out and notice it didn't look like the Plain of Jars down there. All told on that plane, there were five AA crew, the Senator, and six D.C. paper pushers on a free ride. They left early in the morning, so

Curtis and Johnny had gotten their orders at the embassy the previous evening – and stopped by here for a drink before beddy-byes."

Hanny choked on a swallow of beer.

"Wait a minute, wait a minute, wait a minute," said Michael. "Has anybody been searching for this plane?"

"Yes, of course," said Sherm. "Daily."

"Well," said Jedediah, "pretty daily. We fly under contract, y'know. To the company."

"The C.I.A., yeah," said Michael. "Where are you looking?"

"The Plain of Jars," said Jedediah.

"But that's what the flight plan said, right? So why misplace it?" said Hanny. "What kind of shit's goin' on in this place?"

"The right-hand left-hand syndrome, or perhaps you're not familiar with the term? The one never knows what the other is doing. Defines the embassy here to a T. All the divisions. Somebody decided to be careful. Just in case, *quelle doleur*," throwing up his hands, "the plane turns up over towards Burma or perhaps up in China, nobody can be proven to have lied."

China. Michael's eyes slid to Hanny, who had the grace not to look back with an I-told-you-so. They'd gotten their beers. They uncapped them, and they were cold and good – and Chinese. Michael sighed. "Do they or don't they want to find the Volpar?"

"They'd rather not, actually," said Sherm. "On the other hand . . ." He smirked. "You do see, don't you?"

"They don't want a POW spilling his guts out in Hanoi, either," Jedediah said. He sounded disgusted. "So. We *do* want to find it, Michael. If our boys – AA boys – are taken prisoner, nobody on our side'll trade for them. They'll be abandoned. Except by us. We want to know what happened, if they're alive, and if, God help 'em, they're prisoners some-where."

"So does the Army," Michael said.

Hanny finished his beer, smacked the bottle down hard on the table. "Sorry, fellas, but I don't get it. All this secrecy everywhere abounding, yet that crew came in here for a drink and told it all?"

"Well, dear boy, we're telling it all to you, aren't we?" said Sherm.

Michael wondered if he should kick him under the table. Nobody'd ever called Hanny "dear boy" – not that Michael knew about. Hanny's jaw was sliding forward.

Jedediah noticed, too, and came up with a fast grin. "That's what Mam'selle Josie's for. No brass. No press. And the best cover in the world beyond those curtains. Hell, if we couldn't talk freely somewhere in this spy ridden town, we'd all go stark bonkers."

"To be serious," Sherm cut in, "our pilots fly reconnaisance for Vang Pao in little Pileatus Porters, and when they've had the chance, they've headed west and looked. Not far because of lack of fuel, usually, and the fixed-wings can't get down as low as you because they can't pop up as fast if they have to. And they can't stop dead and peer down through the trees, either." He stopped a moment, then finished, "When do you start looking?"

"Tomorrow morning," Michael said. He had told Hanny that much in the cab, so no surprise for him there.

"If I were you, young Sir, I'd file another phony flight plan. The company is going to be unhappy about you."

Michael looked at him. Sherm lifted a suave British eyebrow. Sabotage, he meant, and Michael heard the Colonel's deep voice earlier, "No, I don't think so. Not even the C.I.A. . . ." Plus which, filing false could make both his senior officer and his aircraft unrescuable. And then Hanny made it easier.

"Forget the phony flight plan," he said, his voice edging sarcasm, "all the talkin' you guys do, wouldn't do any good anyway." He cast his eyes around the room, and raised his own eyebrow. "Sure as hell, your company already knows exactly where we're gonna be flyin'."

That's when Jedediah had reached between his feet to pull up a flight bag, set it on the table, and took the maps from it. He jabbed a finger at the western portion of Laos. "Lots of nice green jungle," he said. "Oh, there's war everywhere in this poor country, Laotian against Laotian, hill tribe against hill tribe, even some long reaches by the North Vietnamese, the Chinese. But if you didn't want a Senatorial dove to see the results of the bombing, or to talk to Vang Pao, whom we are advising so mightily and so badly, you'd put the Senator on a plane going west, and then after awhile, tell him the weather's socking you in or you've got engine trouble and can't make Alternate 20. 'Sorry, Senator, we're turning back.' Only they crashed instead."

"Alternate?" Hanny asked.

"No way for you to know that, of course," said Sherm, over kind. "Long Tieng, dear boy. Vang Pao's secret city in the mountains. Alternate to other landing sites, for secrecy."

Hanny managed a nod. "Secret city," he said. "No, I guess I couldn't know that. I mean, nobody to tell me, we've only been here about five minutes."

Oh, shit, thought Michael.

Hanny sat back, and after a breathless moment in which Jedediah caught Michael's eye, asking what was coming down, and Michael cocked his head with a don't-ask-me shrug, Hanny let out a short chuckle and shook his head. "You Brits talk like this to everybody?" he asked.

His gaze locked on Sherm's, whose eyes narrowed. "Far too often, I'm afraid. We're so bloody good at it," Sherm said.

An apology of sorts, Michael judged, hoping Hanny thought the same. Then the two of them smiled.

Hanny called out, "How about another beer?"

The four of them went on talking then for awhile. Personal stuff, some of it, but also giving Michael invaluable in-country know-how. Other men came over now and then, pulled around chairs to perch and talk, too, two or three recon pilots who'd flown in search during the past several days. All so grateful somebody'd come to help, full of help themselves, making Michael queasy, denying to himself that it was anything besides a very long day, knowing it was something else altogether. They offered tips about communications with the Air Force, who flew the Cessna FACs and the orbiting all-country air controller dubbed Cricket here in Laos, Alley Cat at night. They used the maps to warn about this mountain or that rearing up like they'd just appeared out of the bowels of the earth.

"I suppose," Michael said at one point, his second beer set aside, "that there was no may-day from the Volpar."

"Nope," said Jedediah. "Or at least the Air Force doesn't say so."

"Jesus," Hanny said, "it's beginning to sound like the Kennedy conspiracy."

"Not at all, not at all," said Sherm. "Just everybody trying to protect his ass. The plane was where it was not supposed to be."

Just like the Loach, one of these days. Michael hadn't suspected, not once since Hong Kong, not until tonight, that this duty here could run him up against choices. God damned fucking choices. Even if he'd made the right ones in the past, people counting on him had been left behind. He'd thought the last ones, last ones forever, were back in Nam. Now it was the Colonel, decent as they came. The AA men, believing he was the one could find that lost plane. And they had, in addition, provided him with most of the details he'd been missing to reach Kathleen.

Walking home, Hanny no longer limping, Michael had filled in the blanks for him, especially the ones that made it apparent the Colonel was going to be flying with them every damned minute in the air. That's when Hanny had suggested going to Loi Long tonight, and Michael had refused. Hanny knew, too, they'd never find it. He just wanted to be there for Michael.

Michael completed taping the last map into its plastic sleeve, rolled it and the rest up, put the lot inside his small duffle, those of Burma at the bottom. He'd get them all on board this morning. Hanny'd be sitting in the back cabin, and he'd be navigating in any case, so at least the maps would always be at hand. Somehow, he had to figure out the way to ditch the Colonel and do a day flight. And without putting Hanny in jeopardy with the Army.

One thing, for sure. The AA men had made it easy to suggest shifting base to Luang Prabang, and the sooner the better. It would at least put them on target for Burma, and a quicker turn-around. For it was incontrovertible – no way would the Volpar have flown west out of Luang Prabang along the Mekong. Even a naive senator could have identified direction, sun or no sun, if that big river were down below the whole flight out. They had to have flown north, avoiding the Mekong, then west to avoid China. And that's the direction they'd take the Loach and search for it.

He had his second shave, his third shower, cold water now, in less than twelve hours. He got his kit together, went down to roust Hanny, and found him already outside at the curb waiting for the pick up. They shared a cigarette. Everything was dripping but the rain had stopped. They might get into the air. Michael had determined that with the Colonel aboard, no way would he fly in worst weather. Wouldn't be able to search worth a damn anyway. Thing was, if the monsoon didn't lighten up – hell, they were into September, it ought to – they were at its mercy, and God help Kathleen. And that sick baby, if it was still alive.

16

Kathleen awoke with a start, immediately alert. The silence was complete, except for Cho's raspy shallow breaths. He was cuddled into her belly as she lay on her side, facing the windows, his small fist closed round two of her fingers with a great strength, as if hanging on for dear life. Which he was, she thought. He was so sick, where did the strength come from? But she knew. From U-pym's milk.

The moon was sliding in through the shutters, now throwing its light and shadows from a different direction than when she had arrived back from the town, so several hours must have passed as she slept. She must be careful of that, sleeping too heavily. Not safe. Not in the jungle.

When she'd returned from the paddock to the palace yesterday, U-pym had sent up a wail, no knowing whether from shame or just sorrow. The wives had put salves on her sore back, their fingers so kind, their soft voices showing shock and, as never before, a sort of outrage. U-pym, too, sitting cross-legged on the floor by the head of Kathleen's bed, the baby in her lap, patting Kathleen's hands, face, tears on her face.

When the wives went away, promising to return soon, Kathleen and U-pym had held in silence, eyes looking into each other and deciding. "Yes," U-pym had said, sobs still making her words ragged, "I will help you."

So the two had murmured and whispered off and on during the day, Kathleen dozing part of the time. The salves were quick pain killers. She could only hope they were quick healers as well.

U-pym would have gone to town in her stead, especially after what had happened, but Kathleen knew that would have been too risky for U-pym. Once it was found out that Kathleen had escaped, any report that U-pym had sold a sapphire would put her in worse jeopardy than Kathleen, might even cost her her life. So, after dark, the moon not yet up, Kathleen had sent U-pym away with the baby to visit with the other women in the kitchen, had wrapped a Shan shawl over her head and shoulders to protect her back against the rain, and had sneaked out of her window onto the wooden veranda and down to the ground. And while the guard at the gate would probably not have stopped her – after all, her horse was killed dead and she was not carrying the child – still, she didn't want him to know what she would be bringing back from the night market.

She had moved along the rear of the palace and across the back grounds to where the palace wall met the rock face running up the mountain behind. There the wall had crumbled enough space for her to slide between. She used it often in the mornings as a shortcut to go riding, and everyone knew it, and it was all right. On this night, it would keep her intentions secret yet awhile.

It was misting, not really raining, as she entered the town, and the oil lamplight coming from the wooden houses, the basha huts, wavered as if through pond water. She picked her way among them, boots slipping in the mud, heading toward the market. Not fully roofed, the Sawbwa had provided shed roofs to shelter the platforms for the women while gossiping, gambling and conducting business of all kinds. Throughout Burma, the bazaar was the women's world and women's work – and most of the profits as well.

Kathleen would first need the stone merchant, one of the few exceptions to the rule. In Loi Long, the stone merchant was a man. This would be the most dangerous transaction she would make, for after all, why would the Sawbwa's lady want so much money when all was provided by the Prince? She had decided to talk about gifts for the light festival, even ask his advice, perhaps promising to return and buy a number of smaller stones for that purpose.

She walked along the paths between the shops which glowed golden from the oil lamps, the women's laughter rich and low, their eyes and smiles flashing, terry cloth turbans around their heads, their longyis rich with reds and greens or their black leggings shining with circlets of silver round knees and ankles, clicking dice in the game played everywhere: the cloth spread on floor or dirt, its painted animals enticing the gambler to bet and throw multi-faceted dice painted in the same fashion.

One or two of the women recognized her, and news of her presence here at the night bazaar began to be heralded ahead of her, so that soft words both greeted and followed her: "Sayah!" Meaning teacher. "Sayah!" "Sayah gyi!" some even said, giving her, though too young, the honor of calling her a great teacher. Some women came to kneel at the edge of their shops, reaching welcoming hands to her. One took hold of her hand and stopped her, gesturing to the little girl who sat beside her, face lowered shyly. Kathleen was polite, smiled and nodded, but must have shown she didn't understand, for the mother raised the child's face to reveal the split hair lip marring the mouth. The mother spoke softly to the little girl, who smiled up at Kathleen brilliantly and offered her a flower – and Kathleen remembered. A baby she had delivered. Four, four and a half years ago? Yes. Not long after Michael had left, because when she'd seen that poor little mouth, she'd needed him to talk to about it, and he hadn't been there. Now she reached and touched the child's hand, took the flower, bowed to her. She would have caressed that smiling little face, but in Burma, one didn't touch a stranger's head.

She walked on, hearing the tonal language she loved move up and down the scale like music in those soft women's voices, their dusky skins clear and beautiful.

"Miss How! Miss How!" Kathleen turned to see, in the shadows at the back of a shop, the small figure of Daw Kyi. Alive! Kathleen gasped, moved to the shop at once. "Daw Kyi?"

Htin Aung had told her the old woman was dead. Months ago, he'd told her that. Cutting her off, always cutting her off. How many other things had he lied about?

The tiny old woman came forward from her squat to kneel, a cheroot tucked between her fingers. She spit blood red betel juice into an open can, her smile showing black teeth, and reached for Kathleen's hands. "Your baby is sick, poor lady, poor baby." She spoke in English, hard won and remembered for so long after the lessons.

Kathleen took Daw Kyi's hands, managed to smile, to nod. How did she know these things? But then, undoubtedly everyone in the province did.

"What you want, Miss How? I get for you. I help you." And it seemed to Kathleen that from that moment, fortune began to shine on her. Of course, it helped that the moon, at the same moment, still low in the sky, came forth from behind the clouds.

She hitched a hip up onto the platform, curled her legs around, and showed Daw Kyi the cabuchon star sapphire, its color deep blue, not milky. And then, as she sat and sipped tea poured from the small blackened iron tea kettle into small black iron handleless cups, Daw Kyi went away with the sapphire, and it seemed in no time returned with the kyats in exchange, and an aluminum pot with a lid, and a good measure of polished rice wrapped in burlap, and some cooked rice wrapped in coarse green tea leaves, and then she deposited the rice, both cooked and raw, in the pot, and tucked the pot into a worn but big woven bag. After which, wonder of wonders, she pulled forth from the shadows at the back of her little shop a folded piece of plastic sheeting that she no doubt used to protect her own bolts of cloth and twists of thread, and it joined the rest in the bag.

Kathleen tried to get the old woman to take some money for herself, but she would not. At last, Kathleen slipped back down to the ground, hung the big bag over her shoulder – away, she hoped, from the cut on her back – and dropped a low bow to Daw Kyi, her hands lifted prayerfully together to her forehead in a high shiko of respect.

"Go safely," Daw Kyi said, though Kathleen had not mentioned her plans for the uses of the pot and the rice. It gave her the courage for one last question. She asked it in English. "Where is the house of Lim Pong?" And was told it was up the mountain towards where Maung Swe still lay dead. Kathleen remembered it from her rides up there, had somehow never realized it belonged to her Shan guard. Then Daw Kyi leaned out from under the shed roof and looked up at the sky and over at the moon. "Go soon," she said. "Sky change fast maybe. Monsoon not finish, isn't it?" Kathleen nodded, and left, head down, walking swiftly now.

But the walk back up the hill to the palace was going slower and slower, the strap of the heavy bag rubbing across her striped back. And even while it was hurting and she was beginning to breath heavily, Michael was filling her mind, her head, his eyes cradling her like warm blue water, as he'd always listened to her, accepting her, liking her, knowing her. Feeling with her what she felt. That time in the jeep, the worse thing she'd ever told him, was no different.

Maybe it was the child in the market recalling it to her. She had been behind the wheel. He claimed that if he drove he'd surely freeze up, terrified even to get out because they were perched atop the high crown and verge of the cart-road and one wrong twist of the wheel and they'd be hung up perhaps for days depending on somebody with the time and a buffalo to come haul them out. And suddenly she'd asked, "Did you ever help birth a baby? I mean, besides Sally's on the ship?"

Trudging through the dark outside the palace wall, she remembered it. Michael had swivelled his searching eyes from the passing dry bush and huge dusty broad-leaved teaks to her. Somebody always had to be watching for bandits in these parts. She'd kept her eyes on the track, but she'd known his eyes were on her. Finally he'd said, "Yeah, matter of fact. I did." And then he'd told her. How it had been Easter at that commune farm he'd lived on, with everybody deciding to drop some acid and get resurrected, that's how he'd talked about it. She'd had to pick up all kinds of new language to get what he was saying in the time since he'd come to Keng Tung, and now could understand most of it. Anyway. All of them had been depending on Michael to stay cool and be there to talk them down. He'd quit acid within a week of his arrival – he'd said LSD gave him spiders, and Kathleen could see it every evening at the farm, his eyes always moving to the walls at any kind of movement there, even of the harmless little geckos. So he was the one had got stuck with midwifing Dawn Rose.

In telling it, Michael had chuckled, had shaken his head. Kathleen had seen that out of the corner of her eyes while still driving. "I'll tell you, Kath," Michael had said, "that labor seemed endless. I didn't know who to feel sorrier for, Dawn or me." Kathleen had cast him a look of reproof at that, but he was lost in remembering.

"The poor girl didn't even know who the father was. Oh, not me," Michael had hastened to say, "I hadn't been at Rainbow that long. Truly, Kathleen." And for once, he'd sounded very young, younger even than herself, seeming totally unaware of the implication that if he had been, the baby might've been.

"Anyway," he'd gone on, "that little thing squalling in my hands like a scared rabbit decided me to get the hell out of there and within a week I was gone."

And then, in complete contradiction of everything Kathleen knew to be smart, she'd braked and stopped the jeep right there in the middle of that jungle track. "Me, too," she'd said. "Delivered a baby. Three times, so far."

She'd switched off the engine. She needed silence for this, but then couldn't speak it.

"Kath. Ought we to be sitting here?"

"The dacoits around here won't do me harm. You either, not with me."

But his eyes had been roaming again. "That's good news. But if I were a bandit, I'd sure covet a movable jeep." There were some clumps of towering bamboo up ahead, the stems so big around and so thickly crowded together an eighteen wheeler wouldn't have been visible behind any one of them.

And then the words about that terrible first time just bounced out.

His eyes had snapped back to her, and she'd made her gaze firm in meeting them, she caught in a breath. She hadn't been aware of it, but when his eyes flickered down she'd realized her hand was clenching and unclenching the gear shift.

He'd said, "Kathleen," and covered her hand to quiet it, must have felt her trembling. "We have to keep moving."

"I needed you to know. I thought you'd want to know. That, about me."

"Sweetheart, of course I do. I mean – just not now." He leaned forward to start the engine. "Should I drive?"

But then there they were, dacoits, the last of seven of them just stepping out from the bush at the side of the road, three of them carrying rifles, all with huge dahs slung from their hips. One, the heftiest and looked to be the oldest, held an automatic rifle, its belts of ammunition draped from his shoulders in an X across his chest. All wore a hodge podge of uniforms, and all but the leader had sandals on their feet.

"Shit." She and Michael had said it together.

And she said it again now, alone in the night by the palace wall, as she stumbled in the dark and the bag with the rice-heavy pot swung across one of the scabs. But she was nearly at the gap. She managed the last few steps, and thankfully set down her load on a hummock of grass that was drier than the dirt around it. Slipping back through to the palace grounds, she made it all the way back to her room undiscovered by anyone. She'd folded the shawl inside out to hide its dampness, undressed to get back on the bed – and discovered her camisole was stained across the back with blood from the cuts.

Later, the wives found the blood dried on her back and were unhappy with it, saying she slept too actively for her own good. She pretended to a good deal more pain than she really felt, and put on a restlessness that they diagnosed as fever. The possibility existed that they were right, but Kathleen couldn't countenance it. Wouldn't. A sick baby in the rain and jungle and mountains, with only a sick mother between himself and God knew what? No. She then had dozed the late night hours away, while U-pym fed the baby as much as he would take.

And now, at last, the time was come.

She was out of the bed, pulling on her jeans and one of Tom's big loose shirts, tying the laces of her boots to sling them around her neck, and U-pym was beside her, wrapping Cho in a cotton blanket, helping Kathleen tie a long Shan scarf into a sling for him. If her back hurt, she was no longer aware of it. Nothing mattered now but to get away.

All in readiness, the other things she'd hidden in the Shan bags and kept in the trunk were also over her shoulders, and she turned to U-pym. The little woman held out something long and narrow, wrapped in silk – a dah. Like a machete, it would cut her way through the jungle. U-pym knew what jungle required. How many other things had Kathleen not thought of?

She took it, slipped it down into a bag, and whispered, "Only one day," she said, trying to impart confidence. "Tell them a story for only one day, and it will give me time enough. Then say anything that will make you safe. You went to the toilet, and when you came back, I was gone. And that perhaps I had lied about my discomfort, made it more than was the truth, and so you were beguiled, just as the wives were." And suddenly, it swept Kathleen, what she was saying goodbye to. The wives who had kept her sane so often, their care for her a reassurance that the life here was not a nightmare. U-pym who had kept her baby alive.

She pressed the two sapphires she had kept aside for this into U-Pym's hand. To help her get home. Then, seeing U-Pym's wet cheeks, Kathleen lifted Cho from the bed and held him out to his wet-nurse, who drifted her feathery touch down his little face in an anguish of farewell. When she stepped back, Kathleen put him in the sling and shikoed to U-pym, who went down on her knees and put her forehead to the floor, never to see her princeling again.

Kathleen stifled her own half sob, blinked her own tears, and heard the baby's troubled breaths and left. Not out through the window as she'd done earlier, but on silent bootless feet along the wooden corridors to the Sawbwa's quarters, terrified the baby would start crying any moment, telling herself he was full and warm at her side.

She entered the study. Light from the moon filtering in through the half-open shutters illumined walls hung with old photos, one of the young Sawbwa, rifle in his arms, foot on a tiger. How could Kathleen have forgotten about tigers? Fewer in the bush now, but there, all the same, and unpredictable. Another picture of the Prince, slightly older, equally arrogant in his jodhpurs, a crop in one hand, the reins of his horse in another. A third, very young, rifle aimed and ready as he crouched in a howdah atop an elephant.

She crossed the thick rugs to the pistol case, the glass reflecting moonlight. She opened it and hesitated. There were three pistols. She hefted one, then chose the smallest, the lightest. She had enough to carry. She found the smallest bullets, and they fit – she had watched often enough how to load and cock. She dropped the rest of the bullets into one of the bags, sliding the pistol barrel down into a hip pocket.

She went out the window here, lowered her things down to the ground from the veranda and slithered down beside them, still not awaking Cho. Good fortune travelled with her. Just before she went through the gap in the wall, she looked a last time at her prison palace and felt nothing. Which surprised her. She turned her back on it, went to the other side of the wall, put on her boots, slung on the big bag she had left there on the grass, and moved up the hill to find Lim Pong's house.

This time she invited Michael in, having thought out over and over again what she would do next and finding the fears harder to bear than memories. He'd come into her life like a bolt of lighning, no, a clap and roll of thunder that went on rolling and rolling, shaking the deep inside her. Thoughts kept time with her footsteps. Funny. He had been a marvel to her, had tried everything, would dare anything. Had had the courage to seek himself, away from home and money and safety. Thinking of that, of him, had given her the courage to stay in Loi Long when Tom had left. To seek and find her own self, that she'd thought found with Michael, and then knew to be lost with Michael.

Oh, Michael, why didn't you let me go with you? If you had, we'd have children of our own, some with your eyes.

And she wouldn't have Cho. A choice never made. Less than half a life either way. What she had had here, less than half a life. And it was Cho who had given her even that.

She opened the sling to look down on him. He was awake, eyes looking up at her, and quiet. He *knew*.

The moonlight was going fitful, and seemed thinner. Dawn must be on its way. She hurried, needing to be away before first light, walking now along the fence of Maung Swe's paddock, the big silent mound of him visible on the pasture. It made it hard. She opened the gate, went to the shed for the big stallion's tack, not at all sure she could carry it all, and stumbled down to hands and knees, leaning sharply to the side not to land on Cho, bruising a wrist. Nevermind. She got the leather bit and reins, and the blanket saddle that weighed like leather, but she managed and would, if the house was not too much farther. She thought it wasn't. And then, she saw it. Wooden, high up on its piles, and isolated, only a corral on beyond it.

The pony was hobbled and couldn't move fast. Keeping the tack, she set down the rest of the stuff, the baby, too, and strode boldly up to the animal not nearly the size of Maung Swe. She got the bit in his mouth, the saddle over his back, and nudging his belly to get rid of air, she cinched the bands tight. Leading him to the corral gate, she looped and tied the two small bags together and draped them across his withers to hang down either side. He had kept silent so far, and not a peep from Cho.

She put his sling over one shoulder, slung the large bag over the other, and mounted the pony. He snorted. And whickered. Oh, God.

Determined not to panic, she dumped the band of the big bag down to around her hips so that it would dangle on down the side of the horse, and swivelled the sling around to the front so the baby was on the saddle in front of her. She dug her heels into the pony. And then the shout came.

The pony leapt for the gate even as the Shan came off his porch. The pony reared slightly, her fault, hands too hard on the reins. The shy slowed him down, and the Shan was on them, grabbing for the reins, for her. And as he did, he looked full into her face, knew her, and in terror she knew that he'd never believe his pony'd been taken by a runaway soldier, never.

"Get away," she cried out, "oh, get away!" But he hung on, and desperate, she jerked the pony's head harshly to the side, reached back, pulled out the pistol, pointed it, or tried, looking into Lim Pong's glaring eyes, the pistol heavier than she remembered, wavering in her hand. He did not back off, and she fired.

17

Having told the Colonel about last night, what they'd learned, Michael had gone right on into the suggestion that they move to Luang Prabang – today. It had startled Hanny. The Colonel had turned around in the front seat of the jeep and stared at Michael appraisingly. Shit, he never had been good at lying. Not lying now, the cautionary voice came. It was the truth, they'd waste hours everyday in flight if they stayed in Vientiane.

"Right," the Colonel had finally said, and had ordered Willy to turn around and take the men back to the Club to collect their stuff, with the further order to Willy to fly it up by passenger plane and get them billetted in a hotel up there. He had then gone on to observe that if the C.I.A. wanted to know where they were going, they'd find out, so no phony flight plan. "But," he'd concluded to Willy, "you'd best get a guard detailed from the Royal Laotian Army against sabotage. From the minute we put down 'til the minute we take off."

Christ.

The Colonel had suddenly grinned. "Here one night, and I swear you boys found out more than I did in a whole fuckin' week." They didn't mention the kind of place they'd been visiting at the time, but Willy seemed to know that AA and Mam'selle Josie's were a match.

So they were late getting off, especially with Hanny doing extra checks. But the rain had stopped. The Colonel had his own helmet, said he'd needed one, flying LRP's on Slicks. A Colonel flying long range patrol? His grunts must've practically canonized him. He was agile getting in, too. The left seat, as Michael instructed.

Michael rounded the chopper and took his own seat, observed as the Colonel belted in handily and connected his radio, at which point Michael said, "Just so you don't wonder, Sir, Loaches are short on electronic equipment, so we'll be navigating by compass with the Sergeant using maps in the back." The Colonel raised his thumb in understanding, Michael ran through his pre-flights, and warned Hanny, "Ready to crank!"

Hanny was already standing by with the fire-extinguisher. Michael cranked, Hanny jumped in, and they lifted off.

They reached Luang Prabang in an hour and a half, and put down for fuel. From the air, it was obviously a royal city, full of temples and palace compounds. But it was small, looked nice, the Mekong busy with traffic.

North of the city they headed northwest to avoid the Mekong being visible out the left side of the aircraft, and Michael dropped down to begin flying the valleys.

"Binocs, please," he'd ordered the other two men, telling the Colonel to keep his eyes peeled to the left and behind. Hanny knew to look right and behind. Michael watched front and mostly right, no glasses, but they were covered almost three-sixty. After awhile, he started jinking back and forth across the valleys, then running up and down the steep-sided ridges. These mountains weren't all that high, but they sure were precipitous, some of them ending in real dog-teeth, looking knife sharp. The jungle began to go to two canopies, then three.

"Come on, Commander!" The Colonel, over the intercom. "Let's go poppin'!" He'd said on the way out to Wattay that he'd never done it, never been in a Loach at all, and he'd waited long enough. He was hot to trot – his words.

Michael hesitated. He didn't want to insult the Colonel, but still . . . "Sir? Um, are you subject to airsickness, Sir?"

"No problem, Commander."

"Well, you may be surprised, Sir. If you do feel funny, please say so. We'll just go high and stabilize and let your stomach settle. And Sir? We don't have barf-bags, so if you get caught short, put your head out to the left, please?"

The Colonel threw him a good-humored glance. Michael gave a mental shrug. Here's hoping, he thought, and telling the Colonel to forget the binocs now, he turned the Loach sharply down to canopy top, leveled her out, and moved ahead.

Now and then, a tree rose suddenly up out of the green surrounding it and Michael put the little helicopter through its paces. And he took it to the mountainsides as close as he would have without his senior grade passenger, waiting to bank and rise until the last minute, doing it sharp. The Colonel's hands rested on his controls, just the natural place to put them, so Michael could keep an eye on. Nothing like hands to give warning.

Hoping to take the Colonel's mind off but also as a best way to search, Michael decided to give a little lesson in scouting. "There's a trick, Sir, to looking down to the ground through heavy canopy at this speed and level.

You need to try to focus your eyes at some imaginary point below the canopy top, at your best belief of what's ground level. Look for brown, and as far as the Volpar goes, look for dark discrete shapes, glints of metal. Matter of fact, look for anything not natural – sharp corners under growth, for instance. Good way to spot a bunker, but depending on how fast this jungle recovers, maybe a good way to spot the plane, too."

"Yup," said the Colonel. But his hands had started clenching, whitening with each pop-up. And he was licking his lips, his face set and going sallow beneath that weathered skin. Shit, thought Michael, should he say something? He didn't want to humiliate the man. He keyed the intercom.

"Hanny?"

"Yes, Sir?"

"You up for some Monkees?"

Dead silence, then a weak, "Sir?"

So Michael just started singing, soft and sweet, "Here we come . . ." He saw out of the corner of his eyes the Colonel's helmet jerk, undoubtedly with a start of surprise, and Michael carried on until Hanny joined in, doing the drum roll the way he always did with his left hand fingers hard against the bulkhead near his radio mike as they both belted it out, "Hey, hey, we're the Monkees", and on to monkeying around, finished the first verse, and skipped the next verse because neither could remember it, modulating up to do the second refrain.

The Colonel was easing, able to raise his hand to wipe at his upper lip, even show a bit of a smile. So after a closing high "Owww!" and "Watch out!," Michael vamped on into "Take The Last Train to Clarksville" and the Colonel even chimed in on "And I don't know if I'm ever coming' home," with Hanny picking up the falsetto on the "doo doo doo doos" and the train whistle.

It went on like that for the next two hours, lots of green beauty, once in awhile a steepled pagoda sticking up in the distance, almost white. A softer world than Nam, no Charlies down below, no fear beating in the blades. This was happiness, this he could do, was doing, and taking pleasure from it.

And the Colonel was really getting into it – he was an S and G addict, especially "Mrs. Robinson" which began to get a little old by lunchtime. They had taken on extra fuel at L.P., but no harm in topping up the Loach. And locating as many fuel dumps as they could.

"Anybody hungry?" Michael asked, and got a hearty response. "Hanny, we near that fuel dump supposed to be around here? We can get gas, park and eat there." Willy had supplied them with sandwiches.

"Yeah," Hanny said. "Sir. Wind her up and go south about fifteen minutes, turn east and we should spy it, but I suggest we go high to do it."

"Gotcha," said Michael, and did. So it was kind of a surprise that within only a minute or two and from altitude Michael spotted a glint on the side of a ridge. He went down, cruised to it, flew over fast, no fire, did a quick pedal turn, hovered, and they peered. Hanny declared it first. "Looks like a ditched truck, Cam. Sir." And they got going again.

"Marvelous! Marvelous!" the Colonel was heard muttering.

They'd gone south and had just turned east for the fuel dump when the UHF suddenly came to life, startling Michael so he was slow in answering, and the voice repeated, "This is Cricket calling Vientiane flight 7-1." Seventh take-off for the morning, one and only Loach.

"Yeah," Michael responded. "Sorry. Slow on the uptake." He reached and flicked on the Colonel's UHF receiver for him.

"You guys west of the Mekong, right?" And then a muttered but good humored, "Nobody sure as hell else is." Nothing like honest flight plans.

"Yes," Michael answered.

"We got an AA recon down at a STOL site, two crewmen been pole-axed. Can you help?"

Michael's heart sank. "Yeah, maybe," he said, "hold on a minute." So much for pleasure – it meant, after all, not only putting his commanding officer in harm's way but this precious aircraft. He keyed the Colonel. It was his mission, not Michael's, which was the aircraft in flight. All he could do was hope the two didn't conflict. And of course, right now, he knew there was plenty to conflict. Still, nothing for it. "Your call, Sir."

"Can't be helped," he said.

"Not really, no, Sir."

"Then go."

Michael brought up UHF. "If you'll give me the coordinates, I'll relay 'em to my Crew Chief who's navigating us. Give me a second." He keyed Hanny in on the lot, gave him the gist, let him hear the coordinates, which spotted the STOL they'd been heading for.

Michael told Cricket they were on their way, and got Cricket to relay the good news to the downed airmen. Then he went high and blistered, fishing out his Car-15 and its banana clip to thrust them at the Colonel.

"You in harness, Hanny?"

"Just hooking up, Sir."

"What kind of recon're these men doing, way out here?" the Colonel asked.

"Maybe doing what we're doing, Sir," Michael answered, "looking for the Volpar." And now he put on FM and started calling the guys on the ground. In no time, the pilot, Simon Fess according to Cricket, was on the air, whispering, breathless. He said he and his observer had lost their plane to an ambush. "The dinks are at the south end. Where the fuel bladders are – and our plane. We managed to get into the jungle off the strip, but my Porter's a goner." He went silent, and Michael could hear over his mike an AK and then a bang-crump. Shit, grenade launcher. Fess came on air again with a panicked "Shit!" and his voice going high, "We can see you, we can see you, tell us where to go, God – "

The Colonel suddenly came on air. "How about that road over there – two klicks at about 10:30."

Michael turned the Loach to see, too, spoke to Fess, using his best FNG voice. "Okay, now, Mr. Fess, we're gonna get you, don't you worry, easy as cake. Do you know a dirt road off the strip to the northeast?"

Fess did, said he thought they could get to it. Already his voice was quieter. Nothing like a focus to bring a man down.

"Good," Michael said, "you start moving and we'll try to keep the bad guys busy."

He turned the Loach around to the south. "Okay, gentlemen," he said to Hanny and the Colonel, "we're going to swing around across the end of the strip, to the left so both of you can fire." The Colonel had a clip in his weapon, his spare under his thigh. He for God's sake was wearing a grin. And suddenly, an explosion behind them. "Grenade!" From Hanny. He already had his M-16 working.

Looking down, they all saw two bad guys break cover, start running. Not uniformed, guerrillas. One threw his AK away. Jammed, Michael guessed. But the other was still tossing bullets up at them. And then came another grenade, but the launcher didn't seem to know how to lead and again it exploded behind them.

As Michael wheeled back, the Colonel let loose with the Car-15 and dropped the first runner. "Got him!" he yelped. "Turn around, Michael!"

Which Michael did. The rush was even taking him, now, who really didn't want to be doing this.

Hanny had taken out the second AK. When they reached the area from which the grenades had been launched, all was still. Lots of underbrush there. Could hold any number of dinks. Hanny lobbed out one of their own eggs just as a lesson, and Michael headed for the dirt road, eyes roving.

Michael keyed the FM. "Come on, Mr. Fess. You there yet?"

Silence.

"Mr. Fess, come on now."

"We made it!" Fess at last.

Not yet, Michael thought. Too much weight, but no need to say so. The small Lu tribesman would be light, at least. Michael was reluctant to unload fuel.

He came in low and slow to the road and hovered there. Not easy. Nothing but two deep ruts, with the crown between higher than either verge. Too high for the Loach to straddle, and the verges too far apart anyhow.

"All right. Gentlemen," he started, over the intercom, "keep an eye out, please. And let's hope our friends get here before the bad guys come up out of their holes. I will rest our left skid on the crown and hover in balance 'til one or the other turns up. If it's Mr. Fess and company, I'll lower the right skid as far as I can and still allow them to get under the blades to reach us. That's the side the strip is on and they'll be coming from there. When I do that, Hanny, I want you to hang your ass out the left door, we're gonna need all the weight we can get on that side to keep us from rolling over. Got it?"

"Yup," said Hanny.

"But keep your sling on, we don't want to lose you."

So that's what Michael did, glad they didn't have the weight of a minigun aboard after all, and thinking he'd straddled like this sometime before, somewhere, but couldn't remember exactly – and then he did. He hadn't done it. Kathleen had, in her jeep.

Then he saw them, breaking out of the jungle, the little Asian coming pell mell.

"Comin' from the left, Cam!" Hanny yelled through the intercom.

The left? Jesus. How the hell did the dinks get there? Jumped the ditch, asshole. The Colonel and Hanny, both on the left side, were just asking to be hit. At least the AA guys were protected – by the Loach, God damn it, it was taking hits. But now he heard Hanny's M-16. The Colonel had whipped up the Car-15, was working it. Michael went on lowering the skid, putting it down as far as he judged he could go, shouting at the AA men, "Come on, come on, get the lead out!"

They did, ducking way down beneath the blades. Michael could feel the dip as the Lu scrambled in, then almost lost the balance, almost dipped the blades into the ground as the heavier Fess leaped in after him.

Hanny was now yelling, "Didi, God damn it, now! Now!"

Michael jerked aft on the cyclic, yanked in a load of collective, and wrenched the Loach up. It shuddered, hesitated, Hanny and the Colonel still firing, and the Loach still taking hits, thunk, thunk, thunk. Finally, the chopper lifted, and they were airborne.

"How're you little darlin's doin' back there?" he said to Hanny.

"Handy dandy," Hanny answered.

"Colonel?" Michael asked.

"The same," came the answer, accompanied by a quick grin. "Jesus!" he said over the intercom, "this has to be the sexiest damned thing that ever flew!"

Michael shook his head, but had to throw a small grin back even so. If we can just keep her goin', he thought.

"Instruments all look normal, Hanny. You want to put down, have a look? I'll tell you, I wouldn't be too thrilled. Hard enough getting up the first time."

"Let's chance not, then," Hanny said. And they headed for L.P.

Only as the jungle was flowing back beneath them did Michael realize the fear hadn't returned. Anger had, that even this gentler green of Laos held little hunters.

* * *

The afternoon was running out when they got to L.P., and they'd already decided to stay down. Hanny wanted to check the bullet holes. So they'd radio'd a message to Willy they weren't at all sure he'd receive. But he was waiting when they arrived. A miracle man.

The minute the Lu got out of the chopper he bowed his thanks, turned and ran, probably for the can. Fess, young and looking like Opie's best friend with flaxen hair, very blue eyes, and a wide smile revealing crooked teeth, came around the Loach to Michael and grabbed his hand to wring it sore.

"Anything, any time," he said fervently, "I owe you, Mister."

"That's okay," Michael said, retrieving his hand.

"No, I mean it, I mean it! In fact . . ." and Fess reached inside his shirt and pulled out a white brick of what had to be pressed refined heroin. "I'll share it with you," he declared. "Best Burmese horse from Ban Houei Say! You deserve it, all of you!"

Amazed, the three Loach crew looked at each other, and the Colonel and Hanny started to laugh. Not Michael. He'd put the Loach, his two crew, and Kathleen all at risk for a white powder brick of dope? The anger from earlier damned near swamped him, but he held silent, only turned his back on Fess and headed for the small worn Renault Willy had found to rent somewhere, just catching out of the corner of his eye Fess's crestfallen face. "I mean it!" the AA pilot said. "Any time!"

A Royal Laotian Army soldier was waiting with Willy. He'd be guarding the aircraft. Just how the hell Michael would get around the guard was one more darling problem to solve.

Hanny came, reported no mortal damage. It would require major shop work to close up the holes, but they could fly. Thank God for something, anyway. Hanny said he was going to hang around, do some work on it, and Michael grabbed it as an excuse to remain at the airport, too. So Willy and the Colonel went off to the hotel Willy'd found, the Colonel issuing an invitation out the window as they drove off to drinks and dinner at six-thirty, Willy happily having reported a lounge stocked with Scotch and, as the Colonel echoed relievedly, by-God bourbon.

Hanny eyed Michael. "You signing on to help?" he asked skeptically. Michael shook his head. "See you later." And he went looking for the Air America hooch.

He found it, not too far away, an open-aired building that looked like it had taken some mortars in its time, housing their OPs, a TV that was receiving more static and snow than program, and four or five AA guys watching it and drinking beer.

Michael hesitated, then crossed to them. "Um – sorry to interrupt. My name's Cameron. I wonder if uh – " Nobody as much as looked around at him. Michael sighed, raised his voice. "I'm looking for a pad in L.P. Thought you guys might know of one."

Finally, one of the AA men turned from the TV, took in Michael's lieutenant's bars, his army camouflage, and shot a finger at a bulletin board on a wall, immediately turning back to the TV. Still no telling what was on it.

The bulletin board was covered with bits and pieces of paper that were red with Laotian dust and had to've been there for months, years maybe. But there were some keys hanging from nails, too, with labels, so he began shuffling through them, peering to read – and found one that might do. "Meisner's place," the label began. "Apartment, second floor of house, Mr. and Mrs. Fong downstairs, landlord and hooch maid. Leased through October. Any contribution gratefully accepted to defray pre-paid rent – Fong won't refund, the bastard. Double bed, kitchenette." Order of importance, no doubt. It finished, "Gone to Angola. Bye bye."

Michael carried it back to the TV. "Where do I make a contribution to Meisner?"

The same guy sighed, kicked back his chair, went to the desk, jerked open a drawer and pulled out a pint plastic ice-cream container, held it out to Michael. "A map's inside there, too," he said.

Michael took it, saw Meisner's name printed in felt pen across the top, took out a fifty, figuring once Kathleen got there he wouldn't need it for long but the rate things were going who knew how long it'd be before she got there. Leaving the bill for the map, he looked up to find the AA guy watching with disapproval, so Michael added a twenty.

"One week," the guy said. Michael added another fifty to get some more time, decided that was plenty, put the top on and set the container on the desk. He was moving for the door, when he heard, "Cameron?" He looked back. "They're sayin' you were a hot dog in Nam." No answer for that. Michael just waited. "You need any help findin' our boys, just ask."

Michael finally nodded, thinking the world was full of surprises, and left to scrounge up a car and driver. They hung around the AA hooch all the time, apparently. It was getting on towards six, so he put off finding Meisner's place – no hurry any way, was his gloomy thought – and went to the Swiss hotel Willy had found for them.

It looked pleasant enough. When he signed in at the desk, he asked about a phone. The small Laotian desk clerk who had welcomed him effusively and had just finished spieling off all the wonders of his hostelry – river view, very clean, "continental cuisine" in the dining room, electric and water on for four hours in the morning, four hours in the late day, best hotel in Luang Prabang – was devastated to admit to any flaw at all. "Yes, yes, yes," he said, encouragingly, "is phone, Lieutenant!" But then, he had to say, "So sorry. Must abandon all hope. In Luang Prabang, every place in Laos, no phone after four, and sometimes . . ." He shook his head sorrowfully and shrugged.

Thinking about Tom, Michael found his room, and his duffle already there, thanks to the tireless Willy. Tom must be drawn tight with worry. Angry as Michael had been with him the last night in Hong Kong, this wasn't fair.

He rummaged, got the Glenlivet, poured himself a light double which drained the bottle, and grabbed a shave. When he got to the lounge, Hanny and the Colonel were already there, Hanny very relieved to see him. Where Willy had disappeared to never came up. They all had a drink, Michael's a single this time, and discussed plans for the next day. Then Michael begged off dinner to take a walk, pleading he wasn't hungry, and went – leaving Hanny looking appalled. The last thing he wanted, Michael knew, was to sit across a dinner table for an hour with the Colonel, *any* colonel, and make polite conversation. Too bad. Michael had some heavy thinking to do, mainly how to cut Hanny out of it.

He headed off the main drag away from the river. Shops were all wide open. Merchants nodded, smiled, invited him in to look – "no buy!" – and him feeling like Gulliver in Lilliput.

These people were something else. Never tell in a million years that men – and kids, for God's sake, from what was said last night at Mam'selle Josie's – were dying from bombs and artillery less than fifty miles east. Much as he liked them, and he did, very much, he'd seen even back in Burma the indifference felt by the light-skinned plains people in the cities for the darker, smaller hill tribes of their own nation. Worse than indifference. A kind of xenophobic shame. He would be bothered for a long time to come by that Meo refugee camp in Vientiane, by the small hill people he saw scurrying tonight, faces lowered, along these streets in this old capital, having fled down their mountains from God knew what kind of miseries. But the Laotians weren't bothered. Nor were the emigré Chinese merchants in business here. As he walked amongst them, he felt their energy, their cheeriness, with their bright lights pooling down around them, fragile walls against a war coming closer and closer.

There was a fair of sorts strung with Christmas tree lights and he turned into it. Charcoal fires cooked meats that smelled of garlic and hot spices. Meats, in a Buddhist land? Everything changes, Michael thought. Women smoked cigars, legs folded under their sarongs, and sold American black market goods. Music, including rock and roll, blasted from loudspeakers, and every other booth and every square foot of ground offered gambling games, mostly the animal game Michael had seen in Keng Tung on market day, men squatting by the painted cloth throwing dice.

He came out the other side of the fair, looked down a street, saw Chinese signs and headed in that direction. Deep into what had to be Luang Prabang's Chinatown, he stopped at a restaurant. Not that he'd been looking for one. But then, maybe he had. Time to stop running from it and deal with it. What to do about Hanny.

Balanced precariously on a little three-legged stool, he could sit at a table on the street, which pleased him, and he ordered fried noodles, a chicken-vegetable dish, and hot tea. The chicken turned out to be tough and high, the noodles very good, so he ordered another bowl along with salt for the green tea.

Could he really pull it off without Hanny? That's why Hanny was here, for God's sake. But time was running out for Kathleen and that baby. And for them, too. The speed trap today – that's what Hanny was calling the ambush at the fuel dump, a speed trap – it could as easily have been them taken by surprise and caught in it. And then Kathleen would be lost.

Hanny might never forgive him. Ditching his best friend, he'd call it. What happened to trust? he'd ask. But if it went bad, and they got caught, it'd mean years of prison. So be it, for Michael. His gamble, his choice. But Hanny had a baby on the way that ever since the last morning at Da Nang had been at the back of Michael's mind, jumping up and down.

Twilight was gone. Never lasted long in the tropics after sunset. Which settled it. Sunlight meant moonlight. Maybe. They'd avoided rain all day, somehow. The wind took it around them, or maybe the monsoon was really giving up. Thing was . . . yeah, thing was they couldn't wait for a good time. Day time. It had to be at night. Shit, this night. And he'd do it alone.

18

He picked up a cab on the edge of Chinatown. Too bad he hadn't checked out Meisner's place. He'd have to put Kathleen into it sight unseen.

Lord, Lord, he'd maybe be seeing *her* in just three hours. Or maybe two and half. Would she even recognize him? Sure she would. Sure she would, just as he would her. Hadn't he been learning that lesson, the past seven days? Five. Only five days. And he knew now she'd be alive in his head 'til the day he died.

Would it be the same for her? Even if it was, what would that mean? Big difference between memories and a future. What if there was no meaning any more? Without her, before the letter from Richard, he'd already been thinking of green rice and hill tribes and demonstration farms, hadn't he? But would it have lasted? Nothing had much, the past four years.

What would he do if the meaning was gone? Truth told, the best thing he had going for him was flying the damned Loach, taking out dinks. Like today. What meaning in that? And if she ever found it out, it'd take more than a little meaning to hold it together with her, and she would, how not? Still, meaningful or no, he was good at it. Yeah, today proved it. The past couple, three weeks in Nam seeming to the contrary, he was still damned good at it. And there were always plenty of wars going on.

But he should be figuring out how he was going to do it alone, not maundering on about nonsense. What, you think she'll be waiting at the airport for you to arrive on the jet plane so she can throw herself into your arms? Dumb-ass.

He'd monitor the tower and when the air lanes were free he'd go up dark, follow the river west, then north, track time and speed for distance, turn left, pick up the lights of Keng Tung, turn left, and in a while there'd be the lights of Loi Long. Sure, and worry about fuel on the flight back. At least the moon had popped up. To stay?

The cab turned into the airport terminal. He stopped it, got out, and walked into the darkness to the helicopter pad, a brown-out in effect, maybe because of poor power or maybe for safety's sake. First thing he'd have to do was get rid of the Laotian guard. Pay him off to go home, that way he'd at least keep his mouth shut until Michael got back.

But he was nowhere around. Brown-out or no, he could see that. The moon was big and reflecting off haze and clouds. Good light, right now. The Loach creaked. Probably catching a nap in the back cabin. Michael moved closer, only to see something – someone a hell of a lot bigger than that little guard ease out to the ground. Hanny. For God's sake.

"What're you doing here?" He almost croaked it.

"Might ask you the same thing," Hanny said. "Oh, I sent the guard off for some supper, if you're wondering." They stood there on the pad, peering through the brown-out at each other, Michael thinking maybe they'd square off. Didn't want that, he really didn't.

"What were you thinking, ditch me and go off on your own?"

"Hanny – " Michael started.

"Just like that," Hanny was going on. "Get me to this end of the world country, and cut me out. Jesus, Mary and Joseph, you going to sit there, one hand on the stick, the other with a red flashlight, map on your knees, while you try to read it and up pops a mountain thirty meters higher than the fuckin' map shows and you go crunch? Or hell, go one quarter click off course, the moon maybe goes hiding, and there you are, sweetheart, lost in the back of beyond forever. Unh, unh, Michael. Not in the cards."

Michael heaved in a breath. No fight, anyway. "We're never gonna get free of the Colonel in daylight, and the fucking Volpar is in all probability unfindable. Her baby's maybe dying out there."

Hanny stared at him, then he leaned back against the chopper, his arms folded across his wide chest. "Like to ask you something. Have you ever once considered not going? Even for a minute?"

Michael looked at Hanny almost thinking it was funny, as if he really wanted to know, as if it mattered somehow, whatever he might decide afterwards. "No, Neal. I've thought a lot of things, some of them pretty damned black, but never once about changing my mind."

Hanny nodded, straightened up. "So. I've been doing some thinking of my own, and I've figured it out."

"What?" Michael asked, almost bewildered by the shift.

Hanny glanced off to one side. "Guard's comin' back. We'll talk at the hotel."

"But – "

"The hotel," Hanny said, starting away towards the terminal. With a nod to the guard, Michael caught up, and across the tarmac came the cab he'd used to come out here, must've been hoping for the return fare.

They didn't need to say it, both just understood the cab was not the place. They were quiet for the first mile or so, then Hanny asked, "What's she look like?"

"Shoot, if you really have figured it out, you're gonna see soon enough for yourself."

Hanny swivelled around in the corner of the seat to look more directly at Michael. "Beautiful, huh?" he asked, with a small grin. "Must be."

Michael looked him back, thinking of all the parts of her, the whole of her, and shook his head. "Couldn't tell you, even if I tried. How she looked to me."

"Come on, man, talk to me. I mean, I'm here, you know? What's she like?"

Michael turned his gaze out the window at the passing rice paddies gleaming silver in the moonlight, squared by black dikes and lines of palm-trees. "I was remembering something earlier. Straddling that ox-cart track this afternoon reminded me." He gave it a moment. Then, "You ever keep a tab? You know, a count of the dinks you've finished off?"

"Shit, no. Have you?"

Michael shook his head. "Anyway, we'd been driving along a rutted dirt road like that – well, Kathleen was driving, she was a genius at it, somehow sensed ahead of time to avoid it when a wheel was about to slip off into the rut, God, they were at least three feet deep, and I didn't have an inkling. Me at the wheel and we'd've been there a week waiting for a buffalo to come haul us out.

"So all of a sudden, she asked if I'd ever delivered a kid. Well I had, so – "

"Huh?"

"Yeah, never mind. Thing was, so had she. She stopped, even turned off the ignition. She said she had something to tell me. She shouldn't've. Stopped, I mean. That land was never empty, dacoits everywhere . . ." He saw Hanny, watching him, and explained. "Bandits. Or insurgents. All over the place.

"Anyway, what she wanted me to know was, when she was delivering her first baby, both it and the mother died." Hanny whistled in some air. "Yeah. She was ashamed. Sorrowed. And so determined that I know the worst about her, she was trembling. 'I think you should know that two human beings have died at my hands', is what she said. Barely eighteen." Michael swallowed, cleared his throat. "You know what else? She'd found herself a nurse afterwards and got trained in childbirth, always carried a kit around with her in case. We had one with us in the jeep that day."

After a few moments, Hanny said, "Brave girl."

Michael gave a grunt of agreement, and thought, oh, yes. Wanting me to know. And getting back on the horse, learning it right and doing it. He was glad to be done with the story, his voice had been turning difficult, why the hell had he started it in the first place?

Silent again, looking out the window, Michael saw the moon glinting now on the river, knew where he was in the city, and couldn't contain it any longer. He leaned forward, got the driver to stop and let them out. "We walk the rest of the way," he said.

Hanny was paying the tab. "How do we do it?" Michael fairly snapped it. Hanny turned as the taxi drove off, looked at Michael, started a grin, and headed off to the riverside. Teasing him, damn his hide. "Neal!"

And Hanny started, rapping it out. "We do it tomorrow, late day the way we've always planned it. We fly out in the morning, same as usual, but during the day we see . . . hell, I don't know, see a problem . . . something. Tell the Colonel the bullets did more damage than I thought. So we drop him off here at LP and say we have to fly on down to the shop in Vientiane, this one here's not good enough, we may get back tomorrow night, maybe not 'til day after tomorrow. Anybody phones down – like the Colonel," Hanny chuckled, "shit, some Laotian'll be saying, 'who? who? he not here, nobody here that name', and no matter the shouting and screaming, it'll get the Colonel nowhere, Willy either, and they'll chalk it up to Laotian whatever. It'll work, Cam." He grinned a little. "Just thank God for speed traps."

Michael reached, swivelled Hanny around to face him, staring at him and shaking his head at it. So simple. "It never occurred to me," Michael said. And he was close to overwhelmed with the relief.

"Yeah, well," said Hanny, "panic can do that." And sounding very modest, he added, "We only took fire this afternoon, after all. And a retard like yourself, you need more time to think things out." And he started walking again.

They were moving along the river bank now. There was the usual sharp mud smell of Asian tropical rivers in the monsoon. On some docks, families hunkered with noodles or rice cooking over charcoal braziers that had their own smell wafting like mist through the air. And boats skittered everywhere like bugs. And the moon still up there, clean and bright. He could've gone tonight, he could've.

And come a cloud, crunched a mountain, too.

"Right. So," Hanny said, "you gonna tell her what you've been doing the last two years?"

Michael wished he could laugh. "The problem had already occurred to me." His voice went wry. "And of course – she'll want to know."

"It won't matter," Hanny said. Michael looked up, found Hanny with a little smile, so sure.

Their path ran into some godowns now that turned them away from the river. They picked their pace up, the hotel just along the way. "I could sure use a drink," Michael said. "Not the best idea."

They went quiet, now, companionable, felt that way to Michael, anyway. But thoughts sharpened knives in his head. Of Hanny's family mainly. "My turn, Neal," he said. "How come with all this mess you haven't changed your mind?"

Hanny shook his head, finally joked, "Ask me again some night when we get sloshed."

What the hell did *that* mean? But they were at the hotel. They headed straight through the lobby and into the corridor to their rooms, Hanny's on beyond Michael's, Hanny walking on.

Michael was fiddling with his key in the lock, not working worth a damn, when Hanny swivelled around. "Did those what'dy'call'em dacoits turn up?"

Michael got the door unlocked. "Oh, yeah. Kathleen took care of 'em." He grinned sidewise at Hanny. "Told 'em I was a great teacher of pigs and chickens to get 'em to produce more, and needed the jeep."

"That worked?" Incredulous, of course.

"Yup. Man, did we laugh afterwards." His grin went soft. "She has a laugh to tickle a stone. Had. Maybe still."

Hanny was moving again for his room, his own laugh a low rumble. "You and Dr. Doolittle."

Michael was nearly through his door, when once again, Hanny turned around and trudged back.

"Michael?" He looked for all the world embarrassed.

Full of his own confusions, his own scares like a little boy, Michael had to seek his perceptions of Hanny from way down, and it took time.

Meanwhile, Hanny was saying. "Maybe you don't even know it, but you got something going with this girl – about the closest thing to what I guess they call passion I've ever touched. And once this deal's over, and my tour, I go home, run my pop's body shop, and get old on memories, so – " he fetched it up dryly, "hell, y'never know, it might rub off."

There wasn't even a moment and he was heading back to his room, Michael standing frozen, not knowing whether to have forced a meeting of eyes with Hanny or to've looked away.

Didn't matter. His door open, Hanny looked back at Michael, raised his voice. "By the way, thanks for dumping me with the Colonel. You owe me." Had an edge to it. But it sure was the understatement of the earth.

Michael entered his room, leaned back, eyes closed. Full of hope for tomorrow on the one hand, more than since the start back in Hong Kong. But thinking about Hanny, what a bitch. A new wife, a kid on the way, and still having to get it second hand.

He climbed slowly out of his clothes, fell on the bed. Yeah, he and Kathleen had had it the once. Should he be grateful for that? The memories of it had been driving him crazy. Maybe someday. Maybe even tomorrow night. He rolled to his side, bunched the pillow under his face, determined to sleep. He hoped Hanny wouldn't have to be disappointed.

DAY SIX

19

The day had started slowly. Michael had given Hanny a hand repairing the bullet holes in the Loach's skin in the early morning, and before they'd left he tried to reach Tom from an airport phone, only to be told there'd be a forty-five minute wait, so he'd had to let it go.

Two hours later now, and they were flying northwest across the Nam Tha River but staying a couple of ridges south of the Phong Saly Road. The Chinese were building it across northern Laos from Vietnam to China. In effect, it was turning the entire Laotian province of Phong Saly into Chinese territory. Not a good place to be seen, or to go down, either. If Hanny's dark prediction about China was true and worse came to worse, they would search up there for the Volpar, but only then.

The weather kept turning on them so they had to dodge rain storms, find their way out of sudden fogs. The little scout was maneuverable in bad stuff like that. A Volpar would more than likely have plowed straight into the mountainside, so they covered the mountainsides as best they could wherever they were. No luck.

And all the while, Michael couldn't get his head off it. Today, today, God, it sang inside him like an S & G top-of-the-charts.

The intercom woke up. "Sir? Lieutenant?" It was Hanny. "Two o'clock, about four hundred meters."

It was a STOL strip running diagonally up the mountain, built that way so that going uphill on landing would help slow the plane, downhill on take off would lend speed. As Michael slowed and hovered along it, they could see the swath that had been crashed into and through the jungle at the top of the runway. And there was the small propeller passenger plane. Its wings had sheared, its prop blades bent and forever useless. Michael set down. He kept his own blades turning.

The three of them sat a moment in silence, finding it hard to believe that the search was over. Even in just the day and half, it had come to seem to all of them, though rarely spoken, a fruitless duty. Weight lifting from him, Michael had the dry thought that Tom's God had just come through with the blessing Tom had asked for.

That aside, his eyes were roving the area constantly, and so were the Colonel's. Finally, Michael said, "All right, let's have a look. Carry your firearms, Gentlemen." The Colonel lifted the Car-15, but offered it to Michael. Michael shook his head, shut down, and after getting out, took his .38 from its holster. Hanny carried his M-16.

Standing on the dirt strip, the Colonel's eyes were lifted up toward the top of the ridge. "Oh, shit," he murmured. "Michael?" And he nodded up the mountainside. All looked, and there, lifting from the other side of the ridge-top, came smokey haze. A village.

On the ground, it was now the Colonel's command, so Michael just looked at him and waited. "Let's step on it," he said. And all three moved quietly and carefully to the broken Volpar.

They could see into the cockpit and through the torn fuselage into the cabin that the plane was empty. The accident – rather, the crash – had caused the plane to partly disintegrate. But there were bullet holes, too. Whether they'd followed the crash or caused it there was no knowing.

There was a faint trace of charcoal fires in the air, probably from across the ridge-top. Hanny was sniffing high, like a bird dog. "Give me a minute," he said. And he slowly moved away, into the jungle.

The Colonel and Michael watched him go, waited, lost sight of him, and then he was there, back with them. He jerked his head towards the way he'd gone, and led the way back. In not too long a time, Michael could smell what Hanny had detected right away: animal decay.

They came to a sunken bare area, loose dirt scattered around, small mounds of it piled up all over the place. Probably by digging tree rats. They had revealed what was buried there – two bodies, their parts in disarray, their flesh putrid.

"I'll be back," Michael said. He went to the Loach, got out two of the survival kits, and after a little thought, looking back up that mountainside, he cranked.

He returned to the others, and he and Hanny opened the kits, took out the collapsible shovels.

"Don't you have three of those?" the Colonel asked.

"Yup," Michael said, crouched by the grave. Then he looked up at the Colonel, spoke with deliberate formality. "May I speak, Sir?"

"Sure," the Colonel said, sounding annoyed.

"I would greatly appreciate your getting back into the helicopter." He knew he couldn't order him. "Colonel, I'm concerned about that village. And it'll be easier to didi mau if only two of us are scrambling."

The Colonel took a deep breath, sighed it out, gave a loose salute and trudged away. Breathing through their mouths, Hanny and Michael started digging. It wasn't pleasant, but the clothing was still recognizable as such. Both bodies were men, skin discolored, swollen, torn by marauders, but the hair was still intact. Both were white. The shirts had bullet holes.

"Looks like we got us another speed trap," Hanny said.

"You know how old Beaumont is?" Michael asked. And then, at Hanny's inquiring look, "No grey hair here."

Now Hanny peered at one of the shirts, its pocket. Damp with all kinds of fluids by this time, not just blood, the outline of a pair of eyeglasses showed through. With two unhappy fingers, Michael eased the glasses out. "Might help identify him. Doesn't look like much else will."

They scraped wrists into view. No watches. No rings on fingers. No ID tags around wrists or necks. Down by the feet, bare, boots taken, there was a wallet. Hanny picked it up gingerly, tossed it open, and there was a picture of a little family – wife, child, daddy. Which body it belonged to they couldn't tell, but they kept both the wallet and the picture. The only other clue was that one set of clothes was a two-toned grey uniform. AA. Insignia, if there had been any, was missing.

"Okay. Enough's enough," Michael said. And he started shoveling dirt back over the bodies, Hanny doing the same.

By the time they finished and got back to the Loach, they were both running, but Michael didn't lift at once. He keyed the intercom. "We can go up there, Colonel, see what we can see."

"Negative," said the Colonel. "Can you two bring the Loach back here? Find your way?"

"Yeah." Hanny's answer was prompt.

Michael shrugged. "If he says so. I sure could try, but Hanny's got the calculations and the maps."

"I'm not going to send you over that ridge, either one of you. You'd end by being taken prisoner, too, or worse, and you can't speak the language. All told, not a good idea."

"Well, not the both of us, no, Colonel. Somebody has to run the boat. Hanny can do that and I could – "

The Colonel cut Michael off with sharp head shake. "Let's go."

Michael lifted at once, staying low to head sharply away from the ridge and its hidden village.

The Colonel gave it a few minutes, then he keyed the intercom. "Been thinking about it," he said. "You got Long Tieng on those maps of yours, Hanny?"

"Yes, Sir. Marked in by hand at Mam'selle Josie's."

"Can we get there from here?"

There was a silence. Finally, heavily, "Yes, Sir. Some north of Vientiane and east of the Mekong. We better refuel in L.P."

Michael had to swallow against the vomit rising in his throat. That far east there'd be no way to go any place except where this man chose, sure as hell not all the way back west to Burma.

"Michael?" the Colonel was saying. "Contact what do you call it, Cricket? Get them to relay to General Vang Pao that we want permission to fly in. Use it all – Lieutenant Colonel blah blah blah, the United States Military Attaché to Laos, and his two aids."

"Yes, Sir," Michael said, and began radio communications.

No way could Michael belt out rock, Hanny, either. They stayed silent. Luckily, the Colonel didn't notice. He was busy scribbling in the little pad he kept in his breast pocket. When he noticed Michael looking at him, he grinned: "Practicing my pitch," he said. Michael nodded as if he understood.

He should be diddling the throttle, trying to catch a stall, trying to diddle the Colonel. But he couldn't. It was one thing when the search was fixing to go on forever. But not now. They knew where those ten men probably were. But held for what purpose, and in what kind of shape? It really kind of surprised Michael, but he found himself unable to turn his back on them, not even for Kathleen. Kathleen. Which made him about as sick as her baby might be by now.

Here came Hanny over the intercom. "Lieutenant? Everything okay up there? Any mysterious noise?" Trying to open the door for him, bless his heart. "You never know, Sir, after yesterday . . . "

"Everything's just fine up here, Neal," Michael said, his voice heavy, the choice made.

"Right," said Hanny, voice down low, too. "Yeah, right."

They refueled in L.P., left word for Willy where they were going and where they'd spend the night, then flew on down and east. Forever moving in the God damned wrong direction.

20

The sun was passed the meridian, that's what Tom had always taught her to say for straight overhead, and sooner than the day would end in the plains, the sun would sink behind the high peaks on her left. Just a little farther, and surely a creek or a small river would cross the path. There'd been only springs and seeps and tiny streams waterfalling so sheerly down the mountainsides that sure-footed or not the pony would have slipped on the mud and gone down.

There had been a time, even before Cho was born, when she'd thought of Tom with a fierce desire that her child know him and his life. But she'd recognized all along it would have to wait until after the opium harvest for the pack train. It would have made all the difference had she been able to follow the Kha River out of Loi Long into Laos all the way to the Mekong. But she'd long heard tales, had even seen some of it herself, of the narrow defiles, the precipitous cataracts. Not a horse nor even herself could pass along the Kha for much distance.

But now, with summer gone, the days were short in these mountains. This one was kinder than yesterday. Then it had rained off and on, off and on, and thank heaven and Daw Kyi for the plastic sheet. It hadn't kept her and Cho truly dry, but not dripping either, just dampish. And, of course, she'd had the supply of cooked rice so she hadn't needed to boil up any.

But the fire, even if tiny, had been wonderful. Both inside and out. Ever since she'd sent the bullet at the Shan's face she'd felt a cold dreadful thing sitting heavy under her heart like an iceberg. Or what she thought an iceberg might feel like. Unmelting, radiating chill, unremitting hardness, sharp and cutting away little pieces of herself. Or was it a glacier creeping through her, carrying the blackness of the world?

The pistol shot, the cry that followed, still horrified her ears. She feared she might hear them 'til she died. Lim Pong had gone down in front of the pony, but her strength had come from somewhere and she'd dug her boot heels into the pony's sides hard, so hard he leapt forward and over his old master. What made her such a stranger to herself was that she knew that she would do it again, to save Cho.

She'd been unable to control or guide the runaway pony, able only to keep her seat and soften the motion for the baby. The pony galloped down the path to the dirt roadway, around the town and on out the trail taken by the pack train. As if he'd known her destination. Or had taken it so often he thought there was nowhere else to go.

The rain had started after awhile, and the pony'd had to slow down, the track turning to mud that was halfway up his hoof, the bedrock slippery beneath. It was a slow rain, she might have called it an easy rain if she'd been under a roof somewhere, nothing harsh or slashing about it, without wind. They would be all right, it allowed her to tell Cho, which she did, over and over again, murmuring to him, her voice comforting herself as much as the baby.

Once in awhile she would stop, there were sometimes little grassy verges which the pony would graze while she either nursed Cho or pursed half-digested rice into his mouth from her own. He took both with equal immediate hunger, but the eagerness didn't last long. He seemed to grow tired too soon. U-pym had not told her about this, his too-easy repletion. Kathleen had just assumed it was only the meagerness of her own milk that had turned that little face aside. And it was at these times in the quiet, able to hear the insects, the rustling in the branches or underfoot, that she knew her back still hurt. She tried to look at it, couldn't really see, but her shirt showed blood stains. That was all right, that was good, if it bled it mightn't infect.

Last night, before it grew too dark, she had hobbled the pony to a tree trunk where there was grazing, and had walked off with the dah into the deeper forest in search of some woodfalls that would be dry enough to burn. She had thought of that, at least. The tinder box. An old lidded tin, not very big, in which she'd kept tiny treasures when little, painted with a fairy princess on top. She had put into it small packets of needle and thread, and cotton lint, and matches. The dampness hadn't permeated it. Not yet, anyway.

She knew, because Michael had told her, that certain jungle vines and trees had a pith inside that would burn, even in the monsoon. And had told her, too, what the bark looked like, both wet and dry. He had read a survival manual the Brits had used in Malaya during the war, read it when he was only thirteen. That bottomless curiosity of his, and a mind that remembered everything. Showing off, probably, and thank God for it. Last night, before darkness, she had found some of those branches, cut into them, chopped them up.

It hadn't taken fire readily, had used up too much of her lint, too much of her breath as well. But finally, she'd had light and warmth, and the baby had been wiped with rain-wet cloths that she could then rub clean at least a little.

They were all right. Would be all right. The track of the opium train remained clear, the dung showing different from the mud in spite of the showers. After what had happened with Lim Pong, she had decided she wouldn't follow the train all the way to the Mekong. They had a radio, and someone might be sent back home. All that was needed was any river, a tributary, because they all flowed into the Mekong, didn't they? Certainly, of course they did.

All through the night, even when the moon went away, she'd seen the glisten of Cho's eyes looking up at her in bright trust, as if to say, "we are in this together; you will do fine." She'd decided to believe him.

Now, the end of her second day on the trail was almost upon them. She came across a clearing, the blackened earth of an old campfire inviting her. As she'd done last night, she tied up the horse and spread the plastic sheet on the ground, placing on top of it horse blankets, bags, Cho's cloths, everything she had to soften and warm the plastic. And then, using branches she cut with the dah, she rigged half the sheet over their heads like a little tent.

Cho was whimpering. But he'd have to wait, only awhile. She went slightly off the track to squat and relieve herself, able to watch him. She'd laid him on his stomach, and there he was, up on all fours, rocking, always trying. He never gave up, and nor would she. Her eyes were also roving about to find windfalls for the fire. She had just stood, was fastening her jeans, when they arrived.

Two Shan horsemen, without warning, without stopping, rode across her little campsite. Screaming, screaming, she ran to the tent. One Shan leaned from his saddle to grab the plastic and overturn the whole, Cho, too. But she beat him to it, and leaped at his horse's head, turning the animal aside as it knocked her down. She didn't try to get up but flung herself along the ground to cover Cho with her own body, but one of the Shans moved his horse between her and Cho. Now it was he who was screaming. The pistol was in one of the bags. Oh, God damn it.

She recognized them. One was the captain of the pack train, the other one of his lieutenants. She knew the name of the first only, Sai Myaing.

The lieutenant now swung his horse to run down the tent and Cho. With another scream, more of a low growl, Kathleen jumped up, was bolting forward – and the captain ripped out, "No!"

In looking back at him, the lieutenant forgot his purpose long enough for Kathleen to reach Cho, scoop him up, and face her two marauders. They would have to kill her to hurt Cho.

"The prince wants him dead in any case," the lieutenant said.

"Then it will be on his head, not ours," Sai Myaing replied. "Saddle the woman's horse. It will be dark soon. We need to get back."

While the lieutenant did it, and turned out her Shan bags, thus finding the pistol, the captain held his assault rifle ready on her. They let her repack almost all of it, but took the bullets and pistol, the dah. And they would have left the rice and cook pot, but she pleaded and they let her stick them into the big bag along with her journals. Luckily, though why at this point it should occur to her worry she didn't know, they didn't notice her American passport.

They made her mount and left her hands free for the baby, but tied her feet with a rope beneath the pony's girth. She looked across the head of the lieutenant at the mounted captain. "Is he there?" she asked softly, meaning with the train. Both men returned her look with contempt, and she understood – of course not. The prince could not join the train on the trail, how could he, when he was down in Ban Houei Say.

They took the reins from her to put the pony on lead, and kicked their horses, and hers perforce, into a good pace heading in the direction she had been going, towards the opium train.

It was difficult, with no way to control the pony, no time to stop and comfort Cho, or feed him. Did Htin Aung know? And how did he? And how did they? Oh, yes, yes – the radio they carried. He could talk to them, of course, and to the palace. Fool. Oh, heaven. Had U-pym betrayed her twice, then?

Her mind was spinning, terrorized, bewildered, frantic, all these things. But only when they crossed a stream, wide and with a path alongside it running south, did her heart break.

*   *   *

The end of the pack train was not as far as Kathleen had thought. She'd been travelling too fast, catching up. The horsemen were already making camps alongside the trail, building fires much bigger and better than hers. The pack train carried firewood with it. The horses had been unloaded and were tied to rope strings with grain and hay, also carried with them and piled below their muzzles. The horsemen looked up or around to watch as first Sai Myaing, then Kathleen, then the lieutenant rode past. Every so many meters, armed guards were perched on rocks or remained mounted. And once they passed a piece of artillery. A second piece, Kathleen knew, would be nearer the front of the train. Han Shee-fu, a Chinese Shan, was in competition for the heroin market and had in the past raided Htin Aung's opium supplies. And there were bandits, too, and even, encroaching into Laotian territory, the Burmese army. Everybody wanted the precious gum.

They rode well into the length of the train, finally halting near a large tent. The captain's. Two guards had been instructed by the lieutenant to accompany them, and took their watch close by. Watching her.

Her ankles were untied and she was pulled ungently to the ground by the lieutenant, who seemed to carry a dislike for her. Because she'd caused him a longer ride? Because she was Anglo? Or because she'd provided his province with a sickly prince?

Sai Myaing stepped to her. "See to yourself," he said. "When you need to go beyond the light to relieve yourself, you will leave the child by the fire." Knowing, of course, that she would never run off into the night without her baby. He then went into his tent.

There were no other women on the train. There would be some drinking, of course. But Shan men were not usually cruel. Though, of course, if they knew she had killed one of their own . . .

She had to wait for a turn at the fire to cook rice. She would need some while travelling, and anyway, the leftover rice would taste better with the fresh-cooked mixed in. She could see the flash of teeth in dark faces, smiling at her. The horsemen boiled tea for themselves and for the guards, whom they fed, as well. One of her guards thought to offer her a cup. It helped greatly, because whether it was the nightfall or the fear, or that iceberg inside her that was Lim Pong, she was very cold.

She watched as one of the horsemen took some rice on a leaf and carried it back to a ruined stupa they had passed, and left it for the spirit nats. Yesterday and today, Kathleen had seen dingy unpainted pagodas scattered widely in the jungle up or down the ridgesides, but all looked old and deserted, some even with broken htis, and no bell-sounds at all or cookfires rising above them. Perhaps there were no villages close by. That had been a thought that had come to her since she'd been captured – a nearby village might bring women to the train with food or weavings or – for whatever purpose, and if so, if so . . . mightn't there be some hope for her? But there'd been no sign of a village since she'd left Loi Long. Perhaps the opium trail was too dangerous a place to live near? Or perhaps Htin Aung had cleared them out against dacoits for the safety of the trains.

Cho was mewling. If he annoyed these men in the night, it would go badly for her and the baby. She turned towards the jungle, sitting sideways on her hip as Shan women did, raised her shirt and tucked Cho's head beneath, letting him suckle.

Lamplight from inside the tent now fell through the open flap, and she heard something . . . she turned her head slowly, hoping not to be noticed, and saw a Shan guard cranking a box. Oh, God – the generator for the radio. Looking upwards, she could see the antenna stretched between trees. And now she could see the captain talk into what looked like a phone. To his Sawbwa, down in Ban Houie Say?

What if he was ordered to kill the baby? Htin Aung would blame Cho surely for this "episode" of hers. That's what he'd call her try at escape. She rocked, sitting there, feeling that little warm mouth on her nipple, the milk drawn forth by it. There'd be nothing she could do to save him. But she knew if that happened and she was returned to Loi Long without him, she would find herself a pangi tree and squeeze the fruit for its juice and put it into her tea and drink it down and go to sleep and never awaken again.

If there was agony to it – she didn't remember about the pangi tree – it would be put-paid for her stupidities. And that certainty was more righteous and bitter in her throat than the juice could ever be.

21

"What is this shit?" Hanny asked in a whisper.

"Shut up and eat it," the Colonel whispered quickly. He was seated at the long table on one side of Hanny, Michael on the other. Dinner with the General.

"It's not shit," Michael said softly, knowing it would get Hanny. "It's what ate the shit. Those pigs you saw running around on the way in from the airstrip? The local sewer system."

Both men looked at him, the Colonel leaning forward to glare across Hanny. Michael applied himself to his own plate. Hanny gave a little whimper and started playing around with his food. The table was laden with it, all kinds, all equally mysterious. Unfortunately, there was no excuse for Hanny since forks were provided. Bottles of White Horse whiskey and pitchers of beer, really cold and scattered generously down the center of the table, were replenished by the pretty young women who served the table. Michael found himself wondering how else they served this general and his officers. Those at the table couldn't keep their hands to themselves.

The General sat in the center, the three off the Loach lined up along one side of him, and three Meo officers on the other. Across were Americans: three men who proclaimed themselves U.S. A.I.D. consultants, one of whom, Jack Haskell, had driven them into town from the airfield; two self-admittedly C.I.A; and a special forces ranger who was easy-going and already drinking too much. All sat on the floor, which made long legs miserable.

Earlier, still late afternoon when they had arrived off the Loach at Vang Pao's operations headquarters, the General had been in the midst of a screaming fit in some Meo dialect at the three Meo officers now down the table. Two of the A.I.D.'s across the table had been there, witnessing it – not the best way for Americans to endear themselves to the locals, Michael had thought at the time. Vang Pao had interrupted himself to welcome the Colonel warmly.

Just before they'd entered the war room at the back of the General's two-story house, the Colonel had ordered his two "aids" to look sharp, so Hanny and Michael had stood at attention for most of the meeting, though not exactly looking sharp since their heads were lowered – the Colonel had also commented that it was too bad they couldn't shrink.

When they saw General Vang Pao, it was obvious why. He was strong-bodied but shorter even than the Colonel. His face was brown, round, pock-marked, and when greeting the three new arrivals it was slashed by a grin that looked perpetual. It was not. When he learned their purpose here in Long Tieng, it died.

"Why should Vang Pao help find what United State call dove?! Vang Pao is domino for Laos!" His voice was rising, going shrill. "If Meo go down, royal Lao princes go down. All Laos be lost! You don't know that? When North Vietnamese rule Laos, Thailand go next!" He shook his finger furiously at the Colonel. "*Then* Americans come, ooh, la, la, mais oui! To save Thailand! But to help Meo? Oh, no, Nix-one say, must be secret war!" He held the finger to his lips and hissed, "Shh! What kind war is that?" And suddenly he was hoisting his thumb at himself and building to another shout. "Where my guns?! Where my soldiers?! Where my hard rice?! Get me these things, I help you find dove!" He swung and pointed at his officers, and was again screaming at them in Meo.

Given the problems the General had just outlined in English, and remembering those Meo refugees squatting outside Vientiane along with what they had and hadn't seen in Long Tieng, Michael doubted the poor guys could find a fast solution. So he and Michael, Hanny and the Colonel kept their eyes to themselves. Let the General cool off. It had been hairy enough getting into this place, Michael sure as hell wanted to get out.

The secret city sat in a bowl of mountains with a neck of an entrance. The macadam airstrip was busy as with a swarm of bees and as unpredictable. The traffic controller had spoken English with a heavy Laotian accent, and the transmission was bad. Little Air Force O-1's and AA Porters were taking off constantly, the strip so crowded they fairly had to jump up into the air for lack of distance. Several Hueys were down on the H-pad, kicking off cargo or taking on airborne patrols, the soldiers so young they were dwarfed by the rifles over their shoulders. But Michael made it in and settled down. The three on board the Loach were scarcely out on the tarmac, uncreaking their limbs, when a jeep hurled up, stopped, and an American civilian got out.

"Jack Haskell," he said, "U.S. A.I.D." For A.I.D. read C.I.A., Michael thought. Haskell even acted it, full of C.I.A. arrogance, telling them to get into the jeep, that he'd been sent to take them to the General soonest.

Kissinger's boys, an AA pilot had called the C.I.A. at Mam'selle Josie's. And then he'd quoted Nixon saying there was no American manpower in Laos on a combat basis. The pilot had belched out a bitter laugh. "My God," he'd said, "not a week goes past we don't lose pilots." He leaned towards Michael in belligerance, as if it were all Michael's fault. But since he was three sheets, Michael didn't take offense. "This ain't no civil war, baby," he'd said. "There's a fuckin' gook invasion goin' on. The only moral war in the world the last twenty five years, and our esteemed president lets children go fight it."

And there they were, not thirty yards away on Long Tieng airfield. That same pilot had dubbed this town spook heaven. Hanny had been eyeing both Haskell and the pad unhappily. "Sir?" he asked the Colonel, "permission to remain with the aircraft?"

"Negative," said the Colonel, getting into the front seat of the jeep. Then he looked at Hanny. "You're not a crew chief today, Sergeant, you're an entourage. Mine."

They drove down muddy dirt streets, some straight and lined with modern bungalows – in the many hundreds, it had looked like from the air, could've been an American low-cost housing development, except Levittown didn't have tin roofs – but other streets wandered off in all directions with thatched huts scattered along them. Chickens and, of course, the pigs squawked and squealed to get out of the way of their jeep. Young women sat on front steps – all the houses were up on stilts with porches, sandbag bunkers to the side or back. There were few men of any age, except now and then a cluster of Americans sitting on a porch drinking beer, one with a small bear on a leash, another with a monkey on his shoulder. As if there weren't enough of those around. AA pilots, Michael guessed, though none he or Hanny recognized. In the cratered wastelands, kids – little kids – were mock-drilling with sticks. Armed boys lingered on street corners, probably waiting to be airlifted into combat. Michael thought of the Montagnards of Nam, like the Meo here, the hill tribes the only people willing to fight for their land. Sure as hell the troops of South Vietnam weren't.

Maps covered the walls in Vang Pao's headquarters, most of them of eastern Laos, both the northern mountains with the Plain of Jars and the southern panhandle, but Michael saw one or two of the west where the

Volpar had gone down. Encouraging.

The Colonel had let Vang Pao run his anger out against his own officers for a few minutes, then jumped in during a pause. "General? If I may speak?"

Vang Pao swung around, stared, then nodded, wiggling his fingers in invitation. "Sir," said the Colonel, "if you help us find Senator Beaumont, and he is well, I promise I will bring him here to see for himself your tribulations. Yes, he is a dove. But when he sees your children, the damage you are all suffering, at the least he will return home to tell America that North Vietnam has broken all the Geneva agreements, and sending secret insufficient help to fight a secret war about which lies are told every day is sure as hell the wrong way to win it. I can't promise you guns. But better he be found before he's given over to your enemies in Hanoi. Who knows what harm he will be forced to do?"

Vang Pao was listening. So were the two so-called A.I.D. men, who exchanged uneasy sliding glances.

"Sergeant," the Colonel said, "the map, please." Hanny stepped at once to the map of northwest Laos, pointed to the area he could locate better than Michael could. "The Air America plane went down somewhere in this area, Sir," he said directly to Vang Pao. "We know there's a village close to the site, beyond the top of one of these ridges. And there may be others."

"What we need," the Colonel said, "is someone who can speak the languages of the area to visit the villages, or infiltrate them, find out what the people know. General Vang Pao, please. Ten American men may still be alive."

He waited. Vang Pao studied him, finally gave a nod. "I will try find one who can do it." Suddenly, he grinned. "You come dinner tonight, n'est pas? Seven-thirty prompt. Your aids, aussi. We drink, be happy one more night. Tomorrow night, never know . . ." He shrugged, turned back to his officers, effectively dismissing the three off the Loach. Nevertheless, they saluted, crisply about-faced and left.

Haskell'd been waiting out on the porch to take them to their guest-house for the night. Hanny had asked permission to go back to the Loach. Haskell's mouth had set, especially when the Colonel let Hanny go, insisting he come back in for dinner.

Which, given the food, Hanny would no doubt have happily skipped. He would probably call every pig he saw from now on a sewer rat. Moreover, voices were raised all up and down the table, with laughter, jokes, calling to each other, so that the noise bounced off the walls of the room, and it was hot. Everybody was getting sloshed. Flying tomorrow morning didn't seem to matter, if any of them were. For the three of them from the Loach, sobriety didn't improve things any.

A young boy entered, well, was more like pushed into the room. An old Garand rifle held to his shoulder, he went directly to Vang Pao, saluted, and waited like a little ramrod on the General's pleasure.

When Vang Pao did take notice, he pointed out the three from the Loach, and started asking questions, for the boy nodded and nodded and nodded.

"Oh, man," Hanny muttered. He was watching, too.

"Yeah," said Michael. "Looks like our linguist infiltrator has arrived. What do you think? Ten years old or eleven?"

They both looked at the Colonel, who managed somehow to shrug. "War is hell, Gentlemen," he said.

The boy finally came to stand behind Hanny, centered that way on the three. They all swivelled on their butts to look at him. He nodded to each of the three in a kind of bow, then announced, "Me Corporal Boun Nung Gia. General Vang Pao attaches me to you." And he saluted, staring at the opposite wall.

It took the Colonel a second. Finally, he said, "At ease, Corporal." The boy relaxed a little. "Sit down and wait," he added. And the boy sat cross-legged on the floor behind them, face remote, his gun laid across his thighs. His ragged cut-offs were too big for him, tied up by a thin rope, his shirt flapping about his thin upper body.

Michael turned back around to the table, seeing all that food, feeling slightly ill for having eaten it. Suddenly, he jammed his finger into the table by Hanny's full plate. "Shameful!" he declared, no longer keeping his voice down. Hell, nobody ten inches away could hear him in this bedlam, anyhow.

Hanny had had it. "Give over, for sweet Mary's sake!"

Michael smiled a little, gave him a small wink, stretched along the table to a glass full of chopsticks to grab a pair, dumped some rice onto Hanny's plate, was reaching for the platter of spareribs, when Hanny got it.

"You keep loadin' that plate up," he said, "and the kid's as hungry as he looks, we're all gonna be sorry come tomorrow in the air."

"There's a thought," Michael agreed, dismissed the spareribs, and turned with the plate to hold it out to the little corporal. The kid's eyes fixed on that plate, and he struggled very hard not to crave it. "The Sergeant here," Michael said, "feels sick and can't eat this food, but he doesn't want to insult the General by leaving anything on his plate. Would you eat it, please, as a favor to the Sergeant?"

Hanny turned now, too, nodded encouragingly at the kid. The boy's eyes lifted and looked from Michael to Hanny, back at Michael, who smiled. At last, the boy took the plate slowly, trying to keep his dignity. Michael signalled Hanny to turn away, as he himself did – to slide his eyes around back after a minute to find the kid shovelling in the dinner.

The girls were clearing the platters and the beer off the table, replacing the pitchers with bottles of brandy and what Michael would swear were Lalique crystal snifters.

The Colonel leaned over. "Apt to turn into a drinking contest about now, and then to battle plans for tomorrow. Time to go," he said. They all looked towards Vang Pao. He had a girl kneeling at either knee, was laughing raucously, and would never miss them. The kid's plate was empty. Michael took it, the three men stood up, and the kid jumped to his feet, gun on his shoulder again. Might be hungry and too thin, but his muscles were good enough.

Heading towards the door, Hanny stopped by Haskell. "Come on," he ordered, his voice brooking no argument. "Taxi time."

Haskell hesitated only a moment, surprised and not liking it. Neither did his several pals. But nobody argued.

Outside, Hanny simply announced he'd be spending the night with the Loach. The Colonel nodded, told Haskell to take them to their billet first to get Hanny a mosquito net, pillow and some kind of cover. Haskell had already provided them with toothbrushes, razors and soap. Michael said he'd just as soon walk, clear the beer fumes out of his head. And he said he'd relieve Hanny at two.

But the Colonel objected. "You're the one at the controls, Michael, and you're flying in the morning. You need a good night," he said. "And how're you going to find the house, walking. This place is a maze."

"I know!" the kid piped up, pointing at himself. "I walk, too! I protect you!" he said to Michael, having to tip his head back hard to look up at him.

So they walked along quietly together, the boy carrying that heavy rifle. Michael broke the silence. "Your English is very good. You speak many um – " he didn't want to label them hill-tribe dialects – "languages of Laos, do you, Corporal?"

"Yes, Sir," said the kid. "Many. My village is in west. Speak languages from there. Lu, Lahu, Shan, even some Chinese."

"Good," said Michael. Then, "Tell me your name again, please."

"Boun Nung Gia", he said.

"Ah," Michael said, nodding. "Ba-oon Noo – "

The kid grinned up at him. "You call me Donald Duck!" he said. "You know Donald Duck?" And suddenly, he went quacking and waddling out ahead, hands angled ninety degrees up from his hips. "Quack, quack, quack!" He spun around to face Michael. "Me Donald Duck! Ver' good, yes?"

Jesus, Michael thought, he's a child. A fucking child. Wonder if he keeps a talley of his hits.

"Yeah!" Michael said. "Very good. Where'd you hear about Donald Duck?"

"AA hootches got lots of movies!" he said.

Nice. Something in common with Hanny. How could he send this little boy up and over that ridge into God knew what mess? "Okay," he said. "Donald it is."

The kid beamed, turned, and led away, waddling once in a while with a quack.

When they reached the house, they found the Colonel writing on a big pad. Haskell must have supplied that, too.

"My report for Washington," he said, looking up through a swirl of small green bugs. "I'm gonna get a lift back to Vientiane tomorrow. Whatever you find, I'll need orders, and the sooner the Chief of Staff gets a start on the story the faster he can react when you get back with whatever you find out."

Right. Get rid of the man, get stuck with a child, Michael thought without humor.

"I've gotta tell you, Colonel," Michael started, "this deal is just not gonna play worth a – " He was looking around as he spoke, and found Donald missing. "What the hell –?" He went to the front door, looked out to see the boy standing at attention at the edge of the porch, his rifle shouldered. Michael went out to him.

"What're you doing?"

"Keep guard. General order me."

"All night?"

"Yes, Sir!" He hadn't looked at Michael once, eyes forward.

Exasperated, Michael turned back into the house, found a small chair, brought it out to the porch. "Sit," he ordered.

The kid was caught, not knowing what to do, his eyes flying around to the chair, then back out to the street.

"That's *my* order, Corporal!"

At last, the kid backed into the chair and sat down. Michael grasped the rifle. Donald held on to it, but finally had to give it up. Michael slammed the stock down on the porch floor, and leaned the gun softly into the boy's the shoulder. "There," he said. A moment, he sighed, giving it up, and returned into the house.

"As I was saying, Sir," he began, "this kid is just too young."

"He's all we've got," the Colonel said. "And there's no way we can find out what happened without him."

"He wants us to call him Donald Duck!" Michael had to struggle to keep his voice low.

The Colonel closed his eyes, only a moment, then spoke mildly. "His English seems good enough. Did he say anything about his other languages?"

Michael was getting angry. "Yes, Sir. He speaks a number from western Laos. But damn it, Colonel – "

The man just held Michael's eyes. Michael pulled in.

After a moment or two, the Colonel turned back to his report, waving away the green bugs. "Sleep, Michael," he said.

Michael turned on his heel and went into the bedroom he'd be sharing with Hanny if he weren't out at the airfield. But how the hell either he or the Colonel could sleep with that child keeping watch to protect them, for God's sake, was beyond him. He stripped to his briefs and T-shirt, and stretched out on one of the cots, pulling the net down, but his feet hung over the bottom of the cot as usual.

Like the emigré Meo down in Vientiane two nights ago, these children here were running in pictures through his head. That little boy on guard out on the porch, the squads of them drilling on those muddy wastelands. He suddenly wondered if the poet had written about little hunters not to evoke dreams of adventure for English boys, as generations had believed, but to inform the world about the lands and people east of Mandalay, whom he'd known perhaps as well as he'd known India.

He shifted on the cot. It creaked, his weight half again what it must be used to. Tomorrow they'd head west again. Today they'd gone as far west in Laos as they could, almost, only to turn south. It had seemed to Michael that all he'd needed to do was stick out his right arm and he could touch Burma. And then they'd turned again. East. Sure as hellfire going round in circles. For how many times?

DAY SEVEN

22

The first shells started landing shortly after midnight and woke him, even as Donald came running to urge him and the Colonel into the bunker. The two men grabbed their boots and had to crouch their way into it, even for the Colonel the ceiling was too low. And when they were sitting there, backs against the wall, the crown of Michael's head brushed the bottom of the sandbag roof.

The shelling got heavy. Sounded like it could go on all night, Michael thought. "You okay, Colonel?" Michael asked.

"Yup," he answered. "Get some sleep."

Michael was sitting next to Donald, his mid-arm touching the boy's shoulder, and he was soon aware that Donald was shivering. And with each exploding shell, there was a start. Scared to death, Michael realized. Aw, God.

"Hey," Michael murmured, "I'm cold. Are you?" He couldn't really see the kid to know his reaction. Just felt him press against his arm, still trembling, jerking with the shells. Michael put his arm around him, drew him in so that more of their bodies touched. "There," Michael said, "now we'll warm up." And slowly, the trembling quieted, the fearful jerks to the sounds of the shells subsided. Michael lay his head back and felt Donald go to sleep, drifted off himself.

Something scrabbling across the back of his neck brought him to. He slammed it away, and heard it land. Jesus Christ. He hoped it was a roach or even a scorpion. He could abide six legs a hell of a lot sooner than eight.

Donald had slept through it. The shells were not as frequent now. Michael looked at his watch. Almost three. Hoping not to disturb the kid, he shifted his butt slightly – it was going numb. And trying to put any multi-legged, unwanted companions down here in this hole out of his mind, he made a real effort to relax. He must have succeeded. Dawn was trickling into the bunker when he woke up, and the shells had gone silent.

* * *

Hanny hitched a ride in from the airfield to shower and shave. After a huge American breakfast delivered by two girls looking to be all of twelve years old, the three men and Donald went out to the Loach, the Colonel to collect the stuff from the two dead guys and see the Loach off.

The boy's eyes widened on seeing the little aircraft, and he looked at Michael as if at God when told he would be sitting up front with the pilot. The Colonel loaned him his helmet, making a big deal out of getting Donald to promise to return it to him. Too big, of course, it practically rested on his shoulders, but at least he'd be able to hear through the earphones. By this time, Donald was practically beside himself with excitement. Michael thought he might piss his pants if they didn't take off pretty soon – or maybe even afterwards.

Michael got him settled in the peter seat. The Colonel stepped back, looked up at Michael with a casual salute. "See you tomorrow night in Vientiane. If not, radio in why not. If you get back to L.P. tonight before six and can get the phones to work, call the embassy." Tom, too, Michael thought, the news not so good, glad he hadn't reached him yesterday.

Michael cranked, Hanny got in and they lifted off. Michael and Hanny could hear the boy's voice go up and up, rising even as the Loach did, almost to a squeal of wonder. So Michael keyed him in, and began talking about how the little chopper worked. At Hanny's suggestion, Michael by-passed Luang Prabang for refueling and went on up to the town of Nam Tha, at the head of the river of the same name, the town farthest north still in the hands of the friendlies. It would put them into this operation with the biggest load of fuel available.

In the nearly four hours of the trip from Long Tieng, broken only in Nam Tha, he and Hanny sang some songs, even taught Donald a couple. And at last, they approached the Volpar.

"Do you recognize the area, Donald?" he asked. The boy was staring down at the jungle passing below. He shook his head, very con-fused. Finally, Michael reached the STOL strip, and hovered down to about two feet above it, Donald's side facing up the ridge. And the boy broke into a huge smile. "Yes, yes. Yes!" he shouted.

"Look up the ridge," Michael told him. "See the smoke up there?"

"Is Rapet! My village!" he cried. "This landing we build for drug planes ver' long time 'go. Is Rapet!"

Michael immediately lifted again, and Donald's face went crushed.

"It's all right," Michael said, "don't worry, you'll get to go home, I just don't want to park there." And he started doing a spiral turn around and around, looking for a break in the canopy. And finally, he found one, put down, and let the turbine idle to cool off before shutting it down.

Hanny got out and came to stand beside Michael still in the Loach, so they could all talk. "Okay," said Michael to Donald, "you know what to do?"

Donald just looked at him and slowly shook his head. Michael took a breath, sighed it out. "You saw that crashed plane back there," he started, and the boy nodded. "Ten American men are missing from that plane." The boy was nodding. Knew some of it, anyway. "We need to find out what happened to them. Maybe they are in some village . . . your village . . . maybe they're being treated very well . . . maybe they're prisoners . . . maybe they have been sent to Hanoi . . . "

Michael reached over and removed the helmet from Donald's head, unbuckled his harness. "You have to go and ask. Then come back and tell us. And nobody must know we're here. Nobody. Whatever you find out. Very important to General Vang Pao. Do you understand, Corporal?" Donald nodded. Michael continued, "The thing is, how will you explain just turning up . . ." Donald looked puzzled at the phrase. "Explain being here. Coming back home."

"Ah," he said. "No problem," he said, and Michael nearly burst out laughing. No problemeh. Yeah.

"My village make brick – white powder brick." Heroin, like Simon Fess's, Michael thought. "Sell to Vietnamese, Chinese. I no like those people. I like Ameyikans!" He beamed. He half slid, half jumped to the ground. "So. I come back. See my mother, my sister. I whisper I know General Vang Pao, they be proud!"

And then Hanny spoke up. "Sir? I don't think we're going to wait around forever, are we, Sir?"

Man, when he speaks up, Michael thought, he's more right than anybody else in the world. Worried about Asian time. What happened to no problemeh?

"You're right, Chief." Michael sighed again, and said it straight out. "Donald. We can only wait a short time. We might come back, but if you take too long, we will be gone away." Watching his face lose everything, Michael had to add, "For today, for today." Which he knew didn't thrill Hanny to death: sure they'd come back – to a perfect ambush.

The boy nodded, rocking, jigging back and forth, so eager, so excited to get away. Like himself, Michael thought, wanting to move, to get it going.

"Be careful," Michael said.

Donald was backing up, his eyes fixed on Michael. "You wait. You wait." And he turned, ran a few steps into the jungle, turned back. "You make warm last night. I not forget you." And he was gone.

"What was all that?" Hanny asked.

Michael just shook his head.

* * *

They kept looking at their watches. Senseless. They each admitted they didn't know what time it was exactly when the kid had left. They said little, automatic weapons in hand, and when not looking at the time their eyes never stopped scanning, probing the damned jungle, moving, sweeping in slow arcs, hoping to catch motion, color, a startled parrot. It dripped. No rain, maybe it always dripped. Mists had lifted mid-morning. No fog. There was a tiny humming, a clicking, mostly bugs, and once a big dragonfly cruised past.

Michael was still in the pilot's seat, one leg dangling out the door, his foot working in a found rhythm he was hardly aware of. Hanny stood on the ground beside him.

"I'm gettin' bugged driving up and down the same old strip." Michael started it, matching the beat of his foot, his voice so soft it was close to a whisper. "I gotta find a new place where the kids're hip." And then Hanny came in doing Brian going high on the chorus, almost squeaking it to keep it soft, while Michael took the "Get around, get around, I get around" and the "Yeah!" and together they went right on into "My buddies and me're getting real well known. Yeah, the bad guys know us and they leave us alone!" This time, on the verse, bringing in the "oo wa wa-oo, wa wa-oo, oo oo oo oo", and finishing with another set of "I get around, get around, I get around," Michael taking the last deep gleeful "Eeyeah!" Good old Beach Boys.

Still a silence all around. Where was Donald? And what was Michael to do about it? Should he go up there? And if he did, got spotted, what then for the kid? What kind of trouble had Donald gotten himself into? Shit, what to do? God damn it.

"Uh, help me, Rhonda! Help me, help me, Rhonda!" Didn't even think about it, just there it was. "Uh, help me, Rhonda! Help me, help me, Rhonda!" And then as Michael went up a tone, Hanny came in rising from the bass, "Bow, bow, bow, bow" and they finished the last refrain together, "Help me, Rhonda, yeah! get her out of my heart!" And Hanny, "Oh, Rhonda!" Michael was on the roll with "She was gonna be my wife and I was gonna be her man," and Hanny sighing "Oh, Rhonda! Oh, Rhonda!" And Michael, "But she met another guy. Come between us and uh shattered our plan!" "Oh, Rhonda!" went Hanny – and Michael came to and said, "Shit."

Silence again. Where the hell did that verse come from, for Christ's sake. He'd forgotten it was there, he'd swear it.

His foot must've been going again, for suddenly Hanny put his hand on his ankle to still it. When Michael looked at him, Hanny jerked his head straight out at three o'clock. Donald. "There's a mercy," Hanny said.

Michael stepped to the ground and went to meet the boy. He was limping, using a stick for a jerry-built crutch.

"What happened?" Michael asked, stopping in front of him.

Donald looked up at him with a grin and flipped the crutch away. "Ver' bad wound," he said. Then he frowned, his face growing sad, and struck his chest. "I am cadre! Fight with Pathet Lao for communism in east. Bad time. Get wounded. Mother ver' proud, no difference Vang Pao or Pathet Lao. But head of village, make big difference! Vietnamese, Pathet Lao buy many brick!" And he grinned again. "So Vang Pao, he long gone!"

God, he was so mercurial. Michael asked, for lack of anything else at this point, "Where's your gun?" Hanny had by now followed him over.

"I hide!" Donald said.

Michael nodded again. "Well. Are they there?"

The boy nodded back vigorously, with a big smile. "Yes!" And he held up both hands palms forward, fingers spread to count ten. "Ten," he declared.

"Are they all right?" Hanny asked.

Donald shrugged, looked a little apologetic as if responsible for his village, shrugged again. "Two sick." He made a little face. "One try take white brick, get caught. Put in hole, bamboo door on top. No can move much in hole." He looked very sad. "Too many days, can die in hole."

Michael's and Hanny's eyes slid off each other. And then Donald added eagerly, "But nobody die yet! Keep rest in cave! Make white powder brick!"

"Is the Senator – " Michael started, and then realized this kid wouldn't know a senator from a ground hog. "An older man," he started again, then realized hell, Beaumont could be Kennedy's age ten years ago for all Michael knew. "What will they do with the Americans?"

"End of monsoon, walk to Chinese road. Maybe Chinese, maybe Vietnamese come with truck. Pay good, either one, they take Ameyikans. We let go free now?" Donald asked, full of eagerness. "I help!"

"Oh, boy," said Hanny.

"Not now," said Michael, watching the boy's face fall. "In a few days. We have to mount an attack – um – get a patrol – some airborne troops to invade – ." Damn. He couldn't promise that, no way.

Donald was frowning solemnly, nodding in understanding. "You come, I help. But, Sir, I tell you – my mother and my sister, you no kill."

Michael was so moved by this boy. Handling it was becoming a problem. But he managed to nod. "I understand," he said. He looked at Hanny, whose Irish eyes swam, so that he turned and headed for the Loach.

"Well," said Michael, "let's go, then."

Donald looked at him amazed. "I no go!" he said. "I wait, you come back, I be here! You tell General I be big help!"

"I don't know when it will be," Michael said, protesting. "Not long, I'm sure, but – days, maybe – a week – or more . . ." Much longer and the monsoon'd be fuckin' over. Not to mention a dead guy in a hole.

Donald nodded. He was smiling. "My mother need me to do white powder brick for her and my sister." And again as if apologetic, "My father die two years before now. I make ver' good brick!" He started backing away, suddenly reaching to collect his crutch. He never took his eyes from Michael. Then he halted. "You come back?"

Michael nodded. "I promise." Then, to make it real, he asked, "Where do we find you?"

"I come here! Every day, I come here!" He beamed.

"Okay, okay," Michael said quickly. And in a spur of the moment generosity, he pulled off his watch and gave it to the boy. It was too big for Donald and had an expandable band which couldn't be adjusted to make it smaller, but the kid was quick all right. He shoved his wrist into it and pushed it up his arm to his bicep – beneath his shirt sleeve. And immediately looked up at Michael, absolutely blown away.

"Know how to tell the time?" Michael asked. Donald let his eyes show his insult. Michael took hold of his arm, exposed the watch-face. "See how it looks, right now?" he asked. Donald nodded solemnly.

"Starting in two days – two – you come here at this time every day. Understood, Corporal?"

The boy saluted. "Yes, Sir!" And then he beamed, turned, and quacked and waddled for several feet, to finally break into a run, calling back, "You not forget Donald Duck!"

Michael watched until he was swallowed by the jungle, then went back to the Loach and Hanny, who stood there waiting, watching him.

"It's just after four," he said. "Not a bad time."

Michael was suddenly scared to death. It had all seemed so easy when it was impossible.

"You sure?" he asked.

"I told you," Hanny said. "Are you?"

Michael started a grin. "Yeah," he said. "And thanks to you and Nam Tha, we might have the fuel to make it." He got into the Loach. Hanny pulled out the fire extinguisher.

Michael sat there, almost awash with disbelief. Damn, he thought, it's really going to happen.

"Crank, Michael."

He cranked, Hanny stowed the extinguisher, collected some maps and got into the peter seat.

Michael caressed the sticks for just a moment, then pulled in some collective, drew the cyclic back, and hovered up carefully through the canopy to the sky. He banked the Loach around and pointed it west.

"Come on, baby, come on, baby, be good, baby," he was murmuring, and then it was a melody. "Come on, baby, light my fire! Come on, baby, light my fire!" And then paraphrasing Jim Morrison, "Gonna set the night on fire!"

Hanny slowly turned his head. "Dream on," he said.

Michael's grin was huge. "Yeah!" Hanny started to laugh. And together they belted it out the last "light my fai-yer!"

Her face, her body, her hair, so full of electricity. Still the same?
What in the name of God would he say to her in that first moment? Come
on, baby, come on, we're goin' home?

23

Mountains rose on every side, karst peaks jutting up independently of each other. Even this late in the day, some of the peaks held their clouds, wreathed by them, tips showing above, the green jungle below. Now and then, the Loach got caught in it, more like a haze with glaring vision all around, the sun sometimes, rarely, shafting through. Could be that gibbous moon on the river at L.P., fuller now, might turn out helpful after all.

"Like tits on an upsided hog," Hanny had offered about the peaks, though how he knew anything about hogs was beyond Michael. At least he hadn't said it about the pagodas scattered here and there, steeples poking up out of the green. And then without warning he started belting out "On the Road to Mandalay!" until he ran out of the lyrics. "You ever go there?" he asked.

"Oh, yeah," Michael said, "when I caught the Irriwaddy River paddle steamer down to Rangoon, heading back to the States." Had left Kathleen on the wharf fighting tears. The last time he'd seen her.

Mandalay. Due west, and with its pagoda-topped Mandalay Hill rising up out of the red earth plain, as much another world as the one they were in.

Their earlier euphoria seemed to die for good after that, no more songs, tunes gone out of their heads, even Hanny's. Maybe he figured it was Michael's dance so he got to lead. And then, Michael caught him watching his hands on the controls, looked down to see his whitened knuckles, bad as the Colonel's. Feeling queasy, too. Had he really believed the fear was gone? Bullshit.

He eased his fingers. Hanny's eyes, careful now, flicked up to his face. He threw Michael a wink, and Michael was suddenly aware his whole damned body was tight. He began the process Coach had taught him back in high school, relaxing first one muscle group, then another, then another. "You gotta watch the nerves, boy. You don't loosen up beforehand you'll go into a full body charley-horse first minute out there on the mat!"

Richard had been there for him all along, not just that one night at the regionals, sure he had. Michael heard again Richard's voice on the phone a week ago – God, was it that long? – Richard trying to keep it cool, not to sound too concerned, not to close up his little brother again. But he hadn't closed Michael up way back then, either. It was Michael hadn't let him in. Hell, Richard had had Charlotte, and if Michael didn't exactly cotton to his fiancée, it was hardly Richard's problem.

Gran had been there for him too, had even left her own house for the first six months after the plane crash to come live with them. And hadn't Charlotte loved that. Only two months to the wedding which no way was she going to postpone, and full of plans to redecorate, move in and pick up on the richest social life in Shaker Heights, all due respect paid to the deceased senior Camerons, of course. Because of Gran, she'd had to put up with a rented condo as a bride – on the top floor of Cleveland's newest and highest scraper, thanks to the family name, and a view of the lake that looked like it went all the way to Canada. Poor Char.

Michael hadn't let Gran in either, so sure he was the only one feeling left. Except the one time, when he'd found Jocko dying in the street and got him to the curb where he sat with the big collie head and shoulders across his lap, the back end of his body flattened by the hit and run, Michael murmuring, petting, while Jocko whimpered and shuddered and looked up at Michael from his long narrow face. Gran had found him there and sat with him until the collie went still, and when Michael had buried his face in the white coat, Gran had pulled him into her arms and let him cry it out, as he'd never cried for his parents. Oh, once in a while he'd wake in the night with wet cheeks, a dream of Mother spinning away like fog in a wind.

And then, in time, he'd just up and run out on the lot of them. Dad's pre-assumptions, and Richard's. And Gran's love.

She had died early in his first tour. Things were really popping in the Ashau Valley, and it stuck in his craw to ask for compassionate leave to go to a funeral when it was already too late to thank her.

Christ, why was this stuff coming up now? Why was he bringing it up, more like it.

Because you're scared half shitless, pal, and it's easier than thinking about tonight. And if you think you're scared, what about Kathleen? Days, weeks, months of it, maybe. Lord, if it goes bad tonight – if? Too many fuckin' unknowns not to go bad. When it does, she's the one going to pay the higher price, especially with a kid. Well, hell, maybe if we've lost everything else, we at least have that in common, we're each of us frightened for somebody else.

Thing was, what really burned the guilt, if tonight went bad, nobody but he and Hanny knew exactly where those men were. The Colonel didn't. Not even that they were alive.

Hanny flicked on the intercom, looking out and down. "There," he said, jabbing his forefinger down and off at about eleven o'clock. Michael leaned, peered.

It was a pony train, led by an artillery piece. Against guerrillas? The train was long and ragged with stragglers, winding its way eastwards up a switchback.

"Traders," Michael said. "All the villages have travelling bazaars every five days, even here in Laos, probably. You wouldn't believe the stuff you can find. Galvanized kettles and hammered steel dahs – gorgeous. Pink plastic combs out of China and silver buttons and bells worked by Chins . . . Coming east like these guys, they'll be carrying star sapphires and pigeon bloods from the Mogok mines." Before Hanny could ask, Michael added, "Rubies. Huge and deep, dark red."

Tom was right. He had fallen in love with Burma. But it was no Shangri La. Not perfect enough. Not always pleasant. Oh, there'd always been enough rice and no beggars. Plenty full of hospitality and laughter, Buddhist gentleness. But underlying these sweetnesses, always the hands-off Buddhist aloofness. Tom had early defined it for him: the negative reverse of the Golden Rule. "Don't do to others what you would not have them do to you." Michael had thought that was just fine, no problem with that, until deep into it with Kathleen, discovering what was really fine: letting somebody in besides himself.

It occurred to him, remembering Rangoon, the posters everywhere saying in English, "Be kind to animals by not eating them!" But a dog got struck by a car there, it was always hit and run.

The Mekong was passing underneath, a narrower course here certainly than in Vientiane and not so sluggish, showing white water. On the west side were coming more horsemen, paramilitaries from their khakis, rear guard for the pack train, probably. And slung between two horses, Michael could see, through glasses now, a second piece of artillery. All that armament, some of the trade goods had to be opium gum.

The karst was giving way to knife-topped ridges which quickly began to soften somewhat, with a village and its adjacent poppy fields, stubbled and brown in this season, turning up in this valley or that, cookfires for supper beginning to raise smoke. Burma. Michael turned southwest to avoid Keng Tung town. Would miss seeing the farm from the air, too. Not that he'd know it if he saw it.

Could be that train was carrying Kachin black velvet. Kathleen had had a Kachin outfit, had tried it on for him one Sunday morning. Looking perfectly beautiful, hair bound with a turban, her skin luminous against the black velvet trimmed with silver medallions and ribbons of pink and red and purple.

And it flashed in as it had in Udorn, only this time he managed to catch hold. Sunday mornings, and Kath's hair in a braid. The only times he got to see her wear it like that. Services weren't until just before noon to give villagers time to gather in, and Tom would be polishing his sermon in Kaw. Half asleep, Michael would stumble to the kitchen to find Kathleen, hair braided but after the night ravelling out from the one long plait hanging over her shoulder, wearing that tacky terry-cloth bathrobe of hers. Laundry in hill villages was done kneeling on a river bank, using soap made from roots, dirt driven out by banging the clothes on a rock. The robe was more grey than the blue it must once have been, threads all spitting out, and she'd be whipping eggs with a fork for scrambling, head bent, mouth slightly open, lower lip loose and a little full. He'd longed to unbraid that hair and feel the strands glide through his fingers like hot silk. To take that lower lip into his mouth.

A new river came up below them and Michael almost overflew it. Shit. Get with the program, asshole.

It was the Kha, had to be. When clarifiying the maps, Tom had said it rose from a ridge to the northwest, flowed south and east. A waterfall was cascading down a ridge running diagonally through their course.

"Look right to you?" he asked Hanny. Hanny gave a little shrug, but didn't disagree, finally nodded. "Worth a try," he said. They banked around to the left to follow it, and Hanny started unrolling the maps. Time to get to work.

"You got it," Michael said. Hanny handed him the maps, took the controls, and there was the layout of the palace, with Kathleen's room marked by Tom from so long ago. Tom had early on tried to get some of the Loi Long emigré Shans to confirm it, but even their knowledge was weeks or months out of date, and their certainties about the inside of the palace were limited anyway.

But the map locating the palace in its surrounds had pretty good detail. Above the palace was a large fenced horse paddock, then a peach and apple orchard; above that were the dry-rice paddies and wheat fields; and above those, hidden by a wide acreage of bush that was cut by mule trails, the poppy fields too muddy yet to replant. The Shans, under Tom's questioning, had understood the needs of a helicopter, Tom dreaming big even before Michael got to Hong Kong. And they'd recalled a space in the orchard that might work, the paddock being too close down to the palace. Some trees had developed a disease, and the Sawbwa had ordered them cut down and rooted out, more than just the sick ones, making a wide periphery to stop its spread.

Hanny kept altitude as they had decided days ago, high enough to be only a speck in the sky. An aircraft, sure, but maybe Burmese army or even on drug business, and easy to take for granted. And then another ridge dropped away from them, and there in the valley beyond was the town. Loi Long. Never having seen it from the air, still it came back to Michael – the Kha going through its middle spanned by arched wooden bridges maybe five feet wide, the open area of the marketplace, the wooden thatch-roofed houses scattered all about – no town planning here, the clumps of bamboo left for shade. And the other side, tucked against the farther ridge, the palace.

"That's it," Michael said, surging, unable to bank it even though each time up 'til now things had gone bad. But no holding it back, the hope so strong. This had to work.

"That?" Hanny. No hiding the disappointment. He'd taken an R & R to Bangkok last year and probably'd expected to see a building coated in gold and jewels. Even the pagoda on the edge of the town would be showing only a streaky whitewash by this time of year.

No. This palace was a single storied wooden building that rambled all along the side of the ridge, chambers sometimes standing alone or with one or two others, all connected with covered wooden walkways, the whole up on stilts, against the mud, like every other house in town. And inside, dark teak floors and walls, these panelled in cross-hatched overlays, all looking black, as if hand-rubbed for a thousand years. A hundred anyway, an amused Kathleen had corrected him, "and half a coconut shell works really well." Not all the rooms in the central main building were along the exterior, and their walls were constructed like partitions, attached to square and very fine studs, the partitions open at top and bottom for the passage of air. Michael hadn't asked what they did in winter, when the air was cold. Probably rolled the carpets up against the openings. They were all over the place, orientals, Chinese and Persian both. Michael had recognized the patterns because Gran threw them everywhere including going up the stairway.

Now they were coming up on it. Michael looked down, tempted, so fucking tempted to go down now, to try to see her, to have her look up and see him, to – Christ almighty, to wave.

Beyond the palace now, over the empty paddock, on to the orchard, and there in the midst of it, the oval space, their landing pad. Bless the Shans. Everything else they'd said might hold an equal truth.

They were at the top of the ridge, now lit by sun streaking through, the fallow opium fields behind them, and it was five ten on the nose. Ground shadows were lengthening, but at least fifteen more minutes needed before they could set down, as quiet as any helicopter could be. Before the valley would be dark enough so people gathering in for the evening meal would burn lanterns and be light-blinded to the sky and hillside.

Hanny put the little bird into a wide circle and Michael started tracing the plan on the map, speaking it aloud for the hundredth time. All the while, Hanny was free to jump in with corrections or suggestions, but he didn't. He waited until Michael was done and then he said, "One thing, Cam. Ain't gonna be just you. It's us."

"Huh?" Michael was blank only for a second, then knew. "Damn it, Neal, you wanted to say this, you've had since Bangkok!"

"Sure," Hanny said, "if I'd wanted a four day long continuous debate. I didn't. And don't. We're goin' in together."

"Damn it, we're doin' it like we've been talkin' since Da Nang!"

"Let it go, Michael. You conned me into this little exercise way back at Li Li's and how often do I gotta tell you I'm in it all the way. So the hell with all this Superman shit you keep comin' up with. If you think you're gonna hit that fuckin' palace with me left babysittin' the fuckin' plane, you're bats. The End. Finito. Que serra, okay?"

After a long moment, hardly able to speak, Michael said, "Shit."

"Yeah," Hanny said.

Ten minutes later, high enough that some twilight still lingered, the sun fast dying but still barely reflecting down the hill off the ridgetop, they put down and Michael once again set foot on Burmese soil.

Then the wait, the dreaded long wait for sleep to take over the palace. People without electric mostly sleep and wake with the sun. A two hour wait, saying almost nothing, undiscovered. Worse than earlier, waiting for

Donald Duck, no songs, just silence.

In the midst of it, it came to him full blown, shaking him: she'd stayed so long, had a baby by the man, supposing she loved him? And something had just recently happened to make her need to leave. But she still loved him. What Michael had to tell her, about the stolen letters, might just be to her a betrayal of long trust in Htin Aung, might break her heart. How could he not have thought of it before? Realized it.

"You know what?" he said to Hanny. "It's absolutely amazing the time you waste, the crazy things you do, because of what you want to believe."

He could feel Hanny shift weight, probably to turn to look at him. "Where'd that come from?" he said.

"I don't know. Out of a clear blue sky, maybe."

"Looks black to me," Hanny said, all this softly, almost a whisper. "So," he went on. "We're here. And we're gonna do it. Right?"

"Right," Michael said. He blew out his air.

The moon had been shining through for short intervals. Bad news, at least for the start of things. But at last, for the moment anyway, the ceiling closed in, and they slung on their automatic rifles. Michael shielded the torch into dull red by fingers over the bulb, and they went down the hill.

24

Out of the orchard and down to a large rock, around the paddock which held something mounded and stinking in its center – dead buffalo maybe – and on down to the palace wall, all going according to the map.

Supposedly there was a slit between the wall and the rock face at the back of the palace grounds. All the Shans used it, Tom had said. Easier than getting a woman and a child up the sheer rock or over the wall, which was close to nine feet high its whole length. And there was always the sharp glass embedded along the top of it.

Well the gap was there, but only a Shan or a woman could pass through it, sure as hell nobody with the girth of Hanny's chest. Michael's either, matter of fact.

The top of the wall was catching dim light from somewhere, but no sound of much of anything coming across it to the outside where they were. They walked along it a couple of meters, when Hanny stopped, obviously gathering himself. Michael landed a hard hand on his shoulder, grounding him as he was reaching up about to spring. Michael hoisted a thumb. "Glass," he rasped.

"Oh, yeah?" muttered Hanny with an edge, "I don't exactly recall you mentioning that." They looked at each other. Hanny sighed. "Mine's heavier," he said, taking his .45 out of its holster to empty the clip and pocket the bullets. All while Michael was taking off his shirt. Hanny handed the pistol over and Michael wrapped the grip of the gun in a sleeve.

He looked at Hanny, this time with a little apologetic cock of his head. "Yeah, you're sorry," Hanny said, "so am I." He bent at the hips, bracing his hands on his bent knees, and growled, "My, aren't you glad I'm here."

Michael placed his boot square on Hanny's back, and as lightly as he could he lifted to a stand.

There were the shards rising up to flay anybody dumb enough to try to go over the wall. He took a fast look across and around the compound, shadowed, silent, no guards to be seen. The palace showed only a few lights, yellow, soft. No electric. Tom believed there was a generator, but never running for long. Petrol, as he'd called it, too hard to get now that Burma had embargoed Loi Long.

Quickly, as firmly but gently as he could, holding the sound-proofed .45 by its barrel, he began splintering the glass. Only after awhile did he become aware that the pieces were beginning to tinkle as they landed below, one on top of another. Nothing to do about it. When he had to shift weight to reach, he heard Hanny's only sound, a muttered, "Shit." It didn't take long to clear a three foot stretch, and then he banged the cushioned butt of the gun down on the bits still left, crushing them, brushing the powder away. He laid the gun aside and hefted himself up on a soft grunt of relief from Hanny. Michael cleared another foot or so of the wall. Putting on his shirt he hunkered down off to that side to let Hanny come up, and they squatted there while Hanny reloaded the .45.

Michael had worried that the ground might be a longer drop inside the wall or fall away more sharply, but it was the same as outside. He and Hanny could get Kathleen over it if she had any strength at all. Once he found her.

From now on, nothing needed saying. They were about to turn onto their bellies to slither down, when Michael smelled it even as Hanny reached to halt him, and they both froze. Smoke from a cheroot. They looked down and along the wall, and there he came in black calf-length Shan trousers tied at the hips, eyes fixed on the ground, a long stick over his shoulder bobbing a bundle of something, the cheroot in his other hand, marching along on what looked to be bare feet. Oh, man, would he step on the broken glass? But it was against the base of the wall and he was out maybe a foot and a half. Plus which, those feet probably had soles tougher than Michael's army boots. Worse problem, would he look up, see them? Or hear them?

They held their breaths, in unison, had done it often enough when caught on the ground in Nam, and then started breathing silently through their mouths. The Shan got to the gap in the wall, and in the dim light they watched as he slid his bundle through it, then slipped through it himself. If he as much as sent a glance over his shoulder he'd see them silhouetted there. Michael shot a finger towards the ground, and he and Hanny made it down without a sound. A low female laugh came from the palace. A yellow light went out. As Sherm would say, beddy-byes.

Michael led off across the open compound towards the near back corner of the elongated palace. According to the map, there was a kind of passageway along the rear between the rock face of the ridge and the building, the veranda above it creating a roof. Probably used for storage, as was certainly the entire area under the first floor of the palace. Michael hoped they'd find nothing more fragrant than that, but it wasn't unlikely that the kitchen had a hole in the floor to shove garbage through for the pigs sheltered below, not to mention whatever else the pigs ate. Hanny'd love that. But the open space would provide them a safe trip across the palace if they could get through it. Kathleen's room was supposed to be at the far end, not one of the separate hooches but in that back corner of the main building.

They had to duck their heads, less than six feet of headroom. It was as silent underneath the palace as outside it. The pigs must be penned somewhere else. They'd be snorting, snuffling. Now and then, there was a rustle, a chittering. Rats. Sure as God made little spiders, Michael knew he'd be running into cobwebs, but hastily he took his mind off that, looking across the open area towards the front of the palace – and found that now and again as he walked forward, that view was blocked. Rooms walled off for storehouses, probably, maybe locked, maybe opium stocks. They crossed under what must've been the kitchen. He could smell cooling charcoal, fried garlic, dried rotted fish ngapi.

They reached the far corner and stopped. A last hesitation. Then Michael reached up to the veranda floor, hefted himself up and under the wooden rail and sat, legs dangling. A moment, Hanny joined him. Michael's heart was trip-hammering, and not from physical exertion. He looked up at the building behind him. A shuttered window, a dim red glow slitting through it, only a few feet from where the building cornered. Kathleen's window, according to the map. No lights coming from within anywhere else along the porch. A door adjacent to the shuttered window that, on harder look, he found to be slightly ajar. Into her room? If not, if somebody else was asleep inside . . . Should take off his boots, but if it went wrong he'd be in deep shit without them. Anyhow, no denying the door offered the quickest, the only access. He had to chance it.

He stood up. Hanny did the same, put his back to the wall next to the window, his rifle off his shoulder and into his hands at the ready. A last look between them, and Michael turned for the door.

It was a bathroom. A zinc sink reflecting dimly, with a single spigot – cold water only. An Ali Baba jar and dipper for a dip-and-pour bath, but then Michael saw the round head of a shower high on the wall. And a by

God oak-seated flush toilet with a chain running up to a wooden box high under the ceiling. Sure wouldn't live up to Hanny's expectations of a palace, but it beat a wet-sweeper any day. Walking in on you to collect your shit when you weren't done yet. It had happened to him once, at the Keng Tung government guesthouse.

The glow, barely enough to see by, seeped through another door left narrowly ajar. He moved to the door, looked in, and saw one bed with a mosquito net draped around it, and toward a corner a burning charcoal brazier casting light and a little warmth, too, probably.

He stepped through the door, stopped again, trying to peer through the mosquito bar to see who it protected on the bed, couldn't. There was a chest on the far wall, and a small table with – yeah, a mirror above it. The rest of the room was indiscernable, its shadows darkened by the pool of red surrounding the brazier, bouncing off the netting, turning it rosy like thin blood.

He crossed the room, his boots silent but the floor creaking with his weight. Make it fast, make it fast, make it fast. Now, now he could see. And there was nobody there, on the bed. He jerked the bar away and up. Nobody. And then he heard a rustle, a gasp from the corner beyond the brazier.

In two strides he was there, peering, to see a small figure cowering back from him, staring up at him, hand almost covering her face, her eyes frantic and moving over his camouflage flight suit, the pistol on his hip – visitor from Mars. But she seemed the more shocked when her eyes rose to his face, held there, widening. She gasped again. "Him! You are him!" she whispered. "Of the picture!"

Though he understood every word, only belatedly did Michael realize that she was speaking English. "Where is she! Kathleen? The sayah? Kathleen Howard – you know her?"

His urgency frightened her. He tried to calm down, held out a hand to her. Slowly, she dropped hers, and he saw in the dim light a deformed face, one-eyed, it looked like, with lumps. Swellings. He reached to help her up, to stop her cowering, but when he touched her, it didn't frighten her the more so much as cause her to whimper and flinch her shoulder back, getting on her knees as if to protect her body more. Her face wasn't deformed. She'd been beaten.

"Yes, yes," she was saying. She understood him. "Not here now. She go."

It rocked him back on his heels. He swallowed, struggled to keep a whisper. "How long?"

"Two . . . no . . . " and she struggled, too, her English seeming to be fast fleeting. Two what? Weeks? Months? But no, couldn't be – Tom had seen the Gurkha since then. As if to make sure he got it, she raised her hand and showed three fingers. And another one, crooked against the palm. Had they broken it? If she didn't get it set soon, it'd forever be useless. It must hurt like hell. And was it two or three, for Christ's sake, and three what?

"Three?" he asked. She nodded once. "Three what?"

"Three day," she answered.

Shit. Just three days? "Where?" he asked.

"She follow ponies. She follow tracks, and then go river, find doctor for baby."

And suddenly, hope wrenched inside. Ponies. Oh, God, could it be? "Where – " He had to swallow again. "Where are the ponies going?"

"Across big river. Laos," she said. "Phong Saly Road."

He was panting as hard as after a run, and guessed he hadn't been breathing very well for a few minutes. She clasped her hands over her face and began rocking, and he knew what he heard coming from her should have been a wail but she kept it silent. "Poor lady! They kill her. They kill baby. Must be dead."

"Why? How?" He was stuttering, terrified, and meant how did she know this?

Again, she understood. "Lady shoot guard, steal horse." God damn, still Kathleen all right. "But he not dead. He come long time after, and he want know where she go. I not tell, I not tell. Long time, I not tell." And she started to weep, now, with shame and guilt. "End of second day, I tell."

Michael wanted to comfort her, part of him did anyway, the part that wasn't impatience and anger. But he knew not to touch her on the head, and anywhere else might hurt her. And he still didn't know how this woman was so sure.

"Radio, you know radio?" she asked. There was the answer, and he hadn't posed the question. "They send message to Sai Myaing. Captain. Yesterday he send message back, they catch her."

"And?" She looked at him. "Another message? That they've – that she's – "

She shook her head. "But when Sawbwa knows, baby will die. Lady, too, maybe. He beat her before he go away."

Michael let out a breath, almost ground it out of his lungs. "Is he . . . is the Sawbwa with the train? Or here, or – ?"

She shook her head again. "Sawbwa go Ban Houei Say." The Laotian drug center of the Golden Triangle. "But he will know even so," she was going on. "He has radio, too . . . Maybe he give order already. Or maybe they keep her for him."

Michael got to his feet. "God damn that son of a – "

"Ssss! Tone it down." Hanny whispered from the window, shutters open now.

"You get all this?"

"Yeah. Let's move."

A moment, mind skittering, trying to think if he'd found out all he could, and Michael crouched again before the tiny damaged woman. "Tell no one we've come here. They won't be able to guess it, so can you do that? Tell no one?"

She nodded. "I go home my village soon. Lady give me two Mogok stones."

Michael stood up, striding for the window, and heard her soft voice. "Save her."

Out through the window before he looked back in at her. "I promise," he said softly.

"Baby, too? Please?"

He nodded. She couldn't see him nod, of course. "We'll try," he whispered. She shikoed to him on her knees, forehead touching the floor.

They retraced steps under the palace veranda and across the grounds undiscovered. Over the wall, and knowing the way, back up the hill to the Loach in a quarter the time they'd taken to come down it.

Seated in the cockpit, catching their breaths from the long run, they looked at each other. Looked out and up at the moon, too, fitful, with clouds riding across it. Michael cranked and lifted.

"We do same time, same speeds, same coordinates, right?" Hanny, having flicked on the intercom, already using his red-lense flash on the careful notes he'd made coming in.

"Right," said Michael. She'd kept his picture. God in heaven, maybe they could put it all back together.

"Won't be hard to find the train, fires trailing out along the track," Hanny said, "but how do we land? Shit, where do we land?"

"We dance by the light of the moon, little darlin'," Michael answered, his voice hard, not funning.

Hanny peered up through the windshield. "Yeah. Nothin' like blind hope, I always say. So where in the fuckin' jungle do you figure to – "

"Look for a pagoda," Michael said. "I mean, after we sight the train. There'll be one somewhere close by. Has to be. They have platforms surrounding them. And walled-in yards. Cleared spaces, big enough for us."

"And then what do we do? And by the way, you know as well as I do what this extra landing's gonna do to our fuel."

"Neal . . . just shut up, okay?" There was a small moment of silence, and Michael asked, "How much money you got?"

25

Last night, after Sai Myaing had spoken over the radio with the Sawbwa, he had come out of the tent and spoken to her while she crouched there in her little plastic shelter, wanting to know, terrified to know. "He will meet us at Phong Saly Road," the captain had said. "And I am to keep you with us. I told him I doubted the child would be alive in two days' time. He said the blame would not be mine." And he'd returned to his tent where a man prepared him food.

She'd shuddered, cold to the bone hearing his calm death knell. And what was meant about the road? Where they reached it, or all the way to the refinery at Rapet? She didn't know how far that was. Two days, he'd said. It had rung in her head the night through. A long night, her back itching, because after getting damp the camisole would dry, sticking to the one cut. She didn't think it was infected, but how could she be sure, couldn't look to see it. And Cho never satisfied, never easy, hunger or illness keeping him restless and miserable. But she had worked out a plan. Two days. She didn't have two days. It would have to be after dark. She'd be too easy to track, to find, in daytime. They had watched her too closely last night. So that now, making camp for the third time, her second with the train, she knew what she was going to do.

During the day, she had begun it. They didn't stop often enough for her to feed Cho with rice, but she held him inside her shirt, let him suck at her dry teat to pacify him, and he'd gotten used to it. And she'd gotten the men used to her taking one of her bags with her when she left the train to go to toilet. The first time, a guard had insisted on turning it inside out, and found only her journals and Cho's cloths. She'd said her time of the month had come, and from then on they'd left her alone.

While on her pony, she had managed to slip her passport in between the pages of one of the journals and then had buried under the cloths at the bottom of the bag the tinder box and the packet of uncooked rice. No pot, but she could steam it inside teak leaves resting on coals. And with each stop, she had gotten into the habit of placing the baby in a nest of whatever was handy and covering him over so that he looked to be a little mound.

Now and then, taken unawares by her own thoughts, fear would shaft through her. All the plans in the world useless, she could never bring it off, she'd get lost in the jungle, she'd fall and hurt herself and both of them would starve to death. Or good in the jungle as she might be, the Shans would find her in minutes after she tried to run. And Cho, against her side and belly, had felt hotter and hotter.

But now, thank the Lord, they were in camp at last, and Cho had had his fill of her rice which was warm off the fire twice already. No rain, and the men were settled in, even those who had returned feeling blessed from trekking up the ridge to the pagoda, invisible through the jungle but that they knew from past trips was there. Some were gambling, some of them already in hammocks slung for sleep, smoking not cheroots but opium pipes, though Sai Myaing tried to keep them from it. They were burning the Sawbwa's cash crop, after all.

The pagoda had shafted her with hope, for once. Not fear. For while the monks, if monks there were in this remote jungle place, would not be eager to offer her sanctuary, the structure itself could – little tunnels running into its black interior, twists and turns and niches where she could crouch and hide until the captain gave up the search. He would have to in a short time, the refinery was awaiting their gum. And she determinedly resisted thoughts of poisonous centipedes, kraits and cobras.

Only a while more, a little while perhaps. Oh, if she could take a pony – but it would be too noisy, and once they discovered her absence, and the baby's, they would search for her back along the trail first of all. But they had crossed a large stream only two or three hours before stopping. It would lead to the Mekong, and perhaps villages along its banks, and the women there would help her, they would. The pagoda up above would offer paths back to that stream, they must, they must, and she could use them once the captain gave up searching and took the train on towards the road. But she no longer had the dah. The jungle would be difficult without the dah. Oh, God, help her. Please, God.

What was that? A helicopter? Oh, no. No, no, no. He was coming after all. He was coming here. She sat up. Men around her, her guards, were all coming alert. Looking skyward, and now they could all see it – a small creature circling like a bug, black against the moonlit glow overhead.

She tucked the sleeping baby inside her shirt. Glancing around, no one had noticed. She pretended to pat him in his nest, bunched up cloths and the longyi seeming to bunch up around him, over him.

They thought it was the Prince, too, but Sai Myaing who came stumbling out of his sleep from his tent was looking up as if puzzled, surprised. "He didn't radio," he complained. "No one radio'd." The noise of the helicopter dwindled as it left their sight. "Landing up by the pagoda," another man offered.

All right then, all right, she thought. As they came down from there, she would go up. And if it wasn't the Prince, maybe . . . maybe she could bribe the pilot for a ride. She patted the silk pouch hanging from a cord around her neck, the stones inside it. Or . . . or she could stowaway. She had no idea what the inside of a helicopter looked like, but surely there were places she could hide in, behind seats or in a baggage compartment.

Dear Lord, have You answered my prayer? Is this the saving of us?

Now the captain with a bunch of his men were heading off into the jungle up the ridge. As others straggled along behind them out of curiosity, she seized her moment and stole away into the jungle herself. No hue. No cry. No one had noticed.

* * *

They'd made the trip back in almost complete silence, both of them concentrating on figuring out direction and location and God knew what else. Oh, once, Hanny had told Michael to ease up on speed or they'd overfly Keng Tung, but that was all. And in any case, neither had an idea of what was in store. All the plans they'd made for their assault on Loi Long and the palace which had worked like a charm, to what good? But flying the return, at least, they knew what the hell they were doing, had done plenty of it the past three years. And here came the line of red campfires, beckoning them like a string of rubies.

Michael banked around, both of them scanning the black jungle for a steeple, a break in the darkness to a lighter area, anything to reveal a pagoda. And there it was, even lit by some dim yellow glows like those back at the palace.

Going low, he circled it once, seeing shadows cast on the platform by statuary. Shit, guardian chinthe lions and spirit nats and Buddhas . . . but the courtyard had some trees. Jesus – okay, okay, the top of the broad stairs leading up to the platform was wide and empty. And that's where he set down.

He killed the engine. The silence was immense, and then the jungle night sounds crowded in. There was an altar set against the pagoda base with fluttering oil lamps, the lights having somehow survived the wind of the Loach's blades.

They took off their helmets, sitting there, looking at each other. "They'll be up to greet us," Michael said, no strain. But his mind was racing. Probably no monks here without a pongyi chaung, a village school. But was she down there, below? Was this the right train? And if it was, and she was, how would they get her out? Even make contact with her, the damn train was spread along the trail for close to half a kilometer.

The lights were almost upon them before they saw the approach, saw them come through the crumbled stone gate into the courtyard, small men carrying battery lights, some of them, some with small fire torches, the man in the lead carrying a gasoline lantern. They clustered at the foot of the steps, all of them armed and wearing ammo belts. The one with his AK at the ready slowly came up the steps. Michael eased out to the ground, and Hanny followed his lead, came around to join him. Each wore his pistol, but left the rifles aboard.

The man – small, hard-faced, with suspicious eyes that were flickering over the Loach and back to the Americans as if looking for some-thing, someone. "Speak Ingle-ei"?

"Oh, yeah," Michael answered on a sigh of relief. "Yes, we speak English."

"Where Sawbwa? Sao Htin Aung. Where Sawbwa?"

Another wave of relief. The only man in all of Southeast Asia who could've recognized him, and the bastard wasn't here. Michael took the gamble. "He is in Ban Hooy-sooy . . . "

The head honcho grinned, and the men with him tried to be polite and not laugh. "Ban Houie Say," the Shan said.

Michael grinned back, and gesturing between himself and Hanny, he tried again. How did they say it? "Ameiyican," he said, and he saw their faces, even the main man's face brighten. It still seemed to be an open sesame, at least among the Burmese.

Hanny's answer to Michael's only question had been that he was wearing his money belt – the hotel's door locks were a disaster, the safe hardly more trustworthy. Michael had his on, too. So, now, Michael just went with it. "Your Sawbwa told us you would sell us some opium gum."

* * *

She had taken care to leave the track on the pagoda side, and had started right up the ridge. But the jungle got denser and denser, she was stumbling over roots slippery with mud, terrified to fall and crush the baby, and the firelights from the train soon were lost behind her. Breath catching in her throat, she stopped, hoping her eyes would adjust. And they did, a little. Feeling now with hands and lifting her feet high, she again was moving, this time to the right where she knew the path ran from the track up to the pagoda. What had happened to the helicopter? The sound was lost, had been for a while. Because of the jungle, or had it gone to the other side of the ridge?

Little flurries of panic had rushed her. How could they not, on top of her fears of everything else? She needed that helicopter.

Oh, sweet heaven, the path. It had seemed bright almost, the moon reflecting off it. She'd hesitated, then stepped forward onto it and headed uphill. Cho was quiet. The path wound back and forth, small switch-backs where it was steep. Her hands were scratched, and one cheek stung. So intent was she to keep her feet moving and sure that she didn't hear until it was nearly too late: they were coming up the path behind her.

She'd frozen there, glimmerings of light on the switch-back below her. At last, she'd wrenched herself into motion and half-jumped into the dense growth lining the path, afraid to go too far for losing it, almost falling over a windfall to crouch behind it, hugging herself, protecting the baby in the curve of her belly, pulling the shawl over her bright hair and white face, and waited.

It had been endless. She'd given Cho her breast, and he got some milk, a little, anyway. What was taking so long? Perhaps the helicopter *was* on the other side of the ridge.

But here they came back down again. There was laughter, and an odd deepness to the voices. She could hear the captain's voice, speaking English. Something about they would have tea and talk about price. Price?

English. Oh, the pilot. Yes. Wanting to buy gum. But that was good. It was. It would give her time to reach the helicopter, to hide, and be ready. Thank God.

* * *

The smoke curled under the ceiling of the tent, so low that it wreathed Michael's head. Hanny's, too, but he didn't seem bothered, going at the bargaining with such gusto he was picking up the rhythms of the head man's accented English. Five kilos of leaf-wrapped packets sat at their feet. Michael's eyes burned. He'd forgotten how cookfire smoke never could seem to escape through the roof holes in Shan houses. Tent roofs either, it seemed, and he was desperate to get out, go looking, *find her*.

He stood up abruptly, having to keep himself bent over, and all talk went silent. "Hey," Hanny said quietly, but pushing a grin, "I'm really workin' the numbers down here." And then, the message clear, "Be careful, Michael."

"Yup," Michael said. "Keep at it." And he beamed apologetically all around, gestured at his bladder – not hard to believe, they'd been drinking enough tea to float the Queen Mary. And the five Shans sitting cross-legged on the tent floor around the charcoal brazier all beamed back, made a few little friendly jokes, or they sounded like it, and the bargaining started again. Blessed Hanny. Michael left.

He straightened up outside, grabbed some air, and found himself facing another circle of Shans, all of whom nodded, smiled. He made the same gesture, walked through the circle and off the track into the bush. There, he took his leak and slipped some money out of his belt, he had about two fifty in dollars, and Hanny was working on five kilos at no more than sixty per. Hanny could make up the difference.

Michael had decided while sitting there, trying not to cough too much, letting Hanny take the lead, that once out of the tent he'd walk the whole length of the train, if need be. He'd find her, God damn it. Had to.

So that's what he did, now – or started to, when about three meters from the tent he was stopped dead by what looked to be a make-shift shelter of plastic sheeting. Here? It was filthy with spattered mud and streaky mold. Hers. He'd swear it on his own grave, had to be. He glanced around, squatted by it, started pawing through the stuff left under it. A Shan bag, some dirty cloths – he smelled his fingers, and knew. The baby.

A heavy hand landed on his shoulder, he was shoved back, and a Shan kicked at the bundle of stuff, stomped it, and began shouting even as he turned and ran for the head man's tent.

Oh, shit, oh, shit, he'd tipped them to it. She'd sneaked out and now they knew it. He was up, leaping for the tent.

Never quite made it for the Shans pouring out of it, followed by Hanny, sticking his head out through the flap, staring at Michael a little wildly. "Told you to be careful, God damn it! What'd you do, blow the whole – "

"Yeah. No. Shit, she's gone!"

The head man was shouting orders left and right, and Shans were darting this way and that, and heading into the jungle on all sides. Michael and Hanny stared at each other, Michael's mind on the fast track. "Okay, okay," he said, "We gotta move."

He hauled out the two fifty, shoved it at Hanny. "Grab us a couple of kits of gum – they need to believe in us. That bastard Sawbwa can't suspect anything about where she's gone to."

"Huh?" Hanny said, thinking he'd lost it, Michael was sure. "Just do it!" he said. So Hanny turned into the tent with the money and came back out at once with the opium. And together, no one paying them any mind at all, everyone shouting and rushing around, Michael and Hanny walked easily along the track, found the path, started up it, and immediately Michael broke into a lope.

Behind him, Hanny kept pace. The moon was still with them. "You mind tellin' me what the hell's comin' down here?" Hanny puffing.

"She's with the Loach."

"You're sure of that, huh? Jesus and Mary, what is she, some kind of psychic? Or you think you suddenly are?"

Michael didn't answer. They found the Loach sitting silent on the platform, her brown skin gleaming dully under the moon. Michael stopped dead, looking around, no sign of anything. "Kathleen?" he called, softly, surely. "Kathleen!"

Hanny gave him a long look, finally shrugged, slung the packets of gum into the cabin. "Hey, Kathleen!" he called, "you here, girl?"

"Shh!" Michael commanded. "Leave it to me."

"Oh, sure, she can't help but know your voice, right? All these years, and she's still – "

But Michael just called again. "Kathleen?"

She heard only the rumble of their voices talking, but she heard the name. Her name. Crouched way back in one of the corridors of the pagoda, sounds from outside banked by the brick walls and crumbled stucco, still she heard her name.

A trick. The captain had come here, had given them her name, and they were trying to call her out from hiding like a sick dog.

Before, in the jungle, after they had all passed her going back to camp, she had waited some longer to make sure, and then she'd returned to the path, had climbed it up to the pagoda and found the helicopter. Tiny. So tiny, her heart sank. She went and looked in and knew there was no place to hide there, to be a stowaway.

Her breaths coming in sobs, she'd known surely it would be time to die soon. The baby had soiled himself, and the smell came up to her from inside her shirt. Not his time. God damn it, no, not his time. Hands trembling with haste, she lay Cho on the floor of the helicopter, untied the dirty cloth between his legs, wiped him with the clean ends of the cloth best she could see to in the moonlight, caught a clean cloth through his legs and tied it, bunched the dirty cloth down into the bottom of her bag. He was good, quiet except for his breathing. At least they wouldn't be able to smell him.

She'd stepped away from the helicopter to scan the pagoda's facade, saw the black arch beckoning and went to it, into it, going deep into the dark, so much darker than even the jungle, and squatted there, the thought coming to her from nowhere of Michael, always so in dread of spiders. Hastily, she had tucked the baby in tight, no openings for crawlers. And he'd started to cry.

But if she couldn't hear, neither could they. Not that little cry, weep, weep, cries the chimney sweep, my father sold me . . . William Blake, was she losing her mind?

"Kathleen!" Michael called, voice louder each time.

"Listen!" Hanny said. And the voices rose to them above the jungle. "They're coming up here."

"They've figured it out," Michael said. Hanny just looked at him. "If I did, they could," said Michael, in stubbornness.

"Kath! It's no trick, Kathleen! Come on out, now!"

She was losing her mind. Already had. Kath? Oh, sweet Lord. "Kath!" the call came again, and she knew the voice. *Knew* it. As she knew her own. Well, if she was crazy foolish, then she was. God looked after drunkards and fools. She rocked forward and stood up, having to bend over, and moved towards where light seeped in through the arch.

He was facing out towards the jungle now, watching those lights, getting desperate. "Kathleen Howard, you get your ass out here, right now!" Hanny's touch on his arm, he turned, and oh, God, there she came, so slowly, face lifted white in the moonlight. Wearing – blue jeans, good God? And one of the knees ripped. He stepped towards her, hands reaching for her.

This man? Cheeks hidden in the shadows made by the bones above them? This tall man? "Michael?"

Arm cupped beneath a weight inside her shirt, hair in a pony-tail. The vision of a girl went, perhaps lost forever in the woman he saw now. One of his reaching hands touched her hair, her face, a finger brushing across her lips. They were the same. And her hand came up and took his, trembling around his, with a grip fit to crush steel.

"Get with it! Now!" Hanny's voice, gruff, scared.

But she didn't let go. "How – how on earth – how did you come here?!"

"Tom," Michael said, and softening a little he added, "and the woman back at the palace." Quickly, now, he grasped her arm, loosening her hand, urging her to the Loach where Hanny waited. Hanny put his hands under her elbows, preparing to lift her up into the back cabin.

"No!" she said, shrinking from Hanny. She looked at Michael, anguish in her face, and took from within her shirt the baby. Even as Michael reached for it, she was holding it out to him, and he was shocked. Sure, he didn't know much, but this baby . . . exquisite face, head, bright eyes – green like his mama's, Michael'd bet – but too small. All Asian kids are small, he told himself, accepting the baby in his two hands. Weighed no more than a three-week old piglet.

"Michael!" Hanny cutting through it. Now Hanny did grab her, pushed her up into the cabin, sat her down on the right nylon troop seat. "What're they shouting?" he asked her.

She was slow to understand and answer. "To wait," she said. "Oh, but don't! Please, oh – " and she was half getting out.

"Michael!" Hanny half turned, needing help with her. Michael stepped to the doorway. Hanny swung around and got into the cockpit. "Not likely," he muttered.

"All right, Kathleen," Michael said, trying to keep it calm. "No one's going to wait for anyone." She looked so bewildered, so disbelieving. He guided her back onto the seat, handed her the baby, began to strap her in. "Lay him down on the fold between your thighs, head tight into your crotch. There's armor in the bottom of your seat." She did it. He found the Colonel's helmet and put it on her head, put her fingers on the send-receive button for the intercom.

He got in, having to squeeze past her. Rifle shots. Warnings to stop them. God, they had figured it out. They knew where she'd come.

Hanny was already cranking. Michael slapped the bulkhead. "Talk to her!" he shouted at Hanny, and with his fingers on Kathleen's, he moved the switch and felt her start as Hanny's voice came through to her, went off, came back. She nodded quickly.

He swivelled away towards the left door, hefting Hanny's M-16 up into firing position, howled, "Go, go, go!"

The turbine had spun up, now got its speed. Men burst through the trees, the other side of the wall and over it, across the courtyard, nearly to the steps, firing as they came. Kathleen aside, didn't they care if they shot their royal heir, for Christ's sake?

The Loach was taking fire, bullets thunking, but not through the open back. Maybe they did care. Michael fired the automatic well above their heads. As the Loach started its lift three Shans got to them, tossed aside their guns and hurled themselves onto the skids.

Shit. They were brave men, shouting, holding on, dangling now above the ground. Hanny did what Michael would've done, he made the Loach swing side to side, dipped, hoping to dislodge them, and did, one, two. Michael stared down onto the head of the third. "Stupid dink," he muttered, and shouted, "let go!" He pointed his weapon straight into the brown mustached face now lifted to him. Hanny bucked the Loach sharply up. And at last, mouth open in a cry, the Shan dropped off. Not that long a fall, Michael told himself, maybe a couple of broken bones.

He sat down hard and looked at Kathleen. She was bent forward over the baby in her lap – in protection, of course – but she was looking at Michael. As she had not in the first moments. As if at a stranger.

Then she startled, took off the helmet to offer it, and Michael shoved it onto his own head. Too small for him, but any port . . . "Talk," he said into the mike, keying for Hanny.

"Smooth sailing back there?" Hanny asked.

"Y'done good."

Hanny gave a little grunt and turned off.

Michael thought a minute, then keyed Hanny again. "Helmet's too small, giving it to Kathleen. You want to communicate, it'll be through her."

Michael handed the helmet back to Kathleen, shouting above the noise of the blades what he'd just said to Hanny. She understood and put it on. The baby was wriggling in her lap, making faces. The moon was in and out now, but when it was out it was full and bright. Hanny had banked around to head south and was still climbing, or that's what Michael figured.

South and east to Luang Prabang.

Kathleen mouthed, "How long?"

The trip? He held up one finger, then two, and shrugged.

She looked so troubled, looked down at her baby, tickled his mouth with her finger and got him to suck on it. He studied her in the dim light, never wanting to take his eyes from her. It was Kathleen. Slender. Thin, really – face, too strained. But Kathleen for all that. She looked up at him. Could they bridge the years? The different worlds? The changes in each of them? And was she asking herself the same questions?

Then he remembered. Jesus. How could he take her to Meisner's place in the middle of the night? He looked away from her, staring down on the dark jungle, down the dark corridor of five long years. And maybe dark years to come, strangers forever. Even if he could find the right address, strangers just turning up at the gate? He'd have to sneak her into the hotel somehow.

A tap on his shoulder, he turned and found her holding out the helmet to him. Michael spoke into the mike.

"Yeah?"

"Sorry. You best get up here," Hanny said.

Now what? Michael keyed him. "Giving Kathleen the 'phones. Explain to her. On my way."

He keyed receive on for her, clambored back across her to slide his feet out the right door down to the skids, knowing Hanny would be telling her not to worry, that they did this little maneuver all the time. A slight exaggeration.

He shuffled forward through the warm moist wind, reached inside the cockpit, grabbed his own helmet, swung into the seat, and saw the blood. Hanny's left hand on the collective was covered with it, and it had pooled on his left leg and foot. Still was, far as he could tell. Anger took him. "My God, why didn't you call me – " and then he saw the splintered instrument panel. No fuel gauge. No tachometer. No altimeter or horizon.

How long a trip? Oh, yeah. Good question.

26

Michael took the controls. "Got it," he declared. Hanny could only respond, "Yeah," and release.

"What were you thinking, Neal, you should've brought me forward right away!" But the anger was more at himself. He should've taken the damned bullets, not Hanny. And if he hadn't been a fucking sentimental idiot, if he'd fired directly into the Shans, they might've gotten clean away.

Hanny had already found a source of the blood on his upper left arm and was applying pressure with his right hand. "The bleeding's slowing down," Hanny said, "but the left hand's cold, going stiff."

Michael's eyes moved from the panel up, found the hand compass still fastened to the bubble, still apparently working.

"You know where we are?"

"More or less." Hanny's voice was tight, either against pain or weakness or both. "We've been going full out due south. At least the engine sounds like it's blistering. Don't know how long – what – five, six minutes?"

Michael grunted agreement.

"Should turn southeast pretty quick. We crossed the Mekong not long before landing, right? So the next big river's the Nam Tha. Should be comin' up in maybe twenty minutes more. And twenty minutes, maybe half hour, forty minutes after that, Luang Prabang. Depends on the bird."

"Shit." Michael turned the Loach to the right.

"What're you doin'?" Hanny, sharp.

"Goin' back to find the Mekong. We're putting down."

"Come on, Cam. No telling what else those dinks hit. Might not get back up again. And even if we do, we'll be suckin' air."

Ignoring the last – what else? – Michael flicked the landing lights on, off. They worked.

"So, okay," Hanny said, "we've got essential buss." Michael was already flicking on the radio. It was alive. "And radio's okay. But who knows if the igniters'll work. And we won't 'til we try 'em." What he didn't say was, didn't need to, was if the igniters didn't work, they were down for good.

"I'm not gonna fly visuals-only all the rest of the way in whatever fog turns up looking for a glory hole up to a night sky. Especially with you bleeding like a stuck pig, sorry about that. We crunched blind mountains in Nam too often, and you know it. The moon could go any minute. Can you manage to figure out coordinates for a Mayday?"

"You'll be tellin' the world we're way the hell and gone off course. Turn back east, Michael. We can just about intersect on the Nam Tha with a straight line from the Volpar down to L.P. – nobody'd have to know a thing."

And meanwhile, it'd be close to an hour and Hanny could be bleeding to death in the next seat.

"Mekong won't do it for us." Hanny trying to speak with strength. "Too many defiles over towards Burma – we saw 'em, remember?"

He was right. Aw, Jesus. "Yeah. Okay." Michael did a one-eighty, now heading due east. "We find an LZ on the Nam Tha." Unless they were offered one on some creek that happened to turn up in the meantime. "Come daylight, flyin' on visuals into L.P.'ll be a piece of cake. Even if the weather socks us in. We'll stay low, follow the Nam Tha back west to the Mekong and take it to town."

"Can't. Fuel, remember? Shortest distance between two points. We got to go straight, and should now."

Michael said only, "There'll be choices if we need 'em." Sounding stubborn not smart, but never mind. He had to see to Hanny. "Meanwhile, we Mayday, and if we can't start her up tomorrow, someone'll come find us. Settled. Now let's get our location tight."

Hanny knew it for an order, discussion over, and somehow managed the map and the red-lense flash to try to figure out where the hell they were. Probably all the moving around making him bleed even more, but no other way.

Michael keyed on the back cabin. "You there, Kathleen?"

"What happened to you?" She sounded scared.

"We're right here. But we have to land, no danger to it, please believe." As long as the moon stays out. "We'll spend some time down and fly into Luang Prabang in the morning. We're due to come up on the Nam Tha River shortly. When we do, we all start looking for an open space on a bank. The most likely would be on the outer curve of a bow – apt to be a wide flat there, a pebbled strand maybe. You okay with all this?"

She was slow coming back, breathless and high. "Morning?" And then, immediately, "Okay."

"Good. We've got Hanny on the left, you're on the right and rear, I'm forward. I'll let you know when. We'll find it, Kath. Going off." He switched off, started looking, waiting on Hanny, Michael keeping his hands as steady as possible to maintain altitude. It'd be so damned easy to lose it, no way in the dark to gauge it.

At last, seemed forever, Hanny came on, having to clear his throat, his breath sounding heavy through the mike. "Get ready."

"Good," said Michael. But Hanny sounded not good. Michael hoped to God they didn't have an artery blown out here.

There came the river ahead of them, a thin twining snake, glittering under the moon. He keyed on the intercom. "Start looking," he said, and took the chopper in a turn to follow the course south. Might as well get as close to that intersection Hanny'd been talking about as they could while looking. Black banks on either side of the silver. Shit, they didn't find an LZ soon, they *would* run out of fuel.

And then they saw it, within seconds of each other. "There!" "Bingo!" "There!" Sand not mud. Looking like alabaster, bowing out into the streambed in a crescent, for sure no sweet landing pad but adequate.

Hanny dictated the coordinates and Michael began sending the May-day to King, the FAC airborne rescue center flying somewhere over Laos. He was into his third repetition, flicking the radio to receive after each send, circling back over the piece of sand, when at last they got their acknowledgement – so damned fraught with static there was no telling whether the coordinates were being repeated back as trans-mitted or not. If the static played both ways, they might not've been received clearly either way, and if the damned igniters didn't work . . . they either rafted a lot of rapids or had a long walk, neither one good news with a baby and a wounded man.

Michael banked around and headed down. The Loach kissed the white sand. Michael and Hanny looked at each other a very long moment before Michael rolled off the turbine and cut the fuel.

Finally, Hanny asked in a whisper, "Going to try it now?"

"It'll keep," Michael said. "It's a habit of bad news." He switched the searchlight off, left the cabin red on, and turned out of the Loach, looking across the cockpit at Hanny. "Give you a hand back to the cabin in a sec." And quickly, he stepped to look in on Kathleen. The spots reflected off the sand, and he could see her face, see the strain in it. Was panic lurking there? He didn't want to bring it to her.

Bush noises swarmed around them now, odd animal calls, hoots – monkeys, maybe – and the water flowing right next to them made a rushing sound, rocks close to the surface. "We're all right, Kathleen. Hanny's been hurt, but we're going to give him first aid, you and I."

She was scared even more, but she nodded, looked down at once at the baby. She had opened her shirt and he could see beneath it a – what did they call it, a camisole? The baby was beginning to whine a little, his mouth pursing into sucking shapes. As she had before, she placed her little finger between his lips and he immediately sucked it. Then, in no time at all and getting no satisfaction out of a finger, the baby started to cry. Why didn't she nurse him? Because Michael was watching?

The Loach leaned and creaked, Hanny sliding out of the cockpit and down to the ground. Damn. Michael started around the nose to help him. Curious how a man hurting could weigh so much more than a man healthy. He got to him as Hanny finished his turn for the back.

When Kathleen caught sight of all the dark stain on him, the blood, she gasped, made a small sound of distress, and without missing a moment she tucked the wrapped baby down on the floor between the seats and reached for Hanny. Futile, he was far too heavy for her, but he managed to sit on the floor. Michael unscrewed the red lense from the flashlight, leaned in beside him to find the first aid kit and handed Hanny the flashlight.

"Hold it for me," he ordered. Would keep Hanny busy. Distract the victim, first rule of first aid. Or was it the second? But not a hell of a lot Michael could do about shock right now. "Shirt off," he continued. But the attempt to get it off caused Hanny to wince, the blood which was already congealing making the cloth adhere.

"Oh, sure, Neal, piece of cake, nothin' to it, right?" Hanny being sarcastic.

He'll be fine, Michael thought, opening the kit. "Never said that, Hanny. Never did." Kathleen was trying to ease the shirt loose, now, but with no better luck.

"Don't worry, Kathleen," Hanny said, grinning at her, "I've taken worse, and our dauntless commander here's been teachin' survival training for two tours."

Kathleen, meanwhile, had given up on the shirt, was pawing through the kit. "Two tours?" she asked, then added with irritation, "Isn't there something in here that'll dissolve the shirt free?"

Michael pushed her hands away to look, too.

"Two years," Hanny said.

She looked up at Michael. "The Indochina war, Kathleen," Michael said. "In Vietnam."

She was aghast. *"Two years?"*

Michael and Hanny exchanged a look, Michael's saying, see? I knew she'd love it.

"Sorry," Hanny murmured. He was hanging on there to the real world, or maybe Michael's world.

Michael found a small tube of antibacterial ointment. Kathleen used it, softening the blood with it. Michael took out bandages, sulfa powder, and wanting to keep the nerves quiet, went on talking. "Meet Sergeant Hanrahan. He's my Crew Chief. This is his helicopter."

"You call me Hanny, Miss – Kathleen. And it's the Army's helicopter. All I do is keep it running. Cam's the pilot."

Kathleen looked up again, Cam not a name she knew. Confused, Michael saw from his quick glance. Hell, she must be reeling by this time, one shock after another.

She was able at last to draw the cloth away from the drying seepage, and they helped Hanny get the shirt off, his black chest hair giving his white Irish skin the glow of ivory in that light. Beautiful man, Hanny. Scarred up, but who wasn't, from Nam?

Two wounds, damn it. Well, three – an entrance and exit from a hit through the upper arm, but obviously it hadn't struck bone. And a deep groove just above the elbow, the one giving all the blood. It was beginning to ooze again.

While he cleaned the groove, the flesh around it, thinking it needed stitches but not interested in doing it himself, maybe tomorrow morning if things didn't work out right, he suddenly wondered if Hanny still had the stitches in his ankle. God, how long ago was that?

Without his saying a word, Kathleen was collecting the sterile bandages and applied some gauze squares in pressure. All the while the baby screamed, but it was an odd little wailing, not like kids he'd heard at home.

"Been thinking," said Hanny through gritted teeth, "why we're so late? Left Donald late, put down for fuel, got ambushed, managed to fly here, put down, you saw to me and I managed to get the radio fixed. We went up, sent the Mayday, weather was closin' in so we put down again. Somewhere blind." He looked at Kathleen. "Can't send UHF when you're down in the mountains," he explained.

Suddenly Hanny jerked away from Michael, exploding with, "Jesus, Mary, and Joseph, too, you diggin' to China through my arm? Sorry, Kathleen."

"We're next door to China. And we don't know how old this bullet was, you want lead poisoning?" Michael asked, but he decided the wound was clean enough, hauled Hanny's arm out and shook some sulfa powder on the wounds, started wrapping. That done, he went through the kit with more care, found the morphine and the needles. He wouldn't give it to Hanny yet – see how he got through the night – and would save the penicillin for a fever if one came on and they were stuck here. Just wanted to know the morphine was still there, the irony of it not escaping him, worrying about morphine in the middle of poppy land. But too often, back in Nam, kits were raided for it.

He got one of the canteens, poured three aspirins into Hanny's palm. "Drink up," he said, uncapping the canteen and handing it over. Hanny did, but not enough. "Come on," Michael urged, "the more water the better." There was sweat on Hanny's forehead, and once in a while he gave a little shiver. Shit. What would they do about shock? No blankets, no nothing.

Michael closed the kit and looked up to see Kathleen's eyes on Hanny. Finished, Hanny lowered the canteen and Kathleen's eyes followed it. Michael reached for the second canteen and handed it to her. "We've plenty," he said.

She gave a try at a nod, but didn't look much comforted. "Don't refill them from the stream."

"We've got tablets to purify water, Kathleen," Michael said.

Her relief seemed inordinate, but then God only knew how she was viewing their situation. Undoubtedly darker than he.

Meanwhile, she'd sat on the floor, uncapping the canteen and trying to rock the baby, who had worked himself into one of those crying jags Michael had witnessed in babies, giving the impression of great discomfort but making you wonder if it was just a force of rhythm. She tipped up the canteen, took some water, swished it around in her mouth, and swallowed it. Must've been dry, how not, the last hour or so?

She took another swig of water, and this time just held it in her mouth.

As if she were warming it up before swallowing.

"We'll settle the three of you back here," Michael said, "maybe your stuff in the Shan bag'll help cushion the floor. But uncomfortable or not, we're all sleeping in the Loach."

She nodded, her mouth still full. Odd. The baby was still crying.

"And after first light tomorrow, when the mist burns off, we head up." He pointed to the roof, managed a grin. We hope, he thought.

The reassurance died. Her face crumpling, she bent to the baby to put her lips to his and dribble water into that small mouth. Michael's breath stopped.

Michael looked at Hanny, couldn't really read his face, only enough to be sure Hanny was watching Kathleen, too. Hanny knew. He had a kid. While Michael didn't, he'd spent a couple of university years working with farm stock. Kathleen was short of milk. And the poor little woman back at the palace, my God, must've been a wet-nurse? And the baby sick, too? Wasn't that what the Gurkha had said?

Michael looked up at the moon, now clouding over. Hard to tell if the clouds would stay high, or if the usual overcast was moving in.

He wondered if the baby could somehow be fed C-rations. They had some aboard. Nobody in Nam ate them unless lost and starving – which they could well be, shortly. Even so, most of the cans were dated 1944 and any one of 'em could be deadly for all Michael knew. But how do you comfort a hungry baby when there's nothing but water?

Hanny got out of the Loach. "Need to take a leak," he practically whispered, and started away. Michael was turning to go after him, needing to get some input on babies, when Kathleen sighed and said, "Oh, me, too," already sliding out to the ground. "Keep an eye on Cho?" she asked. Then, quickly, "That's his name. Not Joe. Cho."

Nice, thought Michael. "Sure," he said.

She started away, turned back around. "He doesn't crawl yet, but he's trying."

Maybe she'd heard reluctance in his voice, wanting to get away, or maybe it was just a mother's hope. Anyway. "I'll watch him, don't worry," Michael said, and switched the searchlight back on. "And don't get out of sight of the Loach," he added. "With the lights on, nobody'll be able to see you out there, but you've got to be able to see us."

Another moment of looking at him, then she turned and went looking for privacy. She had just stood there back at the pagoda and let him touch her. On the mouth. As if he had the right. As if he *owned* her. But she knew that she hadn't *just* stood there, damn it, because his touch had gone down deep, deep inside, that feeling she hadn't had for years. Take care, Kathleen, the warning like a shout going down deep, deep inside, oh yes. No man would control her ever again. Michael must never hurt her again. She went round a bend and the light disappeared, but she looked over her shoulder and saw it reflecting from the sand. This was far enough.

This time, when she went off into the shadows, it struck him like a blow. The back of her shirt was smudged, but not with dirt. Blood, streaked. Unlike the woman back at the palace, Kathleen hadn't been beaten. She had been strapped. God, how alien their lives had been. For so long. Watching her step into darkness, Michael felt suddenly cold. As if she were walking away from him forever. Immediately, Cho began to fuss.

Michael hitched himself to a seat beside the baby, wondering if he should try to feed him some water, thinking his own germs might not be as safe for him as Kathleen's, wondering if his big stubbled face would terrify Cho. But as the fussing got serious, he decided to try it. He took some water, washed his mouth out and warmed the next sip as he'd watched Kathleen do, then bent his face to the baby's and dribbled the water to his lips. No terror there. Cho worked his mouth and swallowed and gurgled with what seemed to be pleasure.

But then he turned his face away. Michael tried the little finger bit, tickling the corner of Cho's mouth. No good. Just as well, Michael thought, not all that clean anyway.

"Kathleen gone?" Hanny back.

"Yeah. What're we going to feed this baby?" Michael asked.

Hanny sat down in the cabin, leaning his head against the bulkhead. "How about the C-rations gravy?

"Christ, it could be poison!" Michael said. He leaned over Cho, who smiled up at him, right into his eyes. People might call it gas, but Michael knew better. That was a killer smile if he ever saw one.

"We've been eating it for two years. It's not poison, it's just crap." He was trying to get comfortable and not succeeding, flinching with every creaky movement.

"Tell you something, Neal. I feel pretty bad about this."

"Yeah, sure," Hanny answered, "but what's done's done. You gotta get over that, y'know it? Goin' back into things you can't change. What matters is, except to buckle her in, you haven't even touched her, far as I've seen. And the stuff flyin' silent between you is fixin' to shatter something any minute. Holy Mother, give the girl a kiss!"

Hanny chasing passion. "Shut up, okay?" Michael said, gently so as not to trouble Cho, not looking around. Suddenly, the baby's hand grasped Michael's pinkie tightly, surprising with its strength. "Well look at you, little dear," Michael crowed, glad for the diversion. He tried raising Cho's hand. The baby hung on, and when offered Michael's other little finger, grasped it with his other hand and began really having a work out, even able to keep his head up.

"You can't call a boy like that, he'll grow up to be a wimp." Hanny again.

"He will?" Michael asked, this time looking at Hanny, ready to believe anything when it came to the baby.

Hanny shot him a glance. "How the hell should I know?" he said, and shut his eyes.

"That's a mercy, isn't it," Michael said, returning to Cho, "because you are a little dear. So let's see you crawl, huh?" And he clasped the baby in both hands and turned him onto his stomach. Right away – *right away*, Michael thought in wonder – Cho was up on all fours, rocking, able to hold his head up while on his tummy, too. On a thought, Michael cupped his hand between Cho's legs and lifted his rump just enough to lighten the load a little, and the baby immediately began clambering forward. "See? You can do it!" But then, Cho gave a cough, and collapsed face down on some cloths Kathleen had crumpled up to soften the floor.

Michael picked him up at once, appalled at what he might have caused, to lay the baby's chest and stomach against his shoulder, patting his back as he'd seen Kathleen do, but with only a couple of fingers. The coughing got worse, real spasms, frightening Michael. His other hand, supporting the baby's bottom, felt warmth spreading across it. He looked and saw that Cho was letting everything go from the force of that cough. And while it hardly smelled at all, the color was bad. Even lacking any experience with diapers, Michael knew that.

Kathleen was back, reaching to take Cho, murmuring, "I'm sorry, I'm sorry." Michael wanted to tell her not to apologize for her kid, how could the baby help it, and it was probably Michael's fault anyhow. But he said nothing. What did he know of the kind of strictures she may've been under, this girl he'd once known to be fiery quick? The old Kathleen would've screamed bloody murder in defense of her child if anyone had so much as raised an eyebrow at him. Muted. That was the word. And it scared him. But with all she'd done, shooting the Shan back in Loi Long, running from the train . . . the fire still had to be there. Somewhere. Had to be.

27

Holding Cho, who seemed at last to be catching his breath, Kathleen grabbed her Shan bag by its strap and went down to the water to clean him up. Michael sat a moment, watching her, and then, since the moon seemed to be staying out, and to save the battery, he went forward and turned off the lights. A few moments, and he could see her again.

She squatted on the sand – still could do that all right, her knees flanking her face – took one of the white cloths she had packed, wet it in the stream, wrung it out, unbuttoned her camisole and laid the damp cloth around her stomach. Warming it, that's what she was doing. She untied Cho's dirty diaper – she'd made them from squares and narrow strips of muslin, sewing the latter to the four corners. No safety-pins, Michael realized. So much making-do she'd had to learn. She now used the clean parts of the soiled muslin to dry-wipe Cho, then took the warmed damp cloth from her skin to clean him better. As she moved, the moon caught her long white arms, turning them fluid. Grabbing his heart.

She shifted out of her squat to sit on one hip, legs curled to her side, back straight, as she had sat so often years ago, and brought her baby up, lowering her face to him. Bathed in the silver light with the water flowing black beyond them, the moon turning the single line of her faded denim jeans black, and her long braid falling down her back, she and her child could have been a Japanese woodcut. Cho's face was raised to hers, lips almost meeting in a kiss, the baby's eyes wide and wondering on his mother's, hand reaching for her lower lip. Michael thought them the most beautiful thing he'd ever seen.

She let the thankfulness flow. Tom had sent him. No miracle. God hadn't favored a fool. Tom had deciphered her embroidery and had found Michael . . . but maybe he hadn't needed to, maybe he and Michael had been in touch ever since Tom had left Loi Long, but if so, why hadn't he let her know that he and Michael . . .

Oh, Lord, she was so tired. And the baby had to have something to eat, *something*. She still had the tinder box. She'd build a fire and – and she had the rice, she could steam it as she'd planned and – . The sand crunched right next to her and she spun around to look up.

Michael had been drawn down to them almost unaware of himself, his steps silent on the sand, but not that silent because she looked around and up at him, only to look quickly away again. What she'd been doing almost every time their eyes caught, except those odd moments when it didn't just happen, when she seemed deliberately to confront him, things hidden behind her eyes. At the pagoda. And a little earlier before she went off into the night.

"How is Tom?"

"He's fine. Just – fine." He crouched beside her. "I know you're – y'have to be worried – about the helicopter, Hanny – . Frightened. It'll be all right, Kathleen."

Still not looking at him, she nodded, then said, "I've been thinking . . . if we get stuck here – " and she added quickly, "it's possible, isn't it, Michael, I know it is. And if we do, we should look for paths leading up the ridges. There'll be villages. We can get rice. I've got some that maybe we can cook over a fire, but cooked in a pot would be better, and village women would – "

"Kathleen. We're going to fly out in the morning. I promise you."

He'd said that so long ago, made promises. Meant them. Meant it now, she was sure. She set the wiping cloth aside with the dirty diaper, started tying the baby into a clean one, and went on quietly as if he hadn't interrupted. "You need to know."

Just as she'd said it so long ago, Michael's heart stopping with it. Ashamed, determined.

"It's not just for us, but for the baby, too. I feed him the rice predigested, all the hill women do that. The way I did the water – we did."

"You saw me?" Michael asked. "Was that okay?"

She glanced at him, only a glance, and her mouth quirked in a little smile. "You looked for all the world like a great hawk feeding a baby sparrow. What's wrong is – I don't – well – I don't have enough – "

"I know," he said quickly, wanting to save her what she seemed to think was the shame. "Not enough milk. Can he get through the night?"

She nodded, but that was stupid. She didn't know that. She didn't know from one hour to the next how long Cho could get through or if he could get through anything more at all. "But if we get stuck here . . ." she said, "what if we get – "

"We won't," Michael cut in. Then he went on, wanting somehow to connect with her. Not easy. "I guess you gave up on your message. Getting through to Tom, I mean. Not surprised, it's been long enough since Tom got it – plus the time since you sent it . . . "

"Yes," she said, "I did. You saw U-Pym? The woman at the palace? You said . . . " Michael nodded, but she wasn't looking at him, so he said, "Yes."

She picked up the soiled cloths and started trailing them through the water. So controlled. As if she were discussing going to a tea-party. "I was going to run from the train tonight . . . later . . . but then the helicopter came . . . you came . . ." She swallowed hard. "I thought it was him."

He'd never understand, she was convinced of it. How could he? The girl he'd once known, having been used and living with it, the only good thing about her now was Cho, and that would hardly make him understand her better, not his child, after all. Oh, but if he had been, if Cho had been . . .

She looked around and up at Michael, and it all came in a rush, sort of. "I'd planned to follow the tracks of the opium train 'til the Mekong and go down the river to Luang Prabang. But he found out and killed my horse."

"What?" He leaned forward and stilled her hands, not sure he'd understood. Surely he hadn't. "What?" he said again, louder.

"The Prince. He knew there weren't any other horses I'd trust. He'd taken them all for the opium."

"I don't understand, Kathleen." Didn't want to.

"I know," she said. "So I had to kill someone." And that was all.

Michael practically snatched the cloths away from her, his mind spinning in disgust, disbelief, God knew what else. He squeezed the cold, cold water through the muslin, rubbing it. Without soap or warmth, the yellowish green stains would remain.

"You didn't," he said.

"Yes," she said, so softly. "You don't understand, Michael – how can you ever?"

He swivelled on his heels to face her, not touching her, just wanting to reach her somehow. "You did not kill that Shan. He's the one that pulled the plug on you, and the woman in your room, what did you call her? She – "

She was staring at him as if he spoke an unknown language, until finally she said, "U-pym." Oh, right, the name. She stumbled on. "You went to the palace and – and she told you where I was – that's how you knew . . . ? "

"You didn't kill anyone, Kathleen," he said, and watched her eyes change with it. She suddenly dropped her face to her hands and just held still that way. After awhile, he turned again to the water, squeezing the cloths as dry as he could get them. "I think you should know, too, that she told them where you'd gone only because they beat her."

She made a little sound and lowered her hands. "She's all right," Michael added quickly. "She's going back to her village tomorrow." Kathleen managed to nod. How she could manage even to *think* he couldn't imagine, much less . . . hell. And then he asked what *he* needed to know.

"Obviously," he said, "obviously, Cho is sick. And I don't understand. Couldn't the – the *Prince* – " detesting the title, "get you out, down to Bangkok, hell, somewhere with doctors or –." His throat was becoming so tight it hurt. He spread the cloths out on the sand to dry. "He killed your horse?" Heard her sigh.

Nothing to do but try to tell him. Her hands wringing, she started, keeping her voice low, steady. And it wasn't even hard. Because she knew whatever or however she said it, he could never understand. How foolish and stupid she had been for so long. "Yours wasn't the first helicopter to fly into Loi Long. Before it got so bad with Burma, opium deals were made there, not here in Laos. And there's a radio. Yes, he could have arranged it."

Michael was now staring at her. Did he not believe it? Why should he?

She looked at Cho as if the baby held all the answers. So that when she spoke it was without warning and startled Michael. "He said if Cho dies it is his Karma. So he shot my horse and told me to give the child up and get him another."

She lifted her chin, and at last met Michael's eyes. He'd have sworn rage moved within hers, no way to be sure in the moonlight, but if so, the wall she had built up around herself was down for a fleeting moment. A mother's rage, deeper than his own, but not by much, God damn it.

What kind of monster was he, this fucking *Prince*? Michael knew perfectly well the cultural divides between westerners and Southeast Asians were huge – his time in Nam hadn't been totally wasted. But this man – *this* man had to stand alone.

He looked up at the sky. The clouds had stayed high, were scattered and moving well. There might still be moonlight for awhile. The North

Star was below the ridge line, but he knew it'd be visible, too.

He collected the wet cloths and folded them under one arm, stood up, slung the Shan bag over his shoulder. She collected her shirt and was gathering up Cho and struggling to stand with him in her arms. Lord, how exhausted she must be. Michael put his hands under her elbows, lifted her to her feet. She started away from it, from him, up the bank, and stumbled.

She felt blind. Surely there was no point in tears now. Too late for tears.

He saved her the fall, caught her in time by the arm and kept hold of her, walking beside her. To save her another fall in case, though there was nothing underfoot to stumble over, hadn't been, only the flat water-smoothed sand. It occurred to him then that she was barely twenty-three years old.

He was able, now, to see the stripes reddening the skin of her back, running up her shoulders to her neck from beneath the thin material of the camisole, the one scabbed. He tried to keep his hands from tightening on her. "That salve in the first aid kit may ease your back a little."

"It's all right," she said, with a shake of her head. But then she twisted to face him. Another of those moments of confrontation? "Don't you want to know why he had me whipped?"

So. He hadn't done it himself. Jesus, what cold evil. Not even in the heat of anger. Michael looked into her eyes, trying to read her in them, and saw . . . shame? Is that what a beating did to someone? Make them feel to blame for it? "No, Kathleen," he answered her, his voice rising and he knew it and couldn't stop it. "There is no reason why. What, he punished you for wanting to save your child? His child? That's not reasonable. That's nuts!" He stopped himself at last, hauling in, shaken deep inside. He turned her towards the Loach again, started them both up the bank towards it again. But something had occurred and he had to ask it, had to.

"Kathleen? Somehow, even way back, I was under the impression that the – that Htin Aung was educated in England."

"Yes," she said. He felt a tremor go through her, and was glad he still held her arm. "At Cambridge."

Oh, yeah, he stood alone, all right. Not that the Brits hadn't turned out their share of monsters through history. Still, it somehow made it – *him* worse. Michael's own xenophobia, he had no doubt. But he was damned if Kathleen and her baby were going to pay for it any more.

When they reached the Loach, as gently as he could he woke Hanny. He was lying on his right side, curled up, and his skin was too cool and clammy. He was noisy waking up, and Michael knew he hurt like hell. "Shit," he muttered, "just got to sleep." And then aware of Kathleen, he apologized.

"We're going up," Michael cut across it, grabbing Hanny's arm, helping him to the ground.

"Yeah?" Hanny said, shooting him a look. Then he showed a half-grin. Amazing man, Hanny. "Could be you're right. Just be glad I never go anywhere without my handy duct tape."

"What's that mean? Oh, Christ, you've been working."

"Had to know, Cam, had to." Hanny suddenly braced a hand against the Loach. "Came outa the blue. The leads to the starter generator might've been severed. They were." Michael just waited. Kathleen kept still. "Found an old grenade handle on the floor, scratched the spoon, pulled the leads together, wrapped 'em up. So, if everything else is . . . " But his eyes flickered towards Kathleen. He fell silent, then reached in and got the fire extinguisher.

"Never mind that," Michael said. "I want you in front, buckled in." He went around to the right side of the cabin, waited for Kathleen, and boosted her and the baby inside. "Sit down the way you were before," he told her, and buckled her into the seat, handed her the Colonel's helmet.

"Michael?" Hanny, voice soft. "Y'know – you try this now and we could all have a sleepless night down here, worrying about things."

"Nope. If the igniters don't work, you're gonna sit down, hold the flashlight and bloody well tell me how to fix 'em. You need help and so does the baby."

Hanny insisted on remaining out with the extinguisher while Michael cranked. Right, too, with the baby on board and no telling the condition of the Loach, though he kept having to shift weight, probably dizzy.

Alone in the cockpit, Michael ran around all his reasons that this was a good idea, trying to convince himself against the uncertainties, the old fear of mistakes back to stay. But if they lost the moon. If they went bingo on fuel. Then Hanny and the baby would . . . Jesus, no end to the round. Until, thank God, Hanny called in irritation, "Go ahead and crank!" So Michael did. The igniters clicked slowly, the start fuel ignited and the blades turned.

Hanny stashed the extinguisher and got into the cockpit on top of his own blood, not so handily as usual but he did it. He looked at Michael, fetched out a real grin, pointed to the sky. Michael lifted up.

Now all they had to do was find their way home. Like Hansel and Gretel without any bread.

28

The view under the moon was grand, and he turned the Loach so that the North Star, low on the horizon though it was, sat just back of Hanny's left shoulder. Michael had to lean to see it, but there it was. And when high enough, he got on the radio, was acknowledged by King, and cancelled their earlier Mayday. "I'm flying on visuals," he reported. "All instruments gone. And I've got wounded, so we need to be met by medics and an ambulance, and he needs blood. Hanny?"

"O," Hanny said.

"Type O," Michael continued. "I'm trying to keep to a straight course east by south-east from an LZ on what we think was the Nam Tha into Luang Prabang. Hope to be there in under forty-five minutes."

"Gotcha, Lieutenant," said King, "I'll inform Alley Cat."

"Good. But keep listening, okay? Without my ten-mile warning light, I won't know when I start flying on fumes."

The sky stayed pretty clear. The beautiful Loach never coughed or twitched, just went. And about fifteen minutes later, Alley Cat, the night Forward Air Controller, came on the air. "The guys in the tower at L.P. say it's pretty quiet tonight, so they'll put the airport lights on for you."

"Bless their sweet souls," Michael said. And it all worked. Low on fuel as they had to be, the glow from the airport came across the Mekong like a light from heaven. They landed gently at their spot on the tarmac.

A field ambulance was waiting, and two Laotian attendants came running with a stretcher.

"Stay in the Loach, Kathleen," Michael said, getting out. Hanny was already bellowing his refusal of the stretcher, "These two midgets'll dump me out for sure!" So Michael slung Hanny's right arm over his shoulders and walked him to the ambulance, helped him in, and told the attendants to wait, there was a baby needing attention, too.

The driver, who was standing by, erupted. "Clinic no take baby!"

"Well, you got that wrong," Michael said, and he shot a finger at him. "Wait."

He returned to the Loach, to find a man whose bald head gleamed in the lights peering into the cabin. The Brit, Sherm. Wouldn't you know, Michael thought grimly. Here we go.

Sherm turned around as Michael reached him, seized Michael's hand in a bruising grip. "How is Hanny? And we hear you've found the Volpar!"

So much for secrecy in Laos. "Hanny'll be fine if he gets some blood. What's this clinic we're going to?"

"Down by the AA hooch. Two doctors, one a local, the other an Air Force captain. On duty tonight, I think. Mainly triage for us and the Air Force."

Michael was surprised. "Triage?"

"Whether to treat here, Vientiane or Udorn." He couldn't help it now, he looked back in at Kathleen. "You boys do seem to have had an adventure."

"They got blood?" Michael asked.

"We try to keep them supplied," Sherm said, "though it may be frozen. Of course there'll be plasma. Did you? Not have an adventure," glancing into the Loach again, "that's obvious, but find the Volpar?"

Michael studied him a moment. "Yeah, we found the Volpar," Michael said. "And . . . we know where your boys are." He stepped around Sherm to lean into the Loach, collect the Shan bags. "As of four this afternoon," he continued, "ten were alive, though two are sick, and one is down a hole being punished."

"Can you get them out?" Sherm asked, no longer so jaunty.

"I imagine we'll try." Michael slung on the Shan bags. "Hand me Cho," he said to Kathleen. She did, and then Michael helped her down to lead her to the back of the ambulance, nothing more for Sherm. Kathleen was stepping up into it when the driver came over and shook Michael's arm. "Clinic no like babies!"

Michael simply handed Cho up to Kathleen. "The clinic's going to like this one," Michael said, "and we're all going there right now."

Sherm had followed to stand by Michael. The driver seemed to know him. "Take them," Sherm ordered, the driver shrugged, and moved for his seat in the cab.

"Thanks," Michael said.

"You two are kings for a day, dear boy." He stepped back. "I'll be along, see how Hanny's doing."

Michael got into the ambulance. "Go!" he called forward, and the ambulance started up.

Hanny was lying on a stretcher now. He held out a hand to Michael, who took it, and Hanny grabbed hold for a wrist grip. "We did it, little darlin', we got 'em out!" he crowed, and his triumph came surging into Michael through their locked arms, shaking Michael almost as much as Hanny was with shock. Hanny went on, "The rest is up to you." Michael had to chuckle, Hanny still looking for passion.

Michael looked across to Kathleen, obviously nearly wrung out.

"What if they don't let us in?" she asked, and she lifted Cho up higher towards her face and neck as if to protect him from God knows what more evils. She'd already sure had her share.

"Believe me," Michael said, "they will."

She kept her eyes on his, glued to his, like a child seeking perfect trust and almost, almost getting there.

* * *

A nurse met them in the door of the cement building, led Michael with Hanny's arm still draped over his shoulder, to what looked like a small surgery where a doctor, an Air Force Captain, waited in surgical greens. Hanny was guided to a table and the door was shut, leaving Michael outside.

He looked back along the hall to the entrance and Kathleen. The nurse was already heading there. Michael caught up, as she said to Kathleen, "I'm sorry, Miss, we don't treat children here."

"Oh, but – " Kathleen started, when Michael jumped in. "Sure you can. Everybody knows you're the best clinic in Laos."

Kathleen kept her eyes down on Cho. The nurse swivelled around and looked up at Michael, well aware she was being conned. He winked, smiled, making her a part of it. "Please?" And then, "He's very sick."

She hesitated, smiled back, but only a little and wryly, turned back to Kathleen and said, "Come with me."

She led them the length of the hall clear to the end and a very small room. It had a cot, a chest of drawers, a wooden chair with wooden arms, and a sink. "This is where the staff crashes on busy nights. But we're pretty empty right now, so . . ."

She touched Cho on the cheek, the forehead. "Fever," she said.

"I know," Kathleen said.

Michael hadn't known, and was damned glad they were here and not on some damp bank of the Nam Tha.

The nurse went to the sink, tested the water – there was only one spigot. "It's tepid," she said, and to Kathleen, "why don't you put him in it and see if you can cool him off." She meanwhile pulled out the top drawer of the dresser to two-thirds open, tested its stability, dumped what it held which wasn't much, grabbed sheeting from the cot, folded it and lined the drawer with it. "There," she said, "now you can rest when he does." She moved for the door, then addressed Michael. "I'll get the doctor to come back when he's done with your Chief." And sending a smile at Kathleen, she added, "I'm Sally," and left.

I'd call her a little miracle, Michael thought.

They filled the sink, he and Kathleen, and together, Michael supporting Cho's body and Kathleen his head, they inched him into the water. He had a moment of surprise and then screamed bloody murder. Michael and Kathleen shared a look, and both of them hating it, began to push the water over him, Kathleen rinsing it over his head.

He was the perfect boy, soft small mound for testicles to come, little rosy penis, skin creamy, eyes green as Michael had known they would be, mouth and long limbs like his mother's, and though his hair was dark it sometimes caught the light with the brightness of hers. Michael knew he'd fallen in love.

They did it for what seemed a long time, cooing and chirping to him, sometimes letting some water out and putting more in. Until Kathleen felt Cho's cheek, wrapped her hand around his arm. "I think he's cooler," she said.

"Let's give him a break, then," Michael said. Give her a break, too, Michael thought, she looked ready to drop. She picked Cho up dripping, laid him on the cot on some clean diapers and patted him dry. His breath was rasping a little, but when Michael touched his dry skin he was cooler. And then, coming towards them from down the hall was first the rumble of a male voice, then an American southern accent, then an angry spate of orders.

"You know we don't treat infants, Sally! You want half of Luang Prabang around our necks?"

"No, Sir, sorry, Sir, Captain." Sally's voice, and they entered the room.

The Air Force Captain, Hanny's doctor, swept right on, this time to Kathleen, who by now was intimidated and frightened. Michael didn't like his tone of voice to her, and doing what he knew well how to do, Michael stepped into the doorway, turned, and filled up the space, not at attention but not at ease either, just standing there, hands ready to lift to his hips if needed. Hanny'd be grinning like a pumpkin.

"Madam, you will have to remove your child. We have wounded men whose resistance is low and children can be contagious. Moreover, – "

"If I may, Sir," Michael spoke easily, but quickly enough to interrupt. "We understood you to be nearly empty tonight, Sir, and we are pretty isolated in this room."

The captain swung around to take him in, eyes narrowing. "This is Doctor Schramm," Sally said.

Schramm's eyes now flickered down to Michael's insignia. "Not your concern, Lieutenant."

"Sir," Michael said, "we have come a long way to get to your clinic. The baby is an American citizen. Kathleen is his natural mother . . . " He sent a look at Kathleen, hoping she wouldn't react. " . . . and I will be his adoptive father when the papers come through."

Schramm, luckily enough, had turned to look at Kathleen the same moment. Kathleen just looked down at Cho. Good girl.

Now Schramm turned a glare on Michael, who widened his stance just a tad. Obviously feeling caught between the silent pleadings of the women and the guard at the door, the doctor turned it on Sally. "Damn it, I haven't prescribed for an infant since med school!"

"I remember, Sir – with your permission. The equivalents of milligrams to body weight for both pencillin and sulfa. Sir."

A moment, the doctor said, "We're going to have a little talk later, Sally." Then he stepped over to the baby, his fingers finding his stethoscope.

"Yes, Sir," she said, and sent another smile at Kathleen as she took the baby from her for Schramm to examine.

"All right, mother, tell me," Schramm said. Michael decided not to hang over his shoulder. He figured he'd better give him that, and as Kathleen started to talk he headed out and down the corridor to ask about Hanny.

A Laotian orderly came out of the surgery where Hanny had been treated, a tray of bloody bandages in his hands. Michael stopped him, managed to communicate a question, and was pointed in the direction of a room three doors away. He pushed that door open, and there was Hanny in the narrow bed, getting blood, eyes closed.

Michael crossed silently to Hanny, studied him a moment, then touched the back of his fingers to Hanny's cheek – which popped Hanny's eyes open.

"Didn't mean to wake you," Michael said.

"Hey," Hanny said. "How's the kid?"

"Sicker than we thought," Michael said, "but they're looking at him."

"Yeah, well, I knew y'wouldn't let 'em get away with it. Been thinkin'." Sure, Michael thought, all doped up along with everything else. Hanny went on. "Thing to do is order the instrument panel soonest. You know where the serial numbers are, right? Maybe Udorn'll have one we can use. I want to install it day after tomorrow. And don't forget some generator leads."

"Come on, Hanny, you aren't anywhere near good enough to – "

"Hell I'm not. Juice up the old veins and I'm fine. Just do it, Cam."

"Okay, okay. Soon as I get Kathleen fixed up, I'm going down to the embassy, so I'll put in the requisition."

"Know what you're gonna tell him?" Meaning the Colonel, of course.

"You already figured it out. Believe it or not, I always listen to you, Neal."

Hanny chuckled, and this time when he blinked his eyes stayed closed. Michael turned as Sherm hesitated in the door, wanting to come in. Michael shook his head at him, and tiptoed to the door, closed it behind himself and Sherm.

"How is he?" Sherm asked. In spite of all the sarcasm that night down at Mam'selle Josie's, he was genuinely concerned. They meandered a little along the corridor.

"He'll be okay," Michael said softly. "How did you come to meet the Loach, anyway?"

"I was playing some poker at OPs and heard your message. I was down about three thousand Kip, and decided to find out if the rumors about the Volpar were true." He stopped walking, leaned against the wall, looked down the corridor where, as everybody in the place could hear, the baby was crying. "Do tell about the lady, please. A lovely piece of trash."

Michael decided not to take offense. He knew the jargon. It meant any cargo other than grunts, who were referred to as "ass". Michael supposed you could say Sherm was really being polite. Sure. Michael hesitated, decided to go for it. "Sherm? I and um – that lovely piece of trash would very much like to keep it under wraps that she's here. No papers."

He watched Sherm, scared he should've shut up. But Sherm only smiled – a nice smile. "Discretion's the better part, dear boy. I can look into it for you, if you'd like."

"I thought I might get in touch with Simon Fess. He owes me."

Sherm beamed. "Precisely the man! He may look fourteen years old but he's as shrewd as Fagan." He straightened, headed towards the door. "I'd like to tell the boys that our little ones are found." He looked back, asking for permission.

Michael appreciated it. He nodded and begged an exemption. "If you could wait until, I don't know, noon maybe? I need to report to the boss, first."

Sherm nodded, raised a hand in a little salute and walked away.

Michael's relief was probably out of proportion to its cause. What did he really know about the Englishman, after all? But he'd have had to get advice from somebody, so . . .

He returned down the corridor to Cho's room. He glanced in. Sally and the captain were conferring. Michael looked around, found a chair – same as the one in Cho's room – set it against the wall, and sat. But not for long. The Captain and Sally came to the door and Michael stood.

The doctor was telling Sally to try sulfathiazol first – "Of course, if the dysentery's amoebic, nothing much'll work." And Kathleen right there to hear it, damn the man. He was continuing that he wanted fifteen CC's of saline and glucose right now, another fifteen in four or five hours so keep the feeder in, and she'd better try for a vein in the scalp. "Given the dehydration you could have trouble finding one elsewhere," he finished, walking straight past Michael. But unfortunately, he hadn't gone more than three feet when he turned back around.

"Who's your commanding officer, Lieutenant?"

"Sir, Lieutenant Colonel Lewis Wisby, military attaché at the American embassy in Vientiane, Sir!" making it smart. For all the good it would do.

But the captain didn't dress him down. Probably had something better in store. He just went on his way.

Through the door, Michael could see Kathleen and Sally still engrossed, so he sat down again. How long before Cho showed improvement? Any time would be too long. He stretched out his legs, leaned his head back against the wall and closed his eyes. Bet the bastard tried to downgrade him. Wouldn't work. Thinking of what Sherm had said, calling him king for the day, Michael knew the Army needed him, too. And anyway. It was a mystery to him how so many commissioned officers in the military were pricks. When this whole thing was over, he'd resign his commission and go back to being a warrant officer.

* * *

She'd been sitting up on the cot so she could keep an eye on Cho in the drawer, but now she got up and went to the hall and there was Michael, still waiting. He had to have a bed somewhere in Luang Prabang. He should go to it.

Cho was asleep, cuddled in his make-shift cradle. At last. And the drip was running into his scalp. That had been hard. Sally'd really had to struggle to find a vein, and Cho had screamed and screamed. Then Sally had brought in a cup of warm milk – dried milk mixed with boiled water, and Kathleen had managed to get some down him. No bottles, Sally had apologized, but in the morning, when her shift was over, she'd take Kathleen to a market where she could get all kinds of stuff.

It seemed like a dream, but it couldn't be if she thought it might be – could it? And Michael standing in that door against the doctor . . . it had seemed he could do anything.

She knew her hair was poking out all down the length of her braid. She knew she looked like – what had Michael used to say? – a waif and stray. Her jeans were a ruin, her shirt and camisole stained and filthy. She had an eingyi in her bag – but no, it was in one of the ones she'd left behind. She hadn't killed the Shan. The realization kept sweeping her, weakening her knees, but the ice she carried inside didn't seem to want to melt. Oh, that once, when he had touched her on the lips, had seemed a heat inside, or something else, something . . . No matter, there was no way he could ever understand, nor did she want him to. Except for the stones. He'd understand that well enough, the last thing she wanted him to.

She stood in the doorway studying him as he dozed across the corridor in the chair. The sight of him, so near, so real after so long, in the quiet of this place . . . the five years had made a difference. His body had changed. She could see it in the way he moved. Held himself. The Lord knew that while she'd blocked her feelings she'd never even tried to hide from visions of him. Walking, running, dancing. Looking down on her. Always with grace, cut now and then by an awkwardness, unexpected and endearing. He moved now with hardness, sure and ready. He'd lost the flesh, the beautiful flesh of his youth. He was rangier, muscles more wiry, perhaps. He was thinner. And his hair left his forehead higher than it used to. The dark brows still carried straight across, breaking only over the bridge of his nose. The blue eyes were as intense. But now lines grooved each side of the wide mouth – from laughter or from that war? Maybe both.

He must have children by now, he was so good with Cho. That hadn't changed. There never had been a gentler man, young as he had been years ago. But wars did bad things to men, she'd seen enough of that to know, and anybody'd be soft with a baby. Except, his hands had reached for gentleness when he'd tended Hanny's wounds, had lain gently on Hanny to awaken him, back on the river. How could he bear being in a war?

As if he felt her gaze, Michael's eyes opened and he was on his feet in one taut motion, only to let it go as he caught a breath. "Everything okay?" he asked.

She nodded. "You should go to bed, Michael. No need to sit here all night."

He turned sharp eyes on her. Questioning eyes that looked amazed. He glanced up and down the hall, finally tiptoed into Cho's room, took a look at Cho, picked up the wooden chair there and tiptoed it back out to set it down beside his. Then he answered her, patting the chair to invite her to sit, saying, "I've learned to sleep in some weird places, Kath."

How many times now had he used that old nickname? First time she'd heard it in five years, and it twisted her with each use. She sat down. "It's awful you've had to fight in that war. For two years?"

Oddly, he looked away before he answered her. "Don't, Kathleen. I enlisted in the Army. And it was my choice to extend tours."

Why would he do such things? If she'd considered, she'd have realized she had no right to ask, but she didn't stop to think about it. "But why!?" she burst out. "You aren't like that." And suddenly realizing, "Weren't," she added.

That brought his eyes around to meet hers. Was he going to tell her about med-school and Diane this very minute? About the despair he'd felt the day he got his ag degree and didn't know where to go, what to do? "Yeah," he said finally, flatly. "Y'got it right. Turns out, I'm good at it."

A moment, two, and she nodded. "I guess we've both gotten good at things we'd rather not've," she said softly.

He ducked his head to see into her face, forcing her to meet his eyes. He didn't know why he was asking it, or what he'd do whatever the answer. He hadn't known he was going to ask it, but he knew he had the right. "Did you love him, Kathleen?"

She seemed frozen by it. Was it so hard to answer? But finally she whispered, "No." He breathed again. And then she went on, "Never!" in a voice deep, shredded. He managed a nod. She suddenly looked very small in the chair. Damn it, maybe he hadn't had the right.

Why had he come, she wondered. Because Tom had pressed him into it, don't be foolish. But, Lord, why ask that question? Could he have expectations? But there was nothing here for him. Nothing left for anyone. Only how could she hurt him with that? And what of his own family? Maybe she was wrong and there were no expectations, maybe all her questions were only what *she* wanted. Oh, no. Far too late for that.

"You needn't stay the night, truly," she started, briskly now. "And when I get to the embassy, everything'll be fine and you'll be done with it."

"Done with it?" His voice was shocked. And bewildered. All she could do was look at him in sorrow.

He wanted to tell her about the letters. No less than when he was in Hong Kong, he needed her to know that all the shit she must've been living with had come out of yet another and long on-going cruelty. But how to figure out whether that sorrow he saw in her would be helped or made worse? He sighed.

"Fact is, Kathleen, we're only part way there. Don't know why I just figured you'd realize, but why should you, you've been – we'd call it 'in-country' in Nam, out of the world. For five years cut off and – "

"Stop it." Echoing him, wanting something halted dead.

Kathleen couldn't bear this, his pity, his condescension. "Life is life wherever, Michael. Mine went on. As yours did."

No teenager here. Grown up, he could see. And a little tough. So different, yet oddly inevitable from the girl he'd known. Maybe they'd never get it together again, the two of them. He felt himself floundering inside. He sought and relievedly found something concrete to deal with.

"Since the nurse will be with us in the morning, we'd better talk now about what's next." Then, from somewhere, he offered a little smile. "Did you happen to pack along your passport?"

Her passport? "Yes, of course," she said. "it's out of date, but – "

"Never mind that, it may be helpful anyway – at least – " Not now, pal. Somebody could hear and how did he know if an old passport would help make a phony one? He tried to keep his voice low. "This little country has huge misbegotten pride and red tape comin' out the gazoo – well anyway . . . there's a war here, too, Kathleen. Plus which, you have no visa, no entry stamp into Laos, and an out-of-date passport that has an entry stamp into Burma but no exit stamp from there. First question'd be, how did you get here? Maybe you could get sanctuary at the embassy, but how do you get down to Vientiane to do that? The bureaucrats here require papers even for internal flights. And there are road blocks. Worst of all, you've no papers whatsoever proving Cho was born to you. No proof of his citizenship."

If she'd been scared earlier, Michael could see he'd terrified her now. "Cho?" she gasped, "Cho?" her voice rising, starting to stand up.

Michael grabbed her hands, pressing her back to stay. "It's okay, I promise you, it will be okay," he said as firmly as he could. He hadn't known what the hell that business of being "done with it" meant but this was not the time to pursue it. She and the baby were his to see to until he could get them out of Laos, and that was that.

"It's going to take a little time, is all, and you're going to have to stay somewhere besides a nice hotel that'll require your passport when you register. I've got a place for you. Haven't even seen it myself, we'll go in the morning. If it's no good, we'll find another. And a phone, too, and call Tom. It's going to be all right."

He watched her eyes, the struggle to bank her fears. He let go her hands, not wanting her to feel caught, but started to tell her about Tom, hoping the life he'd made for himself would please her, calm her. Even ended up telling her about Hla Swe, how much Tom felt for her, and about the clinic. And at last, quiet came to her eyes.

As his voice trailed off, she lifted a hand to his face. Was she crazy? She had no right to touch him, no right at all, only making things worse. She snatched her hand back, said, "I know you will make it all right. Didn't you get us here?" A sudden cry came from Cho's room. She rose and went in to him.

Michael sat on, mulling it over, her uneasiness, her constant pull away from him. He should've taken her hand right then, right then . . . but hell, it wasn't going to be made in heaven like day after tomorrow anyway. He got up, went to the door and looked in.

She had opened her camisole and put Cho to her breast. Michael caught a glimpse of her nipple before the baby took it firmly in his mouth. Bigger than he remembered – probably because of the baby. But dark, and sitting as high above the curve as he had once known it. She looked up to see him, and turned her shoulder to him.

DAY EIGHT

29

She found herself back out on the upstairs landing of the steps that went up the outside of this two-story house to the apartment. She'd been doing it all afternoon, when she wasn't napping with Cho, and she'd had two showers, *two*, with hot water from the tank on the tower in the compound. Both times, she'd stood and let the water pour down over her, belatedly remembering the family downstairs who might like some hot water, too. The water at the palace came from a cold mountain stream, and got warm only in the hot months when warmth wasn't really needed. Her back didn't sting or itch, and when she'd peered over her shoulder into the mirror she saw the cut was closed up, healing.

The rest of the time she'd spent wandering the two rooms only to end up outside, waiting for him. He'd said he'd be back late this afternoon. He'd warned her maybe very late. And she didn't want him to find her there, didn't want him to think her dependent. But she was. She was.

She hadn't known how much until she'd talked with Tom. Michael had placed the call on the phone that stood just inside the gate to the compound, and it had gone right through. When Tom had answered, not speaking to him Michael had simply handed the phone to her.

"Tom?"

A long silence, and then, "Kathleen? Kathleen!"

"Yes."

"Oh, Sis, little Sis."

She had gasped, almost like a sob. And then everything had come in a rush between them. But towards the end, he had told her about Michael. What he had done against the attackers in Macao. And how the Army had awarded him for valor. And what he had chanced in coming after her and her baby. Tom had spelled that out, as Kathleen had not even tried before. Smuggling two illegal aliens across a foreign border in an American military aircraft while away without leave from official duty. His career in an Army that valued him could've been ruined. His whole life could've been ruined. Might still be, if they were found out. He had left for Vientiane after the phone call, to report to his colonel. Now that she knew about the thugs Htin Aung had sent against Tom, how could she set Michael free of her? Of Cho? They needed Michael.

The baby was talking to himself, happy. What a rare thing that had become in Loi Long. He was in the basket on the table. The merchant in the bazaar must have had hundreds of them, the baskets all this gloppy pink – goodness it had been a long time since she'd thought of that word – gloppy. She wasn't even sure it applied. But the plastic had a loose weave so that Cho could see through and not feel so lonely. He was used to attention, more than she alone could've given him. The women in the palace. And U-pym. Poor U-pym. All those friends gone, Kathleen mourned them and picked up the baby for comfort. He grinned up at her. She'd never see any of them again. What must they think? Some would understand, but not all.

Cho felt cool, the fever gone. She guessed he'd had one for so long she'd gotten used to his heat. Even with sulfa powder dissolved in it, he'd taken to the dried milk dissolved in the water she warmed on the twin hotplate. The bazaar had baby bottles but Sally was afraid of them. They might be used, and TB was rampant, and right then they hadn't been sure Kathleen'd be able to boil anything.

He had given her some Laotian Kip, and she'd found a shop and had had some lengths of cotton stitched up to wear as longyis, wore one now, and while they were sewn she'd found a couple of sleeveless blouses, two camisoles. Her own was drying in the sun out on the stair landing, the shirt, too, washed along with her jeans which she somehow had to keep, for what reason she didn't know. Perhaps only that there was so little left of her own.

But there was everything else here. Everything. And part of her wandering about was to glory in it. To glory most of all in the light. When they had first entered this morning, she had been held still, awed by it just inside the door. The walls were plaster and painted white, and there were glass windows and glassed double doors which gave onto a tiny balcony overlooking the Khan River, a tributary of the Mekong, Michael had said.

And the slanted ceiling was wooden and painted white, too, and there were white curtains at the windows, with little flowers but still mostly white. And plain white strips of cotton strung on a rod divided the bed space from the sitting space – the lengths about eight inches wide and hanging loosely to the floor, to be pushed aside or let waft in the breeze made by the ceiling fan, creating even more light.

Too long a time in that dark palace, the walls dark, and ceilings dark, and floors dark, and in the monsoon the shutters more often closed than not. These floors were painted a wonderful light greenish-blue, and what furniture wasn't painted white was painted to match the floor, and the stripes of the cotton on the couch and the two chairs had the same colors.

She had stood in wonder until Michael had nearly run her down when he'd come charging up the stairs with the things they'd purchased at the bazaar. And now she kept wishing she might never leave it. The bazaar was like Burma, and the people were like Burma, and the weather felt like Burma, and she and Cho could make a life here. She could teach English here, and history, and learn the language, oh easy, it was in the same Tai family as the Loi Long dialect . . .

So much nonsense. Htin Aung'd try to find her. How not? Not because of her. He could get himself another woman, easily enough. Could have, long ago. Never mind the whipping, after what he'd done to Maung Swe she'd known how much he must truly hate her. Not that she hadn't felt that hate for far longer, but it had changed nothing. What mattered now was Cho. If he should learn where Cho was. About Cho. That he was getting well in spite of his father. Yes, he'd come after Cho.

Maybe she'd have to go to the States. But Cho wouldn't have a good life there. She remembered from when she was at school, it wasn't happy for dark-skinned people who looked different.

When she had thanked Michael for protecting Tom, he had seemed startled, said he'd almost forgotten it. And then he told her – ordered her, really – to throw the bolt on the door and not to answer until she found out who was knocking. He'd had the care to get her eggs and bread at the bazaar, and had left her what looked like lots of money, both dollars and more Kip. She must tell him she could pay him back. He must know that she was able to fend for herself.

Was that a car? A slammed door, feet pounding up the wooden stairs. She hadn't quite reached the open door to throw the bolt, when he burst through it. Michael.

He was juggling paperbags chock full, and stood looking at her from amongst them. For the first time, she saw the boy she'd remembered. Last night and this morning, he had been only the man he'd become. But now he no longer wore his battle dress, was smiling hugely, eager and alive – the boy again.

"How's Cho?"

"He's better. Not hungry anymore. No temperature."

He was already turning for the counter by the fridge, set down the bags, only to look at her. "You didn't lock the door."

Quickly, she went and threw the bolt. "I'd been – outside on the landing," she said. "Just before you came."

"Don't forget it, Kathleen," he said, and started pulling things out – marvels of the West – explaining each one. "Paper diapers," he said, "so you won't be scrubbing all the time. I'll get you more when you run out. Some cloth diapers, just in case, and safety pins! Great?" She stood bemused. He threw her a grin. "Kleenex! And look here," holding out a plasticine package of six white rolls, "toilet paper!" The bags seemed bottomless and things started sliding to the floor. He was crowing over each. "Bacon, sliced white bread, butter, coffee, they fly stuff in from the States frozen, can you believe it, and two sirloin steaks, we'll fry 'em, and a couple of real bath-towels, that commissary's terrific, and baby formula and more dried milk with a fresher date, condensed milk, too, it's sweeter, and baby food – lots of Gerbers, I thought maybe Cho might like it, but three baby bottles even so, and dishwashing detergent, it really cuts the grease. Shampoo, soap – Ivory, Kathleen, how long's it been since you had real Ivory – "

"Michael, for heaven's sake!" Kathleen finally coming to. He looked at her questioningly, so bright. "They must have thought you mad," she said.

"Oh, it was only a local guy at the register, what'd he know, I was in civvies. Just some clerk from records, right?"

"Nobody in the whole world would ever mistake you for a clerk from records, Michael." Her voice was dry.

Not that he heard it. He was still rummaging, to bring forth a doll – a striped cotton clown, which he presented with a grand gesture.

She took it and tucked it under her chin. "He'll love it. U-pym made him a rag doll but – "

"I got a camera, too." Michael sweeping on. "We need to take Cho's picture for a passport. I talked to the guy about it. We made a deal. Might take a few days but I gave him your old one and he thinks all they'll have to do is fiddle the dates, and stamp it a couple of times. Cho has to have his own. Wait, wait, wait," still rummaging, "yeah, here it is," and he pulled out a plush very floppy puppy. "Every little kid needs a stuffed animal," he said. "Oh," he went on, and reached in again, "a teething ring. It's got a rattle!"

She hadn't thought she had any tears left, and she didn't, but she was suddenly wiping some away and had to sit on the nearest chair and bury her face in the two soft toys.

He reached clear to the bottom one last time, and brought forth a bottle of Glenlivet. "And this is for me," he said.

He intended perfectly well to share it with her. He looked at her sitting there, knew he'd been a little overwhelming probably. Opening a cabinet, he found a mixed bunch of glasses, took two and the Glenlivet over to the couch and sat. "You're going to have to put everything away," he said. "I wouldn't know where."

She looked up at him above the toys. "It has a rattle," she said, "well, isn't that – remarkable!" She gave a little giggle, it caught, and he laughed with her. Not quite like her old one, didn't go on long enough for either one of them, but it was a laugh, thank God, even if it didn't sound quite under control.

In a moment, she got up and started putting stuff away. She was wearing a new camisole and longyi, soft light colors of green and rose, and she was in bare feet, though she'd bought a pair of thong sandals this morning. Her hair hung down her back loose, unbraided, and shining clean. And now Michael noticed two places set at the little table against the wall. It was like coming home.

He made Kathleen sip some of the single malt, and she liked it. Or said she did. She'd never drunk alcohol before, but since she was a lousy liar, or had used to be, he decided to believe her. And was delighted beyond reason by it.

He had seen Hanny before leaving the airport and reported that he would be released from the clinic in the morning. Then Michael would tear down the Loach at Hanny's direction and ready it for the new instrument panel and wiring. So he could tell her he'd be in L.P. all day, could check on her and the baby.

They stood together at the hot-plate frying the steaks and toasting the sliced white bread on the burners and slathering it with the butter that Michael labelled too strong from being stored over-long but Kathleen couldn't get enough of it, no milk cows in Loi Long.

With Cho close by they sat at the little table, chewing the wonderful freezer-tough steak, and neither asked the other about the missing years. Michael decided both of them were scared of it, scared to tear the evening, tear everything apart. But it would have to be talked about sometime, they couldn't just sit on the dime forever. It was pleasant, the fan turning overhead, the noise from downstairs of children and the Chinese-high voice of a woman, the soft sounds the baby made.

She was the one who broke the little dream first, not about the past but asking about the Colonel. That was easy. It had been easy. Most of it. Michael had gone right in to the embassy from the airport and launched into the complicated story Hanny'd concocted, how last night the Corporal had been late and they'd been ambushed and they'd gone up, only to have to find another LZ, until Colonel Wisby had jumped in, waving Michael to a typewriter, telling him to type up the report and file it. It was only later that the problem about the compass had surfaced. But they'd gotten past it, or at least Michael hoped they had. Richard's words to be careful with this man continued to haunt him, especially now that he'd come to know him. No way could he tell any of that to Kathleen. Scare her to death. Along with the fact that since Hanny had stitches he was grounded and Michael would be flying scout solo for the rescue operation for the Senator.

Except that having heard a little, Kathleen wanted more, so Michael did oblige about what a "dove" was, and what may have been sabotage to the Volpar, and the Laotians keeping the ten men in a cave to sell them to the Chinese. Or to the Vietnamese. And about Donald Duck. Which, of course, horrified her, but which also reminded Michael to show her his new watch.

Afterwards, he dried and she washed, telling him with considerable tartness that she *had* used liquid detergent before, you'd think she'd lived her whole life at the end of the world, which caused them both to stop dead and look at each other, not laughing this time. And then it changed, at least for a little while. He started opening cabinets just to see what all Meisner had here, and found it – a radio.

"Well, will you look at this!" practically yelping it. Kathleen had gone quiet. He plugged it in, fiddled with the dial, and there it was, Lou Rawls doing "Snap Your Fingers." An armed forces broadcast, maybe from Udorn, fading in and out a little, Rawls into it, now. Not exactly the lyrics for this moment, if she took it too seriously she'd feel pushed, but it couldn't be helped, he wasn't going to lose the chance.

He looked at Kathleen, but she looked away. Then the blues rhythm took him and swivelling his hips, he moved towards her, stood apart from her, his body still into it. "Remember the first time we danced?" he asked. "That day by the creek?" He stopped breathing, scared she'd say no.

She barely glanced at him, scrubbing the last dish, finally gave a little shake to her head. But it wasn't in denial. "You must have thought I was – Lord, Michael, such a silly fool."

"No," he said, his voice trailing it, and he took her by the arm, turned her towards him, took the dish away, slipped out of his loafers not to step on her toes, and not wanting to hurt her back he dropped his hands to her hips, pressing her into motion. As he had, that day. And she let him, let the beat take her, too. At least a little. "I fell in love with you that day. Or more in love, anyway."

Did you, Michael? Then why did you leave me behind? Her feet had stopped, but he wouldn't let her body go, moving her with him to the music. And she would never ask him that. Never.

Rawls was going dark and dirty. Michael turned her, turned himself, saw her mouth which had set, go soft again. But he was hearing the damned lyrics now, and she surely was, too. "Let me love you like the lover that you used to know." This time she really broke it, standing still. "Can you let me in through the same old door." God. But the beat went heavy now, the double rhythm driving it, his hips doing the catch, and he decided to go with it, moving out and around her, in a big circle in that white room, turning, hands down slightly behind his hips. "Well I had it but I lost it, now I got a broken heart to mend." She was following him out of the corner of her eyes, her mouth quirking a little. Amused, he'd bet a million. And then her hips, her thighs were moving again under the longyi, its cotton tightening, easing, tightening over that firm round bottom. "I don't care what the cost is, I've got to find my way back in. Snap your fingers, I'll come running!"

What was the matter with her? Why didn't she just walk away from this nonsense?

Michael had just gotten back to her when Rawls finished. A silence as he watched and waited, her face down, but she held, oh, God, she held, and Rawls started "Person to Person." Must be a concert tape or something.

Michael dipped his head to look into her lowered face. And the words got to them both at the same time. "Don't write me no letter, don't even telephone, I need you person to person, bring your fine foxy self back home." She looked up in total surprise, gave a quick little laugh, and they were into it, the crazy song that said it all, both of them laughing with it at every new verse. And it was the old laugh, it was.

Another silence waited out, and the sax led off into "Sweet Slumber." He wanted to bring her in, but he didn't. Still, they moved as if embraced, the smile lingering on her lips. And Cho let forth a call. Michael sashayed over to him, picked him up, laid him in his left arm, moved back to Kathleen, put his right arm around her and the hell with it, give it a try for God's sake, he drew her in, moving, moving, holding them both, woman and baby, tight now, feeling her against him as it had used to be.

"I will hold you in my arms again, once more, tonight." And Rawls ended. They stood there, locked together, and then she stepped back, sharp as if starting from a daze. She reached and he handed her Cho, had to, and she was carrying him away towards the bedroom.

"He's happy, put him down here."

She kept going. Michael stepped, took her arm, turning her – and she pulled away from him.

"What are you running from? That was the way it used to be with us. You know it. Feeling it together and right."

"No," she said. When she finally met his eyes, hers were damned near opaque. "We were just – playing at it, trying to get it back. It was a memory, that's all."

"That's shit," Michael said, angry.

"Michael, listen to me, listen now – you must. There's nothing here for you. Not for anybody."

"No, I sure as hell don't 'must' anything. You've got to tell me. Then I'll understand."

She looked at him across her quiet child, the sorrow back.

"Put him down, Kathleen." Michael turned for the couch, sat on it. "Put him down and come here. There's something you need to know, it'll be a start, anyway."

What was it, she wondered. That he was married? Had children? Would give it all up for her? Oh, God. How could she tell him what the years had been for her, made of her? Show him the stones? Tell him outright? But it would serve only to put it all on him. He had left her, after all. No, she couldn't. He didn't deserve it. He'd been young, wanting to do the right thing. And things just had happened.

He was watching her, waiting there. Listen, that's all you have to do, Kathleen, she told herself. Only listen.

She put the baby in his basket, crossed and sat beside Michael.

30

"Okay. Okay," he had started, had to take a breath, started again. "Tom and I figured it out when I was in Hong Kong. Htin Aung stole our letters, Kathleen."

Letters? Letters? It rolled through her, pounding through her, the blood in her ears like thunder. She almost couldn't hear him go on.

"I wrote you for months after your letters stopped. I tried to come back, but the Burmese Government . . . "

She looked away, seeming to stare at nothing. "Kathleen?"

It was whirling around in her. Too late. Too late. She didn't realize when she spoke.

"Of course," she said, whispering. Michael had to bend to hear her. "That's why you did it. Why wouldn't you, believing I didn't care . . . "

"Did what?"

"Got married," she said, still whispering. And then she looked at him, making it gentle. "Of course."

His voice seemed loud in that silent place, and that was fine by him. "I'm not married. Never've been. Never've wanted to, since you."

And he felt the shock go through her, as if all her electricity had suddenly changed poles. Her eyes were no longer opaque but terrified.

"But he said . . . it was in your last letter."

His last letter? What had he written there? All he could remember were the wild pleas not to quit on him, asking what he'd done, what was wrong, telling her he'd never stop loving her, telling her – and the S.O.B. had read them all. "What did he say, Kathleen?"

Again seeming to look at nothing, she sat there wringing her hands. He'd never before realized what a dreadful gesture that was.

"It was after Tom left, after I moved into the palace," she said, her voice so soft he almost couldn't hear her. "Months after your letters stopped, he came to me with a confession, that's what he called it, he said he knew how long I'd been grieving – for you, you see – with no letters. He said one had come, several weeks before this, and he had taken the awful liberty of opening it because, he said, he said he was sure what it would say and

257

wanted to spare me and that he'd been right, you wrote you were to be married. He said he tore it up. But then he decided I should know, it might make me forget you sooner. He said it all with apology and great sympathy, and looked on with the pity of a brother while I cried."

Now she faced Michael again, looking stricken and ten years older than when she'd turned away. Maybe he did, too.

"But even so, why could I go on believing him? How could I, after it all turned?" She stood up, hands still working. "That one kindness I kept on believing . . . oh, God!"

It was such an outcry it brought Michael to his feet. But he didn't touch her, because he didn't understand. How come this mattered to her so much? The whole thing was an incredible betrayal by Htin Aung, this one lie seemed to Michael just one more part of the whole. Why wasn't it?

She uttered a long shuddering breath. She went to the basket, bent, gathered Cho up, rocking him, head hidden in him. "It would have kept *me* from changing," her voice desolate. "If I'd known. If I hadn't believed him. If I'd only – " Her eyes now flew up to Michael's.

If she'd only believed in *him*. Michael. And he'd only believed in her. One hell of a pair, they were.

She started away, a few steps only, and stopped. Like a cat, startled, caught. She turned back for the basket to lay Cho in it and disappeared with it beyond the fluttering white curtain. But she was back in an instant.

"You should go," she said, "you need a good night's sleep." As if nothing at all had transpired here. What kind of fucking control was that? He felt shaken to his bones.

"Don't be ridiculous," he managed. "I'm staying the night. The couch'll do fine." Her lips parted as if she were going to argue, and he swept on. "You're in a strange place, a strange city, a strange country, you don't know the language, hell, you don't even know the address here!" And no longer waiting on anything, he headed for the can. "I'll be in and out of your way in a sec," he said, and closed the door behind him – and leaned back against it.

He'd worried last night – Lord, was it only last night? – waiting in the Loach in the orchard that she'd feel betrayed when he told her about the letters. She felt betrayed, all right, but it seemed more by herself than by Htin Aung. Michael had watched the truth send her into a kind of grief, watched her take it on herself with why, and how, and what if she hadn't. They'd had everything wiped away from them. Yet the rage she had revealed on her child's behalf she had either totally buried when it came to herself, or it was absent.

The destructive words rolled through him, all the what-ifs, Christ, the waste of them. Letting angst about the past determine the present. He'd done it almost all his grown up years, and now she was heading down the same road. Somehow he had to make her deal with it and forget it. Had to help her do it. And do it himself.

Standing at the toilet, letting his water run, he wondered what else had been done to her, not on this day or on that day but all through the years. Maybe she was right, and what he'd felt, dancing with her, her sensuality, the knowing, was only a try at remembering. Maybe he had lost her after all, that girl so alive in his head as she hadn't been barely two weeks ago. The girl he'd left in spite of her tears.

Doin' it again, Cameron? Goin' over and over it. He flushed the toilet, and caught sight of himself in the mirror. The look of him surprised him. Like her, he wasn't that boy any longer, either.

He returned to the darkened sitting room to find a sheet spread on the couch and a bed pillow. He had the feeling that his anger now – and the angst, too – would be as nothing once he learned the rest.

He loosened his belt and stretched out, not wanting the sheet, his feet dangling. He closed his eyes . . . and Sledge entered, smooth as silk, "When a ma-an loves a woman . . . "

After they'd danced that day, the day she now called herself a fool for, they'd swum in the creek. Fed by mountain waters, it was icy. She'd stripped to her underwear and gone leaping in, shrieking, immediately crouching down in the water to look back up the bank at him. "Let me see you," she said in her smallest voice. He was still in his jeans. "Please?" she asked. "Tom's the only man I've ever seen. When I was ten." A little smile crooked her mouth up, and she ducked her head. "I peeked, but it was only the once. We were a very proper family."

So he'd pulled his jeans off, then his briefs, and stood there, everything just hanging out. She looked at all of him, but mainly there. He let her have her fill, then took a flying leap into the water with her and they played like kids until they were goose-bumped and blue and ran up the bank to throw themselves on the blanket, Kathleen face down, Michael on his back – thoughtlessly.

Catching her breath, Kathleen suddenly sat up. "Now it's your turn. Only fair." And she rolled onto her knees, facing him down by his hip, her hands reaching back to unfasten her wet bra. But he snatched her hand away. "Stop it, Kath." She looked as if she wasn't sure what she was feeling – disappointed or insulted.

Michael had sure known what he was feeling. He craved to see what that wet bra, the wet panties didn't altogether hide, darknesses showing through. His imagination was giving him all the temptations a man could stand. One look and he wouldn't be able to stop what would happen afterwards. But not here and not now, damn it, Kathleen so tight in her innocence and doing it while scared to death of getting caught by some kid with a buffalo, a woman fetching water.

Suddenly, something drew her eyes down his body, and she stared in amazement. He looked down, too, and saw the full hard on. From his vantage point it was wavering in silhouette against the blue sky, and he thought, attach some feathers and it'd turn into a fucking palm tree.

When he'd looked back at her, she'd still been staring at his penis, not so amazed, now, but curious, and her hand was sneaking towards it.

Toughest thing the boy he'd been had ever done, Michael thought now, was to get himself up onto his feet to run back into the water, where the cold had felled his palm tree like an ax.

On the couch in L.P., Michael looked down. No rising, of course. That Kathleen had become a charming girl he'd loved once as a boy. He rolled to his side, bunched the pillow under his head. He'd learned last night that the baby had captured him. And from the moment he'd seen her again, the woman in the next room had, too. No way was he not going to find out the rest.

DAY NINE

31

Michael got out and leaned back into the cab. "I'll take him," he said. She handed Cho over and slid across and out herself. Michael had already paid the driver, and started for the door into the clinic. She was turning to follow when she caught sight of a uniformed paunchy man standing by a jeep. A soldier. American. Looking at Michael's back, and then at her with narrowed curious eyes. A moment, and she hurried after Michael, thinking to ask him if he'd noticed the soldier, feeling oddly unsettled by it. But inside a nurse was waiting and Kathleen had only time to retrieve the baby and follow, again the length of the corridor back to the little crash room.

Michael went to collect Hanny. Michael and Kathleen had come here together because prick or not, Schramm had asked Kathleen to bring the baby back for a check up first thing this morning.

Hanny was perched on the edge of the bed, shaving with a safety razor which sliced him as Michael entered his room.

"Shit," he said, waving the razor, "probably'll give me lockjaw, God knows where they scrounged it from."

"Sorry," Michael said.

Hanny grumbled, took one last pass and wiped his face with a threadbare towel. "And no shower," he went on. "How long's it been since you had to take a spit bath – look at that dinky basin!" He pointed to what was, indeed, pretty dinky.

"Chicken pox, I think."

And Willy entered, a fresh set of camouflage fatigues over his arm. He grinned from ear to ear and crossed to grab Hanny's hand. "Hey, you're up and goin'! Brought you some stuff."

"Bless you," Hanny said, untying the hospital gown.

"Skivvies there, too," Willy said. "We'll clean out your room at the hotel and catch an AA Caribou down to Vientiane later this morning. I've already got the Colonel's stuff out in the jeep. Came up after 'em last night." He turned to Michael. "Figured we'd have dinner but couldn't raise you by phone. The whole evening. Began to worry, matter of fact. And when the clerk this morning said you never picked up your key, I decided I better bring Hanny a change of clothes."

His eyes were watchful. He just waited. What was all this? Michael shrugged. "Room phone must be on the fritz." And he turned immediately to help Hanny who was struggling one-handed to pull on his shorts, Michael wondering what he'd say if Willy pursued him on where he'd spent the night. None of Willy's business, of course, Michael wasn't on standby and Willy knew that, but still, Michael didn't have a ready lie.

Hanny saved it. "Nope. We're gonna tear down the Loach so no time wasted when we install the new equipment."

"Well," Michael said, hauling Hanny's T-shirt down now, "truth is, Hanny's going to straw-boss while *I* tear it down."

"And tell him what he's doing wrong," Hanny chimed back in.

Willy still watchful. Michael decided to confront it, at least a little. "What is it? The Colonel want us in Vientiane early? I thought the plan was to be there tonight, available for the rangers if they get in. We'll probably fly the Loach down if the weather holds. Easier than having a Huey hoist it down."

Willy shook his head. "He's good with that, the day's yours."

Michael nodded, now helping Hanny with his trousers and belt.

"Well, see you guys later," Willy said, heading for the door when Kathleen blew through it into the room on a wave of joyous relief. "The doctor says it can't be amoebic, Cho's responding too well, so he's going to be fine, Michael, isn't that – oh." Seeing Willy, and looking appalled.

"Um," Michael started, "Kathleen, um, this is Sergeant Freed. Miss Howard, Willy." Willy's eyes weren't watchful, now, they were plain sharp. Michael plowed ahead. "Miss Howard was here with her baby last night."

And Kathleen burst in, to warn him, Michael was sure. "I think I saw you outside, didn't I?" she asked. And she extended her hand to shake Willy's.

"We shared a cab here from the hotel this morning," Michael said. Too quickly, damn it.

"Sure," said Willy. "See you tonight. Take it easy, Hanny." And he was gone.

A scared Kathleen looked at Michael. "Did I do harm?"

"No," he said. "Let him think what he wants, it's nothing to do with the truth anyway. It's great news about Cho!"

Hanny meanwhile had turned his back, zipping up his fly.

"Come on," Michael went on to Kathleen. "Let's find you a car. You manage okay?" he asked Hanny.

On Hanny's nod, Michael followed Kathleen outside. They found a cab around the end of the building. "You need the address," Michael said, fishing through a pocket to pull out the crumpled map to Meisner's place.

"You won't remember the street," she said, taking the paper from him.

"Yeah, I remember, it's – oh, shit," he said, and she held it up for him. He squinted. "Pak Khan Road. Pak Khan. Got it."

She started to smile. "You and names. That hasn't changed, has it?"

"We'll be by early afternoon, probably. Maybe go out for Chinese or something."

She nodded, leaned forward and told the driver to go to the bazaar. The driver turned and looked at her blankly. She tried it in another language, and by God, it worked. How did she do that? The cab moved away, even as Michael was bending to tell her that he'd take her to the bazaar later. And then came the belated recognition that she was far better able to manage here than he was. He stood looking after the cab. Hanny came up. "Let's go," he said.

As their cab pulled up to the Loach, damn, there was Willy. He turned out of the back cabin with the Colonel's helmet. "Let's hope Kathleen didn't forget any dirty diapers," Hanny muttered. Michael shoved some Kip at the driver and got out, pasting on a big smile.

"Come to see the damage?" he asked.

"Almost forgot it," Willy said easily, gesturing with the helmet. "Cockpit sure is a mess!" Hanny came up, as Willy leaned in. "What'd you say happened to your hand compass? Looks fine." Yesterday with the Colonel, that little problem.

Michael managed, just, not to cast a glance Hanny's way. "I could use a seat, guys," Hanny said, inching past Willy to edge himself onto the peter seat, saving it again.

"Just went haywire, is all," Michael said.

"Oh. Thought you said it got hit."

He had, damn it. "Talkin' about the gyroscopic, I guess," Michael said. "I'm going to hover over to that big shade tree on down the strip, get Hanny a chair. See you tonight, okay?" And Michael walked around to his own seat, got in, waited politely for Willy to get out from under the blades, and cranked.

The Loach had begun to go rank, so after getting Hanny settled on an AA deck chair, Michael found a hose and a bucket, some detergent and a scrub brush, and got rid of Hanny's spilled blood. Then he tackled the shattered panel, the burned wires.

It got hot. Even with his shirt off he was sopping. Hanny was sitting with his legs outstretched, dressed above the waist in nothing but his bandages, coke bottle dangling from his fingers over the scarred wooden arm of the chair. Doing Mama Cass and "Words of Love". He was soft enough, but Michael didn't know how long he'd put up with it. ". . .longing gazes won't get you where you want to go. If you love her, then you must send her – "

"Hey," Michael said, "enough."

There was silence, and then Hanny started in on Otis Redding's "Dock of the Bay." Nice and neutral, Michael sang along, and they jumped on into a couple of Righteous Brothers things. Late in the morning, Michael took a break, got himself a Coke and sat on the tarmac next to Hanny.

"You want to tell me about yesterday?" Hanny said.

"Yeah," Michael said. "They woke the Colonel up with our Mayday." He and Willy went to the embassy, and they plotted the coordinates on a map of Laos. The Colonel said he damned near had a heart attack when he knew we'd gone down and nobody knew zilch about the Senator and his outfit. Some relief when we cancelled it and flew on in. You were right, we shouldn't've Maydayed. Because yesterday, when he wanted me to plot the Volpar and Donald's village, he dug out the same fuckin' map. And when I spotted 'em on it, boy oh boy if he didn't want to know how come – " and Hanny chimed in, "we got so far off course."

"And you said?" Hanny prompted.

"That everything had been shivved, and the cloud ceiling had dropped, and we'd gone by best guess, and for all we knew we could've been farther north on the Nam Tha – or east – or on a different water course altogether . . . "

"Or anything you could think of, and it probably all sounded like a bad lie," Hanny said. "Including a broken hand compass, I gather."

Michael looked at him. Was he being wry or grim. Preferring wry, Michael sure hoped he was right.

"You're lousy at it, y'know," Hanny finished.

Sounded like Gran when he was in the fourth grade. "Uh huh," Michael said. "Plus which, in the midst of it, Willy walked in and listened, and for a guy who's been comin' across like somebody's Christmas elf, he looked pretty skeptical."

"And then, this morning, here comes Kathleen." Hanny, again, and he suddenly laughed, head back with it. "After you've been out all night."

Michael didn't find any comic relief in it at all. "But he can't really put it together, do you think?" Hanny had no answer. "Hasn't so far, anyway," Michael said, and then gave a little groan, drained his Coke, stood up, held out his hand for Hanny's bottle. "Better get on with it. What you want me to do next?"

"Let it go. We'll see how she flies later." He chug-a-lugged his Coke. "So. How goes the other thing?"

Other thing. Kathleen. What the hell, two years shouldn't make such a difference, but they did when it was Hanny's advantage over him. In good sense, mainly.

"Depends on what you mean," Michael said. "Far as I'm concerned, it's all still there, maybe even more so, I mean we've both – come of age, right? But she's carrying a hell of a lot of baggage, and she's shut down on it. She needs to deal with it, y'know? And I don't have an idea how to help her do it."

"Maybe she already has." Hanny's voice even, soft.

Michael was shaking his head, about to jump in to deny it, but Hanny stalled him. "Michael. That's one good and steady woman. I've never seen the likes of her the other night. She was a rock. Seems to me she's been dealing pretty well on her own for close to five years."

"Or thinks she has," Michael protested. "So I just decide it's none of my God-damned business and forget it? Well, I've been there, done that, damn it." He pulled in, too fuckin' up-tight. "Sorry."

Hanny stood up. "Just thinkin' out loud. Nobody can tell you what to do. Or how to do it. Look, why don't I just go to the hotel and you can have her to yourself."

"Unh, unh." Michael shook his head. "I want you to know where she is. Right now, nobody does but me."

Hanny looked at him a long disgusted moment. He knew what it meant: that he might well be around when Michael wasn't. "They're not grounding me, damn it! Oh maybe the doc here, but there's one down at the embassy. A civilian – I'll be able to work him, don't worry."

Michael managed a little nod, not at all sure Hanny ought to even try, but he wasn't exactly thrilled to go alone, either. He carried the bottles over to a barrel and dropped them in. "You up for dim sum?"

32

No dim sum. The meal turned out to be stew Kathleen had made with a bazaar chicken on the little two-burner. Michael wondered if she'd wrung its neck. He'd watched her do it on the farm, hands strong and swift.

While she stirred the stew up, Hanny held Cho on his knee and Michael took photos of him. Considerably more than necessary for the passport, having fun.

They sat at the little table, Cho in the basket with a bottle. He handled it pretty well, just needing it to be braced. The minute Michael took a bite of stew, they came rushing in on him, the memories of Sundays at the farm, after services. How could he've forgotten the taste? In spite of all the fine ingredients, and they were fine, it really was lousy. Kathleen had cooked it every Sunday, leaving it to keep warm on the back of the wood stove.

They would sit in the open pavillion Tom had built for church and gatherings, the sides lifting up in all but the worst of the rains so that the air moved through, carrying on it the sounds and fragrances of the mountains. Cross-legged on the springy basha floor with all the worshippers – they would start arriving in early morning, all clothed in black – Michael would listen but not understand a word of Tom's sermon given in Kaw, hearing the rattle of the fan palms just beyond the raised walls, and trying to join in in English to the old hymns he retained on the fringe of recall, sung here in Kaw and pulsing with simple harmony and an even simpler marching rhythm, a music that shook him inside and deep.

"Michael? Seconds?" Kathleen, handing Hanny a replenished plate. Good God. Michael discovered he'd cleaned his own. How had he managed it? How had Hanny? And he realized he'd only half heard while Kathleen drew Hanny out as Michael rarely managed to do even over Glenlivet, really getting him to talk – about how a patch of black ice had killed his wife on Route 94, driving to Cleveland from Buffalo one late February afternoon, and how little Eric had been living with his folks ever since, as now Barb was, too. "I never miss a week writing the kid," he was saying. Michael hadn't known that.

Kathleen stood waiting for an answer. About what? Oh, yeah. "Gee, thanks, no," Michael struggled hastily, "you gave me such a big breakfast, remember?" And she had. The one dish Kathleen was good at, scrambled eggs.

Hanny, meanwhile, was plowing into his second helping – only to give it up after a couple of forkfuls. "Say," he said, "you know what? I'm full up, too." He pushed back his chair.

"Wait, wait, wait," Kathleen said, and she brought out some mangos and cut them the way she'd done it in Keng Tung: the sides cut free of the pit and the fruit inside them cross-hatched with a knife so that you convexed them and plunged your mouth into the tart sweet flesh, dribbling the juice down your chin. She'd always served them up at just the perfect ripeness. No matter how often Michael had bought mangos in Nam, they'd never been right. Either over-ripe and going rotten or hard without juice. Now he dived in, mouth exploding with flavor, and grinned at Hanny, telling him to go for it. And watched Hanny's eyes pop.

Afterwards, they all had to wash hands and faces like kids, and then they just stood around in that little kitchen area, final cups of coffee in hand. It's over, Michael thought. It's by God over. Get a few rangers for show and a bucketful of greenbacks, go up there and ransom those ten guys, and like Hanny, he was out of here and heading for the States. Kathleen with him. Had to be with him, would take a little time was all.

He raised his cup in a toast. "Here's to no more flitting shadows." Eyes flicking to Hanny, "No more going through the jungle softly."

Hanny just stood there, studying him. Kathleen suddenly grabbed into it. "Oh," she said. She looked over at Cho and murmured, "He is Fear, O Little Hunter, he is Fear, I remember. Dear Lord, yes, no more of that."

"So here's to Ruedyard Kipling," Hanny said, raised his cup to clink it against Michael's, and drained his coffee. That's how he pronounced it. Rue-dyard.

Unthinking with surprise, Michael stared at him, jaw probably agape in the silence until he caught a look fit to kill from Kathleen. But Hanny only sent him a small down-turned see-there? smile, no reproach in it. And turned quickly, putting a hand down on the counter, setting his cup down, and Michael could see he was gone pale. Of course, he denied a problem. Kathleen urged him to pile down on the bed, but he said he wanted his own bed back at the hotel, and had to pack up anyway. So Michael went down to the phone to call a cab, telling Hanny that if he didn't hear a horn in ten minutes to come on out, he was sure one would be along by then. He was also sure he wanted these two to have a few moments alone. Wanted them to be friends. Though he knew perfectly well from school days that you could put your two best friends together for a perfect match and they'd never take to each other in a million years, but he had to hope.

A cab was promised quickly, Hanny already down and coming to the gate by the time it arrived. They planned for Michael to reach the hotel to pack up his own stuff around three, and then they'd fly to Vientiane. Hanny got into the car, looked out the window at Michael. "She's a keeper, pal. Do whatever you have to." And then he flashed a grin. "Though I gotta admit, she's a mite missing in the chef department." Michael chuckled, was halfway back to the house when Hanny called, "Hey!"

Michael looked back, saw the grin. "I figure you'd like to know. Had an old maiden aunt used to give all us kids books every Christmas. None of us ever opened a one, except me and Ruedyard Kipling. Read it through twice."

Kathleen was doing dishes. He grabbed a towel and dried. Finally had to ask. "Was it awkward or easy?"

She cast him a glance. "You mean alone with Hanny?" She smiled dryly, busy with the dirty pot. "A lot easier than with you," she said. And then she relented. "You're very different from each other, but alike, even so. Big and funny and – I don't know, something inside you that's strange to me. Maybe that you're soldiers, y'think?"

She wasn't looking at him, not really expecting an answer, and he wasn't sure he grasped what she was talking about. So they stayed quiet until the dishes were out of the way. She dried her hands, facing him. "Michael," she said, sounding very determined. "I want to tell you something."

"Oh, yeah?" He lifted with relief. "Fine."

"You needn't feel responsible for me. I can pay you back."

"What?"

She was glancing around a little helplessly. "Whatever all this is costing – when I'm in Hong Kong, I'll be able to pay you back."

"What're you talking about?"

"Why don't you listen? I'm not dependent on you, Michael. I will pay it all back."

He found himself rushing red with a silly kind of fury. "Shut up, Kathleen."

"But – "

"Just shut up. Jesus," and he didn't apologize, "the last thing in the world I thought we needed to talk about was money. You want to argue about money?" Incredulous.

"Not everyone is as rich as you Camerons, Michael."

"Oh, for God's sake." No apology here, either. He ran his still damp fingers through his hair, struggling for patience. "Last night, when I told you about the letters, they weren't what bothered you so much as that one lie. One, out of what must have been many, that he told you. It took you so hard, Kathleen, and I wasn't sure why. I want to know why."

Hating it, he watched her turn from him, wrapping her arms to herself, huddling into them. Like last night, she looked suddenly smaller. Almost frail. "It wasn't even that I hadn't gotten married after all, was it," he said. "You talked about how believing in that one kindness had made such a difference. What difference, Kath?" He needed to confront it. Make her confront it, damn it.

Why wouldn't he stop it, why did he keep pushing, she couldn't tell him, she couldn't put voice to what he was pleading to know. And even if she could, it would hurt him wretchedly. He'd reach out to her, pull her in, *try* her, feel forced to, wouldn't he. And when he discovered the truth for himself he'd think it was *his* failure. Michael had used to take too much on himself, whether deserved or even sensible, and probably still did. It was basic to him.

She dropped her arms to her sides and faced him, firming up her voice and her face. "Of course, you don't understand, how could you?" She could feel her mouth tremble. Damn it. She set it. "There's nothing here for you, Michael. I'll always be grateful to you, you've given me my baby's life, but we're done."

He studied her eyes, her mouth. Both were set to be strong. To seem honest. But she was no dissembler, and try as she might as she held his eyes she couldn't hide from him the fear inside.

"What're you afraid of?" he asked.

It chased her into turning away again, but he reached and grabbed her arm and stopped her. He took her chin in his fingers and made her head turn back towards him. "Is it him? You're still afraid of him?"

She shook her head, twisting it out of his control. "No, it isn't – " Her voice was low, a little ragged. "I don't want to hurt you. Why do you make me!"

"You listen to me now," he said, every bit as determined as she had sounded before. He let go of her, stood back a little. "Look at me." She didn't. God, was there ever a more stubborn woman?

"Look at me," and he waited her out until she did. "We . . . you and I . . . we made a kind of splendor. You know we did. Something fundamental to us. It *was* us. You want to deny it, sure, it'll hurt." The Lord knew, he'd denied it to himself long enough.

"Of course I won't deny it," she said. Impatient, as if he were foolish. She caught in an uneven breath, let it out. "But it can't happen again."

Can't? What did that mean? Anything, lots of things. He decided to go with the one he wanted.

"You're right." Woke her up, anyway. "Back then we were both – all new, weren't we? So, no, it won't happen again, not like that." He was bending towards her, silently forcing her to keep her head up, her eyes on his. Was there hope in them? "But now that we know what became of it . . . it can take us somewhere just as fundamental. A place neither of us can ever get to with anyone else. In four years, I haven't. Nor have you." Didn't ask it. He knew the answer.

He'd gone too far. Oh, shit. Oh, shit. The light was dying out of her eyes. She was backing away from him, beginning to wave her hands helplessly as if to silence him. She turned and moved for the bedroom. She pushed the cotton curtains aside in invitation. "Come in, Michael," she said.

What did she intend? To take him to bed in order to prove something? He followed almost reluctantly, not at all sure what he was going to do.

But that wasn't it. She went straight to the Shan bags in the corner and rummaged in one to bring forth a silk pouch, came back to the bed with it. She looked around at him sideways a long moment, so sad again. For him. She opened the pouch, reached in, brought out something wrapped in cloth, unwrapped it – and dumped a stream of gem stones on the white coverlet.

Michael stared down at them. Huge. He'd say from four to six carats, each of them, but what did he know, really. Cut pigeon bloods the biggest, but some star rubies, too. And sapphires, deep blue cuts, lighter cabochon stars. Seventeen, eighteen, more than twenty of them, dear God. Where did she get them? Mogok stones, of course, but how did she buy them? Tom couldn't have given her that much money when he'd left Burma

– he was always having to be frugal, if not dead broke.

Not really wanting to know, Michael looked up to find her watching him.

"You see?" she said. He could only shake his head. "He left them. By the side of the bed, starting, oh, two and half years ago or so, when he decided – . Never mind. Each time, he left one. Not so many, after all."

Michael thought he'd never seen such a sadness, and had to look away from it because now she never took her eyes away from his. Looking back down at the stones, he wanted to send them flying to the floor to be lost between the cracks of the boards. Never to be found. He saw his fingers reaching, saw them shaking – and heard her soft voice.

"I was his whore, Michael. Before he even started to leave the stones, I was."

He couldn't look back up at her. It didn't hurt him. It broke his heart, the sound of her voice, the desolation in it. Michael doubted she even knew the meaning of the word, the real meaning. Joy, that's what the word meant, for a price. Like Li Li's girls. That bastard would've known perfectly well how little of the demi-monde the girl that had been Kathleen could have known. The stones were to humiliate her.

And then, he understood. "That's what that lying act of so-called kindness did. It made you able to forgive him."

She shook her head slightly, almost relieved he still hadn't understood. She scooped up the stones like jacks to pour them from her hand back into the pouch. She crossed to the Shan bag, and put the pouch back inside it. "So you see, I'll be able to pay you in Hong Kong." She straightened, turned, making her eyes once more impenetrable, and walked past him into the sitting room. "It must be nearly three," she said. "Hanny'll be waiting."

There went the rug out from under him. He'd been so close to it. Worse, she was right, it was nearly three. Michael followed her out of the bedroom. There were other things that had to be addressed.

"Kathleen," he said. And it caused her to turn back around to him. Something in his voice, he didn't know what. "I'll probably not be able to get back here for a couple of days. I'll try, but it may not be possible. So don't worry." He pulled out some Kip, some coins for the phone. She didn't reach for it. He slapped it all down on the table and stepped to her, taking her arms before she could move away from him. And he kissed her. No questing to it, just a kiss. And was nearly sickened to find that sweet mouth of hers dead to his lips. He let her go.

"This isn't finished," he said. "I need to know it all, and you can't refuse it to me. I don't give a shit about the money. Just let me understand. That's my pay."

He headed for the door, stopped, went over to the basket, bent and kissed Cho on the forehead without waking him, went on to the door.

"Michael!" He looked back at her. "You must give it up!" she said. Her face was full of anguish. Suddenly, she was wringing her hands as she had last night. But this time he wouldn't stand for it. He crossed to her and took her hands in his.

She looked down, as if she hadn't been aware of what she was doing. She made her hands go still. There was nothing for it. The bewilderment in his face after he kissed her had told her the pain she was going to deal him. But he would never put it behind him, if she didn't. "All right," she said. "Let me go."

He did. No choice, really. She moved back into the bedroom. She'd said 'all right', so how come the vision he'd had on the creek bank night before last slapped at him again, of her walking away from him forever. But in a moment she returned with a set of spiral school notebooks. Along with everything else, they'd been in her Shan bag?

"Journals," she said, holding them out to him. "Mine."

He looked down at them in her hands, the slim little volumes, precious, terrifying, not sure he wanted to know what was in there. But he did, in the way he'd once known her body, he wanted to know all of it.

"Take them," she said. He was so slow. Now she'd decided, why wouldn't he take them? "Damn you, Michael, take them!"

He took the notebooks, and this time had almost reached the door when she asked, "Will you be safe?"

He summoned up a smile and a wink from somewhere. "I'll be careful. Bolt the door." And he went.

She did as he'd ordered, in a daze. She'd lost him. Why was it as hard now as it had been years ago? He would never come back. Oh, to be kind, to make sure she got to Hong Kong, but nothing more.

She stopped in the middle of the room. Her vision was blurred. She'd believed for a long time that she had no tears left. She stepped to the basket, leaned over it, watching Cho stir in his sleep, and clenched her hands on either side of him. Wet drops landed on his little piece of blanket.

She willed her eyes dry. "We've survived, Cho. We're free. Saved by a good man. You will always know his name, baby. Always."

33

It was past six-thirty. The embassy space allotted to the military attaché and staff was limited, and the Colonel's office pretty tight for seven men, but they crowded in. The Colonel, Willy, Michael and the Air America lift helicopter pilot who was going to insert and extract – turned out to be massive, bearded Jedediah, for heaven's sake – plus three rangers, Master Sergeant Milt Starky and two Specialists, who had arrived from Nam shortly after Michael and Hanny had gotten in. The rangers wore jeans and T's and could've been anybody except for their fitness and the way they moved and the way they were still. Four more of them, all NCOs from the Colonel's old company, were due in first thing tomorrow morning, stuck for the moment up in the Razorbacks on the Trail. Learning this had comforted Michael's conscience somewhat. The damaged Loach wasn't the only cause for delay.

They'd gone over the map and were now sitting the way Michael usually did when wanting to get everything straight, feet planted, arms crossed, and taciturn, while the Colonel delivered his orders.

The embassy should have egg all over its face for not having raised heaven and hell to find Senator Beaumont, but it was still stone walling. "We get one try," he said. "You're no senators, so you find trouble up there you're stuck, and listed MIA in Nam." Nobody blinked an eye. No doubt these guys did black ops all the time. Meanwhile, there were the orders.

They'd stage out of Nam Tha, the town where they'd picked up fuel the other day, a lucky guess all right. According to intelligence it was the safest fuel supply close to Rapet, Donald's village. They'd all be flying up tomorrow via Luang Prabang. Michael and Hanny, if he could con the embassy doc into removing his stitches, would get to the STOL where the Volpar went down by four. Meet the Corporal – and the Colonel broke off. "You trust him, Michael?"

Michael remembered the little quacking mimic, the thrill the boy'd had flying; but remembered, too, the kids drilling at Long Tieng, the two days – tomorrow would be three – that Donald had been home. Who knew what his agenda might be now? "Some reservations," Michael answered.

"Good. I was afraid you'd maybe gone soft on him." Michael kept his mouth shut. He had, of course.

"Mr. Zimmerman," the Colonel now addressing Jedediah, "you will leave here – " He broke off at a knock on the door and Hanny entered.

He stepped to the desk, laid down some papers, edged them towards the Colonel with his big middle finger. "Fuckin' civilian doc. Refuses to let me fly." He looked at Michael. "Sorry, Lieutenant."

"Me, too, Chief," Michael murmured. He got up and moved to stand against the wall. "Sit down," he ordered Hanny, and in a moment, Hanny did.

The Colonel's eyes returned to Jedediah. "Arrive there, team aboard, just before sundown, *but* – I want you aloft at least by five and monitoring the radio from Mr. Cameron from the moment the Loach lifts up. Nothing is predictable here. We don't know enough. According to what the Loach reports and Milt decides, you'll insert and orbit until you're contacted. That work for you?"

"You mean fuel, Colonel?" Jedediah asked. The Colonel gave a short nod. "We'll fly loaded. By the time we pick up, we should be light enough for everybody. Gonna be a little crowded – this Chinook is set up for fifteen pasengers, but without a co-pilot and with Cameron flying, too, we should be in good shape."

"You won't be going alone, Michael," the Colonel in what seemed a sudden decision, surprising Michael and everybody else. "You're up, Juve," indicating the Specialist who looked younger than Simon Fess. Simon belied his looks, maybe Juve would, too.

"Sir," Michael started, "if I may?" The Colonel nodded. "A stranger's apt to spook the kid. Wouldn't we be better off – "

"Nope, it's the two of you. Your command because the boy's yours." Juve nodded, accepting that. "You will recon with him, warily, I do advise, locate the cave and the hole – we gotta get that guy out, too, could be the Senator – return to the LZ and radio your report, to be sent by six P.M. And both of you will assist in the ground mission." Another surprise. All around. Polite looks came to him from the rangers, skepticism below the surface. Michael couldn't blame them. What he knew about ranger missions would fit into a teaspoon. "Under Milt's command, of course."

"Yes, Sir."

"Return station is Luang Prabang. In case of medical problems, it's quicker than here and we'll alert the clinic there. That's about it, Gentlemen. Except that the reason for this operation is the Senator. It'd be nice to get all ten prisoners, of course, but we don't bring Beaumont out, we got problems. Whole country's got problems. One last note. Since he's to be involved throughout, it's worth stating that Lt. Cameron's a two-tour vet of Nam, and a cracker-jack pilot. I've flown with him, and I'd take him with me on the ground any time. Might add that Mr. Zimmerman's no novice, either. Nam six years ago, and in Laos since, right?" Jedediah nodded. The Colonel now scanned them all, while everyone nodded or answered more formally, "Yes, Sirs" echoing through the room. The Colonel looked over at Hanny. "Can you work, Chief?"

"Yes, Sir. Air America promises the new instrument panel's in Udorn and will be up either tonight or in the morning – " He sent Jedediah a sly grin, " – or hope to die. So no problem."

"Well, then." The Colonel stood – and so did everybody else. "See you all at Wattay, noon tomorrow. Have a good night." He flashed that grin of his at the three rangers. "Don't play too hard. Vientiane can be more fun than Disneyland, but save it for day after tomorrow." Loose salutes from all and the room emptied quickly.

No bucket of cash and no ransom either. The Colonel figured, too easy to turn the tables and they could be held hostage, too. So much for those happy toasts earlier in the afternoon. Hanny always did say there had to be a black operation somewhere in this duty. He'd been right. And it wasn't just the CIA scam with the Volpar.

Willy took the non-coms to the steak place. All but Hanny, who went with Michael to Mam'selle Josie's, and Jedediah shared the staff car.

Hanny laid his head back against the seat and let his air whistle out between set teeth. "Jedediah?" he said. "You really been here for six fuckin' years?"

Jedediah turned around – he was in the front seat – and shot a laugh. "Yup. Got a wife and two kids down in Pakse." He turned forward, speaking gently. "It's a nice little town, right on the river."

Hanny moaned a little. "What town ain't on a river in this country?" His eyes slid and met Michael's.

"How come you got stuck with our little exercise?" Michael asked.

"I was in the right place at the right time," Jedediah answered, and again Michael and Hanny exchanged glances, startled this time. And again, Jedediah turned around. "Wells Beagin – co-pilot on the Volpar? – he uh was – is – like my younger brother. Stays with us in Pakse when he's there, and – you know . . ." He shrugged.

Michael leaned forward, hating to do it. "Jedediah . . . did you see the stuff we found?"

Jedediah nodded, managed a smile at Michael. "One was the pilot – the pictures of the family . . . but neither could've been Wells."

Michael had half sat back with a sigh when the car drew up before Mam'selle Josie's. The three entered together, and Jedediah walked on ahead, but Hanny froze just inside the door and Michael stopped with him. The beat was pulsing – on this his third visit, it was clear to Michael that it never did anything else. And the girls on the bar were doing their thing, as were the girls with curly black hair in the booths.

"Never thought to see you enter this place again," he said to Hanny. "You want to go on to the club?"

"I figure if I breathe through my mouth and keep my eyes on the floor, I'll make it to the back room." And with that, Hanny plowed forward, Michael belatedly hurrying after him.

Everybody in the place wanted to buy them a beer. Michael figured they were kings not for a day but for as long as it took. Simon had said he'd be in later, so while they waited they ate french fried rice noodles slopped with ketchup and Mam'selle's friendly attempt at southern fried chicken, and played pick-up-sticks. Michael's hands were pretty steady. He wouldn't've been surprised otherwise, all things considered. And if Simon turned up late, well, that wouldn't be altogether Michael's choice, just almost. He had this strange mix of wild curiosity and dread over those journals, and putting them off gave him another kind of mix – relief and guilt.

But Simon wasn't late. They went into a corner to talk, where Michael gave him the film, telling him that there were a couple of pictures of the woman, too, in case a current one was needed, and by the way, if the guy didn't use them all he'd like the baby's back. Then he asked how long it might take.

"Couple, three days," said Simon, and smiled. "You'll be back by that time with our fellas, right?"

Michael nodded, hoping it was indeed right, and grabbed Simon's hand, wanting to impart big gratitude. Trusting this little Opie wasn't easy. Simon just grinned at him. "The slate's not wiped clean," he said. "This stuff," holding up the film, meaning the passports, "doesn't hold a candle to a life." He suddenly laughed. "Especially mine!"

They left, then, on calls of, "Good luck!" and "Go get 'em, tiger!" and "Bring 'em back alive!" Reminded Michael of that cheering section the last day in Nam. He hoped he wouldn't end up ditching these guys the same way.

Hanny said he was up to it, wanted to clear his head anyway, so they walked the short distance to the Phou Bia Club, not saying much. They were about to split in the downstairs hall when Hanny offered a nightcap, but Michael shook his head. "Got some stuff to do," he said. They turned from each other, and then Michael said, "Hey. The doc say you really are okay?"

"Yeah, yeah, sure," Hanny grumbled, still heading on down the hall, and muttered, "fuckin' civilian!"

"Neal?" At his door, Hanny looked back. "It'll all go, tomorrow night. It'll be fine."

A moment, and Hanny grunted, flicked fingers into a little wave and disappeared into his place.

Entering his own, Michael turned on a couple of lights and the ceiling fan, opened windows and the doors to the shallow balcony, turned and looked at the few thin volumes piled on the coffee table. The dun colors of the apartment surrounding him didn't help much. What would he find in those journals? The ultimate conviction that their lives could never be bound together again?

He went to the kitchen, pulled out a half-empty bottle of Glenlivet, looked at it a minute, then shoved it back into the cupboard. He turned back to the small living-room, sat on the couch and opened the notebook on top.

Had she not kept a diary for long? Five years or a lifetime, there were too few. Or had she saved only some? Inside the top cover there was written on its back in green crayon, "1968 #1." Michael opened the other covers and found in proper sequence another volume for '68, two for '69, one for '70. Had she arranged them in careful order for him?

He set the more recent ones down and reopened the first for 1968.

34

The pages were written in Kathleen's open hand in pencil and bore no other dates at all, as if months and days had no significance. Perhaps they didn't . . .

I have found a secret place. Now I can write and find an American voice that will listen as well – my own – and be my own best friend. I feel like that accountant back at Croftsworth School who was caught embezzling – they said he cheated by keeping double books. And so will I. What I will write here. And in the others, the calendar of the tiny events of my life neatly cast down for him to steal and read. I wondered if he was taking them when they first went missing for a day only to reappear in my absence from my room. But I lost any doubts when he told me about Michael getting married. He would only have done that because he realized I was living with the expectation that somehow, sometime, it would be mended. I die a little inside thinking about those moments. Not just because of the awful meaning to me, but because I reacted like a child, crying out and bursting into tears, while he watched in pity. I should have been ashamed. It was some weeks before I could finally give up any expectations of Michael, or of anything else. Killed them really. It seemed for the best and still does, though there yet are days when I struggle to face the morning. But he was right to tell me – cruel only to be kind, isn't that what they say? It makes the other things acceptable.

Michael took breath and wiped a hand down his wet face. He got up to stand blankly a moment, then went out onto the balcony to look at the river under the moon, letting the light breeze dry his skin. She spoke – wrote, it was as if he were hearing her – of "killing" her expectations.

She'd lived all this time with that kind of death. It was beyond Michael's imagination how one could do that. There always had to be something, didn't there? Christ, *some*thing. A fresh taste, a new piece of cloth. That she'd succeeded explained what he'd felt in her. Or didn't feel. The incredible control.

He was staring at nothing. His eyes returned through the door to those little books on the table. If she lived it, he could sure as shit read about it. With some help.

He went to the kitchen and got the Glenlivet, poured himself what probably amounted to a triple, and downed half of it, carried the rest back to the table and the open journal.

> I will not write here, of course, even to my "best friend"
> where these notebooks will be hidden. Someone might
> read them. It's incredible how in doing the most important
> things one can be absent minded. (Should that be hyphen-
> ated?) Maybe it's cause and effect? These little books
> will allow me to retain my English, I hope. Since I am
> forbidden to teach, now, and can manage it only on the sly
> and in little caught moments, there is no one to whom I
> can speak English except him, and we don't talk. That no
> longer interests him as it once did. He wants only one
> thing from me.

Four and a half pages had been covered by this point and Kathleen seemed to have just noticed because the script suddenly became very small and cramped.

> I must be more frugal with my pages. I remember using
> up these English spirals so thoughtlessly when teaching.
> It seemed then that the Sawbwa had brought aplenty down
> from Keng Tung to me in my village, now mostly gone. I
> think I had better keep those that are left for my own
> private needs. I can tell him that I am running out and will
> not write so often. That will be a relief. I am bored
> recording stupidities just for him to read. But with all the
> paper in the world, I may run out of pencils – oh, surely
> not – and anyway, my secret place won't hold more than

five or so notebooks. God. Oh, God. How long do I think to be here, writing to myself for company, with only another kind of stupidity to fill these pages? For he will fill them through my words, control them as he controls everything, my life, everything. Even my anger that I hide from him, especially in my bed where I try to show him nothing of what I think or feel. I am getting better at that, because I am feeling less and less, I *am*. I try to use the meditation techniques, the breathing, but I'm not good enough at it.

Michael had thought she was a real expert at it, but what did he know about how a woman feels when she's being used as a – a fucking vessel, for the love of God? Like a whore. She'd called herself that, and he'd denied it to himself. Well, she'd been taken like one, but without any hope of joy.

So I've learned to remove myself by will, leaving him nothing but a husk, flaccid and like one dead. I lie there and let him do as he wants to me. That one thing I've come to control almost completely. It is a blessing, but why doesn't it stop him? It frightens me, sometimes. That I will kill everything inside so well that it can't be reincarnated. (More expectations, Kathleen, kept secret even from yourself? Fool. Why should I ever *want* those feelings alive again?)

Michael straightened back from the coffee table and the journal, unable to read any more, not right then, unwilling even to scan down into her next sentence. It was going to get worse, he knew it was. She was writing so honestly, not for anyone's eyes but her own.

He was tired of his own smell. The old sweat from the morning – there hadn't been time for a shower after they'd landed, just time enough to dump their stuff and get on to the embassy – was mixing with the sweat he was oozing now down into the couch.

He went into the bathroom, dropped his clothes on the floor, stepped into the shower and found it still lukewarm. He braced his arms against the wall, leaning into them, head down, and let the water wash over him. It seemed to him a marvel that she had come through those lost years with spirit intact. She'd never once, at least so far, written about faith, what surely would have kept Tom going in circumstances like those. But her every sentence rang with determination to survive.

He turned off the water, dried off, noticed a roach in the corner, realized his damp clothes on the floor would be teeming with bugs by morning, picked them up, took them to the bedroom, had no place to put them and dropped them to the floor again. Naked, hoping to stay dry, he returned to Kathleen's journal, sitting for a moment before forcing himself to pick up where he'd left off.

> The women, his wives, witness and watch and cozzen me
> afterwards. Cozzen, what a lovely word. But these women,
> so gentle and affectionate with me, cozzening the body he
> often leaves sore, even bleeding, bewilder me. I've lived
> amongst the Shans, among all the many peoples here, much
> of my life and now realize I understand them very little.

This set of writing seemed to stop here, and a new pencil taken up to go on.

> Another day. I can't date these entries. The western
> calendar is missing totally from my life, and time runs
> together in a round of monsoon, cold, hot seasons. After
> awhile, I will barely be able to identify the years, I think,
> or even my birthday. Mom and Father used to make so
> much of it, and Tommy did, too. I wish – oh, what a dumb
> phrase, of course I wish, I wish a million things. But how
> I do wish that after the Burmese burned down my village
> and the Sawbwa saved us, the women, the children, that I
> had refused what seemed kindness when he offered
> shelter. But what excuse could I have made? And I had
> no way to suspect that when I entered this palace I would
> become as imprisoned as if caged. For months afterwards,
> I didn't realize it. I taught the women and children here,
> members of his family all of them, and I was taught back
> by them, the joyous children who make me laugh even
> now, the Sawbwa's wives who have shown me their
> weaving skills.

A dark line dug its way across this page. Dug its way into Michael's head. A mark of something changed.

I started this whole idea many weeks ago, several lunar months certainly, and so quickly lost my purpose. The cold season is full upon us, the palace dark with closed shutters to keep warmth inside. Only now can I really write about it. It wasn't long after I began these pages that he came quietly in the night as he always does but this time he was sweet and slow to me. Was it because I had found myself by writing here, had softened myself and he felt it? If so, I don't care, I need these pages, I need my American voice, I have missed it. Such a dummy, though, to believe I was in self-control. But I am resolved now, oh, I am resolved. Never again will I rise to him. I had endeavored for so long to put Michael aside, to stop recalling – no, damn it, Kathleen, be honest *here* – to stop evoking what I once felt with him. I truly believed I had succeeded. Forever. And then this one night revealed that lie. The Prince awoke me and made my body take me away, and I called out a name. Michael. Not prince or sawbwa or Htin Aung or even an endearment. Michael.

The first notebook ran out here. Michael stared at that last page, swallowing a little spasmodically, saliva filling his mouth, wondering if he could keep that damned fried chicken down. But now he found he was unable to cease reading. He opened the second spiral, with "1968 #2" crayoned inside the cover. And her writing went on as if with no break, as if she had to pour all this out to a listener totally safe – herself.

And he pulled from me, calling the women to come. They held my arms out, and one lay across my feet, and he knelt above me and struck me with the flat of his hand over and over, and then when he stopped I looked and saw he was still hard. And before I knew, he spoke to the wives and they all turned me over and he held my wrists and entered me from the back. Not as he had done before when catching me asleep on my side and turned away from where

he comes into the room, but this time as not even dogs
behave. I'd never thought of such a thing. I screamed –
oh, Lord, Lord, I am so ashamed of that – and with each
thrust I whimpered. I think I will never lose the sounds of
it. I wonder if he still hears them. It was like knives
ripping me up, and it went on and on. For days afterwards
I wasn't sure I could heal from it. But I am getting all
right, I think I am. After this one time, the women would
not look at me the next day. He has left me alone, and I
swear to all that's holy – if anything anywhere is, in heaven
or hell – I will never make another sound with him, I will
never scream no matter what he does. I continue to lie
awake under the bar, listening for the whisper of his bare
feet across the floor.

Michael ran a hand over his hair still wet from shower or sweat or
both. And he had had that crazy dream for those fleeting moments last
night that he might try – be able – to recapture her, so easily. Oh dear God.

Tonight for the first time since, I feel safe writing. His
officers have come in and they are mounting an attack
against the Burmese up in Keng Tung, in conjunction with
the Sawbwa's cousin, the Prince of Keng Tung Province.
Htin Aung will command. Maybe he will be killed. That
is what I have come to, that terrible hope.

Again there was a change of pencil. Michael's nausea had subsided.
He was sick, all right, but with a horrified anger that might never be vom-
ited up.

He went away to battle, and they lost and Keng Tung is
occupied, Htin Aung's cousin taken to Rangoon Prison, of
which we hear such terrifying things. I spend much of my
private time, when I have any, trying to understand him.
Is that what he has wanted of me? To occupy not only my
body but my mind? He has shown me kindness. What
caused this devil to come out? He must hate me – or do
many men behave like that? Michael didn't. My good

heaven, why would any man want to, it is such a dirty thing. Of course, it had to be because I called another's name. He felt humiliated. And his wives were witness. I wonder if I will always feel dirty. Sullied. That's what Louisa May Alcott would call me. Not that Louisa May could conceive of this any more than I could. Strange she should come to mind, not the finest of writers.

Now it was Michael's hands that were clenched, to either side of the notebook. He wanted to talk to her, speak back to her, knew he couldn't wait and that if he did it would be stale, it wouldn't help her, it wouldn't help him. He went looking for something to write with, just so he could get it down, hauling out drawers, not bothering to push them back in, opening cabinets to slam the doors closed again. He found a ball-point but no paper. Maybe it was Louisa May Alcott that gave him the idea, that old nineteenth century custom of saving letter-paper. Posed above that last page, he thought perhaps it was as bad a violation, this – of her privacy, of her deepest self. But he had to tell her. He turned the book ninety degrees and hesitated again, uncertain how to address her. Don't be an ass, Cameron, his impatience spilling onto himself, and just started writing across her page, perpendicular to her lines, taking care not to smudge with his hand her pencilled words. And he continued to do this as he continued to read.

It has been several more weeks again since I last wrote. How things have changed. He has left me alone at night, and allowed the palace women to study history and English with me once more. It, plus school for the children which he has also permitted, has kept me very busy with lesson plans and trying to find ways for all to write with so few school supplies. How much faster the days go.

Who'd've thought the bastard could harbor guilt? But Michael wrote nothing like that. Against all his detestation of Htin Aung, Michael had already written her things that tried to make sense out of the man, tried to give her back some balance in her judgment of herself. Michael knew himself to be totally out of balance in his own judgment of the Sawbwa, but to call him the piece of filth Michael believed him to be would only diminish her the more.

Although she didn't always mention it, it was clear from other things that the periodic passages of time were frequent and of uneven duration. Part way into the second 1968 notebook, she wrote that "he" had returned to her bed two nights before with no warning. She had only just become used to sleeping soundly in belief it was all over, and got taken with surprise. "So much for dead expectations!" she said, in a miracle of humor. "But I made no protest," she went on, in obvious pride, "*no sound at all.*" Oddly, she wrote, he left her a gem-stone.

> A huge dark blue cut sapphire. They don't do this fine cutting here. He must have bought it uncut and somehow sent it to Singapore. I didn't know that was possible anymore. But then, perhaps it was done years ago, and comes from a secret hoard someplace nearby. What am I to do with it? I think, keep it. For what? Would it be possible for me somehow to escape? It seems this man is determined to create expectations anew in me.

More humor, wry though it might be, a great relief. No one could live sane, lacking bitterness, without expectations of something. Now the time could come when he'd be able to tell her what he knew had to be still true of her, of her body, of her most inner nature, with the hope she'd hear him.

A new pencil, new day.

> Christmas must be this week, sometime. A few people in the town keep their Thadingyut lights up and lit, likening the Christian celebration to their own light festival. And why shouldn't they? End of monsoon, bright moonlit night, a birth of new life. I have nine gems, five of them rubies and of great value. He comes in the middle of every lunar month. The wives must tell him the right time. *He wants a child out of me.* Why, I can't imagine. He hates me, comes only to punish me, so why? Up 'til now, the pessary has continued to work. Or one of us is not fertile, because this morning I found the silk has gone so transparent it probably provides no protection at all. At least he

has become somewhat predictable so I know when to insert it. The last thing I want in this world is to bear him a child. I've become very thin and not pretty, I'm sure, but it may mean something is wrong with me that will prevent it.

In spite of almost a full blank page, this journal ended with what Michael assumed was the year's end. He wanted to write on it his growing conclusions about Hitin Aung, hoping to ease her, perhaps even to save her. But he didn't. Sometime he'd tell her, with more gentleness than he had in him right now. What that man had done all told made any decent words about him difficult, very difficult.

The next notebook, 1969 #1, picked up some time into the year. Little seemed to delineate her life for her. She began by mourning – "still mourning" was how she put it – the loss of her books when the village had burned, having managed to save only some poetry – Robert Blake, John Donne, Rudyard Kipling, and God help her, Alan Ginsburg, some comfort. It was a book Michael had forgotten when he'd left Burma. Hardly the kind of poetry he should have been sharing with that young girl, ugly, harsh, dark. But she wrote that, though she no longer looked at it, it had once informed her what it was like in the States when she'd been so unaware at school, what it was that had driven Michael to drift, to find Rainbow, and the Haight. How it had been dear to her when she was still getting his letters because it brought him closer. Alan Ginsburg, who could've guessed? She'd never mentioned it.

She even wrote some poetry of her own in this journal, wasting too many pages, of which she was well aware and annoyed with herself. Michael tried deciphering the verses, but they were so marked out and scratched over he gave it up. She never did leave a readable version, just started writing again.

I am pregnant, oh God, I have to admit it, and I think it is into three months. I could do something about it still, I'm sure I could, there are women here in the palace who would help if I could trust their secrecy. Maybe my stones would buy it, I have twenty, now. Ah, Michael, if this were a letter to you, if I knew you would read it, if I knew this child to be yours – . Never mind. In some wonderful and fundamental way it does not matter who has fathered it, this small spot of life inside me. *It is mine.*

"Yeah!" Michael exclaimed aloud and in triumph to find the fierceness he'd been missing in her, so tempted to tell her of the wonder he'd felt holding Cho, washing him, feeding him. Lord, how long it had been since he'd written anything of his innermost thoughts, not since his letters to her. And that bastard had read them in her stead. It would keep. For when the three of them were together.

Her next writing was two or three months later, still in the 1969 #2 book, in which she said Htin Aung no longer came to her bed now that he knew she was pregnant. That he sent her wonderful tasty bits of food, and bolts of silk, and jewelry, these stones set in finely worked silver. Her reaction to all this was confusion, partly thinking it augured well for her child, partly feeling more "boughten", her word, than ever. Michael's impulse was to urge her to enjoy this time, but even as he started he realized with a little shock that it had all taken place a year ago, his comfort offered too late.

The 1970 book didn't begin until after Cho's birth, and was written in sorrow. No question an unburdening was how these journals had best served her.

She started by remembering the exultant weight of the baby resting on her belly, even the light shooting from the Sawbwa's eyes on first seeing his son. But it was all couched in a tone of relinquishment. For she soon went short of milk, and U-Pym had been brought in. Kathleen confessed shame at her own envy, her jealousy, and there was nothing Michael knew to say that would help her with that. And then the baby had fallen sick, and continued to fail.

> He let me know today that I am not to ask him again to let me take Cho out of Burma. As if with no well of emotion at all, as if I were an ignorant peasant or a silly child, he lectured me on the teachings of Gautama about Karma, the futility of fighting it, the necessity to divorce oneself from human frailties and pain. I hated him more at that moment that at any time or for anything else, even – oh not that again, Kathleen. Tom once called the Buddha the most benign of all Asian deities. Not a deity, I said, with the

arrogance of my twelve years to think I could inform
my brother about religion. Well, whatever Buddha is,
the Prince will do nothing for his own son because of
him. And he is coming to me once a month again,
obviously having forsaken Cho's life. One more thing
for me to accept? The loss of this most precious part of
me? Now, at last, it is the Prince I know to be the fool.
For I will never forsake my child.

That's when she'd begun to scheme her escape, or it was what Michael
had to surmise, for she simply stopped writing. The last sentence was less
than halfway into the 1970 book though certainly well into the year, on a
page swollen by drops, not hers, Michael's. He left the notebook open to
the air, drank off the rest of the scotch still sitting in the glass – he'd hardly
touched it – took a leak and went to bed. Except for a couple of nightmares
that fled his memory with waking, he actually slept. No real wonder to
that, he'd had little enough sleep the last two nights.

In the morning, he felt ready. The girl he had fallen in love with was
still present in the woman revealed in those pages. Introspective, not often
humorous, but the old wryness was there, still full of conscience and a
desire to *know*. And with a strength he hadn't known the extent of until
now. Different worlds, good God yes, but bridgeable. He'd be able to
reach her. In time, he would. He'd better, because he also now knew the
extent of his need for her. To make the world, his life, right again, as it
hadn't been for all these years.

And then, shaving before the mirror, second thoughts began to shoot
him down. He was damned sure he had Htin Aung figured out. But maybe
he'd assumed the wrong things or just presumed too much with Kathleen,
suddenly certain he should never have over-written her pages. A little too
late, as usual. He nicked himself and turned for the shower.

Standing under the water gone cold in the night, echoes of the last
journal doubled the shivers, and he became utterly certain what that snake
would do next. Dressed and ready to leave, he sat down at the book still
open to her last written page and added to it some of the stuff he'd held
back, unwilling to chance her losing whatever help he might have for her,
ineffectual or not. He finished with a sharp warning, then hesitated a long
time, unsure how much to confess of what he felt.

Sure, instead, that his words could only fail his meaning, he closed the journal, wrapped all five in some of that plastic sheeting they'd used on the maps and carried them out to give to Hanny, to deliver to Kathleen along with the passports if tonight didn't go well.

DAY TEN

35

They reached the STOL strip before three-thirty. Michael stayed high, but by pinching the cyclic between his knees he could use glasses as well as Juve, and together they spotted the Volpar and, to Michael's relief, the opening through the canopy where he had delivered Donald three days ago and would meet him shortly. He hoped.

He decided to go scouting and headed west for the top of the ridge. On beyond, at the foot of the western side of the ridge, they saw the road, a true road – the Chinese-built Phong Saly Road. Running east to North Vietnam and west part of the way to Burma. Dust was lifting over there. He turned northerly along the ridge top toward where the village should be from the smoke they'd noticed on their discovery day. Juve was the first to see the path under the trees, running directly beneath them. Probably leading from the village to the STOL, though they hadn't spotted it coming up from the landing strip, but the canopy there was thick and high. In any case, with the road so close, straight and wide enough for almost any prop plane, why would the village need the STOL anymore?

And then, before they spied it, downhill to the left was a slash and burn field. Untenanted by either people or crops, it was greenly weeded over, probably overused and worn out. But a path led off from its north-east corner, paralleling the one beneath the Loach. The village had to be at the end of both, and it was – clustered next to a waterfall that looked to spring from a rocky outcropping and dropped down to a stream that edged the road. Lining the water this side of the stream were three metal-roofed sheds, chimneys smoking, the ground around them showing white. Heroin powder. Michael knew even before Juve asked, "Heroin?"

"Yup," Michael agreed, though he'd never seen a refinery before.

"And under those roofs are our guys, making white powder bricks. That's if they haven't already been ransomed."

The time commanded. Michael banked around to head back along the ridge top and spotted two more paths between clumps of bamboo, one leading up from the refinery to the village and a second which ran up and back towards the abandoned field, to dead end at a rock wall that rose towards the Loach and then shallowed out towards the ridge top. "Look there," he directed Juve, and the two grinned broadly at each other. "It's the cave! Has to be!"

Immediately, Michael started transmitting to Jedediah listening back at Nam Tha, locating for him the alternate and maybe preferable LZ, advising him to have a look before he inserted on the STOL. Closer to the village, certainly, and although the cumbersome Chinook might be audible, the field would provide a shorter and maybe more efficient extraction.

Still not seeing a path take off from the ridge top down towards the STOL, he was turning to go find it when Juve lifted his glasses, pointing off towards the west. "What the hell's that?"

Michael peered, saw the dust he'd noticed earlier, a thick cloud now. Yeah, right, what the hell *was* it, a fucking Chinese division coming this way? He beat it westward, found to his relief a pack train, moving west, not east. Just before turning back around, Michael saw an artillery piece slung between two ponies. Shit. Kath's opium train, sure it was, heading back to Burma and Loi Long. Loads dumped now and eager for home, picking up speed. The reason for the dust. But hers had had two pieces of artillery, they'd seen them from the air in the afternoon. And then it hit him. This was Htin Aung's refinery. Sweet Jesus, could he be here? Right now? Oh, knock it off, asshole – the head honcho said he was in the Golden Triangle.

"Sir?" Juve over the intercom. Glancing at him, Michael recognized wariness, if not panic, and was chagrined. His foot must've gone heavy on the pedal. The Loach was beginning to spin. Michael didn't apologize, only regretted he'd sent up some unneeded warning signals for the young ranger.

Nearly four o'clock. Michael turned the Loach due east across the ridge, heading for the STOL and hopefully Donald, on the way reporting to Jedediah the possibility that an artillery piece remained in the village. The team might want all that armament they were carrying.

When they'd gathered at Wattay Airport down in Vientiane, the rangers had been dressed for combat in worn old jungle fatigues, no insignia, and so loaded with stuff Michael didn't see how they'd walk ten yards much less penetrate jungle. A Car-15, twenty-one ammo magazines for it, regular- sized grenades, little minis, small mines that Juve dubbed toe-poppers, and a suppressed pistol, Jesus. And it wasn't three minutes before Sergeant Starky had delivered an even-voiced order to Michael to "remove your bars, Lieutenant". Which Michael immediately obeyed even as Hanny turned away to hide amusement that Michael was taking orders from a non-com. "You'll get yours, Neal," Michael resolved to himself, and wondered wryly what the hell good Starky thought it would do anyway, Donald knew he was an officer.

The flight up to L.P. had been uneventful and boring. After a few attempts to engage Juve in conversation – where you from, how long in-country, whatever – the two had fallen silent. Juve periodically re-checked his equipment, or at least those weapons he could get to, strapped into the peter seat as he was. Not nervous, no nerves in sight, at least not until a minute ago, but rather the care was a habit ingrained by what Michael knew to be the heaviest training in the army.

Michael hadn't even hummed much less attempted a song. The opinion harbored by most grunts was that chopper pilots were crazies, and since they were going in together under his command Michael didn't really want to reinforce any notions Juve might have like that. Anyway, this young soldier was serious. And now was probably skeptical of his superior officer. Not good.

The continuing flight from Nam Tha on to the STOL and the village had been quiet, too, and all the silent miles gave Michael too much time to think about those diaries, what he'd written in them, how Kathleen would react, whether she'd even be reached by what he said. When he visualized her face, which he carried with him now like a picture in his pocket, she wasn't the young Kathleen of memory, but yesterday's Kathleen, the firm line of her jaw raised, her mouth set so tightly the fullness of her lips disappeared. If she weren't open to hearing him, that look promised that the wall might never come down.

"You ever do a ground exercise before?"

The question had come late and sounded loud, even over the headphones, startling Michael. "Yeah," he'd answered. "Two, three times." Juve waited, or his silence indicated that. "Went into a couple of villages to pull out some guys," Michael added.

"In this?" Juve asked, his surprise obvious as he indicated the Loach.

"Well," Michael said, finding a grin to give, "not enough Hueys, the army uses what's at hand. I was at hand. If you can get aloft, you'd be surprised the weight the Loach'll carry. It's space that can get to be a problem." And, since Juve had broken the silence, Michael launched into a briefing on Donald Duck.

"Fuckin' slope kids, kill y'as they look at ya," Juve had said. Seemed his looks indeed belied his nature. Good thing, too, Michael had thought.

Flying up now on the opening in the canopy from the southeast, Michael went low, found it, hovered above it, and dropped in, hearing Juve whisper a couple of expletives and hiss in air as the blades chopped some leaves. Settling softly, Michael shut down, signalled Juve with a finger to his lips and let the silence close in. Nothing. He was getting out when a crackle came from ridge side and there was Donald. Dressed in T-shirt and a sarong caught up between his legs, he came leaping barefoot out of the jungle towards them, pointing to Michael's watch he still wore, wearing a huge grin.

He skidded to a stop and formed up into tight attention, throwing Michael a formal salute. Michael responded in kind. Juve did not, until Michael muttered at him, "Do it!"

Michael decided to ease it out. He smiled. "Howya doin', Corporal?"

The boy's eyes were flickering to Juve. "Where Chief Hanny?" he asked.

"Grounded. He got wounded. This is Juve. Here to help scout. So. You got a report for me?"

"When troops come?"

"Oh," Michael said, giving a little nod, as if he understood such an immediate question. "well, I have to fly back down to Vientiane, tell 'em what you tell me, and then, um, the Colonel, remember him? – he has to decide. You know the army. Slow. But I guess the Americans are still here or y'wouldn't've asked, right?"

A moment, and the kid nodded. "Come," he said, a little abruptly. He turned on his heel to start back into the jungle, up the ridge. "I show you!" he called back, with a return to eagerness. Michael reached inside the Loach, shouldered his Car-15, some magazines and his survival radio, jerked his head at Juve to follow, and the two moved in behind Donald.

Maybe it was the Colonel's pointed warning back at the embassy. Michael was uneasy. Or maybe it was the kid who was uneasy, why wouldn't he be, what'd he know about Michael, after all, and anyway – he might still be worried about his mother getting hurt, or . . .

They moved uphill through heavy jungle for about two hundred yards, slipping on mud-covered snaking roots underfoot, stumbling over rocks rising through the same mud, thornbushes tearing at them on all sides, until, thank God, they came out onto a dirt path, which led directly towards the ridge top. At times, it was wide enough for two to pass, but for the most part it appeared not to be used with much regularity, proving Michael right about the Phong Saly Road having changed things here.

Donald went up the ridge like a little monkey, and twenty-year-old Juve's breath was hardly shorter at the top than at the bottom. Michael couldn't have bragged the same, maybe what came from having seven years on Juve, only he'd thought he was in better shape. When their path intersected the one running along the ridge top, he grabbed the moment to rest, and started asking Donald questions.

"Where is the hole?"

"I show, not far! Man not down hole no more, very sick. He back in cave now."

"And the rest? Do they work making white powder bricks all day?"

"Yes."

"When are they returned to the cave?"

"Late – after four, before dark," and again, he was pointing at his new watch with a proud smile.

"When do the Chinese come?"

"Soon! People Party from Vietnam also!" He beamed. "We have mortar-gun in village, nobody cheat us now!" He started off. "You come, come!"

"Not on the path," Michael said in sudden decision, rising from his crouch.

So once again they went through jungle, only at this altitude it was spaced out with bamboo clumps and some evergreen forest, the needles covering the ground, so it was easier. They had begun to smell the village, burning charcoal, just people, when they arrived at some huge limestone karst outcroppings. Which was why a cave was here. Probably the ridge was riddled with caves. And then they smelled a real stench. Latrine, had to be, except Donald was leading them towards it, the stench getting stronger, until they intersected another, narrower path and reached what looked to be not a dug hole but a sink-hole, with a bamboo trapdoor thrown back, bamboo posts four-cornering the hole's opening. The trap would be fastened down to them, Michael knew. The smell was horrifying.

"Is hole," Donald declared. No horror in him, or shame, just fact. Michael turned away, thinking of the poor bastard stuck down there for what, three days, four? Doubled up in his own wastes.

Donald led away again, but once beyond the smell of the hole, he stopped. It was a little clearing. "You wait, I check cave, see if guards there, come back for you." And he was gone.

They waited, Juve unmoving, quiet, Michael having to shift weight once in a while. His uneasiness was growing, until finally he whispered to Juve, "Let's get outa here." Juve just looked at him. Michael darted a finger due east diagonally back and down hill from where they had come to intersect the path lower down, heading for the Loach, which by now was some distance away. Juve nodded. Acknowledging Juve's expertise in this kind of terrain, Michael said, "You're on point." Not even a nod, and Juve was moving away with the stealth of a jungle animal.

He was fast. Michael sometimes had to choose between keeping him in sight and keeping quiet. For awhile, he chose the former, but after awhile no matter how careful he was, or slow, he was noisy. And Juve disappeared.

Michael halted, listened, and heard what he thought he'd heard: men tracking him. They had no concern, apparently, for stealth. It sounded like a number of them, and he was figuring which would be the smartest way to head, still diagonally or straight down, when a hand fell on his shoulder. He had his Car-15 ready at port arm even as he swivelled – only to find Juve there.

"Damned near – Jesus, man," Michael murmured, slumping in relief. Juve only shot a finger straight down the hill and gestured Michael to go ahead. Michael nodded, but before he turned, realizing he was not an asset here, he whispered, "Your command."

Juve looked at him, smiled a half-crooked smile of what was probably relief, and gestured to Michael again. This time, Michael obeyed.

The surface here was getting more difficult the lower they got from the top of the ridge. Michael started slipping, thought he might slide down the rest of the way which wasn't altogether the worst idea, and then he took a blow to his left thigh that took his feet out from under him. He didn't know the cause, but after a few seconds the pain hit, bad pain, undermining his immediate attempt to stand. He looked down, saw a ragged tear in his left pants leg, blood streaming. How he heard it he didn't know, his breath too noisy, but there was a rustle off to one side. He looked up and saw a little mountain man aiming a crossbow at him.

The man said something aloud, sounded like an order – to get up, maybe? But his aim was steady on Michael. Michael struggled and got his right knee and foot under him, pressing his left hand hard against where the arrow wound had to be and found no arrow there. Must've gone straight through. But when he managed to put weight on his left leg, it held. Didn't break the bone anyway, though it sure as hell had felt like it, still did. The bowman took a step towards him, speaking again, when Juve appeared from behind him, got him in a grip and slit his throat in purest silence, not even a gurgle.

He dumped the body, moved to Michael who now was standing but bent over to try to stop the bleeding, and tore the pants leg to have a look. The men tracking them had gone silent, not encouraging.

"Through the flesh," Juve murmured.

"Yeah," Michael said.

Juve slipped his arm around Michael who was some taller, put Michael's arm across his own shoulders, and started them away. But Michael had decided. "No," he said, his whisper rasping, uneven with the pain.

Juve halted, looking up at Michael. Michael moved away from the protecting arms to stand alone, began taking his shirt off. He whispered. "Sorry. My command after all. Get to the alternate, radio for the team to come in soonest. Tell Zimmerman to hit the ridge down at the southeast and come up it low. You'll know how to talk him in." He didn't even want to look at Juve's eyes, just held out his survival radio, which Juve took. Michael bent over, began tying the shirt into a tourniquet above the wound in his thigh. Fucker was in the same damned place as that bullet he took last year. No help in that. "What I'm going to do," he said, "periodically, I'll loosen this and the blood'll lead 'em a chase. Then I'll tighten it and they'll lose me again. It'll slow 'em down."

"Y'won't make it, Lieutenant."

At least not "Pappy". "I'll lift out of this mess before you do," Michael said. "Go on." And had to repeat it. "Go!" Juve went like a wraith.

Left alone, the blood down to a seep, Michael listened. Thought about it, hard. Heard nothing. He figured they'd find the bowman pretty quick. He decided to give them some blood to follow. He loosened his shirt, and limping badly, the damned leg wanting to give out from under him, stumbling over roots, he continued east down the ridgeside.

The third time he fell, he slipped at least fifteen feet on down across the muddy roots and rocks before he was able to stop, the skin of his hands beginning to shred. He looked back up at the obvious bloody track behind him, and tightened the tourniquet. When he picked himself up and started on, it was at a ninety degree angle on a new diagonal, heading down and north.

He heard when they found the bowman, and after that they were on his trace fast and noisy, again not caring whether he heard, sure from the blood they'd run him down. Immediately, he turned and started scrambling straight back up the ridge, going around them if he could. He came across his own blood, crossed it to go southwest. After a few yards, he stumbled, fell and crawled on all fours into some thornbush where he collapsed and lay panting, trying to recharge his energy. Then the ground beneath him vibrated, and he knew they were coming. He held his breath against panting, and lordy, lordy, they by God went right past. Seven black-garbed Laotians, two with crossbows, the rest with AK's, little hunters all. Donald wasn't with them.

Michael had lost track of where he was. He was bound to miss the Loach now, no matter how he steered, and even passing within ten yards of the strip would miss that as well, the jungle too thick. Oh, kid, shame on you.

If Michael were sure the mission was completed, he'd lay low 'til night, head on down and get away. He knew the right plants to stanch bleeding, even to give a little antiseptic to the wound. He knew how to survive in mountain jungles, knew he'd make it. But he couldn't chance the operation. The village guards had to be suckered away from duty and the Americans.

He loosened the tourniquet going southeast this time. They had to assume he and Juve would be going for the Loach. They'd turn back when they lost the earlier blood, find the new track down, but he didn't keep to it long, going through the same drill again. If they were good, and he thought they probably were, they'd keep close on the blood, not bothering to cast side to side until they tumbled to the scheme. Which could be soon. And he was tiring. One thing might work in his favor. It was getting dark. Of course, this was the eastern side of the ridge, but – had Juve reached the abandoned slash and burn? Had Jedediah inserted yet? Had the fucking radio even worked? Shit. He stumbled, fell, rolled to fetch up hard against a tree and lay there gasping, the leg getting really bad.

Even though it wasn't pumping, just running, and even with the slippery tourniquet, he didn't think he could stop the blood much longer without some kind of stable pressure, some rest.

He scanned the canopy overhead, the lower trunks to see if he could climb any one of the trees – and found it. Bracing himself against the tree he was up against, he got to his feet, dragged over to the low-hanging tree and stood beneath the branch. Couldn't reach it. Have to jump, he told himself, come on, come on. He put his weight on his good leg, lowered slightly, and jumped. Missed, almost went sprawling. Did it again and both hands caught. Somehow he swung up and got his good leg over the branch. Seated astride, he looked up, but the next branch was too far away. He'd have to stick it out here. He looked down, and saw some dark streaks just beneath – blood. He raised both feet up onto the branch, crumpled up the loose shirting and jammed it onto the wound. He slipped his Car-15 into readiness, finger on the trigger, leaned back against the trunk, and waited.

"Come, Lieutenant." Slowly, slowly, Michael turned his head to look down. It was Donald, and now five Laotians gathered in a semi-circle around him, looking up at Michael. "Must come down," Donald said.

"You little shit," Michael said.

Donald was looking straight up at him. No apology. "You take Americans, we have no money for winter. Mother say. Opium crop ver' small this year, Burma kill farmers, we need money."

"We'll pay you! I have orders to make a deal! Many dollars!" Purest nonsense. He'd even asked the Colonel during his first report if the U.S. couldn't pay a ransom, and the Colonel had pointed out that the politicos weren't ready to admit the Senator had crashed in Laos much less been taken prisoner. And anyway, he'd added, whoever carried the dollars up here would likely end up in the cave with the Senator.

A small silence, but then, accusingly, "Why you don't tell dollar deal before? I not believe you! You say when army come, I believe you."

Michael moved only his trigger finger, letting loose with the Car-15 which fired in successive triple bursts. Over Donald, and got one of the guards, who spasmed on his own AK, even as Michael was overrun. Not by the other AK's or by arrows, but by two guards and Donald, who chanced Michael's bullets to leap up and grab his bad leg, tumbling him off the branch and hard to the ground.

And the punishment started.

He was kicked in his soft parts, kicked in the bloody thigh, but never in the head, until even so he began to lose sense. He recovered it, full of pain, being dragged up the hill through the jungle. He let his head hang loose and down, hoping to God the rescue was over. If not, he was in for it.

* * *

They had strung him up by his elbows tied behind him on ropes hung over the branch of a huge shade tree in what had to be the middle of the village. Periodically they would haul on the ropes to raise him up and drop him several feet, all his weight crashing down against his inverted shoulder sockets. He knew they'd tear out before long. The rest of the time men beat him with sticks, but not very hard. Children cheered the beaters on, while what looked to be most of the rest of the village stood by and watched. Donald kept translating from a man who stood on the veranda of the biggest house with some others. Village headman, probably, shouting his question over and over: when would the army come? When? When? And Michael answered over and over, "I don't know." Donald pleaded, his voice very soft: "Tell, Lieutenant, ver' bad time for you ahead, please tell."

Michael's thoughts came in short bursts like electric shocks. Bigger lies pushed him and pushed him, so easy to tell – they will come tomorrow, they will come next week, there will be a whole platoon – but he knew because he'd taught it that once you started talking you couldn't always stop and the truths would surface. Part of him believed by this time that he really didn't know, and he hadn't cried out yet because when he did it would only be worse. They'd think he was softening. Soon, though, soon. Couldn't be helped.

It was dark at last. Light came from torches and a few low-watt electric bulbs, the grind of a generator sounding from somewhere. The team must be away, must be, must be – one little lie, stall, stall . . . but there had to be some guard who'd survived the raid, witnessed and would come shouting the news, so why – Jesus. They were raising him up again, and the shout came.

They let the ropes go and he dropped down the few inches. The men quit beating him. His face was downward. Slowly, he managed to look up, to see what was happening. And had to gather, had to, that it was over, the rescue was done.

Donald had turned away to hear, now spun around towards him. "They take Americans! They take Americans! You know! You decoy!" His eyes catching in the dim light, something happened inside him, for they glowed as he looked up at Michael. And he whispered, "You ver' brave."

But anger went through the villagers like a rumble, and men closed in on him, began beating him with no halt to ask anything, and he heard his left shoulder pop as it dislocated, and the pain started. No lie would help now. A sound was rising in him, through his throat, against clenched teeth. But it was frozen when another shout came. Everyone went quiet. The commands continued. It came from the headman's veranda, but it was not his voice.

"He tells you are only hope of making bargain. Vietnam will like American officer. You must live. He calls everybody foolish." And suddenly, the men who'd been beating him untied the ropes and let him fall to the ground, his face digging into the earth his urine had muddied. The relief loosened his bowels.

A booted foot hooked under his belly and turned him over. There was dead quiet, then a hissing breath. Michael opened his eyes to squint up, the light dim. Asian. Lighter skinned than the Laotians. Staring down at him, eyes narrowing, lips drawing back from teeth. The fuckin' Sawbwa.

Eyes fixed on Michael's face as if he had recognition, too, he bent and ripped Michael's dog-tags off him. He held the ID up and peered at it – he grabbed it into his fist, made a short laugh, then laughed again, hard, triumphant. Swivelling, he stood astride Michael, bent again and grasped Michael's hair, lifting his entire upper body weight against it so that their two faces were close. Michael's arms were useless, the left shoulder an agony. He could do nothing but stare up into that face, remembering the potentate standing on wooden palace steps, looking down on him.

"Where is she, Michael Cameron?"

Michael summoned the energy from somewhere, and the saliva, and spit dead into the Sawbwa's face. Htin Aung let go his hair with a shove, sending Michael's head back down hard against the packed ground of this village plaza. Then he lifted his leg back over Michael, and Michael watched his boots stamping away, heard his voice shout high-pitched infuriated orders.

And then the men set upon Michael. Damned dinks. He struggled as four of them took hold of him and two more stripped him completely. They tied his ankles to the ropes still dangling from the tree overhead. He tipped up his head to see them flip the ropes apart across the branch, and then he was swept upwards, upside down, with his head just brushing the ground, his hands staked, his legs spread apart. He was very afraid now. What was that bastard going to do to him? But he knew.

Htin Aung came to him, a young bamboo stripling, flexible, whipping against his boots. "I knew it not to be happenstance. Americans coming to buy opium from the train where *she* was? And carrying her away? I knew, and faulted her brother for it. I knew, but not that it was you." Htin Aung bent slightly to put his face into Michael's vision. "Where is she?" he barked.

No cold evil here tonight, not for Michael. Dear God. How soon could he start lying?

He could feel something tickle his balls, flip his penis, and then he heard the whistle, felt the hit.

"Where?" The hits were steady and worse and worse, setting him afire, excruciating. "Where?!"

It seemed a very long time but it wasn't, before Michael started the groans that all too soon rose to screams.

DAY ELEVEN

36

The phone just rang and rang. When she had talked with Tom two days ago, he'd said he'd be at home every morning. But yesterday morning there'd been the clinic, and after Michael had left in the afternoon the phone didn't work. And this morning, not even the servant was answering the phone.

Tom'd said the chancellor of his college had influence with A.I.D., whatever that was, and he'd see if the man couldn't get him a quick Laotian visa. Maybe he had. Maybe Tom was already on his way here.

Kathleen shifted Cho in her arms. She couldn't believe it, but he did feel heavier. The diarrhea was disappearing, and so was the cough. Only a few more tablets of sulfa, and then –

She nearly reached the stairs up to the apartment as the cab entered the compound and pulled up. He was back, oh, thank the Lord, he was – but it was Hanny. Hanny.

He stood and looked at her. His black hair hung over his forehead, his black eyes unreadable. But she knew. She sank down to a step, just staring at him. Quickly, he paid off the driver, came to her, bent and raised her up. "Let's go inside," he said.

He made her sit on the couch, still not speaking. Putting aside a small package he'd brought with him, he took the baby from her and lay him down. Then he rummaged and found the Scotch, poured her a little and urged her to drink it. But she just held it in her hand, looking up at him. "Tell me," she said.

"I told Michael I thought you were steady as a rock. I believe that, Kathleen." He took a deep suck of air.

Don't count on it, she wanted to say, but she managed to hold his gaze.

"The army thinks he's dead," Hanny said. "Killed. But I'm not sure." It was as if she hadn't had a breath in an hour. She gasped in two, three, her hand shaking drops of Scotch on her longyi. She set it down.

"Why . . . aren't you sure?" she finally asked.

He hesitated, then sat down beside her, hesitated again and took her hand. "I'm so sorry, Kathleen."

She looked at him in surprise. "Yes, of course. You're like brothers. Why aren't you sure?"

"Truth? I don't know. He did a brave thing, Kathleen. He drew off all but two of the prisoner guards so the rescue worked. The Senator, all the Americans, are back safe." Her eyes glued to his, she hung on every word. "Michael was wounded. In the leg. He used his own blood to make false trails." Hanny stopped, turning away from her. "Juve – the ranger who was with him, Michael sent him to call in the team – Juve says he was just topping the ridge, about to transmit, when he heard Michael's gun – "

"How – " she interrupted.

"A carbine. Its fire is recognizable. Juve says it was followed by an AK – another kind of automatic rifle."

"Also recognizable," she said.

He nodded. "Russian made. He heard nothing more." Now he picked up Kathleen's glass and drank off the scotch, stood up and began pacing spasmodically.

"Then why, Hanny?" she persisted. If only he were right.

He finally stopped, faced her, shaking his head. "I don't have a reason, just – I need to see for myself. Michael's good in jungle. He could've gotten away, be down somewhere, nursing the wound. Needing help." He caught in his breath. "Last night's Air America helicopter pilot and two other pilots Michael and I know – one's the guy getting your passports, they're not ready yet, but – "

"Hanny!"

"Yeah. Anyway, we're going back up there today."

Kathleen's breath came in sobs, now, hands to her mouth, her eyes dry.

"The Colonel won't okay it," Hanny went on, "but he's signed me out on R & R, and he's turning his back on where I take it. Young Juve wanted to go, too, but the Colonel nixed it. The whole team went to Nam this morning, but Juve left us some schematics, where everything is up there." He sat down beside her again. "If he's alive, we'll find him,

Kathleen." He fell silent, slowly turned his head and looked at her. "I've gotta tell you, though. The Colonel's convinced if he were, he'd have reached the Loach and have flown out. But hell, they could've shot up the Loach out of anger after the rescue . . . you know, anything . . . "

She nodded as Hanny started pacing again.

"So." He picked up the package. She could see now the wrapping was clear and inside were her journals. Oh, dear heaven . . .

Hanny was holding them out to her. "Michael gave me this. He said – he said if anything happened, I was to get them to you. He said, Kathleen, twice, that you were to look into them. Look into them, Kathleen – it's what seemed to be the most important thing in the world to him just before they took off."

She took the journals, sat looking down at them, her mind skittering everywhere, bewildered. All too much. And she didn't want them back, not ever.

"Last thing he said, you shouldn't bother with the first one." She could see Hanny didn't know anything more, couldn't answer any questions about it. He didn't know.

"I'll see you tomorrow," he said. She barely felt Hanny's kiss on her cheek, and then he left. Belatedly, she was up and across the room to the door, to the stair-landing. He was walking away from the building to the gate and the phone. "Hanny!"

He stopped, turned, looked up at her. He nodded, waved and went on. And she heard the low groan in her own throat as it rose and grew and was becoming a scream except she clapped fingers against her mouth to silence it. Got herself back into the apartment.

*　*　*

As the sun rose higher, its light streaming in through the openings in the woven bamboo, it turned the hole into a stinking steam bath, and he began to remember with longing being bone cold in the hours before dawn .

The whip had broken him, of course. It had seemed forever that he'd held out, but finally, finally, hanging there upside down, he had shouted out the lie, "America! She's gone to America!"

It had stopped it. Htin Aung had stood back, looking down on Michael's face. "Tell me!"

Michael could hardly say anything more, his mouth dry, his throat

307

rough from his screams, but he by God managed. "Took her to – to Chieng Mai. She flew from there to the States . . ." Htin Aung was listening. Wanting more? Christ, get on with it. "Through Bangkok," he was whispering, now. "Brother met her in Bangkok, took her to the States." The one detail too much.

It was the longest moment he'd ever spent. Htin Aung brought the whip down on him again, with the shout of, "Liar!" And again the whip and "Liar!"

It seemed to be the more torturous for the short respite. Michael's breath came in sobs. Htin Aung leaned down towards his face, hissing, "Her brother is in Kowloon! The White Crane Triad told me by radio this morning. But she is not!" The whip landed again.

Michael struggled for breath. "You do this . . . much longer . . . you'll have done your worst . . . and nothing left to threaten me with." If the bastard hadn't already accomplished that.

It worked. Htin Aung tossed that fiendish piece of bamboo aside to stride away, calling out some commands. Immediately, men lowered Michael to the ground, his ropes still attached to the tree, causing him to cry out again when his swollen balls got caught between his thighs. Htin Aung spun back around.

"It is not over. You will not have a pleasant night. I will hear soon if she is in Macao where the brother keeps a Burmese whore. Is that what you will do to Kathleen? Turn her into a whore? You disgust me!"

He shouted more orders, and this time he went up into the house. The men who'd let Michael down now untied him. It was a great relief to his bad shoulder, which had been twisted by the stake the left wrist was tied to. Donald was there, too, kneeling beside him, eyes full of reproach. "You not tell me about this 'she'. Who is this 'she'?"

"He keeps this up, Donald," Michael's whisper was hoarse, "I'm not gonna be worth much to the Vietnamese."

"Not matter no more. He buy you from us, Lieutenant."

Sweet Jesus. "Please, Corporal. Get me out of this."

The kid looked really sorry, shook his head. "Prince own refinery. Sell heroin to triads. Everything here come from Prince."

Then Michael was forced to his feet, shoved forward to walk. But the feet were so swollen his balance was precarious and they had to drag him as they had up the ridge. Even so, even so, he took in that house. And then he saw the antenna. Barely visible in the dull light, it stretched from a window across to a tree, and on to another tree, and on. No wonder the bastard could talk to Hong Kong. With a generator and that length antenna, it could be a powerful long-range radio, but probably they could only speak at pre-scheduled times. Soon, he'd said. Yet tonight? Tomorrow morning? And when the damned Triad didn't find Kathleen at Tom's clinic, what then? If he could get to the radio . . .

He was dragged a long way, the dislocated shoulder making it a nightmare, and every foot of it the stench he recognized got stronger and filled him with a new horror. He wasn't being taken to the cave, but to the hole.

They didn't bother tying his hands and feet again. They held his head up, kicked his legs out and into the hole, and pushed him down into it, clapping the woven bamboo trap down to fasten it tight above him. Nothing to be done about it. Not even Donald stayed.

* * *

Michael tried, or thought he did, to use the stuff Kathleen had taught him. Meditation, never had been any good at it, but for awhile he'd conned himself into believing he was doing it, losing immediacy, leaving. Probably just going in and out of consciousness, and when alert in a fury with himself. Hanny'd been right, some lousy liar he was – said too much – too many unnecessary details'll catch you up every time. Brother taking her to America was a prime example.

The moon was up when he heard the voice again. "Damn you, where is she?"

Michael raised his face to see only a shadow above him.

"Why do you want her?" Of all the dumb questions. He knew why. He'd written Kathleen why, for God's sake. And what the man said next affirmed it. For after a little silence – amazement, probably – he laughed, a short laugh. "I knew you to be a callow American boy from your letters years ago, full of your own gonads. It seems you still are that fool. Though after tonight, you've hardly a gonad left, surely."

That sickening upper class Brit accent went on and on. "I have heard from the Triad. She is not in Macao. But after they killed his whore, they gave Reverend Howard a message from me. An offer to trade – you for his sister."

Michael's mind spun with it. God help Tom. He almost didn't hear what Htin Aung said next.

"He will be watched, but of course, he may not know where she is. For your sake, you had best tell me."

There was a long silence. Michael turned his face down, trying to control his breathing so the fucker wouldn't hear his fear. Then Htin Aung leaned down, his voice almost intimate. "Don't misjudge me from my speech. I am not English."

Michael couldn't help it, he looked up again. Even in this light he could see the man's face, see those creamy perfect teeth as he spoke. "I grew up in Burma. Came of age, in Burma. I know things to do. You think about that tonight. All night." And suddenly, the moon was bright again. The man disappeared.

Over and over again through that long night, he pleaded with Tom: don't lead them to her. Don't do it, Tom.

It had rained soon after their exchange, and at first Michael was grateful for it, lifting his face to the openings in the trap over his head to lick the drops from his lips. But after awhile he'd realized that the ground he was sitting on was becoming a soup, the water with no place to drain. The soup a foul mix of mud and feces, not much of which his own. God help his wounded thigh. Only good thing about it was that the cool paste seemed to soothe his testicles. They were ballooned and raw, and his penis felt frayed, burned like hell when he pissed. No doubt all his lower body surface sitting in shit would become inflamed, too. He'd tried shifting his weight but couldn't. His knees were bent almost to his chest.

The first time left alone he had tried to worm his right hand up between his body and the rock wall of the hole to reach the trap, but couldn't. So he'd ducked his head and lifted his shoulders against the trap, his only lever his single good leg. But even doubled up, it wasn't good enough, the trap too strong.

Toward morning, shivering, the cramping inescapable, his shoulder, his genitals, every damned part of him had pulsed with pain. In moments of sense, he'd known that even if he got free, he might never use his left arm again. He might even lose his leg.

Now, under the sun, he was sweating, steaming alive, losing the little body moisture remaining to him.

He heard giggling, children's voices, thought he must be hallucinating, and then the sunlight dimmed and he heard *his* voice. "How was your night? Nightmares or pretty dreams?"

Htin Aung let the silence linger. "You must listen to me, Cameron.

For I have remembered. One of those letters Kathleen wrote you. So many letters you never received. 'Are you still afraid of spiders, Michael?' That's what she wrote. 'You were always the one who spotted them, out of the corner of your eye, and would jump a mile.' Unfortunately, Cameron, you can't jump even an inch, now."

What? *What?*

"Tell me, Cameron. Where is she? *Tell me!* The children – you hear them? – they have been up since dawn light, gathering them."

Another long silence. Oh, Jesus, could the man really do this to him?

"The boy Boun Nung Gia will stay by you, in case you change your mind." A heavy sigh, and as he had in the moonlight, the man disappeared again.

Almost unable to breathe from his terror, terror like nothing he'd ever really felt except in his worst acid fantasies, Michael squinted up, and heard the giggling, the little tippy-taps, the scrabbling, and black *things* came trickling through the openings in the trap, creeping, *falling* onto his face. Oh, God. Dear God. He ducked his head and felt them land in his hair. He wanted to close his eyes, but when he did it was worse. He had to see, had to watch. Sweet Jesus, Jesus, Jesus, let me die.

"Sir? Sir? Tell! General Vang Pao not like this. I not like this. I make sure they do not poison. But they will bite. You must tell!" Donald.

They crawled down his shoulders and across his belly and into his crotch and into the crack of his ass. They were big, some of them, but not all. They clicked. And the biggest ones, some very big ones, even squeaked. No more, no more, please God. He opened his mouth to call out, "Laos! Laos!" but one entered between his lips so he spat and clamped them shut against the words and the spiders, and heard the howls echo inside his head.

* * *

"Sweet hour of prayer! Sweet hour of prayer! That calls me from a world of care . . . " Singing softly, eyes moving again and again to the journals on the table, she sat in the soft chair and rocked Cho in her arms. He'd been fussing ever since Hanny'd left, nothing suited him, even through the noon meal with the Chinese family downstairs. Han Lien, the mother, had fallen for Cho, and both yesterday and today had invited Kathleen to eat with them. She would have refused today but had no excuse that wouldn't worry the kind woman. She'd had to force herself to eat, and the time had seemed endless. When would she know? Not 'til tomorrow? She didn't think she could bear that.

The old hymn that she loved so much was working its magic on Cho. It had been Michael's favorite, too. He'd told her. When he was little and his parents went out in the evening – they did that a lot, he'd said – he'd throw a world class tantrum for being left behind, and his gram would take him to the old rocker in the guest room, hold him on her lap and sing to him until he fell asleep. As Cho was.

It always came back to Michael. Everything. Everything.

She settled Cho in his basket, returned to the package to look at it as if it might bite her. Finally, hands trembling, she tore away the plastic wrapping. One journal slipped to the floor. She picked it up, opened it – 1969 #1. Don't bother with it, Kathleen. But why should she bother with any of them? What had he wanted from her? That she read them again, go through it all again? Why had she ever brought them out with her. . . given them to him? Except she couldn't have told him the truth of it. Oh, God . . .

Maybe he'd written her a note. Quickly, she upended each of the journals, even the first one, shook them with the pages dangling. Nothing fell out.

He came for you. You must do as he asks.

She opened the journal labelled 1969 #2, starting at the beginning of it to leaf through the pages, not knowing what she was looking for, picking up phrases of her own here, there, some seeming so childlike, now. She had never reread these notebooks.

At last, more than halfway through, she turned a page and saw. He had written across her own pages, and something inside her twisted at the sight of that unforgotten script of his, slanted, letters firm and elongated, beautiful.

> He does not hate you. And it wasn't the humiliation you
> believe you gave him that turned him. Dearest Kath, there
> is a kind of man who, when denied what he wants most,
> turns on the one who denies him, punishes most the one
> whose love and respect as well, perhaps, he most desires
> but cannot attain. He wants too much of you and cannot
> forgive your refusal of it, wants from you what you gave
> to me, what he knows you gave to me from our letters and

your journals. He loves you, Kath. Pervertedly. It is not
you, not your blame for that humiliation, but his own
nature. With some men, love is only a fine line from
cruelty. Perhaps they stem from the same root, and one
branch grows crookedly. Who knows why. But believe
this. Only lack of love can sully someone. You were not a
victim of that.

Once finished with this, she went back and peered through his lines
to hers to make sure she knew what had prompted him. And that's when
her tears began.

Turning the pages, being gentle with them, she found little exclama-
tions scrawled here and there. "No, no, remember what I wrote before!"
And, "Yes. There, you see?" And, "Kathleen, you have not changed one
iota!" And a longer entry, where she'd written that school was permitted
again.

Pity him, Kath. If I am right in what I wrote earlier, he was
as bewildered by what he did as you were. A man in
conflict, maybe, not wanting what he felt with you, feeling
a loss of control with you, feeling under your power and
hating you for it even as he loved you. I have no doubt he
still does.

His longest entry came in a new volume, when she wrote that she
was pregnant. Her tears were unstoppable, now.

You wonder why this man who hates you so would want
another child with you. You misjudge his feelings for you,
Kath, I truly believe you do. But even if you are right.
Even if he does hate you. That is not what drives him to
you. He truly has no interest in ever seeing Cho again. To
him, the boy is dead. But I know you understand that.
What I think you don't realize is that you, his son's mother,
are in no way tarnished by what the Sawbwa perceives as
Cho's weakness. That is Karma, only Karma. What Sao
Htin Aung wants again from you is your strength for his
blood line. In addition to his perversion of love, he

admires you, Kath – more than he would wish, I am
certain. And it probably leads him to an additional resentment – you are not Shan. His life has been strange, after
all. Boarding school with English aristocracy – people not
known to respect dark skins. Then he had to return to a
remote and uneducated land. You must seem the perfect
compromise – literate, with beauty, and a life as exotic as
his own. And strong. How could you not be, he must
think, for you have withheld yourself from him.

This took up several pages, ending far beyond her own entry that
prompted it. And it was his last major entry until the blank pages that
ended the 1970 notebook. She couldn't seem to stem the tears.

He wrote the time and date, something he hadn't done before. Early
yesterday morning. She couldn't verify the date, but it had to've been. Just
before going off on the mission. The realization had her gasping for a
moment. Then she was able to read it.

Listen to me, Kathleen. It has settled in me through the
night, a conviction that you *must* be careful. Sao Htin Aung
will raise heaven and earth to get you back. Not the baby.
You. We can withstand him together, you and I. But if
something happens to me, don't dismiss my warning lightly.
Tell Tom. Go some place where Htin Aung cannot easily
find you. And lose your fears, sweetheart, that your very
nature has been destroyed. It fills these pages. It flows
between you and your child. If you will accept me, it will
bind us together again, as it once did. Michael.

She was sobbing now, trying to get control, but that was gone, all
gone. And the baby was sobbing, too, sensing something, hearing her sobs,
a sound new to him.

She went and picked him up, carried him to the chair again to rock
him, managing finally to stifle her own sobs not to feed his, but the tears
kept running, running, and she didn't know whether she was really rocking
him or rocking herself for comfort.

She couldn't sing them any more, but the words still went through
her head. "In seasons of distress and grief, my soul has often found relief.

Sweet hour of prayer! Sweet hour . . . "

He had to come back. They had to have a time. She had to *know*, and in the whole world there was only one who could inform her. Michael.

37

He came back to the world on a shout, shivering violently, maybe from fear of the soft pats on his cheek or at discomfort from the waterfall pounding down cold and hard on the back of his head. Immediately he was rolling away from the touches and over on the dislocated shoulder, and the pain made him cry out again. Ten seconds, twenty, and he realized he was spread naked on a big smooth rock basin. Scoured out from eons of falling water.

What was he doing here and where was here and – oh, God, oh, God. His eyes flew wide to find Donald squatting by his head, reaching to pat his face again, and the restored memory was raising more than a shout in the back of his throat. He slapped away Donald's hand, rolled back to his stomach and began gagging and frantically rubbing his hands through his hair while the water poured through it, and watched bits and pieces of black stuff, some hairy, watched whole spiders, some struggling to get out of the current, get carried away off from him by the water, and he spat, the taste in his mouth from hell, and pieces of black came out of his mouth, too.

He'd had to open his mouth to breathe when they began to enter his nostrils, and once they were in his mouth he'd done the only thing he could. He'd killed others by pressing his body against the stone walls of the hole with them in between. He'd been bitten, and now those bites were swollen, most of them itching, but some painful.

He sat up under the waterfall and started scrubbing his pubic hair, then turned onto his stomach again, careful of the shoulder this time, spread his buttocks and let the water run between them, spread his legs and let the water cool his swollen balls. They throbbed. They felt like mush.

He raised his right arm and let the water pound into his armpit, held his left arm up in spite of how it hurt to do the same there. He lay his head side to side and let the water clean first one ear, then the other. Then he just sat under the falls, certain he'd never feel free of them and clean again, and rubbed at his toes to get rid of the shit underneath the nails. For the first time he noticed the small groups of men squatting nearby, watching him, smoking cheroots or chewing betel, spitting the red juice, even smiling a little in encouragement.

Had he told, then? And been released as his reward? God forgive him. He'd never ask it of Kath.

He struggled to his feet, balancing poorly. Something touched his arm, and he jerked back so sharply that he stumbled and almost went flat. It was Donald, who held out his hands palm up to say no harm meant. Then the kid gestured, wanting Michael to look, and there up on the bank were his clothes, looking damp but clean, and even his boots. Donald acted as crutch for Michael to go to them. Michael pulled on his briefs and eased them over his wounded thigh, up his hips, almost couldn't do it, but once they were on they even gave him a little support. He looked at the pants, too damned tight in the crotch though he'd never thought so before, and knew how they were going to feel, so he put on his T-shirt, his shirt, sat down in gingerly fashion and pulled on his socks. He looked up, and there was a villager standing above him, holding out a folded sarong. Michael took it, nodded his thanks, shook out his boots – nothing there – and eased his feet into them.

Next thing, he had to do something about the shoulder, then about the arrow wound. God knew how septic that had become. He'd tried rubbing at it, front and back, under the falls, but it was too painful.

He looked up the banks lining the waterfall and found some stunted trees, forks low, finally found one with a fork high enough, about eight feet above the ground. He signalled Donald for help again. The kid was there at once and supported Michael up the rough bank to the tree. Michael placed Donald's hands on his body to steady him, lifted his left hand up with his right and jammed the wrist between the branches, the hand grasping a knot. He grabbed one of the branches with his right hand, swung his feet up, placed his right boot against the trunk, started leaning the weight of his body back, let go the right hand, shoved hard and threw his body back with force, and gave a helpless yelp as pain shot through him. But it worked, the books were right, the ball joint slid into its socket. The men down below were all applauding. Shit. It was still sore, but the major pain was gone like magic.

He wrapped the sarong and tied it with a knot in front the way Burmese men tied a longyi. When he looked up, Htin Aung was standing there to one side of the stream, face and eyes expressionless. Good thing he hadn't tried to remember how to tie the knot, had just done it automatically, or that would've been one more humiliation.

The village men were on their feet, a few had already gone, and all the rest but two were fast going, shikoing to Htin Aung. Sure, the big boss, but more – the Royal Prince. The two who stayed carried AK's.

Eyes never shifting from Htin Aung, Michael thought it strange that hatred could come so easy and love could be so hard. "My wound needs debriding," was what he said.

Htin Aung lifted an eyebrow. Purporting to be amused, Michael decided. "And you honestly believe I'll supply you the knife?"

They both were silent. Htin Aung was slender, shoulders good, and not a lot shorter than Michael. A fine figure of a prince, all right.

"After your silence in spite of your little companions earlier this morning," Htin Aung finally spoke, "I have no hope left that you will ever tell me where she is."

Michael sucked in a breath of relief, hoping the bastard wouldn't understand the cause: thank the good Lord he hadn't given her up. He felt the need to lean back against the tree, and did.

"But it's no matter," the Prince was continuing. "Her brother disappeared last night. The White Crane Triad lost him. And may be sure they'll never receive Rapet heroin again. But of course, all is not lost. He carries my message to Kathleen."

"She'll never give you the baby. He's everything to her."

"The child doesn't interest me."

Michael gave a little grunt. Stupid son of a bitch. "You should be informed, Prince, that even in the short time she and I have had to talk, it's become clear to both of us that it's too late. We've lost whatever future we might once have had together. She'll never trade. Not for me."

Htin Aung only gave a short laugh. "You know, I'd have been sure who had taken her even if you hadn't turned up here. Maybe not the first, but on second thought, I'd have known." He cocked his head, seeming sincerely interested in Michael, for the moment. "Intelligent." He nodded. "I'd even have to say your letters evidenced a certain literary influence, callow though they were. But there's a flaw, for all that. A touch too much arrogance." He started a slow smile that Michael was certain the man believed intimidating. "I'd have thought the past several hours might've taught you a lesson in that regard. But if you're persuaded you can convince me Kathleen won't trade for you, you remain as arrogant as ever."

Michael felt a drop of water inching down his neck, brushed at it, saw a small spider fly off him. He jerked, banging hard back into the tree trunk. Might as well've been a hot coal.

Htin Aung's smile broadened. "Perhaps a small lesson after all." The smile went. "We leave for Loi Long at first light tomorrow. Your only decision will be whether to sit in the saddle or make the journey belly down over the horse." He went, too.

"We go cave, now." Startled, Michael turned to find Donald right there, holding out a stick like the one he himself had used as a crutch four days ago. Only four days ago. He carried his Garand at the ready under his arm. He gestured with it, showing the direction.

Michael accepted the stick and limped ahead of Donald down to the path below, where the two armed men waited. They were in quasi uniforms, taller than the locals. And then Michael realized: Shans, attending the Prince, no doubt. They followed close behind on the path as Michael and Donald walked towards the cave and the village.

The bastard knew Kathleen almost as well as Michael did. Neither could doubt for a moment that she'd return to Burma for Michael's sake. And Colonel Wisby had made it clear. A black operation had no official existence. Unfortunately, that meant no cavalry on the horizon. He was going to have to do something smart, but God only knew what.

* * *

Cho had fallen off to sleep again, and she had read what Michael had written over and over. Each time renewed her tears. She knew they came from a well with a reservoir more than four years deep, but even so part of her felt shamed by them, as if she had no right to them.

Karma didn't exist. She no more believed in it than in Santa Claus. What she did believe – perhaps the single most important thing her Protestant upbringing had provided her – was that everyone made his own fate. Sometimes not deserved. But always self-created. And Michael knew it to be true, too. He believed that together they could make it a good fate. Could they? She knew with awful conviction that she couldn't do it alone. And the tears stopped.

Now she was bent over the small kitchenette sink, tossing cold water on her hot eyes, hot cheeks.

Steps on the stairs. It couldn't be, couldn't, but she was running to the door, face still wet. She unbolted the door, threw it open – and it was Tom.

His eyes moved over her face as if wanting to etch it forever into his mind, and a smile started. But suddenly his face drew down, and he pulled her gently, so gently into his arms and laid his cheek against hers. She felt him shudder. He was weeping, her big brother. Two of them stood weeping.

A few moments, and she pulled back from him to look his face through and through as he had hers. He was going grey, this good man, and there was sorrow in his eyes. She took his hand, led him into the apartment and closed the door, almost walked away from it but remembered and bolted it again. "Michael found this place for me. Isn't it wonderful?"

He turned to her, nodded a little, trying hard, she could see, to smile. But he didn't succeed. "He's not here, is he," he said.

Odd. It wasn't a question. She shook her head. "A mission – the army sent him on what he called an operation . . . " It was too hard, damn it. Even to say it.

"And he hasn't returned." Tom's voice was careful and the certainty puzzled her. Probably her red eyes. He lifted a thumb to either cheek and wiped her tears. "Sis. Little sis." He grasped her arms. "Last night, some Chinese from a triad came looking for you at the house. I'd already gone up to Macao. The chancellor had gotten me a Laotian visa, and – " his face working as he spoke, an agony that was equally agonizing for her to watch. "My cook . . . and his wife . . . they frightened them. Poor things. They denied you were there – the truth – they told them where I was, and those bastards went up to Macao, found me – with my friend. They broke into our clinic – hers, really, where she did so much –."

Kathleen thought of the Scotch, which was still sitting out on the counter. She loosened his hands so tight on her arms that they hurt, went and poured some whiskey into a glass, carried it to Tom. He gulped it not quite down, and she drew him to the couch, sat beside him.

"They – what they did – they shot her." He swallowed hard, and finished off the Scotch. "I didn't go back to Kowloon. Dr. Fitzhugh – he's a good man – he not only got me the visa in miraculous time, he laid on a plane at a field the other side of Macao. It just got here. Thank God you gave me this address, I don't know what – "

"Tom!" Kathleen couldn't help it, she was appalled. "Could anyone – are you sure no one followed you?"

Again he was trying to smile at her, trying to reassure her. "No, it's all right. They'd gone. The police came. And much later I took her poor little car, she wouldn't let me buy her any better . . . I took it like a thief, drove it without lights for several blocks, spent the rest of the night at the airfield in the car . . . They gave me a message, Kathleen."

Was there always going to be fear like this?

"You are to go to Chieng Mai, the Pagoda Hotel, and someone will come for you – I guess to take you back to Loi Long. You must be there in five days."

"Well, they're crazy," she said, and jumped to her feet to go stand over the baby. "Whoever they are, crazy! I will never go back there."

There was a silence. She turned to look at Tom, his face, his whole body showing his huge sadness. He stood up, came to her and looked down at Cho. "He's beautiful." He reached to her cheek again, a sweet touch. "Kathleen . . . "

"Tom? For heaven's sake – "

His hand dropped. "Htin Aung has Michael."

She stared at him. "You believe that?" She turned away, not aware for several seconds but then realizing she was wringing her hands. Never mind. "I don't. It's just a trick to get us back. Me. How could he know Michael's missing? And how could he have him, anyway? Htin Aung's off making opium deals for his Laotian refinery up near China, he – " Hands lifted to her mouth, her mind speeding through it. "That village! North-west Laos, he said . . . " She swung around back to Tom, managed some-how a nod. "Yes. He has Michael." Another moment, the two looking at each other, and then she started moving. Faster and faster, picking up the baby, a clean bottle, speaking fast, trying not to sound in a panic. "We have to get to the airport. Right now, Tom."

In a passing moment, she saw him staring at her.

"Please! You can believe me, Tommy! He's alive. And we have to get to those pilots before they go! Oh, I'll explain on the way!"

She had nearly reached the door. "There're coins on the table. Go call a cab, the number's on the phone box out by the gate. I have to leave the baby!" She had unfastened the bolt when she remembered. "In the other room – my boots! Bring them!" And she was out the door.

Han Lien must have read the need in her face, for she didn't ask anything, just accepted Cho into her arms, nodding as Kathleen spoke breath-lessly. "Everything he needs is upstairs. Use the bottles above the sink. Just put the milk in them and warm them in a pan of water." Han Lien's spoken English was poor, but she understood it well enough. "I'll return for him tonight or tomorrow," Kathleen finished.

She leaned and looked long into her bright Cho's eyes. "Let him go and get me another, Kathleen." The dreadful words resounded in her head. She kissed Cho. God, help me to do this.

She looked back up at the Chinese woman, and had to add, "It may be a man who comes," trying to keep the tremble from her voice that she was feeling throughout her body. "The American soldier you saw here yesterday and the day before?" Han Lien nodded. "Or the one who came this morning?" Again a nod. "Or my brother who just arrived . . . " She had to swallow.

Han Lien reached out a small hand and touched Kathleen's hand. "Kathareen, you be awright?"

Kathleen nodded, knowing she would not, could not ever be, without Cho. But he would be all right, and so would Michael. She wrenched a final look away from her baby, and left.

* * *

"It's Rapet! The same village!" She stood there, her voice rising, wanting to scream at them. But the four men around the table in the Air America building stared at her as if she were half-crazed. She had remembered the AA building next to the clinic, had found the men there, and had just named the village where Htin Aung's heroin refinery was, matching it to the name of the village that had held the Senator prisoner.

She pleaded with Hanny. "Didn't that boy ever name the village to you? Did he?"

Hanny looked away, eyes roving. "Yeah. He did. What'd you call it – Rapet? That's it."

"Well the Sawbwa's there, Hanny! He is!"

The others continued to look skeptical – a burly bearded man called Jedediah, and baby-faced Simon, and the bald one with the English accent she'd seen at the clinic two nights ago, named Sherm. But Hanny nodded. He believed her. He knew where they'd been, where Loi Long was, and the palace. "But Michael'd rather die, Kathleen, than stand for a trade."

She knew that. But she wouldn't allow it. "It's not his choice, Hanny," she said, keeping her eyes steady on his, hanging on the silence.

"Nor your choice either, my dear," Sherm said, so condescending she could've killed him. "It's our choice. We fly the aircraft, you know."

They looked so smug. She'd exploded. "Damn you all!" She looked at Hanny and pleaded. "He's your friend. Your brother. I'll obey your orders, I'll do anything – but if nothing else works . . . I'll be there, don't you see?"

Hanny finally nodded again. "So. We just got saved scouring the jungle. Cam's probably in that damned cave. What the hell. We hit the village after dark and bring both him and his lady out."

Kathleen sagged against the table, when Tom spoke up for very nearly the first time. "Sergeant? If you've got an extra AK, I know how to use it."

Hanny looked at him in surprise. "I thought – sorry, but aren't you a missionary?"

Tom smiled. The only harsh smile Kathleen had ever seen in him. "Not any more," he said.

* * *

The four of them sat on the floor of the Huey while Jedediah and Sherm piloted them up to the STOL strip this side of the ridge from Rapet. The flight seemed to go on and on, too noisy to talk, too easy to think. How could she give Cho up? And her secret voice, small, imagined, ashamed, lied and said she wouldn't have to. Michael would come for her again, he'd bring her out of Burma again. Until another stronger voice cut it off, told her not to be a child. He might not even be here much longer, the army could send him anywhere. "Do you truly think the Sawbwa will give you the run of the palace again? You'll be kept somewhere out of the way," the secret cruel voice hammered, "and he'll come once a month to jam himself into you, and if you're lucky you'll have another son to be your only life – until *he* sends him away to boarding school –" Oh, dear God. But Hanny'd promised to bring Michael and herself both out . . .

She looked across the cabin to where he sat looking out through the open hatch to the darkening jungle just as Michael had on the flight down from the pagoda. Hanny must've felt the weight of her gaze, her hope, for he turned his head towards her and even in the dim light she could see him drop her a wink. Then he pointed at his watch, held up his hand to show five fingers. Five minutes? Was it the helicopter shaking so, or herself? Htin Aung was a devil. The men could be fooled by him. Destroyed by him. Whatever she did, she'd have to do it quickly, just take things out of their hands if need be.

* * *

Michael sat on the dirt floor facing the bamboo wall that covered the entire front of the cave. It had a small hinged door in it with easy to lift latches, requiring armed guards on duty all the time to keep watch over the cave's prisoner.

Talk about arrogant. He remembered the times, teaching the kids survival, he'd held forth on how to resist torture, how to endure the pain by keeping a conviction that it wouldn't last forever. How to give up a little, only a little, then hold out, and give up only a little more. What he hadn't taught, because he hadn't known, was that while the pain and the fear of it were endurable, terror might not be. And fear of that terror could destroy you. Because even if the terror did not go on forever, you never forgot it. It changed you, deep inside. It informed you indelibly so that what you once were, you were no longer.

Michael realized he was rocking back and forth like one demented. He was scrunched up away from the cave walls, knees bent, arms holding legs to chest. He wasn't tied up. Just safe. As twilight had come on, he'd noticed something dark scuttling along the edge of the floor against the wall. Both his heart and his breath went into triple time until he saw it was a scorpion, decided to leave it alone. More poisonous than spiders, but not anywhere near as terrifying – not to him, anyway. The place was probably loaded with spider nests. In the dark, he knew with a devil-ridden certainty, they'd come darting out of the recesses. He suspected his heart might not live out the night. He was damned sure if he spotted any of them they wouldn't.

Forget that. Forget it. The damned wound was pounding, front and back, and Michael thought he could smell it now. Would the leg even hold him if he needed to make time? Forget that, too – nothing to be done about it. Think about what to do.

The two Shan guards had left, probably to eat, replaced by a villager armed with a long-bore rifle. He sat a ways off from the cave opening. Michael could hear him coughing, spitting. Even in full darkness, anybody within twenty feet would hear the squeak of the bamboo door swinging on its split bamboo hinges. Maybe in the middle of the night. The best of guards could doze off then. Maybe –

Here was Donald, with a plate of rice. He slid it under the door where there was space enough. Michael spoke at once. His only hope was

Donald.

"Donald, listen, okay?" But the kid was already turning away. Michael unwrapped his limbs and got on all fours, managed to stand up. Grabbed the stick and made it to the door. He could hear Donald's voice, low. And then, peering into the last of daylight, Michael saw the villager walk away. Donald stood there, looking after him. Michael hissed, "Donald!"

The kid turned, returned to the door, and opened it. "This no good, what Prince do to you. I no like. Rapet no like. We go Long Tieng now." And he stepped back, motioning to Michael. Bless him, God bless him, Michael was outside.

Donald was already walking away, on the path back along the ridge top. Michael stood there, not knowing how to do this. Finally, he just said it. "I have to see the Prince."

Donald froze, looked around, came back, and hissed his words softly. "You crazy! You want more spiders?" Michael couldn't manage to control his shudder or hide from himself what uncoiled deep inside him like a worm. "Or maybe he only kill you this time!"

Thinking it was finished, the boy was just turning back around again, unwary – and Michael grabbed him, his hand circling that small throat.

"Be still. You gonna be quiet?" Donald nodded. "You do what I tell you?" Another nod. "I mean it, Corporal. Kill you as look at you."

"Yes," the kid whispered. No trusting him, naturally. Michael had already done that and look where it had gotten him. But silencing him with a blow could as easily kill him, he felt so fragile in Michael's hands. And that Michael couldn't do. So he shoved Donald free, at the same time relieving him of his Garand. Easy enough, like dealing with a toy soldier.

The kid faced him, sure as hell not lacking courage. "You ver' foolish. Sawbwa ver' strong. Ver' bad man."

"Ain't that the truth," Michael said. Donald didn't get it, just looked puzzled. But Michael wasn't puzzled. He just wasn't sure he, Michael Cameron, wouldn't just up and cut and run – that's if his damned leg permitted it – in the next minute. Because he was not sure who he was, was not trusting of himself anymore. But he went on, "You go to the helicopter, wait for me – unless . . . it's still in one piece, right?" The kid hesitated, figured it out, nodded. "Then go."

"You no get down to chopper without me. No can do it!"

"Yes, I can. I will."

Donald just stood looking at him, shaking his head back and forth. They both started at hearing some laughter on down the side of the hill, men coming home for supper perhaps.

"Rapet need opium." Donald pleading. "Prince give for Rapet. Rapet need Sawbwa."

"There's always somebody to supply opium, Corporal. The Union of Burma'll be doing it soon enough."

Donald just looked at him through the falling darkness, sadness written on his face. "I no can help you do this." And he turned on his heel and started away, ultimately running away – only to stop, turn and look back at Michael. Michael waved, trying to make it a release, and immediately, the Garand ready under his right arm, his left using the stick because he couldn't manage without it, he moved off the path into the jungle and headed in the direction of the village.

He knew, really knew, only one thing. Not how he was going to do it – the only ammo he had for Donald's gun, after all, was in its single 8-round magazine – or even whether he'd be able. But Htin Aung had sent an assassin after Tom, and it was pure luck the attempt had failed. He'd killed innocent Hla Swe. It appeared he could harness the power of Chinese triads at will. Sure as hell Michael and Kathleen couldn't count on a convenient invasion of Loi Long by Burma. If Michael didn't see to it, they would likely spend months, maybe years, in hiding, with Kathleen afraid. She'd had enough of that to do her forever, and anyway, one of them abiding fear – himself – was plenty.

So here went nothin'.

38

Hanny'd left the Huey the moment they'd set down. Jedediah kept the blades turning, waiting for his return. Nobody spoke. Maybe the message had been a trick after all, and Michael might be at the Loach, suffering, or . . .

"Started right up!" Hanny, back again. He looked in at Kathleen, shook his head. No Michael. Jedediah killed the Huey's engine. They sat in silence, waiting for the last of the light to gᴜ, for their night vision to kick in, hearing the creaks and ticking of the cooling turbine.

They had decided back at Luang Prabang to make sure up front that the Loach would still run. The AA men had said the Huey could take the weight but if they were all going along – "And it seems you are," Sherm giving in with British dryness – it could get a little tight on the return trip. Anyhow, as Hanny'd said, the Army'd kind of like to get their little helicopter back.

It was Hanny's command. They sat there, the men seemingly unmoving and unmoved. Kathleen wondered how men at war stood the waiting before battle. But that's what they were doing now, weren't they? All of them. It *was* a war, and the wait was hard.

"Time."

They all jumped out, Hanny lifting Kathleen down. He'd given her strict orders to stay right behind him, hold onto his belt. They all carried lights, bulbs shielded by red glass. She was the only one without a gun, armed only with her secret resolve that if she had to trade she'd promise the Sawbwa anything he wanted to get Michael and the other men out. She'd deal later with what would come.

✷ ✷ ✷

Michael was lost. The fucking lanes went with no logic amidst the houses, which faced in all directions. Soft yellow light leaked through shutters closed against night air and mosquitos, forcing him to dodge from house to house under the cover of veranda overhangs and the spaces beneath the stilted houses where pigs rooted and dogs whined. None noticed him, miraculously, the pigs too busy eating garbage, the half-starved and parasite-ridden dogs lacking the energy. And he was tiring, having to travel half-bent over because of the low headroom, his leg dragging more and more.

He'd halted to grab breath when at last something smart occurred to him. From then on, he scouted the travelling ground before he left shelter and did the hustle from house to house with his eyes lifted.

There. It swung slightly in a breeze, catching a nearby glow – the radio antenna. He followed it, saw where it entered the wooden house through the crack between loose shutters. He sneaked under the house, collapsed against one of the posts and listened, the smell of garlic frying over a charcoal cookfire having a warmth that seemed to embrace him.

At least two men overhead. They sounded like men everywhere did, laughing at stories they wouldn't want their wives to hear. Michael hadn't heard Htin Aung's voice in circumstances exactly helpful for recognizing it, but this was the only wooden house he'd seen in the village, it housed the radio, and last night had seemed to house the headman. Where else would Hting Aung be accomodated?

Michael thought fleetingly about hefting up onto the veranda, trying to take a bead through a window, but knew the leg wouldn't allow it, not quietly enough. So he moved on out from beneath the house into the center plaza and over to the tree which had enabled the delivery of so much pain last night. He rested against it, looking up at the house, spotting two automatic rifles leaning up to one side of the closed door.

He was going to have to call the bastard out. And kill him in cold blood.

You think you can do that, Cam? Hanny's voice, echoing inside his head. Since when did Hanny become anybody's fucking conscience?

He was trembling, God damn it. From the effort to get here, no doubt. Still. Take a breather, that's all. Just a breather.

* * *

They'd gotten to the top of the ridge with no alarm sent, Kathleen panting, but she'd done it. And they'd reached the cave, only to find it empty. The smell, the glow of cookfires reflecting off mists told them where the village was. Voiceless, they moved that way and on into it, no real lanes, houses hodge podge. Then Hanny stopped them with a raised hand, and they all stood, trying to smother the sounds of their breaths, their hearts, knowing, every one of them, that they were lost.

* * *

"Htin Aung, you bastard! Get out here!"

Everything went silent, then footsteps pounded across a wooden floor, the door banged open and the Sawbwa, followed by the headman, burst out of the house. Htin Aung reached for a rifle blindly, his eyes seeking Michael. Michael lifted the Garand, finger tightening on the trigger, determined to take out both men on the veranda in an arc of fire. His gun was thrown up and off his aim. Donald.

The headman just stood there. Htin Aung had his AK now, firing it before he aimed it. Michael threw the boy down – who knew whether to get him out of the line of fire or to free up the Garand – and Htin Aung's bullets got Donald as he hit the ground, even as some AK's fired from off to the side of the plaza. The Sawbwa doubled up, his gun falling to the veranda floor, blood spilling from his gut, even as the headman disappeared inside without a gun.

Michael was sprawled at Donald's side, pressing into the boy's neck for a pulse he couldn't feel. Aw, kid. Maybe it didn't mean anything, Michael just might be missing it. Something made him look up and around. And there, for the love of God, came four men, Tom leading them, and Kathleen.

"Don't! I am here!" Kathleen, crying it out, running for the house, blocking the other men's line of fire, then calling something, perhaps the same thing, in Shan.

Oh, God, not after all this. She was beautiful, running. Never, God damn it. Michael looked towards the house to see Htin Aung reaching for his rifle, only fleetingly distracted by her.

As if in slow motion, not knowing he had the strength or even the agility, Michael was up and moving, got to the house, up the steps, to flick the Sawbwa's gun off the veranda with his own. Then Michael pointed the Garand at Htin Aung's head.

"It seems you win, Michael Cameron." Htin Aung's voice husky and, in these straits, his English highly accented. But his eyes didn't blink, firm on Michael's.

"Take it as Karma," Michael said.

Only now did Htin Aung's gaze waver and move past Michael to Kathleen at the foot of the steps, Tom beside her. Michael scanned the yard to see Hanny and the three AA pilots making a half circle, guns pointing out. But if any villagers were interested, they weren't showing themselves, nor were the two Shans who had guarded him earlier. Probably getting drunk on palm liquor and fucking a couple of village girls.

Htin Aung's eyes were seeking Kathleen, seeking . . . what, for God's sake? Absolution?

She looked into his eyes and saw the truth that Michael had given her, and knowing it flooded her as her tears had earlier. Knew, too, that the Prince had been doomed always, with her, no matter his treatment of her. A thing his silent plea told her he still didn't understand. She could never have come to life for him. Only for Michael.

Watching Kathleen, the look passing between her and Htin Aung, Michael hesitated, frozen – the whole of them all seeming frozen, oddly one-dimensional, like a picture on a wall. And then everything jerked into motion, the stalled train released, as the Sawbwa turned his palm up towards her. She spoke to him in soft Shan. Giving him the absolution he was praying for? Shit.

Michael supposed they could take him down to L.P., maybe he'd live through the trip, maybe they could even patch up his belly so he'd survive. Michael had no cold blood here, just blood burning up with fever and the evils this one man had perfected.

"Turn away, Kathleen," Michael said. He looked at her and waited.

Kathleen had offered Htin Aung the only peace she could. So she did as Michael ordered, and turned away. But she could see that Tom did not, was watching with cold, remote eyes while Michael finished the job Tom and Hanny had begun moments before, for they both had shot at once. This time, the sound of the single rifle was thunderous to her. She never did turn back to see its damage. She stood and clutched herself for warmth, shivering, and aching with a new sadness for all of them. But finally, wonderfully, triumph washed through her: Cho would be back in her arms before midnight.

Hanny was moving across the beaten ground to the tree and the body there, so small, like a child's. And now Michael passed her, limping badly, to go there, too. Her eyes sought the stranger who was her brother, to realize that what had seemed remote in him a moment ago might have been shock. She looked after Michael, also a stranger?

But he stopped, turned, came back to her. "What did you tell him?" he demanded.

She looked up at him, at that ravaged face, into his eyes. No stranger there, but something alien lingered. Frightful things had been done to him, she saw that. His eyes shifted like one ashamed.

"Oh, Michael, what did he do?"

He looked at her straight on, breathed out a short chuckle that had little sound. "Spiders," he said, as if confessing a sin, "he sicced spiders on me."

She saw now the swollen places on his face, above one eye, the corner of his upper lip, and felt his horror. Though not his terror. That would always be his own. She reached a hand up to his cheek, and he turned his face into it. When he looked back at her, something had been diminished by her touch. He'd been eased.

He'd never get used to it, not Michael. He'd hate forever being afraid. But the shattering could be repaired. And she could do that, make that happen for him. Her certainty of it was another triumph. A joy. Because even five years ago, she'd never understood what it was that made him feel so gifted in her.

He still waited for a response: what had she said to the Prince? Would Michael understand? It would be enough if he'd try. She felt tears rolling down her cheeks, no stopping them. But her voice was steady.

"I told him his son was healthy, that his blood line would continue."

He looked at her a long, long time, and finally gave a little nod. "Well," he said, "he's our son, now, so what's the difference." And he was limping away again towards the tree. And Tom was following him.

"All right, my dear, we're leaving now," said the English voice, kind for once, and she felt an arm around her, felt herself pushed into motion, saw Jedediah walking ahead of her, Simon on her other side. She tried to look back for Michael, but Sherm wouldn't let her. "They'll be along," he was saying, "we have to get away from here. The village won't sit on their hostility forever. Hanny will take care of him."

Hanny rose from where he knelt beside Donald, turning to reach for Michael.

"Is he dead?" Michael asked.

"I don't know. But if he is, he is, and if he isn't, he's home." He grabbed Michael's arm and put it around his shoulders. And they both turned to find Tom there.

"I can see he mattered to you, but you're not alone," he said to Michael.

What the hell, were they going to hear about Jesus now?

"The triad came through the kitchen. With guns. And I swung her around to put her behind me, but others fired through the window and she took the bullets. Not I." He looked down at Donald, back up at Michael. Tears were in his eyes. "Nor you."

No Jesus talk. No what-if-I'd-done-this or what-if-I-hadn't-done-that, either. Tom just accepted the way it was. Of course. What he'd learned in Burma. On the other hand, he'd fired his AK just fine.

Michael put his other arm around Tom's shoulders. "I can use both of you," he said, and they started him away from that nightmare tree, half dragging him as he'd been half dragged to it in the first place.

"You look like hell, darlin'," Hanny said. "Been missin' a little sleep, have ya?"

They reached the edge of the plaza, headed off between houses. All around them, even the dogs remained silent. They'd have time to find the path down the STOL.

How soon would the mother find her boy? How soon would she be washing his body? Or would she be bandaging his live bleeding wounds? Michael would never know. What if the kid hadn't fallen in love with him? What if he hadn't fallen for the kid? Quack, quack, quack. Fuck it. Never in a zillion years would he learn just to accept things.

DAY TWELVE

39

The Colonel finally came to see him at the clinic on the third morning. Willy had been in and out, and Hanny had sat by the whole time. After his fever broke, Kathleen and Tom had gone down to Vientiane, Kathleen travelling on her false passport, Tom with her birth certificate that he'd brought with him from Kowloon. They were going to park in some embassy office until Richard cut the red tape back in Washington. Wait until Kathleen got a new – and legal – passport, and Cho did, too.

Of course, the State Department had no records of her entering Laos, no record of a birth certificate for Cho, and there were only so many strings Richard could pull with State. Michael sure hoped Kathleen was a better liar than he was. About how the hell she'd gotten here, and who was Cho's father. She'd told Michael there were family factions in Loi Long who might want Cho, the last heir, so the sooner she got out of Laos the better. What remained would be to convince the Laotian locals to overlook all these "irregularities" and provide stamped visas and entry permits into Laos. Simon said dollars would help. Of course. Michael's sole contribution.

Hanny had been there with him since breakfast, saying goodbye. "I'll write you," he'd said, "just not every week." He was going to finish out his enlistment at Fort Rucker. Obviously, the Loach wasn't needed in Laos anymore, and neither were they. Michael hadn't yet really come to grips with that, or with deciding what came next.

"And I'm gonna bring Eric and Barb down." Hanny a little red in the face. "What the hell, if it gets too hot for her, pregnant and all, I'll get her an air conditioner. Thing is, while I think you and Kathleen've got it made like yin and yang, I figure even for you guys it's gonna take some work. So I can do that, right?"

"What the fuck do you know about yin and yang?" was all Michael could think to say, really pleased for Hanny going to make a passion of his own.

"Shit, man, you think I've spent more than two years in-country for nothin'? And by the way, how're you doin' down there?"

"You would remind me," Michael said. Every time he thought about it, he didn't know whether to laugh or die a little. A real match, he and Kathleen. She might not want him to get it up, and he wasn't sure he could. All that prick Schramm would say was, only one way to find out, give it a try. Sure. It was Hanny had the better answer. "I got into a lot of mean fights, growin' up in the Cleveland flats. Lotsa low blows. It takes more time than you think it should, but it'll come back. I promise you." Yeah? But even if time cured him, there was no guarantee it'd make things work for Kathleen. He'd written on her pages that everything would be all right, that she would be all right, but hell, what'd he know, really.

Hanny had just announced he was flying out this afternoon when the Colonel arrived. "Morning, Chief. Lieutenant," he said.

"Sir," said Michael, lifting up a little on his arms but not really trying to stand. He was in the chair, leg stretched out on a stool, and once there they wanted him to stay put. The Colonel waved him back – which landed him a little off center and gave him pain in a different part. The Colonel perched on the bed.

"Thought you boys'd be interested. Senator Beaumont has announced to the press that in spite of his little run-in with the locals, his fact-finding mission uncovered no – none – zip American involvement in any war, secret or otherwise, in Laos."

Michael and Hanny were looking at him agape. "But did you tell him about Long Tieng – the Plain of Jars – shit, Colonel – " Hanny, giving it a try.

The Colonel shrugged. "The White House got to him. Probably the Paris negotiations – also supposed to be secret." The three looked at each other. The Colonel shrugged again. "Well, anyway, thanks to you two, he's alive and kicking. And the Army's off the hook. Uh, Chief. . . if you wouldn't mind?"

Hanny was at the door at once, looked back at Michael. "I'll be outside," he said. What'd he think, Michael wondered, that he'd need to call for help?

"Lieutenant." Again not Michael. How come? "The doc – what's his name, Schramm? – he wants you transferred out of here and into a major hospital for physical therapy for your leg. We can make it the U.S., Tokyo or Clark in Manila." Michael nodded. "Before you state your preference, however, there's something else comes first." The man looked regretful. What was going on?

The Colonel sighed. "I'm totally convinced that you are deserving of at least a Silver Star for valor and gallantry in the rescue of the Senator. Certainly he is. In all likelihood, without your actions, and sacrifice, there would have been injuries, even loss of life. No doubt loss of Senator Beaumont. Unfortunately, I'm going to have to lose the paperwork."

Whoops. He knows, thought Michael. Richard warned me.

"You're just lucky you aren't going to lose the Army – dishonorably."

The silence was long. Michael finally cleared his throat. "Um . . . Sir? Could you explain?"

The Colonel just cast him a dry look. "Come on, Michael. The story was too good for those AA pilots to bury, and the weekly party was two nights ago. Remember the party?"

Shit, yes, he remembered. Sandy, was that her name, the Major's wife? Or was it Jackie? Shit.

"Obviously you've suffered considerably. I gather not only for duty's sake, however, but for the sake of a young woman as well. Not my business why you came to Laos – what did you tell me, to get to know the hill tribes?"

"Sir, that was true – partly, anyway."

The Colonel nodded, believing it. It lifted the onus a little, Michael thought.

"Problem is, Lieutenant," that again, "you have used and endangered Army property for private purpose. That includes the Loach, Chief Hanrahan, and, I might point out, yourself. In fact, both the Loach and Chief Hanrahan took some damage in the process." His eyes flickered, barely, down to Michael's crotch. "As did you."

Christ, he knew it all. But how the hell – even the AA pilots didn't know about flying into Burma or the opium train.

The Colonel reached into his pocket and pulled out a small plastic baggie to dangle it in front of Michael's eyes. It held a wisp of copper-colored hair. Kathleen's hair.

"Found it caught in my helmet," the Colonel said.

Michael couldn't admit it. Kathleen caught in falsehood would never get her damned passport, and he'd never get out of Leavenworth. But he couldn't face out a lie to this man, either. So he just sat there, stuck in the goddamn chair, and looked the Colonel in the eye.

As if he understood that nothing more was going to be said, the Colonel nodded and stood up. He held up the baggie, looked at it, looked around the room, walked across it and dropped it – and its contents – into the wastebasket. "So. No medal. No dishonorable discharge, either. You performed your responsibilities well. And with honor."

Another sigh. "The doctor says you probably can get a medical discharge if you want it. 'Course he's only Air Force, but probably right even so. Except it seems to me the Army's due a little something. Your record indicates good work as a survival trainer. No flying, Lieutenant, but then you probably know that, the foot may lack the facility now."

Michael managed a nod. He hadn't quite dealt with that, either.

"It's a special forces camp on northern Luzon in the Philippines – lots of hill tribes there." And he smiled. By God, he did. "We can send you over to Clark Air Force Base Hospital. When they let you out on pass, you can hop down to the Rice Institute, get a little warm-up on your schooling. Third world agriculture, wasn't it?"

He'd sure done his homework. Michael hadn't realized all that old stuff was even in his records.

"So," the Colonel was moving for the door, "what do you say, Michael?" He looked back at Michael sitting utterly stunned, now. "Up to you. You want to go to Clark?"

He could've thought, here we go again, pal, one more person with expectations, with a hell of a lot more certainty about you than you have, trying to fix your life for you. But Michael knew that for a crock.

Every time he'd made a choice, cut out, doors had slammed shut behind him. Done it to himself, hadn't he, and they were closing now. But this time, for good or bad, deserved or not, the only one really beckoning him to come on ahead, come on, come on, was himself.

The Colonel waited. Michael could hardly speak, finally brought forth a little cough, a nod, and managed, "Thank you, Colonel, Sir. Maybe someday it'll pay off for somebody. I'll sure as hell try."

The Colonel started out – and through the doorway. Michael could see Hanny standing there with Tom and Kathleen. She was crying. Oh, boy, no passport? Her hair glowed.

The Colonel stopped dead, then leaned back into the room, almost whispering. "Jesus, Cameron – having a girl who looks like that and she's worth going to the mat for, too? You're one lucky bastard." He swivelled towards the hall, then once more, leaned into the room. "Almost forgot. You're demoted back to warrant officer. Only we'll make it a three instead of a two. I guess you deserve that much." He shot a finger at Michael. "But don't ever try to diddle an old hand."

Not when he has an aid like Willy, Michael thought.

Michael watched the Colonel drop a little nod at Kathleen, hear his boots marching all the way up the corridor and out of the clinic. "What's wrong?" he called through the door.

Kathleen smiled at him, tears or no. "It's all right", she said. "We got the papers. But Hanny's leaving . . . "

Hanny stood in the door, looking at Michael. "There's a roadhouse, probably two, outside the base at Fort Rucker," Michael said. "Take her dancing. And ask the DJ to play Percy Sledge."

Hanny's face went stern, the way it always did when he felt swamped. And then, before he headed up the corridor after the Colonel, he did a very unlikely thing. He blew Michael a kiss.

EPILOGUE

They drove up the dirt road, lane really, that curved along the mountainside. A low mountain, the house only about a thousand feet high, sitting on a shelf deep and wide. They'd seen it two days ago from the helicopter, and later the pilot steered them to the right guy at the Bank of Manila down in Baguio. Now here they were with the bank's agent at the wheel. They sat in the back seat, Michael's hand covering Kathleen's.

Into their second month in the Philippines, and moving ahead on all fronts, as Michael would say. Except the one they had yet to try. Maybe from shyness, or fear of finding out. Because if they tried and it failed them . . . There was only one thing each knew for sure: the place they were heading, neither could get to without the other.

Bushes, unkempt, overflowing with little trumpet flowers – creamy with touches of pink – lined the road, the fragrance overwhelming. "What is it?" she asked.

"I don't know," he said, puzzling over it. He'd smelled it before, couldn't recall when or where . . .

"Almost like oleander," she said.

And then he remembered. "On the freighter, coming out to Burma," he said. "We were given wreaths to wear on our heads in Fiji, New Caledonia . . . tiare, that's what it is. Only what's it doing here? Not native to this altitude, has to be a transplant."

"It's marvelous," she said.

The car pulled around the house and stopped. They looked at each other, almost scared. The agent got out, went up the wide steps to the wrap-around veranda to unlock the center set of double louvered doors. Doors like it ran the full length, this side of the house. From the air, the veranda had been hidden by the roof, but they had been able to see the long center portion with wings at either end jutting diagonally out, the fall of water below it, the land flowing down the mountain, ruined terraces dropping to the town. A small church, there, with small fields scattered up the opposite mountainside. They had looked at each other, the discovery catching their breaths.

Michael had been released from the hospital five weeks ago, and since then had done much better, hardly limping anymore except when he was tired, because of the beach.

Kathleen had taken a small suite in a little hotel there, funky motel really, only about an hour from the mountain camp where Michael trained the kids. He would come down on a Saturday, stay 'til late Sunday, driving an automatic he'd found because his leg wasn't yet flexible enough for a clutch, and walk the beach. A couple of miles up, beginning to run it now, and back thinking of Kathleen waiting with the baby on the porch that sagged but smelled of salt, watching for him. The sittingroom had a fold-up bed, and that's where he slept.

Sometimes they'd go out to dinner, even, recently, dancing at a place up the road – he could manage slow dancing – and a maid at the hotel whom Kathleen trusted would stay with Cho. Kathleen was being dated for the first time in her life, and it pleased Michael very much to give that to her. She'd shopped and bought her first dresses since boarding school. Even wore high-heeled sandals to dance in, which she'd spent some time getting used to. Michael thought her legs purely elegant in them. A week from today, Tom was to fly in from Hong Kong and perform the wedding ceremony.

They'd started their search of northern Luzon three weeks ago. Just for fun they'd used a helicopter service out of Baguio. A lot of these mountains were jungled, but a number had been terraced and cultivated for decades, maybe centuries – there were indigenous peoples here as well as modern Philippinos. While Michael did survival training, Kathleen was learning Tag-a-log, getting pretty good at it. But for one reason or another, house, land, lack of a town, nothing had suited. Until here.

There were five hundred hectares here. And the town below meant farmers, who might go shares. It was to be a co-op – an experimental demonstration farm co-op. If it went, it would improve everyone's life. Including their own.

They'd make a three-partner company, after all Tom was the one with know-how about third world politics and economies, how to handle graft and pay-outs. So they'd decided he'd have to have his own rooms for privacy, with a study where he could write in his spare time. They hadn't shared any of this with him, of course, and knew better than to refer to his world-wide reputation as a spare-time thing. But they also knew he'd come be with them, that he needed to leave Kowloon behind, and Macao. And they needed him.

Finally the agent's key worked. He threw open the doors for them and returned to the car where he sat with his head back and dozed. They entered like children into a castle, breath bated, hopeful. It was shadowed, high-ceilinged, the outer walls all louvered doors. But the inner solid walls could all be painted white.

They crossed to the opposite side, opened those doors. The veranda this side of the house was deep, its louvered walls running along both wings.

They moved to the railing, looked out, looked down, looked at each other. It was crazy, this house. Everything could come into it, for it reached out, embracing the world.

Her eyes were a deepening green. His were steady, waiting, going hot. They both wanted it. Not the house, though that, too. It. Each other. Desperately.

They looked through the house to where the car was parked, the agent was still dozing. They looked back at each other, her lips curving up, his widening into a grin, daring each other. And the daring made it happen.

He turned her back to the railing, lifted her to sit on it facing him. She pulled up her skirt, he got unzipped, opened her thighs and pulled her panties aside, while she lifted her legs high to clasp around his waist, her eyes closed, head going back, breath short as his. They were ready, both of them, more than ready. He slipped inside her, she was easy as satin, and he pulled the bottom of her in towards him. They clung, pressing, grinding, and exploded. Like in three minutes, for God's sake.

They held together clinging, panting, her face down in the corner of his neck, his forehead resting on her hair. They didn't check out the agent. Who cared? But they did, finally, look at each other. And she knew. They both knew.

"Welcome back," he said. He slowly grinned. "Me, too."

She started to smile, started to hoot, and they laughed in mutual glory. Only then did he peer over her shoulder down from the height to the ground, to pull her roughly off the rail and onto her feet.

"Jesus," he said, "what if you'd lost balance or – my God."

"You had me tight," she said. "You had me oh so very tight." And they laughed again.

She smoothed down her skirt, knowing the agent couldn't miss the wrinkles, but the hell with it. She turned in Michael's arms, leaned back against him, hugging his arms around her, and looked out to the mountains, low but rising beyond the town and its small church steeple, aware of the mountains at their backs.

"We'll call it Tiare," she said.

"I told you." He was patient. "It's not native here. It's a transplant."

She thought of Michael growing up in that well-to-do Cleveland suburb, of her own growing up on a remote farm with little plumbing and no electricity among an unknowable people. She thought of his schooling and hers, of the years apart, of war and helicopters and fear and kindness. Of murder and the life that followed. She thought of all the wondrous things that could grow in strange soils.

"So are we," she said.

* * *

Photo credti: Paul R. Cooper

Suzanne Clauser was a founder and serves on the Board of The Antioch Writers' Workshop in Yellow Springs, Ohio, where she and her husband reside. The Clausers have traveled extensively in China, India, the South Pacific and throughout Southeast Asia, and have lived in Rangoon and Upper Burma, where parts of *East of Mandalay* take place. In addition to being an award-winning writer of TV movies and miniseries, Clauser also created her own hourly primetime series. Her scripts have attracted a lengthy list of stars such as William Shatner, Johnny Cash, Jane Alexander, and Henry Fonda. *A Girl Named Sooner*, her first novel, was made into a critically acclaimed film.